His Secret

GINA A. JONES

Edited by Kirkus editing service

Author photo by Tana Elliott, T E Photos

Cover design by Indie Formatting Services

Formatted by Indie Formatting Services

Paperback: 978-0-9993893-0-0

eBook: 978-0-9993893-1-7

For Amy, my forever friend.

A NOTE FROM THE AUTHOR

I'm so excited for you to join me on this escapade of 'His Secret.' A secret: Something that is kept or meant to be kept unknown or unseen by others. When I wrote this story, I had no idea how far my imagination could take me. I'm sure it will raise some controversy for some, others will find their own true self in my words. However, it is only a story, a story from my heart. The heart is what drives us. That is what I need from my characters. I need their mavericks, their dissidents, their adventures, their conflicts. As a writer, I am not trying to change the world, but only entertain your thoughts for a little while. My writing is inspired by many things, music, friends, past experiences, family, food, and sometimes, just something someone said. But my biggest inspiration comes from my husband, and I will no longer apologize for being the romantic that I am. If you want to be treated romantically, then you must entertain romantically.

So, sit back, relax and prepare yourself to be taken on a journey. I ask, that when a song has been written into a scene, download, YouTube it, and take a little break, while listening to the song and put yourself there. Go there and discover...His Secret.

Gina xoxo

PROLOGUE

THE PASSERBY: TEN YEARS EARLIER

"911. WHAT'S YOUR EMERGENCY?"

"Yes, I was passing by this house and, uh..."

"Sir. Sir, are you there? Is there an emergency? Can you give me your location?"

Rain turns the grey sky to black. The wind howls up a horseshoe lane and into a large house, slamming the double doors open and shut. Gargoyle creatures each hold a ring knocker in its mouth. Inside, the house is bare—except for one picture, which hangs over a large field-stone fireplace. A man in dress blues is kissing with his bride. They are happy. In love.

"Sir, are you still there?"

"Yes. I just saw someone run into the pasture."

"Have you been in a car accident?"

"A house. The sign at the gate says Fairbanks."

"Are you the owner of this house, sir?"

"Ah... no. I was driving by, and the rain was pouring hard, so I had to pull over into a driveway."

"Are you hurt, sir? Did you run off the road?"

Screams from in the background.

"Someone's screaming. I think they are hurt," says the caller.

"Sir, I have your location at 5952 Oak Road."

"Um... I guess. I'm not really sure where I am. I was just waiting for the storm to pass, and saw someone run across the field. It's storming really badly, and the doors to this house are open. I think something really bad just happened."

"Can you tell me what happened, sir?"

"I don't know what happened. I was just waiting for the storm to pass. I heard screams, and then someone ran from the house. Oh, my God. I think I hear a baby crying inside."

"Sir, you say you hear a baby?"

"Yes. I'm on the porch, and the doors are swinging open and shut in the wind. There it is again—a baby is crying."

"Sir, dispatch is on their way. Please remain on the line."

"Yes. Yes, I will. I'm inside now. I can still hear the baby crying. I think it's coming from upstairs."

"Sir, can you see if the baby needs help?"

"Yes, I'm upstairs now. I think the cries are coming from behind the door I'm standing at."

"Sir. The police are almost there. Can you hear them?"

"No. Not yet. I'm going inside to get the baby."

The cries become louder as the passerby opens the door. A baby lies in a crib alone, crying. "Hey. What's the matter? Where are your parents? I have her. It's a baby girl, about two months old, I would say. She's crying, but appears unharmed."

"Sir. The police should be there."

"Yes, I hear them. They are outside. Up here! There's a baby."

"Police."

"Yes. Up here! I found a baby alone and crying. Someone went running and screaming from the house."

"Sir, put the baby down and walk from the room."

"Officer, I didn't do anything. I was checking on the baby. I'm the one who called."

"Sir, the police are there. I'm going to hang up now."

"Yes. Okay."

Another officer enters the room. "We have a dead body floating in the lake."

PART I

Spring: A time for change, a time for growth. Wake the youth, with their wobbly legs, and direct them into this special place, where time is meant for them. Go, and remember that all faith is blind, and let that faith lead you to your fate

— GINA A. JONES

1

LE CORDON BLEU CHEFS HAVE WORKED IN SOME OF THE MOST prestigious restaurants in the world; many of them are Michelin-starred, and One of the Best Craftsmen in France (Un des Meilleurs Ouvriers de France-MOF). *"Un des Meilleurs Ouvriers."*

"Julia?"

As I quickly shut the laptop, "Frère Jacques" hums quietly from my throat, "Yes, Pastor Tom, I was just going over this morning's daily devotions." There I go again, lying.

Please, Father in heaven, forgive me once again for this lie I have just told Pastor Tom. "I will be right down. I'm just updating my profile on Angie's List. Just give me a minute."

"Okay, Julia. Cathy has worked hard at another breakfast for the family. We need to be respectful by being on time."

Walking over, I open the bedroom door. "I'm sorry—I should be down there helping her," I say quickly, shutting the door behind me, and pass him on the stairs. I enter the kitchen, giving Cathy a quick wave, which has become my show of apology every morning lately.

"Cathy, please take a seat and let me take over. I was just looking up some delightful breakfast entrées upstairs." *Crap, another lie. Father in heaven; please forgive me again for... yet another lie.*

"Oh Julia, that sounds great. I loved your blueberry crêpes yesterday. Plus, I need to meet with the ladies' aid group at church. If you can manage to get the girls fed and onto their lessons, I would so much appreciate it." She unties her apron, and tosses it on the worktop.

For a woman who spends her entire life preaching to other women the importance of a wife's role, "Your family comes first, your husband comes first," she sure seems to run amok, letting me take on that role.

They both would be appalled if they knew of my dreams of moving to Paris—and working in an upscale, fine cuisine restaurant... one that also serves wine. *There I go, judging again.*

I'm about to silently pray for this *sin* of judgment when it hits me. That's all they do—judge.

"Did you see that dress she was wearing? It was sleeveless. Bare shoulders should not be allowed in church. Or outside the home, for that matter," crooned old Agnes, our piano player from church, last Sunday. Forget the fact it was a hundred degrees with no air conditioning. I wonder what God has against bare shoulders? The men go shirtless all the time when they play basketball in the parking lot. I have never heard anyone complaining about that.

Pondering what to do with the two-day-old carrot cake, I hear Cathy yell from the garage, "Julia!" I rush out while tying on the apron.

"Yes, Cathy. What's wrong?"

"Do you smell that?" she asks, her nose in the air.

"Smell what?"

"Smells like someone is smoking cigarettes."

"Here, in this garage?"

"Well, I didn't really smell it until the garage door opened."

"Oh... yes. That would be Mr. Stouter from next door. I think he's trying to quit again. I saw him sneaking a few puffs behind the shed. He tells Mrs. Stouter he just can't seem to get the new puppy housebroken. If you ask me, I think it's the real reason he got Mrs. Stouter a new dog. So he can sneak a smoke."

She waves her hand. "Oh, poor woman. Are you sure you don't mind making the mini quiches for my ladies' group tomorrow morning?" she asks while getting into the car.

"Not at all. Go on. I got it covered," I say, swishing my hands at her.

"Thank you, Julia. I love you as if you were my own daughter. You know that, don't you?"

"Yes, I love, you. And the girls, too. Now get going." She backs the car out, and I rush back to the kitchen.

"Cathy," Pastor Tom yells. "Cathy!"

"She's left, Pastor Tom, for ladies' aid at the church." I say, searching through the fridge. "Can I make you some eggs benedict?"

"What?" Popping only his head in the doorway, he fumbles with his tie.

"She left. I can make your breakfast." Sensing his need for assistance, I shut the fridge and meet him in the doorway. Grabbing his tie, I say the little rhyme. "The fox chased the rabbit around the tree two times." I wrap the tie around twice. "The rabbit ran down his hole." Slipping the end through the loop, I pull and tug it straight. My hands then run down the front of his chest, smoothing the creases in his shirt.

"Thanks. Cathy left already?"

"Yes."

"Well, she could have told me." He grabs his Bible from the counter, along with other needed items, shoving them into his leather satchel. "I have a meeting with the deacons. We're meeting at the coffee shop."

"Would you like some breakfast?"

"No. I will have some there. Tell the girls bye for me," he says, throwing on his sweater. He walks out the door.

"Put God first... then your family," is the mantra preached every day in this household. I see that God's always first on this list of priorities. Did God intend for women to use this time, tea tootling on God's holy sanction, complaining about their husbands and gossiping? All while their men sit in coffee shops, discussing the football scores—and their nagging wives?

"Morning, Julia. Where are Mom and Dad?"

Natalie, the eldest daughter, walks in and plops herself down at the table. "Your mom's at ladies' aid and your father just left for a deacons' meeting. She rolls her eyes. I agree, with an inward roll.

"What's for breakfast?"

"Well, how about carrot-cake French toast?" She shrugs her shoulders, showing no enthusiasm for the fine culinary arts. *And, children—obey and respect your parents.* I see none of this, either. "Where's Paige?"

"She's still in bed," she says, rubbing her eyes with a yawn.

"Well, get her up. I need to feed you two and get your lessons started."

"Paige," she screams.

"Natalie, I could have done that." She makes another eye roll.

Natalie, sixteen, and Paige, fourteen, both have been homeschooled for the last two years... by *me.* Cathy loves all the compliments though. "How do you do it, Cathy? Running all those charities, along with the church functions, and never missing a moment by your husband's side?" This is where I would love to speak up.

Well, you see, Natalie was actually kicked out of private school. How these rumors haven't surfaced is beyond me. *And I, Julia, have done all the teaching.*

When Natalie was fourteen, she became quite the little rebellious teen—smoking pot and hanging out with... *boys.* Actually, I envy her, the way she stands up for herself. I will never forget what she said to her parents. "It's easier to ask for forgiveness than permission," she said. Clever girl.

Paige shuffles in, looking every bit as enthusiastic as Natalie. Her eyes are half-closed, and her hair is knotted. She is wearing pink sweats, and a T-shirt with the caption, *I am not to be ignored.* Of course, it will be long dresses, and hair pulled back tight, before Mommy and Daddy return.

"What's the point of being home-schooled if we have to get up early?" Paige whines.

"It's not a reason to become lazy, Paige." And on the one hand, I want to scream and say, "How did you both become my responsibility?" But, it's not their fault—not really. Whatever you allow, will continue.

I really do love both these girls, and Tom and Cathy. It's more than just an obligation. I owe the DeLuca family. They took me in after the death of my parents. I was at least Paige's age: fourteen. They were both killed in a car accident the week I was at church camp. I've been with this family ever since.

"What's for breakfast, Julia?" Paige asks, yawning.

"Carrot-cake French toast," I tell her, setting two plates on the table.

"I think it's another one of her... experiments," Natalie says, and rests her chin in her palm.

"Just try it. Who knows? You might like it," I say.

Both girls drown their plates with syrup before taking the first bite. I watch them both like they are lab rats. "What do you think?"

"It's pretty good," Natalie says, shoving another bite. I look at Paige.

"I like it, Julia. It's really good."

I am now satisfied that my clever use of the old carrot cake that was growing stale was not detected. "Make it quick, girls, and start your lessons for the day. I want you both finished before you head to the Y."

"What! Can't we finish when we get back?" asks Paige, whining again.

"No. I, too, have things to do."

After the girls finish their breakfast, and begin their lessons, I run up the stairs, two at a time and into my room, where I complete my profile on Angie's List.

Name: Julia Ellis

Age: 21

Female seeking a full-time nanny position. Qualifications include homeschooling K-12. Certified swim instructor, piano instructor, and Bible-lesson teacher. I can start anytime. References available upon interview.

I finish, giving all contact information, including my email address and cell phone number; however, my finger hovers above the "send" button. I feel like it's going to jump up and bite me. *Just do it.* Tap.

There, it's done. Now... how to tell Pastor Tom and Cathy? I feel guilty. I shouldn't, though. You would think that they would be glad for me to get on with my life. However, that's not the way things work around here. Oh no. "A young lady should never seek her independence. It will only cause her to end up in a life of sin," says the church. "A lady's place is in the home, raising her children, supporting her husband." My question is—what do you do in the meantime? Raise other people's children, perhaps? So, becoming a nanny will be no different. This will be my defense. I need to save for Paris, if I'm going to study at a culinary academy. Yes, I know there are fine schools here in the States, but Paris is my dream. Plus, if I'm clear across the pond, I'm a safe distance from the eyes of judgment. God will be my only judge, and we have an understanding.

The music downstairs changes from old hymns to alternative rock. Katy Perry sings of kissing a girl, and I find myself tapping a foot to the beat. Pulling up my saved window of Le Cordon Bleu, I once again read every page, my eyes devouring all the information my brain can absorb.

Filling in the needed information for applying, my finger hovers over the send button once again. *Just hit the dang thing.* Tap. I did it. It's done. My finger releases, and then the alarm goes off in my head. *What if they send information to the house?* Because at that exact moment, I realize that my home address was in the application. *Is it better to ask for forgiveness than for permission?*

I rush back downstairs and find Natalie seated in the living area. She looks up.

"You do it?" she asks. She looks cute, yet cunning with that smile of hers.

"Yes, I did." I sit down next to her on the couch, and my shoulders relax.

"Good. Then when I turn eighteen, I'm moving in with you to study fashion."

"Oh, Natalie, I knew you had ulterior motives." I poke her in the ribs. "Is Paige in the tree house?"

"Mm hmm."

Glancing up at the clock, I see it's one hour before we leave. "You'll be done in an hour?"

"I should be."

"Okay. I'm going to check on Paige." She blows a bubble with her gum, and I smack it.

Walking out back, I stand under the huge maple tree where Pastor Tom built the girls a tree house when they were little. I stand on the first nailed board, and lightly caress the carvings of all our names—Julia, Natalie, and Paige. Paige was no more than seven when we carved these. Both, Natalie and I helped her, yet she protested the whole time, "I can carve it. I can carve it. it." It's in times like these that I can't imagine leaving the girls.

Pushing open the trap door, I poke my head up into the tree house. Paige lies on her tummy, her feet dancing in the air, with her pink Beats wrapped around her head. Shaking her head to the music, she smiles at me. I raise one finger letting her know one hour. She gives me a thumbs-up. I wink back.

I glance around the walls of our childhood tree house, and see the girly curtains flutter in the breeze. I think back to the day Natalie picked out the material—pink with sparkles. Everything had to have sparkles. Even back then, she was a whiz with fashion. Natalie would design the interior, I would make the entrées, and Paige would pick the music for every tree house party we ever had. I miss those days. I'm going to miss these girls.

Now, back in the kitchen, I decide if I have enough time to make the mini quiches Cathy wants for her ladies' group. I don't mind doing this... I love it, really. I get to work, but not before changing Pandora to French café music.

Holding the bowl on my hip while whipping the eggs, I move about to Anita Kelsey's cover of "Sway." This is my favorite time of day... *my time*. Not that I don't love being with the girls... it's just—well, I get to do *my thing*. And the great thing about it is that I'm doing something for someone else, making little quiches for Ms. Cathy's group. Lightens up the guilt.

Natalie walks in wearing her handmade beanie, her long blonde hair tucked inside. Loose strands hang from each side, and her body is adorned with a beach wrap she made from a design she saw on Pinterest. Large, movie-star sunglasses cover her delicate face, and her hipster, gypsy-style, glitter handbag hangs off her shoulder. Another design by Natalie.

"I'm going up on the roof to sunbathe."

I think her limited fashion options have helped tap into her creative side. She took one of her father's old T-shirts, cut off the sleeves, sliced up the middle, added straps for the shoulders, and made a stunning, little beach dress. Of course, her parents have only seen it while she is also wearing a sweater. They think it's just a long T-shirt skirt.

They weren't too keen on the beanie. They said it made her look too *hipster.* The look she is *really* going for. But the guilt set in when it was clear that Natalie's feelings were hurt. (She told them, "I crocheted this by myself. Grandma taught me.") Then they told her it was lovely, and how proud they were of her for spending time with her grandma. Like I said—clever girl.

"Okay. But first, Natalie... hand over the cigarettes you have in your bag. Poor old Mr. Stouter has once again taken the blame for you." Pulling the sunglasses down just a bit, she rolls her eyes and pulls the pack out. I take them, stuffing the pack into a plastic grocery sack before throwing in the trash. "I'm afraid your mother might try doing an intervention on him."

Once she leaves, I finish up with the quiches, then put the kettle on for a mug of tea. I have adopted a lot of the European words and ways. I should probably learn French, if I'm going to be hanging out with the Parisians. Trainers are what I call my tennis shoes. A jumper for when I'm chilly, and the girls laugh when I say, "Make sure you have clean knickers on."

I found that people in the U.K. love using the word "cream." It's used for every color when reading from my favorite English authors. "I wore the cream dress with cream tights." Or, "Once my body was fully creamed, I put on the cream dress with cream tights." I would think in a country so liberal there would be more vibrant colors.

Biscuit for cookies, the loo for toilet, the boot for my mini's trunk.

And once, when my mini cooper overheated, Paige looked at me as if I were insane when I told her to put up the bonnet. Some began asking if I was actually from England, although I don't have an accent.

Now with the quiches poured into the muffin tins, I stretch plastic wrap over the top before placing the tins in the fridge. An hour has passed, and both girls rush out the front door. I'm about to walk out myself, when I catch sight of myself in the hall mirror. My long dress is sleeveless, so I grab a light cardigan from the closet along with my little white trainers, and meet the girls out front.

Natalie, who recently got her learner's permit, sits in the driver's seat. She holds out her hand. "Keys, Julia," she commands, smiling. I hand them over, and walk to the passenger side. Paige, in the back seat, smacks her gum and bobs her head to the music from the pink Beats still wrapped around her head. Natalie cranks the radio, and pulls the car away from the curb. The windows are rolled down, and Taylor Swift shouts from the car, "I knew you were trouble."

Since the girls are home schooled, the state requires a form of physical education. Both are avid swimmers, taught by me. I offered to give them swim lessons at the YMCA. They jumped at the chance, when told that otherwise they would have to join the girls' church softball team, of course wearing long dresses while playing.

Natalie carefully pulls into the parking lot, gives a great demonstration of parking, and turns off my little mini. "God, Julia. I so want this car."

"Natalie, do not use the Lord's name in vain," I preach, still feeling my own transgressions from all *my* little lies. She huffs, and rolls her eyes.

"I'm sorry," she says, holding out the keys to me.

"Oh, just leave them in the ignition. I'm going to take a walk on the boardwalk out by the hospital to do my devotions." I truly need a long talk with God... and hope He understands.

Looking back at Paige, I smile. "It's good that you're a tiny thing. Not much room back there." She really is a little cutie—sandy blonde hair, like Natalie's before she discovered peroxide. Light freckles across her nose give her an even more youthful look. Natalie, too, had them at one time. I guess we outgrow a lot of things.

"Are you staying, Julia?" Paige asks, removing her Beats.

"You know, Paige, I don't mind you listening to your music, but it would be nice to have a conversation with you occasionally."

"I'd rather she keep them on. Keeps her from hearing some of my shit," Natalie says.

"Natalie... your mouth," I gasp.

"It's true. She would probably tell on me."

"No, I wouldn't, Natalie. I would blackmail you."

"Little stain," Natalie hisses.

"Whore," Paige retorts.

"Girls... enough," I scold. "I have enough to pray about today. I guess I will throw you two out in the lot.

"Are you staying, Julia?" Paige asks again.

"No, she isn't. Didn't you hear her?" Natalie says, getting out of the car.

"I'm going to the boardwalk... to sort things out."

"Like what, Julia? You know I wouldn't tell on Natalie... or really blackmail her... right?"

"Yes, I know. You're very lucky to have a big sister, you know." I wish that I had had a sibling when my parents were killed."

Paige lowers her head.

"Yes, I can't imagine not having Natalie if Mom and Dad died. I'm sorry, Julia."

"Okay. Get going, and I'll be back to pick you girls up." She shoves her Beats down into her bag and runs up the sidewalk, her flip-flops snapping on her feet. *Can I really leave these girls?*

I park my little Mini behind the hospital and leave to begin my morning walk. A few years ago, the city made this amazing boardwalk, which connects the park to the hospital five blocks away. It's actually a long bridge, with several turns through swampland. It's also quite the bird and nature preserve, being that if this bridge were not here, none of this would be visible.

I start my walk, and see two gold finches balancing on the twig of a briary raspberry bush. How light they must be, for the twig doesn't bow. Their morning song is so crisp, and finely tuned. This makes me think of God's promises... for His eye is on the sparrow, He surely is watching me.

A little squirrel scampers up a tree so effortlessly, moving from branch to branch. I then spot a groundhog wrestling through the thick weeds and briars underneath the tree. Yes... this is truly such a precious glimpse of God's work. *Speaking of God.* I drop to my knees, raise my hands to the sky, and silently pray.

Dear Father in Heaven... where do I begin? I need answers and guidance. I need direction. Father... please forgive me once again for the lies and... omissions I have committed today. Lying to Pastor Tom about what I was really searching for on my computer. Lying to Cathy about looking up recipes, and about Mr. Stouter. Please forgive me for not telling Pastor Tom and Cathy my plans of becoming a nanny, and leaving for Paris. Forgive me for the judgments I have put on others today. I pray for the girls to behave, and to be there for each other when I'm gone. And... even as I'm asking this, Lord, I must remember that it is Your will. What is Your will for me, Lord? Is it to become a chef in Paris... or a wife and mother? It is only through You that all things are possible, and I will obey Your will for me. I just... Father, I need something... something to let me know... a sign.

"OH, SHIT!"

Opening my eyes, I see a man on a bike who is racing toward me, but instead of jumping out of his way I freeze and cover my eyes.

CRASH.

Quickly, I open my eyes and see that the man and his bike have crashed into the wooden rail, breaking through and sending them down into the briars.

"Oh, sir. I'm sorry. Are you okay?"

"What the hell are you doing?" he yells up at me.

"I... I was... praying."

"We're you praying that you'd kill someone today?"

"What? Well, of course not. Why would I ask God to kill someone? I... was asking for... guidance." Why do I feel the need to tell him? Obviously, he's in no shape to listen.

"Maybe you should ask for guidance of *where* to pray. I don't think in the middle of the boardwalk is the best place." He rustles in annoyance, a tangled mess of bike and briars. Foul language spews from his mouth like vomit.

"Do you mind not using that language?" He looks up at me. His annoyance so palpable, it gives me a pang in the chest.

"You're kidding me, right? I could seriously be injured, and all you have to say is... *watch your language*?"

"You're right. I'm so sorry, sir. Here, let me help you," I say, reaching down to him.

"No, I can get up myself. You've caused enough difficulties for me already."

"Is your bike broken? I will pay for it." He pulls the bike free from the tangled mess, and I'm amazed when it's lifted above his head, and placed back on the boardwalk. "Here, give me your hand," I insist once again, extending my hand to him. He grabs it, but when he pulls himself up, I reach for the railing, which is missing, and I lose my balance, landing on top of him. Lying on top of his chest, I'm increasingly aware that it's bare, and... sweaty. But not bad sweaty. I mean... he doesn't smell like sweat. Actually, he smells good—like earthy soap, and a slight musky.

I lift my head slowly from his... good-smelling, wet chest, when my eyes meet his. The irises are deep blue, wrapped in a hazel ring. Absolutely gorgeous. How can a man have such gorgeous eyes? It's not fair. I just... stare into them.

"Are you all right?" he asks.

"Uh... um... yes. I am. I... just forgot to hang onto the railing. Because... it was... it was..."

"Gone?" he finishes, mockingly.

"Yes... it's gone. I mean... broken."

"Yeah, I know. I ran through it to avoid hitting you."

I stare into his eyes like I'm lost in the abyss and then quickly push myself up, when my sweater becomes caught on briars. "Ouch."

"At least you have a sweater on. How do you think my bare back and chest feel?"

Divine. Of course, I don't say it out loud. I hope not. Dropping my head back down to his chest, I see cuts and abrasions. "Oh, you're bleeding."

"Yeah, well that's bound to happen when you crash into a wooden rail and fall into a pit of briars."

"The groundhog," I say suddenly.

"Groundhog? What the hell are you talking about?"

"Do they bite?"

"Yes. They can be quite mean if provoked. Excuse me, but why are we having a conversation about a groundhog?"

"I saw one down here earlier. Just before you... I mean... just before I made you crash. Do you think maybe... you might have fallen on him, and he could be hurt?"

"Seriously? You are more worried about a fuckin', damn groundhog than you are about me?"

"I suppose you're right. I sound pretty silly." *Julia, just shut up and get off this man's chest.* "I think I'm stuck. There are briars stuck in my sweater."

"Hold still and let me pull them away."

"Okay... thanks."

He cautiously rips briars from my white sweater, and I cringe listening to the wool tear "Ouch. That one must have been stuck clear through," I say, looking up into his eyes again. *Those eyes.* He looks at me, too, for a moment, then continues with the briar removal.

"Better?"

"Yes. Thank you."

Placing my hands on his chest, I push myself up and stand, then reach for his hand.

"I can get it from here," he says, rolling his eyes. Feeling a slight embarrassment, I turn away. My hair becomes tangled from more briars. "Ouch."

"Don't move, it will just get worse."

"Then what shall I do? You're not going to leave me here, are you?"

He stands, stomping on the weeds as he approaches.

"Take your hair out of that... hair thing," he says.

"You mean, take out my hair tie?"

"Yes. It's the only way you're going to get out of that bush."

Reaching up, I feel the mass of briars and stickers poking into my head. Pulling on the hair tie only makes the situation worse. I put my fingers in between the hair tie and my ponytail pulling out each tendril.

"Here, you're making it worse. Let me get it." Now, with his chest inches from my face *again*, he reaches up, untangling my bird's nest of a hairdo. I must look like a real sight by now. Finally, my hair comes spilling over my shoulders, and I watch his expression as he carefully pulls the remaining leaves and briars out of it.

"Thank you," I say breathlessly. *Why do I sound like I'm out of breath?*

"Now, I'm going to lift you up onto the boardwalk. Don't move. Okay?"

"Uh huh," I breathe out, again breathlessly. He places his hands around my waist, and, with the slightest effort, my body is lifted and placed on the boardwalk. I watch as he turns himself around, places both hands on the bridge behind him, then swings his legs over his head, completing a somersault, landing on his knees. *Wow.* I've only seen this done once while watching footage of military boot camp training. *Not sure why I was watching.*

I see his legs, bloody with abrasions and then... his little, tight, black bike shorts. His back is also a bloody, scratched up mess. Quickly, I remove my sweater as he stands. "Here, let me clean some of this blood off," I say, dabbing his back.

"No, I'm fine. I've been through a lot worse. I'm going to jump in the lake and clean it off, anyway. May I ask why you are wearing a sweater? It's eighty-five degrees."

"My dress... it's sleeveless. My shoulders were showing." He looks at me, still waiting for my answer.

"Okay. Whatever."

"Again, I'm very sorry sir," I say, as he turns around and reaches for his bike.

"May I suggest that you pray somewhere else? I, and that groundhog, were not prepared for this little calamity today."

I crane my neck over the edge of the embankment, checking for a smashed, little groundhog. "I'll keep that in mind." He shakes his head and walks his bike down the path. I watch until he's out of view.

BACK AT THE Y, I'M WAITING FOR NATALIE AND PAIGE IN MY LITTLE MINI. I'm not even sure how I got here. I am still obsessed by his blue eyes. *And his chest.* I've never touched a man's bare chest before. Do all men's chests smell like his? I don't think his scent will ever leave my memory. I must search for that scent in the body wash aisle.

The car door opens. "Julia... holy shit!" Paige exclaims. "Natalie, come look at Julia."

"What the hell happened to you?" Natalie says.

Forgetting that my hair's a mess, my dress is torn, and my sweater lies bloody on the seat, I say, "I met a man today."

"And he did this to you?" Natalie asks.

"Oh... no... no, he didn't."

"So... did you piss off his cat?" she jokes.

"What? No. He didn't have a cat."

"Then why do you look like this?"

"I made him crash his bike. Then I fell on top of him. He had eyes."

"Yes, Julia. Most people do," she says, looking at Paige.

"I mean... they were gorgeous, blue eyes."

"Oh... so now we're getting somewhere," she says, smiling.

"Hey, don't be using those words," I say, coming back to Earth. Natalie grins.

"What words, Julia?"

"You know that... cat thing."

"I can't say cat?"

"Of course, you can say cat. Just don't say the word before it."

"His?"

"No. That... cuss word."

"And what cuss word would that be... Julia? Come on. Say it," she coaxes.

"No. I will not." She continues to grin ear to ear. "Piss. Don't say piss."

"Oh my God, she said it," Natalie laughs. "I think I just peed a little."

I turn the key in the ignition, and put the gearshift into drive. Paige pairs her phone to the Bluetooth of my stereo and hits Taylor Swift's "Today Was a Fairytale."

Hmm... maybe it was.

2

On the drive back to the house, I am put on the witness stand—interrogated by both girls. Paige, for once, is not even wearing her Beats. I'm sure that every song played is to get my goat. *Or maybe every song makes me feel... in love?*

"Come on, Julia. Tell us more about... Mr. Blue Eyes," Natalie swoons. She must truly be intrigued. She didn't even ask to drive home.

"I was praying on the boardwalk when I heard someone say, 'Oh... poop.'"

"What? No! He said, 'Oh, poop?'"

"Well... not that word exactly... but the *bad* word."

"Oh, you mean 'shit,'" she says nonchalantly, as if she were saying, "The sky is blue."

"Natalie!"

"Oh, go on, Julia. I want to hear," she whines.

In the rearview mirror, I see that Paige is staring at me in eager anticipation, her mouth agape, and eyes glued to mine. I tone it down for her young ears.

"Oh... that's about it, really. I looked up, and he ran over the side of the boardwalk to avoid hitting me. I tried to help him up... and that's when I fell on him. End of story." I shrug my shoulders.

Natalie raises her eyebrows with the expression, *really?* I raise mine as if to say, *Yes... really*, tilting my head to one side, toward Paige. Eventually, she catches my drift and responds with, "Okay. Whatever, Jules."

I pull into the driveway and park my little Mini off to the side, giving Pastor Tom and Cathy access to the garage entrance. Both girls remain in their seats, like they might miss me spilling my guts if they leave. "Come on. Let's go. I need to start preparing tonight's dinner." I'm the first to exit the car. They follow—stuck to my side. "That's all. Really," I say.

Paige, satisfied, places her Beats back on her head and disappears from the kitchen. "Okay, she's gone. Spill it," Natalie commands.

I crane my neck around the corner, just in case Paige is listening. I don't see her. "Okay, but not now... later. I really need to braise the lamb before putting in the oven." Of course, it's not really lamb. I substitute beef. I can't imagine eating a cute, little lamb. It sounds so... sadistic

She stands, arms crossed, head slowly nodding. "Okay... later," she says, then turns on her heel and leaves the kitchen.

I pull the lamb—I mean beef—from the fridge, then grab a large skillet, pouring in a little olive oil. Setting the temp to high I unwrap the meat, and notice the little scrapes on my hands from today's earlier mishap. I wonder what he's doing now. Is he also tending to his cuts? Thinking of me? *What an odd thing to think.*

I decide to clean myself up a before preparing the lamb curry and head to the upstairs bathroom. Closing the door behind me, I gasp at my reflection in the mirror. "Oh, good Lord! I'm a pathetic mess." My long hair hangs like a mop, covering my shoulders and back. The top of my head looks as if I've been shocked by an electrical cord. I look like the Bride of Frankenstein... minus the grey, lightning-bolt streaks.

Smoothing the top of my head with my hands, I step back and inspect myself. Essentially... it's not bad. I've never notice the highlights in my chestnut-colored hair, or the long, loose waves that frame my face. I like it. I look so... free—and maybe... pretty? Perhaps I should wear it like this more often, instead of a tight, pulled-back ponytail, or bun.

I turn my face from side to side and study how I really look. Did he think I was pretty? Why am I even thinking these things? He's probably home repeating every curse word he can think of as he pulls out each thorn stuck in his skin. *His... skin... his chest. Stop it, Julia!*

I wash my hands and face, remove my dress, and toss it into the hamper. Wrapping myself in a towel, I leave the bathroom and saunter down the hall to my room. I change into another long dress and make my way back to the kitchen. My hair is still down and bouncing about, swishing at the small of my back. I feel uninhibited.

I get all the other ingredients for my fake lamb curry, adding them to the huge, cast-iron pot—bay leaf, cilantro, garlic cloves, fresh ginger, plum tomatoes, and chopped yellow onions. Setting the heat on high, I glance at the clock... four o'clock. It must be an awfully long ladies' aid meeting, and deacons' meeting. I check my phone for any missed messages... none. *Typical.*

A mouthwatering scent, which is emanating from the stew, now permeates the house. I lift the lid and stir the stew lightly with a wooden spoon. My mind wanders off once again.

What would it be like to be preparing this dish for the bike man? Still stirring the pot, I have visions of him walking through the door after a long day of work. What does he do? Would he come in... *shirtless?* But, I'm sure he has an important job, and would be wearing a suit and tie. My thoughts drift off.

He walks in. "That smells divine, Julia," he would say, kissing me on the cheek.

"Thank you..." What's his name? I will just call him Dear. "Hard day at work, Dear?"

"It's always a hard day at work," he would say.

"Well, you're home now, and I will make it all better," I say. He wraps his arms around me, and then asks how the children are. I would say, "Oh, they are perfect little angels... because they're ours." I would then help him loosen his tie... because I'm sure he has such an important job that he must wear a tie. And of course, he has me tie it every morning, because he hasn't yet gotten the hang of it. At least, this is what he tells me. But I think that he likes me doing it for him.

Our children come running in from playing outside, a little boy and girl—clones of us. We're also expecting again.

"How are my darlings today?" he asks our children.

"Daddy! Daddy!" they call to him. He picks both up in his strong arms, and kisses their fresh, outdoor-smelling heads. I find myself more in love with him every day, and I close my eyes just as I'm about to kiss his lips.

"Julia."

"Yes, Dear?"

"Dear?"

I open my eyes. The stew is starting to smell scorched. I'm still standing over the pot and holding the wooden spoon. Turning around, I see Pastor Tom.

"Oh, you're home. I'm... just... preparing dinner."

"Is something wrong? I've been calling your name for ten minutes." He is looking at my hair. I put down the spoon, cover the pot, and then smooth my hair back.

"Oh... no, I'm fine, Pastor Tom. I was just... just wondering if I have enough spice in the lamb curry," I stammer. I grab a dish towel and pretend to wipe food off my hands. He's still looking at my hair with an appalled expression.

"Shouldn't your hair be tied back? After all, we wouldn't want hair in the stew." Without saying a word, I rush upstairs, retrieve a hair tie from the bathroom drawer, and with shaky fingers, make a messy, loose bun on top my head. Before returning to the kitchen, I check on the girls.

"Your father's home. Make sure the music is changed back and... Natalie, take off that bikini," I tell her through her open bedroom window. She's sunning herself in a yellow bikini, lying between the two upstairs dormers.

"Shit," she says, reaching out her hand. I take it, and help her through the window.

"Stop saying that word." She quickly throws on her cover, then pulls on a large T-shirt. She grabs her cell phone, and turns down the volume to the wireless speaker she has it paired to. Paige, I'm not too worried about. I'm sure she's in the tree house, listening with her Beats on.

"Mom home yet?"

"No." I leave her room, and head down to the kitchen. Pastor Tom is now sitting in front of the TV, flipping through the sports channels. "The girls are just finishing up their last week of finals. I can't believe it's almost Memorial Day. Summer is upon us." I feign small chatter as I pass through the living room.

"Cathy home?"

"No. I haven't heard from her yet. I'm sure she'll be here soon." He glances at his watch, and continues flipping the channels.

At six o'clock, the utility door opens and Cathy walks in, weighed down with bags from the mall. What on Earth would she have in common with anything from there? Surely not her fashion.

"Oh, something smells wonderful, Julia! What is it?" she asks, walking past me.

"Lamb curry." I watch her stuff bags into the hall closet.

"Oh, good. I'm starved."

"So are we," Pastor Tom says, walking into the kitchen.

"Well... let's eat," she says, patting his cheek. Not a kiss... just a pat.

"So, where have you been all day, Cathy?" he asks.

"Oh... just out with the ladies' group, visiting folks in the nursing homes."

I glance at the hall closet door.

"How was your meeting with the deacons?" she asks in return, taking a bite of stew.

"Okay," is his only reply. "Julia, this stew is delicious." It's clear he's avoiding any further questions from Cathy.

"You look awfully tanned. Did you play golf today?" she queries.

"Oh... just a few holes. Julia, is there bread with this?"

"Yes, it's still warming in the oven." Excusing myself from the table, I walk to the oven and pull out the bread. As I'm slicing it, I watch this family dinner carry on. The girls are both rolling their eyes. Tom and Cathy each tell about their day, while also telling obvious, little white lies, and I laugh inside. *Will my little daydream turn into this? Just keep dreaming of Paris.*

~

IT'S DARK AS I PREPARE FOR BED. I AM WEARING MY FLANNEL PAJAMA bottoms, and a T-shirt, when I crawl out of the window, and meet Natalie between the dormers.

"I miss you, too—so much. I've got to see you before you go back." She's FaceTiming her secret boyfriend, Sebastian, a foreign exchange student from Paris that she met at the Y. Cathy and Tom would freak out if they knew. He is another reason that she wants to go to Paris with me. Lucky him.

"Can you sneak out tonight?" Sebastian asks. Natalie looks at me. I give her a doubtful look, raising my eyebrows. Then, I consider the fact that he will be leaving in two weeks.

"One hour only. I mean it, Natalie." She smiles, then kisses my cheek.

"Thanks, Julia. Sebastian, give me a minute. There's something that Julia and I need to discuss. I love you." She kisses the phone and then ends the call. "Okay Jules, spill it."

"I already did. Really, that's all that happened." I lay back on the shingles, stretch my arms above my head, and stare up at the stars. She does the same.

"Okay. Maybe that was all that happened. But how did it make you feel? I mean... you seemed so... love-struck just from looking him in the eyes."

I burst out laughing. "I was not! Was I? What... exactly is a love-struck look?" I ask, turning my head to meet hers. She smiles at me.

"That look that you have right now. It's mapping out your life ever since you ran into... what's his name?"

"I don't know."

"You never asked his name?"

"He never asked for mine, either."

"So, you're not going to see him again? Do you want to?"

I consider her question, and then counter with my own. "What's it like, Natalie... to kiss a guy?" I ask this in full confidence that she can answer, knowing that she and Sebastian have kissed... several times, I'm sure.

"Oh, Julia, it's like everything changes. The way you feel about everyday, normal stuff. It's like... different. Everything is extra-special, all because of that kiss." She's talking up to the stars now. "Before, when getting ready in the morning, you thought nothing of it. Then it becomes all about him. How you want to look, how you want him to see you."

This I know from the noticeable change in her from the first day that Sebastian came into her life. Before that day, she was just Natalie. Then, overnight, she became Natalie, conformed. She had her hair lightened, and her eyes were enhanced with shadow and mascara. Not that she wasn't lovely before. It's just that now, it's all enhanced.

"It's like that one kiss gave you something to build your dreams on." She rolls on her side, and looks straight at me. "The dreams of what you want for your future, who you're going to be, what your babies will look like, what their names will be. Oh, Julia—it's transforming!"

Just like my daydream in the kitchen. I was married, cooking dinner for my family, with my babies running in. But he and I never kissed in real life. So why do I feel like this? Was it from the feel and smell of his sweat, as my face laid against his chest? Was it the way I looked into his deep, blue eyes? Was it the way he looked at me when he was untangling my hair? Or was it the way he picked me up, making me feel protected? Whatever it was... my life feels different.

"Tell me something, Julia. What's it like to have never been kissed? I mean, you're twenty-one. Don't you want something to build your dreams on? I know you want to study French cuisine in Paris... but without someone making you feel special... is it enough?"

At this moment, I'm not sure how to answer her. Thoughts of cuisine and Paris have been my only purpose. Thinking of him today, my dreams have changed. I did feel... special, and pretty, all from just our short time together. And in that time...... everything changed. But did it change for him? I look at Natalie, who is still waiting for my answer. "I guess... I don't know how it feels. I will have to tell you after I've been kissed."

"You're still thinking about him, aren't you?" she says with a smile.

"Yeah. I guess I am."

She gets up, shoves her phone into the pocket of her jean shorts, and swings her leg over the trellis. "I'll be waiting to hear about that first kiss, Julia." She climbs down the trellis, jumps to the ground, and disappears under the stars. *She'd better be back in an hour.*

I climb back through my window, open my laptop, and check for any updates on Angie's List. So far... nothing. I give myself a pep talk. It's only been one day, but still I stare at the screen, waiting for something to pop up. When I grow cross-eyed, I shut the laptop, and crawl into bed. I know I will be awake until I hear Natalie climbing back on the roof, and into her room. But in the meantime, I lie awake and think about... bike man.

～

DROPPING THE GIRLS OFF AT THE Y AGAIN THIS MORNING, I'M EAGER, almost giddy, to head to the boardwalk. Of course, I tell myself it's only a routine for my daily devotions. It has nothing to do with the fact that... he might be there. Well... maybe a little. *I hope he is.*

I park my Mini and walk with anticipation to the boardwalk. I get a little perturbed when I'm blocked by a group of mommy-and-me dates, which are crowding the bridge with preschoolers and strollers. I say a little serenity prayer, and then glide through.

No little birds, or squirrels, or groundhogs get my attention today. Only one thing inhabits my thoughts. *Him.*

I turn the last curve, and see the broken railing. Yellow caution tape has been hung at the crash site. Walking over, I touch the remaining railing, and the spot where he picked me up, like it's... holy or... sacred. Looking around, I scan the area in hopes that his bike will come flying by. What if it does? Will he stop? Will he even remember me? And, what will I do? Jump out in front of him, and say, "Remember me?" Lord, I'm stupid.

Another group of mommies and babies pass by, followed by a few joggers and fast walkers, and then my heart beats faster when I see a bike approaching. I narrow my eyes as the bike gets closer. Seriously, what am I going to do if it's him? I haven't thought this detail out very well.

The bike is now ascending closer, and the memory of his chest against my cheek triggers a response somewhere deep inside me. It's something I've never felt before. It feels divine and... sinful at the same time. Quickly, I pull out my hair tie, shake my head, and let the long waves of my hair fall over my shoulders. The dress I wore today is quite a bit shorter than usual—a design by Natalie—and my shoulders are... bare. No little white trainers today—I am wearing leather, thong sandals. Oh... and my toes are painted bright pink, too. It's just as Natalie said: "Love changes the way you feel about yourself." All because of him, I feel pretty and special, making this average day a fête of me. I'm decorated.

As the bike approaches, a tingling feeling penetrates through my skin, hitting me deep somewhere in my core. What *is* happening? I'm scared. I'm going to jump. Because, if it is him, I'm a mess of hormones, and I won't even be able to talk. But if I jump, he will have to save me. Will he save me?

My breasts feel swollen, and my inner thighs are... clammy. My hands are shaking, and my mouth is dry. Oh, good God, what the *hell* is wrong with me? And why did I just say *hell* in my mind? If this is love, why does it feel so... awful... and exhilarating at the same time? *Because it's love.*

Just a few more feet. He's close, and my heart is about to blow out of my chest. He's not slowing down. He races faster... and so does my heart. *Quick, act normally, Julia.* Slowly, I tilt my head to the side, tossing my hair over my shoulder, and look him in the eye. "Oh, it's you. The foul-speaking bike rider."

As he whizzes by, he looks at me as if I suddenly grew an alien head. It's not him, and now I feel like a complete fool. First, I look around, making sure that no one else has witnessed my foolishness, and then place my elbows on the wooden rail, watching as the yellow caution tape flaps in the breeze.

I'm quite confused. I don't know what I expected. *Yes, you do, Julia. You expected him to be thinking about you all night, like you were of him. You thought for sure that he would come here, hoping to find you. Really, Julia, don't try to fool me... because you can't... I am you.*

"Don't be so down. He's thinking of you," a woman's voice says.

Glancing over my shoulder, I see a short, ample woman standing with her back to me. "Excuse me? Were you talking to me?"

"I believe we are the only ones here, Dear."

"There was no one here a second ago," I say. Because there wasn't. Where'd she come from?

"A lot can happen in a second," she says with a chuckle while holding her hand out to the greenery. A small, gold finch lands on her hand. I walk over, slowly, and watch in amazement as the little bird eats seed from her hand.

Her gaze is focused off in the distance, not on the bird. It pecks away, scattering seeds to the ground. His little head jerks from side to side, and then he flies away.

"You said something a minute ago," I say. "Something about he's... thinking of me? What did you mean by that?"

"Just what I said. He's thinking of you, too." She places her hand into the pocket of her jacket and pulls out more seed, still looking straight ahead.

"Who's he? And how do you know what I was thinking?"

"Well, you were, weren't you? Doesn't really matter how I know." She turns towards me, and it's now I see the heavy, white cataracts that cover her eyes. She's blind.

Another little bird lands in her hand, and pecks at the food. Usually, it would be easy for her to guess my thoughts by the disappointment showing on my face. But... she's blind.

"Tell me what kind of bird is in my hand, Dear," she says.

"Um... I think it's a wren. I don't know birds very well," I say, giving a small laugh.

"Yes, I think you're right. It feels like a wren." I wonder how she can tell. "Here, give me your hand." Lifting my hand, she pours some seed into my palm. "Now, hold it out." I do... cautiously. Within moments, a little sparrow lands and feeds from my palm.

"Wow, I didn't know this was possible." As I admire the sparrow, I also look at the big smile on her face. I wonder what she is smiling about. She can't see the bird. "You're right, you know. I *was* thinking of someone."

"I know," she says. "And he's thinking of you, too. Somewhere out there, someone is thinking about what it would be like to be with a person like you." She's not speaking of someone in general.

The little bird flies off, and I rub my hands together, shaking out the rest of the seed.

"You came here because you're looking for something different in your life," she continues.

"What makes you say that?" I ask, wondering how she can read me.

"Easy. Your breathing. It gives signs of frustration and irritation. It was not until I made you aware of the little birds, did it change."

"I was hoping to meet someone here today. It didn't happen."

"Maybe today is not the day." She turns, feels for the railing, and cautiously finds her surroundings. Looking at her now, I think that she must be at least in her seventies. "You can't make things happen when it's not time. That's not up to you. Sometimes, what we learn, and who we become in the process of waiting, is even more important than what we're waiting for."

"I don't even know what I'm supposed to be waiting for, or who I am supposed to become." I slump back against the railing, then watch her feel for her cane. "Here, let me help you."

"Oh. Thank you, Dear." With her cane, she feels for her surroundings. The cane bumps against the built-in bench, and she feels her way to sit down. "Come here, Dear," she says, patting the spot beside her. I do.

"How long have you been blind?" I ask her.

"I don't even remember. A long time, I guess."

A small breeze stirs my hair and tickles my nose. Grabbing the long locks, I pull them over to one side and begin twisting, giving my hands something to do. "Your hair is very pretty," she says.

"Oh... thank you," I say, and wonder how she can tell.

"It smells long."

"You can tell that it's long by the smell?"

"Yes, it smells like fresh lilacs, and I've never smelled them here before. So, it has to be your hair blowing in the breeze." I study her. She's so observant.

"You know... for being blind, you sure see a lot," I say. She smiles. "I'm not blind, but seem to be in the dark so much. I feel lost most times, and feel as though I'm waiting for... well... I don't actually know what I'm waiting for." I feel close to her, and yet I don't know her. It's like she appeared from nowhere.

"Don't worry, God is never blind to your tears, never deaf to your prayers, and never silent to your pain. He sees, He hears, and He will deliver you."

I find it strange that she is telling me these things, because, truthfully, I'm beginning to wonder if He does hear me.

"You're having doubts, Dear? Just remember, when you are going through something hard, and wonder where God is, remember that the teacher is always quiet during a test." I look at her face—worn, yet so gentle. I want to touch her face, because even though it's laden with wrinkles, I have the sense that it would feel like velvet.

"Thank you," I say, and cover her hand with mine. "It's nice talking to you." I hesitate before speaking again. "I want to study French cuisine, and be a chef in Paris."

"Oh, how exciting!" She gives me comfort. Natalie is the only one I confided with. The fear of judgment keeps me silent.

"You really think so? You don't find that... immoral of me?"

"Why would that make you immoral?"

"Well... it's just some people feel that a woman shouldn't have such a career... or career at all, for that matter." It feels good to say this out loud.

She squeezes my hand. "They are not to judge. They have no idea what storm God has asked you to weather." Her face is so sweet, and angelic. I feel at peace with her.

"Thank you. You have no idea how uplifting that is to me."

"Ask yourself this, Dear. Consider what you're doing today. Is it getting you closer to where you want to be tomorrow? Complaining will change nothing. Take action, make a change, and never look back."

Thinking back on the day before, when I placed an ad on Angie's List, I have definitely taken forward action, steps in the right direction. "Well... I think I have. However, those, too, come with ulterior motives."

She chuckles. "Sounds like the perfect plan."

"Thank you for your words of encouragement. I must get going. Can I help you with where you need to go?"

"Oh no, Dear. I'm fine. You go on, and don't give up on that dream. You hear me?"

I stand, placing a hand on her shoulder. "I won't... I promise," I say, hating the fact that I have to leave her now. "Again... thank you."

As I walk away, a peaceful feeling runs through me. I see a clear picture of my future, guided and mapped out before me, and for once, it feels good to be lost in the right direction. Maybe it's been the only direction for me all along. My dream is no longer a dream... it's a plan.

A few more feet down the boardwalk, and it hits me that I never asked her name. I spin on my heel, turning to walk back toward her, but she's gone. It's only been a few seconds. There is no way she could have moved out of my sight. *She's blind.*

My cell phone pings with a notification, and I glance at it. It's an email alert from Angie's List. Tapping the screen, I quickly open the message.

Dear Ms. Julia Ellis,

I have read over your qualifications for the nanny position you are seeking. We need your services for a ten-year-old little girl. This also will be a live-in position, so I hope this arrangement works for you. Please email me back ASAP with a time, so we may set up an interview and discuss further arrangements.

Thank You
   L. O'Shea.

3

THE DRIVE HOME IS QUIET. NOT EVEN THE GIRLS ARE SAYING MUCH, BUT I'm sure Natalie has a list of questions for me when we get home. Right now, I'm formulating a strategy of how to go about breaking this to Pastor Tom and Cathy. Maybe I should say nothing until after the interview. After all, there's a good chance I won't get the position. *But there's also a good chance... I might.*

The email said this was a live-in position. I never considered that might be the case. This is going to be awkward. Yes... I expected long days, and possibly some late nights... but living with people I don't even know? And would they feel comfortable with me, as well?

Pulling into the drive, I take a deep breath. "I got a response for the nanny position," I say to Natalie once Paige has left the car. She smiles.

"I thought something was up."

"They want me to move in," I say in rush.

"Even better." Her grin turns devious. As I watch her eyes light up, I just know that her pretty little head is spinning with sneaky thoughts.

"Don't look so eager to get rid of me. Aren't you going to miss me?"

"Julia, I'm going with you when you leave for Paris. So... yes, I will miss you for now, but you are my ticket out of here, and my ticket to be with Sebastian. And the way I see it... you will need my help as a nanny's assistant... free of charge, of course."

And there it is... the ulterior motive spreading like wild fire in the dry hills of California. Well, at least she has a plan, even though it hangs on the tailcoats of *my* plans. Even more reason to worry about what Pastor Tom and Cathy will think. Like I don't have enough to worry about!

"So, when is the interview, and where?" she asks, with wide eyes.

"I need to email back a time at my earliest response. It sounded urgent. But Natalie... there's a good chance I won't get this job. It's just an interview."

"Oh... you will get this job, Julia. No one out qualifies you, "she says, checking her reflection in the visor mirror.

I smile at her. "Thanks, Natalie. That means a lot. Really, it does."

"Now, let's go send that email," she says, getting out of the car.

Running up the stairs two at a time, I try to catch up with her. She's already in my room, lying on my bed on her stomach with the laptop open, scanning my emails. "Hey... that's private," I say, quickly turning the laptop around.

"Like you would have anything to keep private, Julia." She rolls her eyes.

"I might. Okay... I don't. But that's no excuse for you to go through it."

She rests her chin in her hands. "Just open the damn thing and set the time for tomorrow."

Sitting cautiously down in the chair, like it's about to be pulled out from under me, I open the email. I read it again, biting the hangnail on my thumb.

"I need to ask the location first... don't you think?"

"Who cares? As long as it's far from this Bible-Belt, corn-growing Indiana town," she says, rolling over onto her back. Her iPhone sings Taylor Swift, and she pulls it from her pocket. "It's Sebastian." She taps the accept button as she gets up. "Hello, Babe... *tomorrow*," she whispers pointing to me as she leaves the room. I hear the bang of her bedroom door, and start my response to Ms. O'Shea.

Dear Ms. L. O'Shea

Thank you for the consideration of my employment as your nanny. I will let you know how soon we can meet, once I know your location. I live in Warsaw, Indiana, so I hope your location isn't too far. Not that this is a problem; it's your convenience I am considering, since your email seemed urgent. Also, Ms. O'Shea, you stated that this is a live-in position. I hope we can further discuss the living arrangements upon meeting. I hadn't planned for this employment to be live-in; however, I am not opposed. I'm looking forward to our meeting.

Kind Regards,
    Julia Ellis

I hit send and begin to shut my laptop, when a ping comes through, signifying an email alert—her... email alert—Ms. O'Shea's.

That was fast. How desperate is she? I mean it's only for one child. And she wants me to live with them. Then the worries of why taunt me. What if she's handicapped? Not the child, but the mother... *or maybe both.* Not that it would matter—but would I qualify?

The location. She has an Irish name. Could this possibly be a nanny position in Ireland? Would I want to move to Ireland? How far is that from Paris? I could be closer to my dream place... and far from the eyes of judgment. *This is getting better.*

I open the email and begin to read, biting the hangnail again on my thumb.

Ms. Ellis

Thank you for your prompt response. We are located at 5952 Oak Road, just thirty miles east of you in Ft. Wayne. So, I hope this is not a problem for your commute for the interview. I will be happy to answer any questions you have about the living arrangements. One thing I can tell you now is that you will have your own room on the west wing of the manor, with plenty of privacy. You are correct about my sense of urgency—the sooner the better. Also, Ms. Ellis, this position is for long term. We can further discuss this at the interview. Will tomorrow morning at ten o'clock work for you? Again, thank you, Ms. Ellis.

L. O'Shea

Ms. L O'Shea

This time will work. See you tomorrow.

Julia Ellis

AFTER GIVING MY MINI A FULL TANK OF PETROL FOR MY HOUR-LONG drive, and dropping the girls off, I once again look over the directions before starting Google maps. It seems clear, so I tap the app and pull out of the station.

The first twenty miles is a straight stretch down the highway, and I think back to last night's conversation with the DeLucas. I can honestly say... it went much better than I thought it would.

Pastor Tom appeared totally fine with my leaving, given the fact that Cathy will have to step back into her role as full-time mother. Of course, having one less female in the house will probably be a little relief, with all the hormones raging every month, especially now with Paige entering adolescence. The poor man is totally outnumbered. Then, the father in him was concerned for me, asking questions such as—Who are these people? How well do you know them? Do they attend church? And if they do... what denomination? I have no answers for those.

Cathy's concerns were about Tom. He would have to play less golf and help her with the girls. *Strange*... I didn't seem to need his help. Then she turned to me with tears in her eyes (which made me tear up as well), and said, "But it's like you're my baby, too."

Natalie, ever mischievous, sat in a chair pretending to be looking at a country and craft magazine, which was actually only the cover from one of Cathy's magazines. If you looked inside, it was the latest issue of Cosmo—like I said earlier: clever girl. Yet, she was supportive, and made such responses as, "Oh Julia, I'm so happy for you... but I'm going to miss you. I will spend some nights helping you. I'm sure you're going to need some help... right?" At this, I turned my head slightly and narrowed my eyes at her, then agreed that there will be days I would love having her around.

After the conversation ended, Paige, who had been oblivious to all of this, removed her pink Beats and said, "What's everyone talking about? Why is Mom crying?"

To which Natalie retorted, Paige needs to be more involved with her family, which scored points with her parents—Little Miss Ulterior Motives. I then exhaled. The truth was out—partly. I still hadn't mentioned my plans for Paris.

I'm shaken back into reality by the commanding voice of Google maps, alerting me to stay right at the fork, and continue on I-24. Quickly, I use my turn signal and make my way into the right lane. According to the directions, I will arrive at my destination in twelve minutes. I debated on telling Tom and Cathy *after* the interview, but then there was the possibility that I would not make it back in time to pick up the girls. I desperately wanted to use Natalie's theory—*It's easier to ask for forgiveness then for permission.* But I just couldn't do it.

After a few more turns, I find myself driving up a long, paved driveway leading to a house that looks more like an inn. She did say manor... so I guess this is it. I park my Mini in the horseshoe-shaped drive and peer out the windshield. The house is enormous, with a colonial look, with white, painted bricks, and black shutters that encase every window... all twelve of them—and that's just the front. A large front porch sits bare with no outdoor furniture, or even a plant. I would think the mistress of the home would at least adorn the front with some feathery ferns, or large pots of geraniums. Not even a bit of land-scaping—just grass growing right up to the house.

Switching the engine off, I grab my purse and folder, containing my certifications and references. I give myself one more assessment in the rearview mirror. Not sure what look I should go with, Natalie gave me a light application of makeup. She applied a dusting of blue eye shadow to my eyelids, and some pink gloss to my lips. To me... it's a bit much. My hair is in a French twist—more of a professional look. I'm wearing a blue, pencil skirt with a white blouse; a red, white, and blue scarf is tied around my neck. I look like a flight attendant for American Airlines.

I exit the car and walk slowly toward the front door. They are huge, double-hung, wooden, black doors, each with a brass creature holding a ringed knocker in its mouth. I look for a doorbell button—however, there isn't one. I grab one of the knockers and start to bring it down, when the door opens.

"Hello, you must be Julia," a woman with a heavy Irish accent says. Well, I did get the Irish part right.

"Yes, I am. And you are..."

"Lisa. Lisa O'Shea. Please come in, Ms. Ellis." She backs away from the door, gesturing for me to come in. I do. I wait for her to shut the door, and follow her down a long corridor. "I take it you had no problem finding the place? I hope it wasn't too much of a drive for you?"

"Oh no... not at all. I just wasn't expecting the house to be so isolated."

"Yes. When people think of Fort Wayne, their first image is always the city," she says. I love her accent. She seems older than I would have thought for having a ten-year-old. She has to be at least in her sixties—but a pretty sixty, I have to say. Her figure is trim, and her hair is cut in a shiny, red bob that swishes from side to side when she moves her head.

Her eyes are the bluest of blue. "I'm heating the kettle for some tea. I hope you'll join me?"

"Oh, yes. I would love some."

"Please come with me, Ms. Ellis. I will just make our teas, and then we can take them to the back patio for some fresh air while we make friends. Do you have a particular fancy?" I'm sure she's referring to the tea. Oh... she's so proper. *I love it.*

"Earl Grey?" I ask.

"Yes," she smiles.

As we make our way to the kitchen, once again I'm astonished of the lack of furnishings. Bare walls, with no photos of the little girl—or even a family pet, such as a dog or cat. There are no family vacation pictures. The place is classic, clean and... sterile. Not much of a lived-in atmosphere. A large, fieldstone fireplace showcases the entire front room, and could be such a beauty, if there were at least one piece of art, or a family portrait above the mantel. Nothing. *Perhaps they've only just moved in.*

The sound of the teakettle whistles as we enter the kitchen, steam erupting through the spout. "What a lovely kitchen," I say. It really is grand in an old, palatial way. The room is huge, with tall, upper cabinets that are stained like black walnut. A granite worktop, with a more than ample working area, is at the center of the room. I could *so* work in this kitchen, filling it with the much-needed aromas of each season. Summer salads with fresh cucumbers, and strawberries. Apple pies, and coffee cakes, in the fall. Winter would bring the wafting scent of a Christmas goose, glazed in butter, with cranberries.

"Oh, that it is, Dear. You like to cook?" she asks.

"Oh, yes. I plan to study at a culinary academy, and hopefully become a chef." I decide not to elaborate much more on the topic. Right now, I should focus on this interview only.

She pours the water into two cups on the granite worktop, each with a tea bag placed inside. "Do you need any sugar—or cream, perhaps?"

"No, thank you. I like it plain."

"Very well, Dear," she says, handing me a cup that is set on a matching saucer, with a small spoon. Grabbing her cup, she walks to the glass doors, which give a beautiful view where a garden could be. But giving of my earlier thought, perhaps they've only moved, and after all... it's still only May, which means there is plenty of time to start one. "Are you okay with the patio, Ms. Ellis?"

"Yes, that will be lovely," I say, grabbing my saucer and cup, and following her out. The back yard is bordered by a three-foot stone ledge. Some of the stones are beginning to crumble away, yet the ledge is perfect, in its old, crumbling-ruin way. A grassy field stretches far into distant hills. I wonder how large the estate is.

"So... tell me about yourself, Ms. Ellis. I read your qualifications. However, I would like to know more on a personal level," she says, and reaches for her tea.

I cringe a little, wondering how much I should reveal. But of course, she is putting her trust in me with the care of her little girl... so I should be upfront and honest. "Well," I start, "what my resume doesn't say is that I was orphaned as a young girl—fourteen, to be precise. My parents were both killed in an automobile accident." She grabs her chest.

"Oh, my, I'm so sorry to hear that. That must have been devastating for such a young girl."

"Yes, it was hard. I had no siblings so... I had to grieve alone. Luckily, I had the DeLucas—Pastor Tom, and his wife, Cathy—taking me in, and raising me. I was at church camp the week it happened. They have two girls, much younger than me, so I practically raised them as well. I adore them—they are each like little sisters to me."

"Well, thank the heavens for them," she smiles.

"Yes, I was blessed with their family. Also, our church favors home-schooling, so, once I finished my state-approved education, I then earned my certification to teach as well... in a home-school setting. I have no bachelor's degree to teach in public or private school—I just want to make that clear."

"Oh, that's wonderful. However, Sidney does attend public school. But there are subjects she could use some tutoring in. That will come in very handy."

"Sidney? That's her name?"

"Yes. That's where her father was at the time of her birth—Sydney, Australia. So he named her Sidney."

"Oh, what a sweet story. It's so nice for a father to be involved in naming his child," I say. Her eyes quickly dart away from mine, and her smile fades, like maybe I said something wrong. She grabs up her teacup.

"Yes. Well... tell me more about yourself. You say you're a swimmer? Can you give lessons, as well?"

I feel that, for some odd reason, she is trying to change the subject. "Yes, I do. I taught both girls, and they, too, now teach. They're both avid swimmers. I give Bible lessons as well... if that's okay with you, Ms. O'Shea." The moment turns awkward when she looks away again, not responding. I regret bringing up religion, but this is something that I know Pastor Tom will ask about, and I will need to have an answer for him.

She sets her tea down, and I wait for her response, which seems to take longer than it should. "Sidney would love swim lessons. There's no pool here on the property, but perhaps you could take her to the public pool?" I blink a few times, noticing how her questions seem to be directed... almost *detached*. Such as "On the property," instead of "We have no pool." And something about the way she speaks of the little girl... calling her by name and never says, "My daughter." I wait just a few more seconds before responding, wondering if she has an answer for my question of the Bible study. When she says nothing... I speak.

"Yes, I could take her to the public pool. That will not be a problem." She sits up straight, then taps her spoon on the saucer before setting it down.

"Ms. Ellis, I think you are perfect for this position. I need to know how soon you can start. I'm moving back to Ireland, and I will not be returning. My mother is very ill, and I must care for her."

"Oh... well." I swallow, and shake my head. "Well... I'm elated, Ms. O'Shea, that you feel I'm perfect for the position. However, wouldn't you want to take your daughter with you?" I'm sure the confusion on my face is noticeable. Perhaps they are divorcing. Why would she not be returning to Ireland with her own daughter?

"Oh, I'm terribly sorry for the confusion, Ms. Ellis. Sidney is not my daughter. I am her current nanny. Sidney's mother died when she was a baby. You will be working for her father, Mr. Fairbanks. He is gone most of the time. Travels the world for his business."

My look remains deadpan, I'm sure, for she seems to be evaluating my thoughts. I struggle with my next words. "Oh, I'm so sorry to hear this. How terrible it must be for her... losing her mother as an infant." I blink, realizing that what I just said could be an insult to her, if she has always been her nanny. "I mean... I mean losing her mother at such a young age. I'm sure her father has made great accommodations for her. May I ask how long you've been her nanny?" I'm backpedaling now, sounding ridiculous.

"I've been with little Sidney for two years. Yes, Mr. Fairbanks has done... well, he has done his best, I'm sure. But fathers can be different than mothers," she says, looking away. "I don't ask too many questions, Ms. Ellis. I see to it that the little girl is well cared for. That is what Mr. Fairbanks compensates a nanny for." And as she says this, I get the feeling it's for my benefit, and is not her true opinion.

I grab my tea as she waits for my answer of how soon I can start. So, I finish the last drop, set the mug down on its saucer, and answer, "Yes, I can start right away."

Her eyes light up. "Oh, God bless you! You are an angel, sent from above." She pulls a necklace out from under her blouse, and kisses it—rosary beads. Catholic—I wonder what Pastor Tom's take will be on that. "Let me show you to your quarters, and then we can discuss anything else that you may need to know."

She and I grab our cups, and I follow her back into the kitchen. "Just set your cup in the sink, Dear. I will clean it later. Follow me, please."

We climb a staircase off the back of the kitchen that leads to a landing on the second story. From where I'm standing, I see only two doors down a long hallway. "This will be your quarters, Ms. Ellis. This here is your bath," she says, opening the door. "And down here to the right, will be your bedroom." She opens the door, and I'm dumb-founded at the large room—complete with a fireplace, and a window seat. It has an old English flair with a four-poster bed, and a dressing table in the corner. Off to the left is another door.

"Is this a passage to another room?" I ask.

"No, Dear. This is your closet. I hope it will fit all your things?" Opening the door, she walks in and turns on a light. I follow and assess the closet for myself.

"Oh, my. This has to be the biggest closet I've ever seen." My mouth drops open, and I will myself to shut it. "Oh, this will do perfectly. More than perfectly."

"Oh good. I'm glad," she says, walking out of the closet. "Now, shall we go back downstairs and discuss the... how soon you can move in?"

"Yes, Ms. O'Shea."

"Please call me Lisa." I nod with a smile, and follow her back down the stairs. Once in the kitchen, she turns quickly toward me and starts making suggestions. "How about you join me tomorrow early morning, when little Sidney is preparing for school? I can show you where her school is when I take her, and then I will make you familiar with the rest of the duties."

"Oh, that sounds great. I can't wait to meet her. But I'm sure she's going to miss you, after you spent two years in her life. I just hope she will warm up to me."

"Yes... I will miss the little lass. And... just give her some time, Ms. Ellis, on the... warming up part. She took some time taking to the likings of me."

"Maybe she feels threatened by someone taking the place of her mother?" I say. She looks at me, wringing her hands together as if there may be another reason. However, she does not speak on the matter. She turns to rinse the teacups out.

"Oh, little girls can be quite fickle," she says, and sets the cups in the drainer.

This is the second time that has felt awkward. I begin to wonder about it, and then shrug it off. Perhaps she's testing me. "So, how early do you need me to be here?"

"Is seven bells too early for you, Ms. Ellis?"

This means that I will need to be up at four to be on the road by at least six. Before she thinks I'm hesitant, I quickly respond. "Not at all. I will be here."

"Marvelous."

She walks me to the door, and I thank her for accepting me for the position.

"Oh no, Dear... thank you for accepting the position." I'm about to walk out when she speaks. "Oh, bloody hell. I forgot to go over the compensation with you. Oh well, we can go over that tomorrow. Just have your bank account number handy. Mr. Fairbanks deposits each week into your account. This is much easier for him than writing a check, given that he's out of the country so often.

"Okay, not a problem. Goodbye, Ms. O'Shea. I'm very excited to start." Instead of saying goodbye, she places her hand on my shoulder. I'm expecting her to say something, or to at least smile. But she does neither. So, I turn, and head for my Mini.

When I reach the car door, I notice that she is still watching me... strangely. Something doesn't feel right. The sky turns an ash grey, and just as I'm about to open my door, I'm startled by a crow landing on the hood of my car, cawing, and thrashing his wings at me. Quickly, I get into the car and shut the door. The crow hops closer on the hood, jerking his head, and looking at me with one eye. "Shoo... shoo," I say, starting the car.

Before putting the car in gear, I look over at her once more, and give a small wave. She places a hand gently on her throat before returning a weak wave back.

Yes... something doesn't feel right.

4

———

I CURSE THE DARK CIRCLES UNDER MY EYES THE NEXT MORNING WHEN I look into the rearview mirror. I lay awake all night, consumed with worry about oversleeping. Then, when I wasn't consumed with worry, I was filling in the gaps of what seems to be a mysterious situation going on at the house of Mr. Fairbanks. It's not every day that a crow lands on my car, warning me off.

The rising sun blinds me, so I pull down the visor to avoid its glare as I pull up the horseshoe drive. I park, kill the engine, and curse once more at the dark circles as I check myself in the mirror one last time. *I don't want to frighten this little girl on my first day.*

The door again opens just as I'm about to bring the knocker down. "Good morning, Dear," Lisa greets me with a smile. *How does she know when I'm right at the door?* "How was your drive this morning? I hope it was splendid."

"Yes, it was another pretty drive... once I hit the country. Everything is blooming with color. Full of life," I say, and follow her down the hall into the kitchen.

"Yes... that it is, Dear. Sidney shall be down shortly. She is getting ready for school. May I offer you a cup of tea?"

"Yes... thank you. That will be nice," I say nervously. "I guess I'm a little anxious to meet little Sidney. I just hope she will like me. Most children do. I head up many of the grades at our church. Listen to me ramble on so," I say with hushed laughter. "She's just a little girl. Nothing to be frightened of. It's not like she's going to come down here with fangs and claws." For Pete's sake... I sound pathetic. *Just calm down, Julia.*

"I'm sure she will like you, Ms. Ellis. Sidney is quite... eccentric. Not saying that she's peculiar. It's just... well, I'm sure you will make your own assessment. She likes to keep to herself, mostly."

"Perhaps being without a mother has made her shy? Maybe I can help... being that I have no mother myself." She looks at me with a frown. There it is again. I've said something wrong.

The teapot whistles, and she turns quickly, grabbing it. "Like I said yesterday, Ms. Ellis..."

"Please, call me Julia," I say.

"Julia. Yes, well, like I said yesterday, just remember that you are only here to care for her, and not to get caught up in family concerns. That is what Mr. Fairbanks is paying you for." She pours water into the cups, and then hands me one. "You wouldn't want to confuse the little girl," she says, throwing me a sympathetic look.

"Oh, no. No, I wouldn't want to do that." I feel confused.

"Good. Well, then... just make her happy, and see that she is well cared for. The rest is up to her father to see fit."

"Yes. Yes ma'am." I grab my cup, bringing it to my mouth as if to cover this... again awkward moment.

"Well, good morning, little lass. This here is Ms. Ellis." I spin around from the worktop, and my eyes land on the most beautiful little girl I have ever seen. Her dark, shiny, long hair falls over her little shoulders like a princess's. Her eyes are emerald green... they are gorgeous. Her skin is flawless, with an olive color adults envy. She is truly a lovely little girl.

"Hi there," I say, walking over and bending down to meet her. "I'm Julia. Please... just call me Julia. I'm going to be your new nanny." Her eyes move from me to Lisa, then back to me. I hope I haven't said anything wrong. Surely, she has been told Lisa is leaving. Is there no communication in this house?

"Say good morning to Julia, Sidney," Lisa says.

"Good morning, Julia," she says, taking a seat at the table. I look to Lisa, who is now pulling out a plate from the microwave.

"Blueberry pancakes, your favorite," she says, setting the plate in front of her.

"Oh, they're my favorite, too," I say, hoping to break the ice. Sidney looks up at me, and then turns to her pancake. I look to Lisa with desperation in my eyes. She raises her eyebrows as if to say, "give her time."

THE DRIVE INTO THE CITY TAKES TWENTY MINUTES. SIDNEY HAS REMAINED quiet the whole time, sitting in the backseat and gazing out the side window. Lisa makes casual talk about how beautiful the spring is, and how school will be out soon. "You'll have the whole summer to get to know Julia. Doesn't that sound fun, Sidney, making a new friend? Julia gives swimming lessons. Wouldn't you like to learn to swim?"

"I do," I say, turning around, and giving her a smile. She looks from the window.

"Yes, I would like that," she says, then returns her gaze to the window.

"I can teach your friends, too. We can all go to the pool together. Would you like that?"

Without turning her face from the window, she says, "I have no friends."

Feeling the moment is heading down awkward alley *again*, I continue to smile at her. "Well, I tell you what... we are going to make lots of friends this summer at the pool. I know two girls who are dying to meet you. Their names are Natalie and Paige. I live with them, and they want to come and see you."

"Why?"

"Why? Because they love meeting new people, that's why. Would you like to meet them?"

She shrugs. "I guess."

I feel Lisa's hand cover mine. I look to her. "Give her time," she mouths.

She turns into the parking lot of Wayne Elementary, parking the car at the curb. "Oh, is this your school? I would love to see your room." She looks to Lisa.

"I think it would be nice, Sidney. Why don't you show Julia your room, and then introduce her to your teacher?"

Sidney has a moment of hesitation before she answers. "Okay."

"Really?" I smile, overly pleased. "Oh, I would love to see your teacher. You know, Sidney, I'm a teacher too." She grabs her book bag and opens the car door. I get out, and walk with her up the sidewalk. Lisa waits behind in the car.

As we walk inside, I notice that none of the other little girls talk to her. They are all chatting with each other, but none talk to Sidney. Maybe she is right about having no friends. *Well, I'm going to change that.*

She leads me to a room down the hall, where she hangs her bag on a hook, then takes a small desk next to the window. I stand in front of the classroom, and watch as she sits alone. Other girls chatter with each other, but none with her. She is truly the prettiest little girl in the class That alone should make her a magnet to her little mates. Perhaps, there is more going on here.

The teacher enters, a very young and attractive woman, and I make my way to her desk, introducing myself. "Hi," I say, and extend my hand. "I'm Julia Ellis, Sidney Fairbanks's nanny... or new nanny." She sets a canvas bag of books on her desk, and shakes my hand.

"Hello, I'm Mrs. Gensinger. Ms. O'Shea told me Sidney was getting a new nanny. I'm glad you came in today. Perhaps you would like to stay and observe?"

I look over at Sidney, now pulling a reader from her desk. "Just a minute, let me talk with Sidney."

"Sure, no problem," she says, and tells the rest of the class, who are still buzzing around, to have a seat

Walking over to her desk, I bend down, meeting her little face. She looks up at me with those beautiful, emerald eyes. "Your teacher asked if I would like to stay. Would it be okay if I arrange to stay tomorrow? Ms. O'Shea needs to show me things... or I would stay. I really would like to get to know some of your friends."

"I told you... I don't have any friends," she says, turning away.

I look around the room. "Oh, I'm sure there are lots of little girls who want to be your friend. They just don't know you yet."

"You don't know me," she says, and looks back to her book.

"Well, not yet. But I can't wait to know you better. Tell you what... I'm going to leave with Ms. O'Shea, and have her show me all the things you like to do. Then, I'm going to think of new things that we can do together. While I'm gone, I want you to think of things you would like to do with me. Okay?"

She shrugs. I open her desk, looking for a pad of paper. "Do you have a pencil?" She reaches in her desk, and hands me a pencil. "How about at recess, you take this pad outside with you and write some things you would like to do?" Maybe this exercise will take her mind off not having any friends to play with. She gives a slow smile and nods her head. And with this small accomplishment, I feel a piece of the wall chipping away.

When I return to the car, Lisa is on her phone, and appears to be upset. "Yes, Daniel, I will book it tonight. Please tell Mum to hang on. I will. Tell Mum I love her. I love you too, Daniel. Bye." She ends the call, and pulls a tissue from her purse.

"Is everything all right?" I ask, getting into the car.

"Oh, Julia—my mum has taken a turn for the worse. I must leave tonight. I hope you are prepared to stay."

"Well, I only brought a few things with me... but yes, it's not a problem. Please, do what you must. I'm so sorry for your situation."

"Thank you, Julia."

"Would you like for me to drive home? You seem pretty upset. Please, let me drive." We switch positions in the car, and I pull out of the parking lot. As I make the drive home, Lisa begins writing down information while telling me.

"Okay. Sidney will need to be picked up at three o'clock each day. The school calendar is on the corkboard in the kitchen. Her last day is in June... I'm not quite sure the date, actually. Oh, listen to me make such a fuss. I'm so sorry to leave you like this." She dabs under her bottom lashes with the tissue.

"I understand, Lisa. We will be okay." I smile, touching her shoulder.

"Oh, thank you so much, Dear. I emailed your bank information to Mr. Fairbanks, which he said he has received. He will deposit seven hundred pounds—excuse me, seven hundred dollars each week into your account. There is also an expense account to which your name has been added. This is for all household items, and anything Sidney needs... and, oh... the groundsman will need to be paid out of this account. He takes care of the lawn and any problems that may occur, such as broken tree limbs, and what have you. Any traveling expenses you have are to be paid from this account also."

Seven hundred dollars a week. I try not to show the excitement on my face, especially at such a sad time. But—seven hundred dollars a week! Holy moly! What kind of business does this man own? I exit onto the freeway and make the last stretch home.

"Let me make you familiar with the rest of the house," Lisa says, as we enter the front parlor. We make our way to the kitchen, where she shows me the corkboard with Sidney's school calendar. "Here on this paper is all the contact information you need to reach Mr. Fairbanks— his mobile number, and the number of his main office in Ireland. Of course, I never use this number. I always just ring his mobile."

"Is he Irish, too?"

"Oh, no, Dear, he's American. He has other offices overseas, as well. He usually lets me know which continent he's on."

"Sounds like quite a traveler."

"That he is. Now let me show you the rest of the quarters." She leads me through the corridor to the great room—the one with the beautiful, bare fireplace. I could practically stand up inside, it's so tall. She opens two double, mahogany doors. "This here is where Mr. Fairbanks conducts his business when he's home." There are large, floor-to-ceiling bookshelves covering an entire wall. A large picture window shows a rolling, green pasture extending at least ten acres or so. I didn't see this from the patio the day we had tea. It's absolutely gorgeous. Opposite the window sits a large, mahogany desk with a large, dark-brown, leather chair. How inspiring it must be to have this view when looking out that huge window. I would put my desk here, too... if I had one. "This is where you can always find him when he's home."

"Is he home often?" She shakes her head, then looks at the floor.

"Sadly, no, he's not."

"This must be hard for his daughter," I say. She takes a deep breath.

"Yes, it probably is hard for her. However, she seems to make do."

Make do? How sad.

She pulls open a drawer on the desk, and takes out a leather portfolio. "This will be the account onto which your name has been added for expenses. The bank has been notified of your name in case your signature appears on these checks. A new box of checks should arrive soon with your name on them. In the meantime, it's quite all right to use these." She places the book back into the drawer. "This is the only drawer you have access to. The others remain locked, with Mr. Fairbanks holding the only key. Come now, let's make our way upstairs."

We walk up a stairway, which spirals around to a hall at the top. "This is Sidney's room," she says, opening the door.

"Oh, it's lovely." The room is painted pink and lavender. It has a white bedroom suite, complete with a canopy bed, and matching window treatments. White bookshelves cover one wall, just like in her father's office. "Oh, I would have loved a room like this when I was young," I say in awe, looking around. "Did you help her decorate it?"

"No... this is the way it looked when I arrived two years ago. Now, follow me and I will show you the master's quarters—Mr. Fairbanks's room. Because he is not home very often, the room can get quite dusty and stale. I like to freshen it up with some polish and fresh linens."

My phone rings. I pull it from my pocket and see Cathy's name displayed on the screen. "Hello, Cathy?"

"Oh, Julia! Thank God I reached you." She sounds desperate.

"Cathy... what's wrong? Is everything all right?"

"The girls—I can't find them."

"What do you mean, you can't find them?" I look down at my watch. They have swimming lessons in less than thirty minutes.

"I've hollered for them, but no one answers. I yelled for them to get ready for swim class. I've even checked their rooms. They're not here, Julia."

"Cathy, calm down. Paige is in the tree house with her Beats on. Go out and get her. I'll get a hold of Natalie," I say, knowing exactly where she is.

"Oh... okay. Thank goodness." She ends the call, and I quickly send a text.

Natalie, get rid of that cigarette and get off the roof, your mother is coming up to your room.

Shit... thanks, Julia.

I slide the phone back in my pocket. "Sorry... just some urgent business at home."

"Is everything all right on the home front?"

"It will be," I say, rolling my eyes.

We walk down the hall. Lisa opens the door to Mr. Fairbanks's room displaying a huge, mahogany sleigh bed, with a matching chest and dresser. The room seems dark and dreary, with the thick, heavy drapes that cover the windows. There are only two words to describe this room: *No life.* "I haven't dusted or changed the linens in a few weeks, nor has he been home. So, I'm leaving this to you, Julia."

"Yes, not a problem." *I will also be giving this room some life and light.*

I'm sitting in the great room, writing my list of ideas for things to do with Sidney, while Lisa makes plane reservations and packs for her trip back to Ireland. I was hoping to spend a few more days with her, but due to her mother's illness, I will be taking her to the airport once we have picked Sidney up from school. She wants to say goodbye. I'd be lying if I said I wasn't nervous. In fact, I'm terrified.

Setting my list of ideas on a small end table, I walk over to the large, bare fireplace. I run my hands across the smooth, concrete mantle and along the fieldstone, wondering how old this manor is. Maybe the year it was built is carved into one of these stones. Stretching up on my toes, I look for any carvings, and jump at the loud clang of metal hitting the slate hearth. I turn around and look down at the fireplace tool set I have just knocked over. I hope the slate is not cracked. With my nerves still frazzled, I hear a thump against the window. I jump again.

Carefully placing each tool back into the holder, I feel the floor for any cracks. There don't appear to be any. *I'm lucky.* I then make my way to the window to see what on earth crashed into it. There on the ground is the crow. It's still alive... and cawing at me. This is really getting creepy.

I scream when it flies up and hits the window again.

"Is everything okay in here?" Lisa asks, running in. "I heard such a clatter. Are you all right, Dear?"

"Yes... clumsy me knocked over the fireplace tools. And a crow at the window scared me. I'm sorry... I didn't mean to alarm you," I say, still feeling shaken.

"It's best we be leaving now to pick up Sidney. I just hope the wee lass will forgive me for leaving so soon. But I must be on that plane tonight."

She leaves the room, and I crane my neck out the window. The crow is gone, and a cold shiver runs down my spine. I get a strange feeling that something bad happened here once, long ago.

～

I'M STANDING AT THE SECURITY GATE, WATCHING LISA TALK TO SIDNEY. She is on her knees, meeting her at eye level. "I'm sorry to leave so soon, Lass. I will miss you. But I know Miss Julia will do her best for you." They both look up to me. I nod, giving a look of sympathy as I walk over and lay my hands on Sidney's shoulders.

"I'm here for you, Sidney. Anything you need, I will be here for you." I brush her shiny hair back from her face. She nods and looks down. I try not to show my nervousness, but I am trembling inside.

The last call for boarding is announced. "That's me. I must go now," Lisa says, and kisses Sidney on the cheek. She dabs under her lashes with a tissue, then walks to security. Before walking through, she turns and gives us one last wave. We both wave back. And just like that... she's gone. I look down to Sidney, who is looking up at me. Here I am, with this little girl whom I barely know. *Please, Lord... be with us.*

I am about to reach for her hand when she hands me a folded-up note. "What's this?"

"It's the list you wanted me to make today." I inwardly smack myself for forgetting. With all of today's untimely events, it slipped my mind. "I only have one thing on it," she says. And when I open it up and read what it says, I see why.

"A horse? You want a horse?" She smiles a big smile, and nods excitedly, and I feel another stone fall from that wall. *I must find a horse.* "Come on," I say, taking her by the hand. "You mean, take you somewhere where there are horses, and let you ride them?" I ask, as we leave the airport and walk to my Mini. She climbs in the front seat and buckles her seatbelt.

"No, I want *my* own horse to ride at *my* house. There is plenty of room. You can get you one too," she says, so sincerely. She's breaking my heart... especially since this is the most she has talked since I met her. I start the car and drive out of the airport parking lot.

She watches me as I drive onto the freeway, not saying another word. I don't want her to clam up now. I must keep her talking, if we are to ever break the ice with one another. "So... why a horse? Have you ridden before? Has your father taken you horseback riding?" I'm bombarding her with questions.

"No, I have never ridden a horse. That's why I want one," she says, looking up at me with those killer eyes, and I'm about to melt. *Hmmm... I'm going to have to think about this one.*

"I'll tell you what," I say, turning off the freeway, and onto the last stretch of our drive home, "give me a few days to think about it. I mean, this is a pretty big request, and—not that I'm not up to the challenge, but horses don't grow on trees." She gives me a hopeful smile, and I see two of the cutest dimples in her cheeks.

"Okay," she says. Not another word is spoken the rest of the way home.

I thought that maybe we had broken some ground in the car. However, once we are inside the house, she disappears to her room. I look at the list of foods that Lisa left on the corkboard labeled "Sidney's favorites." It's full of your typical kids' food. Chicken nuggets, waffle fries, mac and cheese, applesauce, and any kind of soup. *Any kind of soup?* This gives me an idea.

Before walking upstairs and asking if she would like to help me make lemon chicken soup with rice, I raid the cupboards, making sure I have all the ingredients. Once my raid has proved fruitful, I go to the top of the stairs. I tap lightly on her door. No answer. I tap a little harder, and still she does not answer. Is she mad at me? "Sidney?" She still does not respond, so I open the door and peek inside. I don't see her. This is where I assumed she went after I saw her climb the stairs.

I begin to panic, and run to her father's room. "She misses him, and went to his room," I say quietly to myself. Opening the door, I still don't see her. I'm about to yell her name when the phone on the nightstand rings. "Ah, she's playing a game with me." I walk to the phone. "Oh, gee... I wonder who that could be," I say, and answer the phone. "Mr. Fairbanks's residence," I say in a silly voice. There is no answer. "Hello," I repeat.

"An inmate is calling from the Indiana State Prison. Will you accept the charges?" says an automated voice. I assume it's a mistake, and hang up. "That was weird." *Sidney!*

I run back down stairs, and look every place a little girl can hide. Panic rises in me even more when I still don't find her. The phone rings again in the kitchen, and I jump. Running to the phone, I answer it again. "Fairbanks residence," I say sternly. There is a slight pause.

"An inmate is calling from the Indiana State Prison. Will you accept the charges?" Again, I hang up, and run up to her room. Walking in, I still don't see her, but I hear strange voices coming from her closet. I slowly walk over, and press my ear to the door. It's her... and she's speaking in different voices.

"Sidney?" I say quietly. The voices stop, and she opens the door. "What were you doing?"

"Playing."

"Are you alone?"

"Yes."

"Then whom were you talking to?"

"No one. I was just playing." She hangs her head in embarrassment.

"Oh. Well, would you like to help me make some soup?" I ask, quickly changing the subject.

"What kind?"

"Lemon chicken with rice. I would love the help. It's kind of lonely down there."

"Okay," she says, and I take her hand.

Sitting at the table, just me and this little girl, I watch as she crushes crackers into her soup. I wonder if she's ever had a close relationship with another female. Does she have any aunts, or even a grandmother? I conclude my answer is no, or they would be here with her instead of... me. I just hope I can make her happy. What was all that talk in her closet? She clearly seemed embarrassed to be caught. And who was calling from the prison?

I'm startled when the sound of a chainsaw begins buzzing somewhere outside. Sidney continues to crush her crackers, not affected by the sound. "What's that?" I ask.

"Probably Gus."

"Gus?"

"The groundsman."

"Oh... yes, the groundsman." I walk over to the patio window, and see an old man with a chainsaw cutting a dead limb from a tree. "I suppose I should introduce myself," I say, and walk out onto the back patio.

I find an opening in the stone wall, and make my way over to the older gentleman. His back is to me, and I don't want to startle him... especially with a running chainsaw. The limb falls, and he backs away. When he turns around, I hold out my hand. "Hi, I'm Julia, the new nanny. You must be Gus." He turns off the chainsaw, and sets it on the ground. Wiping his hands on his coveralls, he then shakes my hand.

"Yes, I am. It's nice to meet you. Has Ms. O'Shea gone?"

"Yes. She left today. Her mother is ill. So, now it's just me," I say, smiling.

"She's been after me to cut down this dead limb for some time now. Would you like me to cut and stack it for you? This ash wood will be great for burning in the fireplace this winter."

"Yes, I suppose. Could I help you?" I would hate to see this old man carry all this wood. He looks feeble.

"No, it's quite all right, Miss. I will just load it up in the wagon, and haul it with the four-wheeler."

"Are you sure? I am glad to help."

"I'm sure. Just doing my job."

"Well, please have some lemon chicken soup. I just made it."

"Now *that* I will do," he says.

"Great, I will put some in a bowl for you." As I make my way back to the house, I hear him yell, "I will mow the field tomorrow. Better get ahead of it now, before it gets too long. I've been telling Mr. Fairbanks that he needs to put that pasture to work, and get some sheep, or cattle, or something."

I spin around with an idea hitting me like a bolt of lightning. "What about horses? Would this field be good for a horse?" I ask, walking back to him.

He looks out to the field. "Yes. There's a small barn on the other side, and the fence is still in great shape. There's plenty of clover, and alfalfa to graze on. It would do a horse just fine."

I can hardly believe the next words coming out of my mouth. "Do you know where I can get a horse?"

"As a matter of fact, I do. A friend of mine just went into the nursing home. His family is selling his farm, and he has an old horse. She's not good for much, just grazing, but too nice to put down. You'd be doing that old mare, and the family, a favor."

"How much?"

"I'd say she's worth at least five hundred dollars."

Hmm... five hundred dollars. I don't have enough in my account, yet... but I could use the account for the household expenses, and then pay it back with my first paycheck. I look back to the house. Sidney is watching us through the glass door. Looking back to the pasture, I can *so* see a horse out here grazing, living out the rest of its life making a little girl happy. "I think I would like to buy this horse," I say, and then take a deep breath. "How soon could you get it here?"

"I can bring her tomorrow, if you like."

"Yes. Tomorrow will be perfect. But please, don't say anything to Sidney... it's a surprise. I'll get that bowl of soup for you, Gus," I say, and walk back to the house.

Gus now has the wood stacked next to the stone wall, and I make the "button your lip" gesture when he sits at the table to eat his soup. He winks, and smiles over at Sidney, who is helping with the dishes. I know that I'll be awake all night with second thoughts.

DAY TWO, AND I'VE MANAGED TO PUT A SMILE ON SIDNEY'S FACE WHEN she sees the Mickey Mouse, blueberry pancakes I have set in front of her. "What do you think of these?" *Just wait until she sees the horse. I hope I'm not sucking up too much. I totally am.*

"Wow, Mickey Mouse," she says.

"Yep. I used to make them for Natalie and Paige."

"The two girls who want to meet me?"

"Yes... you remember. How about maybe this weekend?" She shrugs.

"Sure," she says, pouring syrup on her pancakes. Her mood

instantly turns uninterested. "Are you staying with me at school today, like you promised?"

Oh, shoot. I plumb forgot. I've already planned with Gus to be here when he delivers the horse late this morning. "Sidney... please don't be mad, but there is something very important I have to do once I take you to school." She looks up at me through her lashes. "It's a surprise," I say with the hopes to get on her better graces.

"For me?" I begin cleaning the breakfast dishes.

"Yes, and don't ask me what it is. It's a surprise."

"Then will you stay with me at school tomorrow?"

"I don't see why not." I smile, and tell her to finish up. "We don't want to be late."

She quickly eats, and we leave for school.

I take her to her classroom, and talk with Mrs. Gensinger about tomorrow's stay. Now to get home, and write a check for the horse. *I must be crazy.*

When I pull into the drive, Gus is already there with a horse trailer hooked to his truck. I get out of the car, and go to greet him while he backs the horse down the ramp. She's a lovely horse—brown, with white patches, and white on her legs. It looks like she is wearing boots.

"This is Holly." The horse whinnies, shaking her head back and forth.

"Hi, Holly," I say, petting the side of her face. "Sidney is going to love you."

"I'm going to walk her to the barn first, Miss Julia." He tugs at her bridle, and she obeys. She knows that she has found a happy home.

"I'll go and write the check. Whom do I make it out to?"

"Brian Coy," he hollers back.

I still can't believe I'm doing this as I write the check, sitting in the big, leather chair. In the memo, I write "horse," sign my name, and tear it out of the checkbook. Closing the book, I place it back in the drawer, and repeat to myself as I walk out, *It's easier to ask for forgiveness than for permission.*

Gus has Holly in the barn, getting her used to her new surroundings when I walk in. This is the first time that I have been in here.

Looking around, I see that it's perfect for one horse. "You have a place to buy her feed?" Gus asks, guiding her into the stall.

"I haven't thought that far ahead yet. Can you suggest a place?"

"Tom's Feed will deliver. I don't think you'll be fitting much feed in that little toy car of yours." *Lord, Julia... you have not thought this out at all.*

"I guess you're right. I will have to set up an account there." How's this going to look in the household expenses? Horse feed?

"The owner threw in her saddle, and bridle for free. I don't know how long it's been since anyone has ridden her. Are you familiar with saddling up a horse? I can help you out, Miss Julia."

Right now, I'm praising myself for skipping swim time at camp, and taking horseback riding lessons instead. I was sixteen, and had filled out in the chest a lot more than the other girls. I was very self-conscious at the time. Natalie says she would do anything to have boobs like mine. I have since grown into them. "It's been a while. Could you oversee me, and make sure I do it correctly?"

"No problem, Miss Julia. I wouldn't want to see that horse throw you. Course, I think she's too old to put up a scuff."

As I fasten the last buckle under her belly, Gus congratulates me. "I'd say you haven't forgotten." I smile with pride, and tug at her reins to lead her out of the barn.

"Okay, Holly. Let's see how much you like to be ridden." Once we are out, I pat her on the rear while stepping up into the stirrup pad. She swings her head toward me, so I calmly talk to her. "How are you doing, girl?" Stepping up, I swing my leg over her, and sit lightly down into the saddle. She backs up a little, but then obeys when I pull on her reins to turn. In no time, we are galloping at a slow stride into the pasture.

Gus is leaning on the fence when we return. "Looks like you two are going to be fine."

"Yes, I think so."

With Holly now grazing in the pasture, I follow behind Gus to pick up a few bags of oats at Tom's Feed. I set up the account and delivery days, then check the clock on my dash. It's time to pick up Sidney. I can't wait to see her sweet little face when she sees Holly.

She's waiting on the curb of the sidewalk as I pull up. "How was school today?" I ask. She removes her backpack, and tosses it in the back seat.

"Same as every day," she says, while putting on her seatbelt.

"What's that supposed to mean?"

"I sit alone at lunch, and alone at recess." Looking up at me with those emerald eyes, she intertwines her fingers, and gently lays them on her lap. "So... where's my surprise?"

"It's in the backseat," I say.

She reaches back, and grabs the plastic grocery bag. She looks at me, furrowing her brow. "Apples and carrots?"

"Yes, apples and carrots." I put the car in drive, and move away from the curb. She studies me intently as we leave the parking lot. I'm trying very hard not to laugh.

"Why would you buy me apples and carrots?"

"I didn't buy them for you. I bought them for Holly."

"Who's Holly?"

"She's someone who wants to meet you." Staring straight ahead, I try to maintain my serious face, but on the inside, I'm dying to shout out, "I got you a horse!"

She studies me like I'm insane, and maybe I am. Writing that check today was pretty bold, and I just hope it all works out. Surely, her father wouldn't mind if she has a horse. All rich, little daddy's girls get whatever they want—right? Especially a little girl whose mother has passed, and whose daddy is gone all the time. Guilt presents. Well... I've spared him the shopping this time. He should thank me. *I'm only convincing myself.*

We pull into the drive, and I can't take it anymore. "Grab the bag of apples and carrots, and follow me to the barn." She unbuckles her seatbelt, grabs the bag, and gets out of the car. "Come on. Holly's in the barn."

"Why is she in the barn?" She looks at the bag, and then at the barn. Her eyes widen to the size of saucers, and it hits her. "You got me a horse!"

I jump up and down with excitement. "Yes... I did." She takes off running to the barn before I have a chance to stop her. "Wait, Sidney! Wait for me... you don't want to scare her." I dash after her, and praise myself for wearing jeans today. I've been wearing them since leaving the DeLucas' house.

I beat her to the barn door, then start with the rules on how to handle a horse. "Please... just let me see her, Julia," she says, jumping up and down. I open the door, and see Holly crunching on her oats. "Oh, she's so beautiful. Is she really for me?"

"Yes... all yours." She walks over, and I tell her to introduce herself, calmly. "You don't want to spook her." She starts with a light pet on her nose. Holly shakes her head, and Sidney jumps back. "It's okay. She's just moving to keep the flies off. You can pet her." She cautiously pets her again on the nose. "So, what do you think your dad will say?"

She shrugs. "I don't know."

"Do you think he will be mad?"

"He'll probably never see her." This is *so* not what I expected her to say.

"Would you like to call, and tell him about your new horse?" She shakes her head. "Well... how about when he calls you? You can tell him then."

"He never calls me. Can we ride her now?" I watch her take a carrot from the bag. Holly wastes no time taking it from her. She Sidney smiles up at me, exposing those cute dimples.

"Your dad never calls you... ever? Not even to say that he misses you?"

"No. Can we ride her, Julia? Please?"

Huh... strange.

Once Holly is saddled, I help Sidney up, teaching her the proper way to mount a horse. Her eyes are full of wonderment, and I think those dimples are going to bust through her cheeks as I lead her out of the barn.

I walk Holly slowly down the pasture, telling Sidney to hang on tightly to the horn. She's doing quite well. I don't think her smile has faded once. Holly stops to graze on some wild clover, and I look back to see how far we've gone. The pasture is bursting bright yellow with dandelions. But as I look to the sky, I see thunderheads forming. The wind begins to pick up.

"I think a storm is coming. We better get her back to the barn," I say.

Closing the barn door, I look up at the weathervane turning in the wind. A crow lands on top, and starts its cawing at me once again... looking straight at me. "Come on. Let's hurry." I grab her hand, and run to the house. By the time we make it to the door, the crow lands in front of it, and I shoo it away with my foot. Just as I shut the door, lightning streaks across the sky.

After dinner, I help Sidney with her homework, and pray that the lights stay on. The storm has become quite fierce, with a heavy rain, and a wind that is causing the lights to flicker. I search the kitchen drawers for any candles, just in case we lose power. I find some, along with some matches, and then light them so I'm not struggling looking for them in the dark. The phone rings, and I walk back to the kitchen to answer it.

"Hello, Fairbanks residence."

"An inmate is calling from the Indiana State Prison. Will you accept the charges? Press one to accept. Press two to decline."

This is the third call from this automated voice. My curiosity now hovers with my finger over the number one button. Instead... I hang up. *Could her father be in prison... and that's why he never talks to her?* "Okay, young lady, I think it's bedtime." She looks out the window. Rain pelts hard against the glass.

"What about my horse?"

"She's safe in the barn. You can see her in the morning."

I watch her brush her teeth, and then turn off the bathroom light after she leaves for her room. "No... leave the light on." I flip it back on.

As I tuck her in, she smiles up at me. "Thanks for the horse."

"You are quite welcome. But you will have to help me with her. A horse is a big responsibility." She nods. "Good night."

I walk back downstairs, blow out the candles, and then head up the back-service stairs to my room. I'm almost to my bed when lightning fills the sky, and the loud boom of thunder quakes throughout the house. A shiver runs through me as I get into bed, and the thought of the phone calls do nothing to shake it away.

～

BOOM! MY EYES OPEN TO COMPLETE DARKNESS. FLASHES BLIND ME FROM the lightning as I look at the digital clock. The power must be out. It's still storming, and I have no idea how long I have been asleep. Pulling the covers up to my chin, I look out the window into the darkness. Lightning flashes, and my blood runs cold when a silhouette stands before me. I lie still, listening as my heart pounds. Lightning flashes again, and the silhouette reaches out and touches my hand.

"Julia?" Oh, thank God. It's Sidney.

"What's wrong? Are you scared?"

"Someone turned the bathroom light off."

"Oh... the power is out from the storm. You need to use the bathroom?"

"No. I just like it better when the light is on. Can I sleep with you?" I throw back the covers, and reach for her. Within no time, she is fast asleep.

As I listen to the steady rhythm of her breathing, I hear something downstairs. Holding my breath, and craning my neck, I hear the sound of glass clinking. It makes my blood run cold. I slide out of bed, being careful not to wake Sidney, and I pad to the door. I listen. Someone is walking around downstairs.

As I walk down the stairs, I mentally *will* the steps to remain silent. Somehow, I manage to reach the bottom without making even one creak. Lightning flashes, and the image of a person stands in front of the glass doors... on the inside. My body trembles with fear, and the pounding of my heart is so audible, I'm sure that whoever is there can hear it.

Lightning flashes again, and I push myself up against the wall so that the light will not cast my image. I also hold my breath, so they cannot hear me breathing. *Think!* I have to do something. Should I run upstairs and lock the door? What if they hear me? The thought of

Sidney waking, and coming down the stairs looking for me, terrifies me. *God... please make her stay asleep,* I silently pray.

Lightning flashes. The person is still there. With my body embedded against the wall, I make a quick decision, I have a few seconds before the next flash. Quickly and quietly, I move against the wall, successfully making it to the great room, all while in the dark. *Now what?* The answer comes to me. As I make my way across the wall, I feel for the stone fireplace. When my hands find the roughness of the stones, I carefully feel for the poker in the tools' cradle, trying not to rattle it, or knock it over.

With the poker now in my hands, I walk toward the kitchen. Lightning flashes, and the person has not moved. I only hope they are facing the window, and not me. I draw the poker up high, and quietly move closer. I am now only two feet away. Lightning flashes, and I bring the poker down hard on their head. They fall.

"Ow!" they cry out before hitting the floor. "What the hell are you doing?" It's a man's voice.

"Who are you? What are you doing here?" The poker is still gripped tightly in my hands. It's dark, but I know he is still on the floor.

"I own this house, and I'm here to find out who in the hell wrote a check to a name I do not recognize for a damn horse."

"Mr. Fairbanks?"

"Yes! I am."

"Oh, my God, sir, I'm so sorry. I just thought..."

"What—that you'll just beat the hell out of me standing in my own house?" Lightning flashes, and I see him on the floor. He's trying to stand up. Even though I can't really make him out, I reach out and find his arm.

"Here, let me help you up," I say, and feel for the kitchen chair. I pull it out, and help him up to sit in it. "Are you bleeding? Do you need an ambulance?"

"I can't tell. It's dark," he says with sarcasm.

"I'll get you some ice." I feel my way to the worktop, running my hands along the kitchen counter until I reach the refrigerator. I open the freezer and instead of grabbing ice, I feel for a bag of frozen peas.

"Here, I have this for you," I say, and feel my way back to the table. He's sitting in the chair, and I grope for his hand. "Here, take this and put it on your head." I feel his hands come over mine. The lights come on, and now I'm face to face with him. My eyes are looking straight into his. Those... eyes. Bike man.

"Praying girl?"

5

"Mr. Fairbanks?"

"You've already said that," he hisses, while glaring straight in my eyes, with the bag of peas on his head.

"I know. I mean... you're Mr. Fairbanks?"

"Yes. Why do you find that so hard to believe?"

"I guess—because, I've met you before... well not exactly met, but rather ran into, or...

"Yes, the memory of our acquaintance hasn't escaped me. You seem to have a way with your graceful, first impressions." He tries to sit up and begins to sway, becoming unbalanced.

"Here, stay seated. I think you're dizzy. Let me check your head." He sits back down with my assistance, and I move behind him, gently feeling his head for a bump. His hair is short, cut in a crew cut with the top a little longer. With my fingers lightly massaging his head, I feel a small lump, and he winces. "Sorry. I don't see any bleeding, but I think you should keep the bag of peas on it. It will help keep the swelling down."

He moves his hand to the back of his head, placing the bag on the bump, and I'm suddenly aware that my fingers are still in his hair... stroking his head. I quickly drop my hands to my sides. "Let me get you some ibuprofen." I remember finding various medicines in a cupboard while searching for the ingredients for the chicken lemon soup. I make my way over to the cupboard, open the cabinet, dump two pills in my hand, and fetch a glass of water. When I turn around, the look on his face reminds me that I'm only wearing a T-shirt and panties. And I'm sure he got a good view while I was reaching for the ibuprofen. He quickly looks away.

I pull down on my T-shirt while holding the glass of water and pills in my other hand. Holding my legs together, I walk toward him, when he glances up. "Get a good look?"

"I don't know what you are talking about. My vision is pretty blurry," he says, with more sarcasm. Whether his vision is blurred or not, guilt tugs at my heart for bashing him over the head, and I take a seat beside him. He throws back the pills in his mouth and swallows them with the water.

"I really am sorry, Mr. Fairbanks. It's just, I wasn't expecting you to be home... and the storm had me freaked out. I was only—"

"Yes, you were protecting my home. I understand."

"And your daughter," I say. His face softens as he looks at me.

"Yes. Sidney," he whispers.

"She's asleep in my bed. She woke up and got scared when the bathroom light was off. She crawled in bed with me and fell fast asleep. I can go get her. I'm sure she will be so excited to see you."

"No, that won't be necessary," he says, looking down. I now see broken glass on the floor. He must have had a glass in his hand when I hit him. "There's my hundred and twelve-year-old scotch all over the floor. What a waste," he says.

"I'll clean that up. Can I get you another?"

"No. I think I will just go to bed." He gets up, and I help him to stand. With my arm around his waist, he embraces me. I look up into his eyes... those beautiful, deep, blue eyes, encircled with a hazel ring. There's a long pause as we stare into each other's eyes. My heart races, and I begin to feel stupid. I'm at a loss for words. *Say something.* I'm about to speak when he does.

"Thank you, Julia," he says, looking into my eyes.

"You're welcome. I just feel so awful for... Wait! How do you know my name?" He just looks at me with surprise.

"What do you mean, how do I know your name? Ms. O'Shea told me. Plus, it was written on the check you signed for the horse. The bank notified me right away, with the image of the canceled check. Ms. Julia. Ellis." He moves closer with each enunciated word. By the time he says, "Ellis," we are nose to nose.

"Oh... right... that," I breathe. I can smell the oaky scent of his scotch from his warm breath on my face.

Feeling a little awkward, I step back and use the excuse of the broken glass. "Just let me clean this up, and then I can help you upstairs."

He releases his arms from around me, and I move to the laundry room to get the broom and dustpan, along with a mop, and bucket of warm water. He watches as I sweep up the glass, and mop the scotch up from the floor. I feel intimidated. Perhaps he's judging my cleaning abilities. Because clearly, there is nothing interesting about watching someone clean a floor. Unless she is doing it wearing nothing but a T-shirt and panties. *Oh good God, Julia.* Give the man a good show, and maybe he won't be so upset about you buying a horse, or bashing him over the head. It's obvious, by the smile on his face, that his vision has returned. I roll my eyes and return the broom and bucket to the laundry room. I look for a pair of pants, or pajama bottoms that might be left in there. I find none, since I put everything away before bed last night. So, I walk out, once again tugging down my T-shirt.

"Can I help you to bed now?" He raises his eyebrows, as if I am suggesting more. "Do you need help walking up the stairs?" I clarify. He turns his body away from the table while still sitting in the chair. He opens his legs, and reaches out to me.

"Come here, Julia." His voice is low and seductive. I love the way he says my name, like he's known me for years. Staring into his eyes, I walk slowly toward him. When I reach him, he places his hands on my hips, holding me. My heart races, and my breathing practically stops. It feels like minutes pass by before he says anything. "Yes," he whispers. "I would like help up the stairs... Julia."

Why does he say my name like that?

He stands. I wrap my arm around his waist as he leans on me, and we make our way to the stairs. Walking up, he has one arm around my shoulder, and with the other, he uses the railing. We reach the top of the stairs, and I'm expecting him to let go... but he doesn't. He continues towards his bedroom, and I'm feeling very, very nervous. He must notice my trembling. "I freshened your room up yesterday. There are new sheets on the bed, and I replaced the heavy drapes with sheers. I picked them up when I was buying apples and carrots." I am rambling, and my voice sounds high pitched, like a mouse's. Truly... I'm nervous. We reach his door, and before he opens, he looks at me.

"Apples and carrots?" he asks.

"Yes, for Holly."

"Holly?"

"The horse."

"Ah, yes—the horse," he says, and walks into his room... still holding on to me. Maybe he's waiting for me to let go? I help him over to the bed and quickly release my arm from around his waist. He walks over to the window *just fine,* and inspects the sheers. He runs his hands down the silk, and then turns, smiling at me. "Nice," he says, and begins unbuttoning his shirt. Before I can turn and walk out, he has it off, and tosses it on the bed.

"I see you must be feeling better. Good night, Mr. Fairbanks." I will myself to turn away and leave the room—however, my eyes are rooted on his chest. I remember falling onto it. I breathe in deeply, remembering his scent. He walks over to the bed, pulls down the duvet, and then looks up at me with a cynical smile.

"Thank you... Julia," he says in *that way* again, and begins to unbutton his trousers. Quickly, I walk out and run down the stairs. When I reach the back-service stairs, I take them two at a time, running to my room and shutting the door. I lean against it and exhale. *What is wrong with me?*

~

THE MORNING SUN SHINES BRIGHT THROUGH THE GLASS DOORS, SHOWING no signs of the wicked storm from last night. I'm making breakfast for Sidney—blueberry pancakes—and I am having my third cup of coffee. I never went back to sleep last night, and it didn't help that Sidney took up most of the bed. I wanted so much to wake her and tell her that her father was home, but then decided it would make another great surprise—first the horse, and now her dad. Hopefully, I'm on a roll.

She walks in and the first thing out of her mouth is, "Can I ride my horse before school?" I give the excuse that Holly is sleeping, because the storm kept her awake all night. Then I tell her I have another surprise.

"What?" she asks with wide eyes.

"Just sit and eat your pancakes, and your surprise should be here in a minute." She glances around the room, and then shrugs her shoulders.

I haven't seen Mr. Fairbanks this morning, and I'm not about to go up to his room. Then, I begin to worry that he might have a concussion, and I should check on him. No... he seemed fine when I left... *more than fine*. Finally, he walks into the kitchen, wearing jeans and a black T-shirt, and smells freshly showered.

"Surprise!" I shout. She looks up from her pancakes.

"You mean, Jonas?" she asks.

Jonas? His name is Jonas. God, even his name is sexy, and he's the father of this beautiful little girl. Yet... she calls him Jonas, and not Dad. Why? Nor does she seem thrilled to see him. She just returns to her pancakes.

Jonas gives me a quick glance while pouring a cup of coffee. Never does he look at his daughter. He walks off to his study with a paper folded under his arm, carrying his coffee. *What's going on here?*

I grab my cup of coffee, deciding I need some answers, and walk into his study. I find him on the computer, and am about to speak up when I see Holly grazing out in the pasture. Fearing he will bring up the issue of the horse, I ask my questions carefully.

"I made plans to stay with Sidney at school today, but perhaps you would like to take her, since you've returned home?"

"No, that's fine," he says, never glancing up from his computer.

"Are you sure? I thought you might want to take her to school."

He looks up from his computer. "I believe that's what I'm paying you for."

"Yes, sir," I say, and shyly grab my hair, which is down, braided to one side. He looks at me, and my eyes go straight to the floor.

"Is there anything else, Julia?" I look up. His elbows are propped on the armrest, and his fingers are steepled at his lips, waiting on a response.

"Would you like some breakfast? I made Sidney pancakes, but I can make whatever you would like," I say, still playing with my braid.

"No, thank you." He returns to his computer.

"Are you sure? It's really no problem. I don't have to leave for another thirty minutes..."

"I said no. Thank you," he states, cutting me off.

"Okay, then," I quietly say, before turning and walking out.

As we drive to school, I consider ways to start a conversation about this strange relationship between Sidney and her father. But how do you discuss such a delicate subject with a ten-year-old? "So... you call your father by his first name?"

"Yes," she says.

"Are you happy to see him?" I ask lightly. She shrugs her shoulders as her only response. "When was the last time you've seen him?"

"I don't remember. Can we ride Holly when we get home?" I can see this is going nowhere, so I drop the subject.

"After you do your homework." She pouts a little, and then agrees.

I pull into the parking lot of the school, park my Mini, and we head to her classroom. She has not forgotten about my staying as she pulls me to her desk, dragging over a chair for me to sit next to her. Today, she is all smiles, exposing those cute little dimples—which she must have gotten from her mother. That cynical smile Jonas gave me last night had lots of character. However, dimples were not one of them.

Mrs. Gensinger tells the class to quiet down, and then tells Sidney to introduce me. She stands, taking my hand and walks me to the front of the class. "This is Julia. She's my best friend. She bought me a horse and is teaching me how to ride. She makes me blueberry pancakes shaped like Mickey Mouse, and lets me sleep with her when it storms."

Once her introduction of me is finished, she looks up at me with a big smile on her face. This is not the little girl I brought to this classroom just a few days ago. She now has confidence and pride in herself. I smile down at her, brushing her hair to the side.

"Why, thank you, Sidney," I tell her, and we take our seats.

THE CLASS RUSHES OUT TO RECESS, AND SIDNEY PULLS ME TO THE SWINGS.

"Can you push me, Julia?" She hops into the swing, and I give her a gentle push.

"Higher," she says, and I run, pushing her over my head.

As I watch her swing, I notice a little girl leaning against the pole of the swings. She watches us, shyly. I bend down and talk to her. "Hello. What's your name?"

She puts her finger in her mouth, and bites down on her fingernail while looking at the ground. "London," she says quietly.

"That's a pretty name. I like it."

"Thank you," she says, twisting her little body slowly back and forth, still with the finger in her mouth. I can tell she is very shy, yet is reaching out.

"Would you like to swing? I can push you, too." She runs to the swing next to Sidney's, and I give her a push. The two little girls now swing side by side, and Sidney gives her a smile. Maybe this can be the start of a friendship.

Lunchtime has finally arrived, and I'm starving. Sidney wants us to eat our lunch under the large oak tree in the playground. Before we leave the classroom, she walks over to London. "Want to have a picnic with Julia and me? Julia made us turkey wraps, and grapes."

The shy little girl nods her head yes, and Sidney takes her hand. *How sweet.*

We sit under the tree eating our lunch, and Sidney tells London all about her horse. "Do you want to come to my house, London, and ride Holly? She's really a pretty horse, and Julia is a good teacher."

"Yes, I do, but I have to ask my mom," she says.

"Julia can ask her. Right, Julia? You can ask her mom, and London can come home with us."

"Yes, but what about spending time with your father? He just got home. Don't you want to spend some time with him?"

"No. I want to play with London. Jonas never plays with me, anyway."

"Well, maybe that's because he's very busy and doesn't have much time, but I think he would still like to spend some time with you." Even after I say it, I realize that, judging by this morning's display of father and daughter relations, proves she's probably right.

"No, he doesn't," she says without a blink. "Will you please ask her mom? Please, please," she says, getting up, and jumping up and down. I look to London, who also has a pleading look on her face.

"Yes, okay. I will ask London's mom. London, what is your last name?" I ask, so that I will have a proper way of introducing myself, other than calling her, "London's mom."

"Anderson," she says, and a smile brightens her face.

At three 'o'clock, I'm standing with Sidney and London on the curb, waiting for her mother to pick her up. A black Hummer pulls up to the curb, and London points. "That's her... that's my mom." When the woman doesn't get out of the car, I walk over to the driver-side window.

"Hello, Mrs. Anderson?" A woman with long, blonde hair, and large sunglasses, turns to look at me.

"Yes?"

"My name is Julia... I'm Sidney Fairbanks's nanny. We would like for London to come over after school today. Sidney and London have become such good friends, playing so well together. Sidney has a horse, and—"

She rips off her sunglasses, and glares at her daughter. "London, get in the car right now."

"But, Mommy!"

"Get your ass in the car, right now!"

"Mrs. Anderson? Is something wrong?" I ask, very confused by her reaction.

"My daughter knows better than to hang around with a girl like that," she says, looking over at Sidney.

"Mrs. Anderson... I ask that you watch your tone and language around these little girls."

"That child is a spawn of the devil. Her father should have moved her out of the country when she was born. Then maybe she would be spared the omen that she is known for."

"What are you talking about? How could you say that about her— or about any child, for that matter?"

"London! Get in the car now," she says through gritted teeth. London lowers her head and walks over to the car. She is barely in, when her mother peels away from the curb. I look over to Sidney, who is now in tears.

I rush over and bend down, looking at her tear-stained face. "Sidney, I know that was an awful thing for London's mother to say, and it's not true. You are a wonderful, loving, beautiful girl. Sometimes, awful people say awful things." I wipe her face and kiss her forehead. She sniffles, and catches her breath.

"She's not the only one who says that about me," she says between sniffs.

"What? What do you mean? Other people also say bad things about you?" She nods and covers her face with her small hands. The shock makes my face feel as if it will never return to its normal state. What is wrong with these people? How could someone be so cruel to a little girl?

I take her in my arms, giving her a hug. "Hey, pay no attention to those people. Obviously, they truly do not know you, or how sweet you are. They are missing out on so much, not knowing a wonderful girl like you." I release my hug and take her by the shoulders, then lift her chin. "You hear me? Pay no attention to those people." She nods, and I take her hand. "Come on, let's go home and ride your horse." And with that, a slow, rising smile brings those two dimples out.

As we get in the car and buckle up, I make a suggestion. "You know what I always do when I hurt inside," I say, starting the car. She looks up at me and shakes her head. Her eyes are still red from crying. "I like to give a gift to somebody. How about we buy Holly a gift?"

"What kind of gift would she like?" she asks, her nose a little stuffed-up from her crying.

"Sugar cubes. Horses love them." Wonderful—her big smile is back.

∼

WHEN I REACH THE DRIVE OF THE MANOR, I SEE THE FLASHING LIGHTS OF the mail truck parked in front of the mailbox. Before pulling up, I park my mini and get out of the car to retrieve the mail before driving up the lane.

"Good day, Miss," the postal carrier says. "I haven't put the mail in your box yet. You've got quite a bit that I'm still sorting through." He reaches back and grabs a few more letters from the plastic postal bins, and wraps them with a rubber band before handing them to me. "Here ya go. Looks like someone has been busy writing. I don't see a lot of handwritten letters anymore. Today's folks do all their greeting through emails and such."

I take the bundle of letters. "Thank you, sir. Have a good day."

"You, too. Bye, now." He tips his mail carrier's hat, smiles, and drives away.

As I walk back to the car, I glance down at the bundle of letters. I notice the return address in the left-hand corner of the envelope on top. Removing the rubber band that is wrapped around them, I sort through all the letters and see the same return address, stamped in green ink, on all eight of them. There, in the corner of each letter, is the name Indiana State Prison, and they are all address to Mr. Jonas Fairbanks.

I replace the band around the letters before getting back to the car.

Sidney is holding the box of sugar cubes we bought before leaving town, so I place the letters in my purse. I'm curious if she knows who might be in prison.

As soon we park the car at the house, Sidney bolts out with the sugar cubes, and I know exactly where she's heading. I yell to her, "Sidney, wait until I take the mail in. I need to show you first how to feed them to her." She stops, stomps her way back, folds her arms with a pout, and looks up at me.

"Hurry up, then!" she whines.

"Follow me to the house and change your school clothes first. I need to give your father the mail." I just hope he is home... and maybe explains the letters from prison. She runs in before I even make it to the front porch. Once inside, I pull the bundle of letters from my purse and walk to the study. Jonas is still as he was this morning—planted in front of his computer. I knock on the doorframe. He glances up from his computer.

"Mr. Fairbanks?" I remain at the door.

"Yes? What is it, Julia?" *God, I love the way he says my name.*

"The mail came. These all came addressed to you," I say, pulling them from my purse. He looks at the bundle of letters in my hand.

"Okay, just set them on my desk. I will look at them later." He turns back to his computer.

I walk in slowly, and stand in front of his desk for a moment before setting them down. Maybe I should drop them on his computer, getting his attention, and then he will explain. Feeling that would be a bit too brash, I set them on the side. "Did you have any lunch? May I make you something?" I ask, hoping he will look over at the letters.

"Yes, I did have lunch," he says, not looking up.

"I had a wonderful time with Sidney at school today," I say, trying to get his attention.

"I'm glad," he says, pecking away on the keyboard.

"She made a new friend today, London Anderson. Do you know the Andersons, Mr. Fairbanks?" I ask, wanting to tell him about Mrs. Anderson's behavior, and what she said about his daughter.

"No, I don't, Julia. Now if you don't mind... I'm really busy here." He removes his glasses, and pinches the bridge of his nose. I start to leave, but then feel that he needs to know about today's situation with Mrs. Anderson.

"There was a situation with Sidney today that I feel you should know about." He folds his arms across his chest, and sits back from his computer.

"A situation?"

"Yes. It made her very upset—and it upset me, as well." He swivels around to face me. His arms still folded.

"What did she do?" he asks, making Sidney the accused.

"She didn't do anything. It was the mother of her little friend, London... Mrs. Anderson," I say, while petting my braid, which is becoming a nervous habit around him. "Sidney wanted London to come over and play after school. So, when I waited for Mrs. Anderson to pick up London, I asked her if it would be alright." He now notices the letters on the desk, and picks them up. Thumbing through the bundle, he tosses them back down, and runs his hands through his hair.

"Go on, Julia," he says, as if I'm a bother.

"She scolded her daughter for even playing with Sidney. She called her a spawn of the devil. It was just awful, and Sidney started to cry. I didn't know what to say or do." He turns his chair back around, holding his head in his hands, and mumbling something I can't make out. "I know it's none of my business, but maybe you should talk to your daughter, and assure her that she's not. Maybe... you should have a word with Mrs. Anderson."

He stands up and walks over to the big window. I see Holly grazing out in the pasture. Now that I know he has seen the letters, I continue. "There have also been a few phone calls from the Indiana State Prison." He snaps to attention at this, and there is anger in his eyes. "Of course, I didn't accept," I quickly say. "Would this be the same person?"

He moves away from the window and walks over to the book-shelves, opening a small cupboard containing a bar, and pours himself a glass of amber liquid—*hundred-year-old scotch*? He takes a drink, sets the glass down, and then walks my way. When he's inches from me, he softly runs his finger along my cheek, and looks me in the eyes.

"You're absolutely right... Julia," he whispers, and I once again smell the oaky scent on his breath. My heart races. "It's none of your business."

6

Kiss me. Kiss me. His eyes remain fixated on my mouth. With his thumb, he lightly brushes across my bottom lip. I feel hypnotized. I've never felt anything like this. I want him, but I don't know what for. I want to touch him, *but where?* I'm not hypnotized—I'm paralyzed. *Move arms, move.* Touch him... touch his beautiful face. I'm not breathing.

"Who are you really, Julia?" he breathes my name. "What do you pray about?" My face is now cupped in his hand, and his thumb continues tracing across my bottom lip. My lips are slightly parted, and my breathing is audible with each rise of my chest. My hands are petting my braid—*I think.* No—more like squeezing it. I want them to move up, and touch his face. I want to feel the light stubble of growth that peppers his jaw. I want to run my fingers across his sexy lips.

"Jonas," I breathe out so softly, it's hardly a word. His hands smooth down my face, and then he takes my hands in his. Like he's reading my mind, he runs them across his strong jaw. He closes his eyes and breathes in. Is he breathing in the scent of my hands?

Still with his eyes closed, he continues to rub his face across my hands. I'm afraid they will become sweaty. *I'm sure they are.* My hands begin to tremble, and he opens his eyes. "Do I make you nervous,

Julia?" He smiles—roguishly. *I like it.* His eyes are hooded, seducing me. I swallow hard.

"Um, just a little," I say in a rush. "Paris," I whisper.

"Paris?"

"That's what I... I pray about." How I even remembered what he asked is beyond me. "A chef," I squeak out like a mouse. He looks at me with a sweet smile this time.

"You want to be a chef... in Paris?" I nod. My head moves in small, quick up and down movements, afraid if I speak, the mouse voice will squeak again. He still holds my hands, and I remain frozen to the floor. I don't want to move from him, and I'm not sure if he's going to advance this moment. I remain motionless, except for the heavy breathing in my chest.

He releases my hands and gently touches my braid. With his thumb, he caresses the herringbone pattern of my hair. I watch as his thumb enjoys the feel of my hair. Like a breast, it's something feminine for his pleasure. It's erotic, and I'm baffled how I would know what erotic feels like.

"I like that," he says. I think he's referring to my braid, but then he adds, "that you pray for your career." Of course, he would. He's all-things-business. "What else do you pray for...Julia?" Why does he say my name like that? Like it needs to stand out.

I need to speak, so I mentally will the mouse voice to cease. "Guidance," I whisper. "The ones I love and care for. People I don't know." He furrows his brows at my response.

"Why would you pray for people you don't know?" His hands move from my braid and take my wrist, gently. He lightly rubs his thumbs up and down with such a feathery touch it almost tickles—*almost Erotic.*

"I pray for people who are lost in this world. Those who don't know Him," I say, watching his thumbs caress the inside of my wrist. I peer up slowly, and look him in the eyes. *Those eyes.* He tilts his head slightly, trying to discern *who* "Him" is.

"God?"

"Yes. Do you pray, Mr. Fairbanks?" My voice is breathy.

"Once." He cups my face in his hands again, and I smell his body wash. The same smell as when I fell onto his chest. I'm stare at his chest through his tight, black T-shirt, remembering just how it felt.

He moves in close. His eyes are fixed on my mouth, and I think he is going to kiss me. *Yes.* He closes his eyes when his lips are just inches from mine. I close my eyes, too, waiting to feel the moistness of his gorgeous mouth when our lips meet. I feel his warm breath on me.

"Okay, I'm ready for you to show me how to feed Holly the sugar cubes," says Sidney, loud and demanding. I jump back from Jonas's light embrace on my wrist. He remains in his spot, and I watch as his lips form that roguish smile again. There's a strange glint in his eyes, and I really can't tell if it's sarcasm, or humor. Probably both.

"Okay," I say, sounding guilty. She's changed into her play clothes—jean shorts, and a pink tank.

"Can you make my hair like that?" she says, pointing to my braid—which I'm stroking again.

Feeling the need to break the tension, I take my braid and make a pretend mustache on top of my lip. "Like this?" I say teasingly at her. She giggles.

Looking back, Jonas walks to his desk and collects his tumbler of scotch. "I promised her that we would give Holly a treat. I thought it would cheer her up after today's episode with Mrs. Anderson."

"Well, looks like it worked. She seems fine now," he says, and tosses back the rest of his scotch. He then leans against his desk and crosses his arms—glaring at me. I glance over to the bundle of letters and he follows my gaze. Whatever is in those letters has taken him back to another time, and made him distant. He takes the letters, unlocks the middle drawer with a key he pulls from the pocket of his jeans, throws them in, and slams it shut. And just like that... he's back behind his computer, no longer smiling, or looking at me. I turn and leave the room with Sidney.

HOLLY COMES TROTTING UP THE LANE WHEN SHE SEES US WALKING INTO the pasture. Sidney is calling her name while shaking the box of sugar cubes. "Holly, I have a gift for you," she says, running toward her. Her hair bounces in two braids from bangs to ends in a herringbone pattern, just as she requested. I follow behind her, still bewildered by what had occurred just a few minutes before with Jonas. He never looked up again once he sat down and got back to work. *What is in those letters?*

"Hold your hand flat, like this," I say, demonstrating as I lift my open palm to Holly's mouth. Her velvety lips nuzzle the inside of my hand, triggering a memory of Jonas's soft, caressing touches on the inside of my wrist. Soft, yet erotic. I remember the way he started cold and harsh, then melted down into a gentle moment. The look he had in his eyes, fierce and angry, when I mentioned the phone calls from the prison. The way he took the letters and threw them in the drawer. *The drawer that I don't have a key for.*

"Okay, let me feed one to her," Sidney says with excitement, breaking my thoughts of that surreal moment with Jonas. Taking her small hand, I pull her fingers back to create a flat palm, and drop two cubes into it. I extend her arm by the elbow, reaching up to Holly's mouth. Holly's lips nibble inside Sidney's hand, making her flinch.

"It's okay. That's how she picks it up. She has to use her lips. She won't hurt you," I say, reassuring her. Sidney attempts again, and this time she's all smiles and giggles, showing those dimples. With her other hand, she gently rubs Holly's nose.

"I like how soft she feels," she says.

"I think she likes it when you pet her nose."

"Really? I hope she likes me."

"Oh, she does. She knows you saved her life," I say, rubbing Holly's cheek.

"How does she know that?" Sidney asks, looking up at me, and squinting from the sun.

"She told me so," I say.

"Horses can't talk, Julia."

"No, they can't talk with words, but they can talk with their eyes." I take Holly by her bridle, pulling on the cheek piece. "Look into her eyes, and tell me what she is saying."

Sidney turns her head and looks into Holly's eyes, calculating her answer. "She says she's happy to be here. She says she really likes the gift I brought her today. She says this is where she wants to stay all her life." Sidney nods her head with assurance.

"Then, she shall stay," I say, patting Holly on the cheek. "You're a good horse, and a good friend, Holly." I grab her bridle and turn her around so that we can walk through the pasture when I spot Jonas, standing at his study window. He's been watching the whole time... I feel it. Even though he sees me and knows I've caught him watching, he doesn't move away. He leans against the window frame, and continues watching us... watching *me*. Feeling a little awkward, I smile and give a small wave. He returns the wave and then walks away to where I can no longer see him.

"You want to ride her?" I ask Sidney. Of course, she does, and I help her up.

"What about her saddle?" she asks.

"I think you can ride her bareback today. I'll hold her bridle, and we will just walk the fence line." I make a stirrup with my hands, and she gracefully pops up, swinging her leg over Holly, just like I taught her. "Perfect," I say, taking Holly by her bridle and leading her to the pasture's edge.

We walk for at least three miles, and I can't believe how much property there is on this pasture. It's surrounded with farm ground, and tractors are out, tilling the fields. A small woods over the hill is the only patch of trees I see. Soon, this pasture will be barricaded with tall stalks of corn, or maybe velvety soybeans.

In the distance, I hear a dog barking and worry that maybe it's a pack of wild dogs. I listen intently and hear only one. Maybe, it's just a stray. I stop Holly, fearing she may become spooked, and throw Sidney off. So, I pet her, and talk to her, keeping her calm, and I listen for the dog. Then, in the near distance, I see a lab trotting in our direction. He has a collar, so hopefully he is tame and... *nice*. Being that he is only trotting toward us, and not running to us, perhaps he's just a little curious. But I would hate for him to scare Holly, and hurt Sidney. I must address this situation and take over.

"Hey, boy," I coo at the dog, extending my hand. He sniffs at my hand first, and then Holly's legs. "Good boy. What are you doing out here? Are you lost? Let me see if you have a tag." The dog sits, and I'm relieved this meeting is going so well. Holly too, is behaving.

"Can we keep him?" Sidney asks, hanging tight to Holly's mane.

"No, he's not ours. He has a collar. We should find out whom he belongs to."

"But if we can't, then can we keep him?"

"I don't think your father was very happy about the horse. Lord only knows what he'd do if I brought home a dog."

"Oh, Jonas wouldn't care. He doesn't care about anything I do," she says. And that's another thing I need to address. *Why does she call him Jonas?*

"No, I don't' think so—and it's *may* we keep him, not *can* we keep him," I correct her.

"Okay... *may* we keep him?" I roll my eyes.

I check the dog's tag and read his name. "Toby," I say. "What are you doing out here by yourself, Toby?" The dog lifts his paw. I take it, greeting him with a shake. "Do you want to walk with us?" Hopefully, we will run into his owner.

Up ahead, in the distance, I see smoke rising. "Come on Toby, let's see what's up there." I say, and take Holly once again by her bridle. The dog behaves, walking obediently beside us, and is panting heavily. Perhaps he's come a long distance. Of course, it is a hot afternoon for May.

Our journey takes us a little farther, when I see fire burning in along the fence line. I just hope it's a controlled burn. I forgot to bring my cell phone, after my *episode* with Jonas.

An older woman is controlling the fire, raking the ground and smothering the blaze down to a smolder when it reaches out from the fence line. She looks up and sees us. I wave. "Toby," she orders. "Toby, get back here." The dog alerts to her command and trots off.

"Hello," I yell. "He found us, and I was hoping we could find where he came from." She scolds her dog when he walks back to her. "He seems sweet... Toby. I read his tag. I think he might need some water, though." She looks up giving us a perplexed look, first studying Sidney, and then myself. "Hi, there. I'm Julia Ellis, and this is Sidney..."

"The Fairbanks child," she cuts in.

"Yes," I say, confused, looking up at Sidney. The look the old woman is giving her is almost... *ghostly*. "We were just taking our horse for a walk, and—"

"I hope that horse didn't hurt my dog," she says, cutting me off again.

"Well, of course not. You can see he's fine. I was more afraid of the opposite. Afraid your dog would spook my horse," I say directly, but then add, "but he was very gentle, and didn't bother my horse at all." I hope this will get us on neighborly grounds.

She continues to stare at Sidney in a peculiar way. "I didn't get your name?" I ask.

"I didn't give it," she says coldly.

"Well, we must be neighbors. I'm the new nanny for Mr. Fairbanks —and like I said, this is Sidney, and I'm Julia. We met Toby," I say, smiling at the dog, being polite so maybe she will tell us her name. She doesn't.

"Thanks for bringing my dog back."

"Oh... no problem." Looking over at the dog, I can see he's still panting. "I think he might need some water, though. He might have been running awhile before he found us."

"She is a pretty girl, despite everything. I always wondered what she would look like," the woman says.

"What?" I ask, assuming she is talking about Sidney. She is still looking at her—more like *studying* her. "Yes, she's a beautiful little girl," I say. "Excuse me... despite what?"

"It's just a shame about her mother," she replies, not answering my question. I look at Sidney, who is petting Holly, and playing with her mane.

"Yes... it is a shame," I say, not sure that "shame" is the proper word to use. *Tragic* should be more like it. Of course, I'm not sure how Sidney's mother died. Nor am I aware how much Sidney knows, so I decide not to question her any further. But I think she senses my curiosity, and turns to the dog.

"None of my business, anyway," she says. "I'm not one to get all caught up in town gossip. People should just keep to themselves. Come on, Toby. Sorry my dog bothered you," she says.

"Not at all," I say, as she walks away. "Maybe we'll see you again sometime?" With her back to me, and walking away, she only raises her hand in the air as if to say, "Probably not."

~

THE MUSIC COMING FROM THE HOUSE AS WE ENTER THROUGH THE GLASS patio door is *horrendous*. I don't think I've ever heard anything so terrible in all my life. And I've heard some pretty crazy music coming from Natalie's room. There is almost a satanic eeriness about it. Sidney seems oblivious to the sound, and jumps up on the counter, reaching for the cookie jar. "No, it's too late for a snack. Dinner will be ready in no time."

Knowing I would be out all day as Sidney's visitor at school, I prepared a beef stroganoff in the Crock-Pot, and, judging by the savory smell, it's *more* than ready. All I need to do now is make the noodles. But first things first... silence that horrible music.

I follow the sound to the great room, where I find Jonas sitting in the big, leather chair. There's a glass of what appears to be more scotch gripped loosely in his hand about to fall. He's awake, but appears lethargic. His eyes are glazed over as he stares at the stone fireplace. I search for some sort of remote to turn off the music that is blasting through the sound bar hanging on the wall.

"Mr. Fairbanks," I yell through the music. His eyes move up slowly to my face as I bend over to look at his. "Are you, all right?" He stares into me. The smell of alcohol is strong, and I wonder how much he's had to drink. I take the glass, which practically falls into my hand, and set it on the side table. There, I see his cell phone, and discover that the music is coming from his Pandora app. "Judith" by A Perfect Circle lights up on the screen. Grabbing the phone, I quickly swipe the app out, and the music shuts off. *Silence.*

"Mr. Fairbanks, have you been drinking all day?" He doesn't answer, but only rests his head against the back of the chair. He stares into the fireplace, and I catch a faint whiff of smoke. *It's too hot for a fire.* Glancing over, I see the smoldering ashes of paper. I walk over and bend down, looking at what has been burned. A piece of paper with the corner not yet burned catches my eye, and I pull it out to see what still remains. "Indiana" is the only word left visible. He's burned the letters from the prison.

Something has put him in a terrible state. Will I be able to deal with this? Sidney stomps in, demanding to eat. "How much longer? I'm starving," she says. I must do something. She shouldn't see her father like this.

"Just give me a minute, Sidney. I think your father isn't feeling well," I say, clearly knowing what is wrong—*he's drunk.* "Could you go find the package of noodles in the pantry, please?" I am hoping to divert her attention, but she walks over to Jonas and touches his arm.

"Jonas... what's wrong? Are you hungry?" I'm a little puzzled by the concern she shows for him. This is the first time she has acknowledged him since his arrival home. Maybe I should just watch, and observe their way of interacting. What I have seen so far is... totally not the normal relationship of a father and daughter. But perhaps, with her mother deceased, her father gone most of the time, and her being raised by nannies, this is the only thing she knows.

He looks away from the fireplace and into his daughter's face. She still holds his arm. He takes both of her hands in his. "Do you like your new horse?" She nods with a smile. "OHolly, that's her name?" She nods again, showing those dimples. "Did you thank Julia for getting her for you?" I'm about to interrupt with, "I didn't buy her with my money" but instead, continue to just observe. She looks over to me.

"Thank you so much for Holly, Julia," she says.

"You're very welcome, Sidney—but actually, your father bought her." With this revelation, she turns back to her father.

"Thank you, Jonas, for buying Holly. You can ride her if you want to.

Julia will teach you." He looks to me and smiles sweetly, and then turns back to Sidney.

"You would never want to leave your horse, would you?" he asks in a coaxing way. Why is he asking her that? Where's he going with this?

Her face turns suddenly hard, and the happy dimples vanish. "No— I would never leave Holly. I love her!" she shouts. She is now pouting, but it's not a spoiled pout. Her bottom lip protrudes, and begins to quiver. She is getting ready to cry, and I feel sorry for her. Is he trying to upset her in a cruel way—threatening to take away her horse? But why? *Because he's drunk.* I need to intervene.

I'm about to open my mouth and speak when he begins to soothe her. "Shh," he says smoothing her braids. "Holly can stay here forever. But you have to take care of her, okay? You can't expect Julia to do all the work. Plus... Holly will end up liking Julia more. You want to be her favorite, right?" Sidney nods, wiping away the tears that are running down her cheeks.

"I will... I will take care... of her. She will love me," she says, now in choking, sobbing gasps. I'm confused. Feeling protective of her, I decide that this must stop.

I move two steps forward and take her by the shoulders, turning her around. "Sidney, you *are* Holly's favorite. Remember when you looked in her eyes?" She nods, still gasping. "Tell me what she said to you," I say, and then look at Jonas, with a look of disappointment.

"She thanked me for saving her," she says, sniffling. "She said she wants to live here forever."

"That's right. I heard her say that, too," I say, looking at Jonas, and not her. "Now, please go to the kitchen and find the noodles for dinner. Are you still hungry?"

"Yes," she whispers.

"Okay. Let me talk to your father, and then we will have dinner." She wipes her face with the back of her hand and walks out of the room. I turn to Jonas. He sees the anger on my face.

"Look, I wasn't trying to upset her," he says.

"No? Well, that's exactly what it looked like to me, Mr. Fairbanks," I hiss.

"Look, you don't understand—nor do I expect you to."

"Well, *make* me understand. Tell me what's going on here. It's something to do with those letters," I say. Quickly, he stands up from his chair. The drunken haze has evaporated. Our eyes lock. I'm not about to back down. I demand some answers. However, I'm forcing myself to say the words.

"Trust me, Julia—you don't want to know," he says through clenched teeth. I blink rapidly and swallow hard.

I take a deep breath and *will* myself to take some sort of control. "Okay. I understand that whatever *it* is, is your business. However, you hired me to take care of that little girl in there, and I plan to do so, to the best of my abilities. Even if that means protecting her from you." My mouth feels like cotton, and I can't believe I'm standing up to him. I'm not even petting my braid.

"It's not *me* she needs protection from," he says. Confused, I spin my head looking back to the burnt letters in the fireplace. "Yes, I hired you to take care of," he hesitates, "my daughter." I look to him again. He senses my confusion and sees that I want answers, but he offers none. "I'm going to take a quick shower and be down for dinner. It smells wonderful." And just like that... he leaves the room. Subject closed. *What. The. Hell.*

PART II

Summer: The frondescence of spring has reached its fullness, and summer will take over this season. Seeds are planted, and growth and nurture will give two of these things—fresh new fruits giving life, or... fiendish briars cutting old wounds.

— GINA A. JONES

7

As I am cleaning the dishes after dinner, I let Sidney help with the drying. Actually, she insists, and Jonas disappears into his study. It's been pretty quiet since Jonas came back downstairs, freshly-showered and smelling of soap, and of mint... all manly. I'm sure the mint is to mask the all-day scotch-drinking, however I kind of like the smell of scotch—oaky, with a hint of almond.

All through dinner, I tried not to think of the previous episode in the great room, and move forward on to how best reset the dynamics of this... *family Even though Lisa warned me not to meddle.* Several times, I caught Jonas looking at me... at us—Sidney and me. I couldn't tell what was on his mind, but whatever emotions the letters fueled in him, have now disappeared. But, somehow, I need to have a background to go on —if I intend to fix it. *Should I... fix it?*

"Sidney, you did a great job helping me. It's late, and it is bedtime. Go brush your teeth, put your pajamas on, and come back down to kiss your dad goodnight," I tell her. She frowns at my last request. "I think he could use it. He's had a bad day, and a kiss from you will make it better." She acquiesces with a roll of her eyes, and then drops the dish-towel on the counter before heading upstairs. *I must start somewhere.*

She returns in pink pajama bottoms, and a pink-and-white striped

T-shirt. "Are your teeth brushed?" I ask. She smiles in an overly-large, toothy grin. I cup her little face, and inspect her teeth. "Great job, Miss Sidney. Now, let's go kiss your father goodnight."

I'm expecting him to be at the computer when we walk in, but he's not. Standing and looking out the big window into the darkness, he turns when we walk in, and smiles at our presence. "Sidney is going to bed, and she wants to kiss you goodnight." I say.

"It was her idea," Sidney says, halfheartedly. "She says you had a bad day... and I should kiss you."

"She did?" he asks, but looks to me. "Yes, Sidney, I did have a bad day." She walks over to him. He bends down, and she kisses his cheek. I'm waiting for him to kiss hers. He doesn't. *Well, it's a start.*

"Goodnight, Jonas," she says, walking back to me. *Jonas—another topic. Do I address it?*

"Goodnight, Sidney," he says.

"I'm going to help Sidney to bed and then heat the kettle for some tea. Would you like some, too, Mr. Fairbanks?"

"Yes. I would, Julia. Thank you."

Once I have Sidney tucked into her bed, and the bathroom light down the hall is left on, I return to the kitchen and set the stove to heat the kettle. It whistles, and I fill two mugs with tea bags dropped in. I set mine on the counter. Then I put the other mug, and a teaspoon, on a tray, along with sugar cubes, and cinnamon, and honey, and then walk back to his study, where Jonas is still standing at the window. "Here's your tea, Mr. Fairbanks. I wasn't sure how you like it, so I brought a tray with some sugar, honey and cinnamon," I say, placing the tray on a side table. "Oh, I forgot the cream."

"I don't take cream. Thank you." He looks to the tray. "Where's yours? I thought you were having some, too."

"Oh, yes, I will be taking mine upstairs."

He sprinkles a dash of cinnamon in his mug. "Please, Julia. Won't you join me?"

"I thought you might need to be alone. I... I'm sure you have work to do," I stammer.

"I always have work to do... *Julia*." God, there he goes with my name again. "But right now, I want to have tea with a beautiful girl."

Beautiful? He thinks I'm beautiful?

"Please, will you join me?" he asks again, and walks to a chair in the corner. He sits and crosses his legs, placing one foot on his knee. He sips his tea and looks up at me. "Please."

"Okay... If you're sure I won't be bothering you."

"You won't be bothering me. Now, please—I insist."

"If you wish." I walk back to the kitchen to get my tea. When I return, he gestures for me to take the chair across from his. I do, and sit cautiously down. The leather smells new and is cold on my shoulders, being that I changed into a spaghetti-strapped tank top, and yoga pants. *I thought I was retiring to my room.* Crossing my legs, I hold my arms tight across my chest, trying to hide the fact I'm not wearing a bra, and bring the mug to my lips. He watches me and smiles.

"I want to apologize to you about earlier," he says. I'm not sure if he's referring to the incident in *here* earlier, or in the great room. Both are very confusing to me.

"Oh, no need. I'm sure you have a lot on your mind." *I have no idea what's on his mind.*

"Yeah," he half-laughs. "There is a lot more on my mind than I planned on at this point. Though," he hesitates, and sets his tea down on the table between us, "I should have been preparing for this."

This?

He uncrosses his legs and places his elbows on his knees. Dropping his head to his hands, he rubs his face, and then runs his hands through his hair before looking back up. "I've made so many mistakes, Julia." Why is he telling *me* this? I have no idea who he really is. "It's just... you always think you have plenty of time," he says, looking again out into the darkness. Is he referring to the death of his wife?

"How did she die?" I ask. He looks back at me, and I see turmoil in his eyes. "Your wife—Sidney's mother. Ms. O'Shea said that she died when Sidney was a baby."

He takes a deep breath and reaches for his tea. "Drunk driver," he says, and takes a sip from his mug.

"Oh God, I'm sorry. I shouldn't have asked."

"No, it's okay. I'm glad Ms. O'Shea told you that." Again, he rubs his forehead and looks out into the darkness.

"So, I assume Sidney has no memory of her?"

"No. Sidney does not know her mother."

Silence fills the room for the next few seconds, and so I bring my mug to my lips again. I want to ask more questions, but feel I should wait for him. Perhaps this was their anniversary... or the anniversary of her death? When he remains silent, I remind myself that *he* wanted me to stay and have tea with him. I'm sure it wasn't to sit in silence. So, I press on.

"Do you think maybe there should be some pictures, or something to remind Sidney of who her mother was? I noticed from day one that the walls are bare. Out of respect, I think there should be a few pictures of her." *Plus, I'm dying to know what she looked like—stunning, I'm sure.*

"I don't have any of her," he says. "She took them with her when she left."

She left? "Oh... I wasn't aware you were divorced."

"We weren't. She left when I was abroad, and I came home to an empty house. Sometimes, memories are the worst form of torture." He brings his mug back to his mouth and looks over the top of it at me with those gorgeous eyes of his. I too, bring mine to my lips, pretending to be sipping, but really, I'm only trying to hide. From what, I don't know. *His gaze on me?*

"So, tell me about yourself, Julia," he says, setting his mug back down.

"What do you want to know? There really isn't much to tell," I say.

"Why Paris?" he asks, placing his elbows on the arms of the chair and making a steeple of his fingers, running them along his lips. I can't help but watch his fingers move across his bottom lip and wish they were my tongue instead.

What the hell, Julia? Why did I just think that?

"Well," I swallow. "It's always been a dream of mine... Paris. They have one of the best culinary schools. I want to study French cuisine."

He smiles at me. "Little girls with big dreams become women with visions," he responds. Does he think of me as a little girl with a dream, or a woman with a vision?

"And another plus is that being in Paris will keep the eyes of judgment off me." He furrows his brows. "It's just... where I come from, people aren't too keen on a woman having a career. 'Not too keen' is probably putting it nicely—more like *appalled*," I say, with a quiet laugh.

"Well, do what one of the greatest women in history said to do."

"And who's that?"

"Eleanor Roosevelt. Do what you feel in your heart to be right. For you'll be criticized anyway," he says with a wink, and reaches again for his mug. "Please, don't take this the wrong way—if Paris is truly your dream—but I really don't see you fitting in."

I flinch, a bit offended. "What makes you say that?" I ask.

"Your rectitude would not blend well with the snootiness of the Parisians. Their *froideur* can be quite brash. Trust me... I know," he laughs. "That's actually a compliment."

I like his laugh. There is comfort in it. In just this little bit of talking to him, I feel... surprisingly, comfortable. I really don't know why. I know there is something tearing him apart every day, and it has to do with his wife, her death, her leaving, and those letters. What happened? How could she leave carrying his baby? Well, I'm not sure if she was pregnant then. Was his business such a priority, it came before his wife and their unborn child? Was his devotion to his business the reason she left him?

"What is your business?" I ask. "What's the name of it?"

"I don't own a business. I buy businesses that are struggling, dichotomize them, and then sell the spare parts."

"Oh," I say, not really sure what that means. "I see."

"I work for an investor who acquires companies through corporate raids. He buys large stakes in corporations, and uses shareholder voting rights to undertake great measures, increasing their share value. These measures might include downsizing, replacing top executives, or liquidating the company. Mostly the latter, and then that's where I come in. I sell to competitors of those companies for a great compensation of the difference."

"The difference?" I ask, feeling all the more stupid.

"Their gain on the market, now that their competition is gone."

"Like a hostile takeover?" I ask, not sure if this is correct.

"Yes, you are correct, Julia. However, those of us in the business world like to call it an *acquisition*." He smiles. "But more about you. You are... religious?"

"Well, I wouldn't use the word 'religious,' per se. In fact, I hate that word. I'm a person of faith. Religion can sometimes destroy faith. Religion is a manmade word for 'law-of-faith.' However, we are saved by grace, and there is nothing we can do to change that. If you don't accept the gift of grace, then you can never have faith."

He's looking at me as if it's the first time he's ever laid eyes on me. "I like that. You're a very wise girl, Julia."

Slowly, I bring my mug to my mouth. "Thank you, Mr. Fairbanks," I say, before sipping my tea.

"Call me Jonas."

"Jonas." I breathe his name.

"Julia." My name floats seductively off his lips.

We sit across from each other, yet I feel every part of him touching me with those eyes. Nothing is being said. It doesn't have to be. We are talking through our gazes. My eyes scream, *Teach me—teach me why I feel this way about you*. Why do my breasts swell, and my nipples ache, protruding out to reach his touch? Why does my belly tingle, and my core ache down low in my loins, making me wet for him?

Gone are all the questions I wanted to know. Why does his daughter call him Jonas, and not Dad? Why is he silent about her mother? Why did Mrs. Anderson think that Sidney is the spawn of the devil? Why did the lady at the fence-line think she was pretty, despite something? *Despite what?* Why did he make Sidney cry with the threat of making her leave her horse? My heart is full of greed—greed only for him. I want him. *Does he want me?*

"Julia." His voice reaches me from somewhere far in a tunnel.

"Yes?" I whisper.

"You are right about me having a bad day, and a kiss might make it better." I am speechless, and my eyes are blinking rapidly. Does he want me to kiss him? "Will you kiss me before you go to bed?" he asks quietly, his blue eyes resting on mine.

"Yes," I whisper, and I wonder if he heard, because the word barely escapes my mouth.

"Come here," he says. He sets his mug down and reaches out for me.

I set my mug gently on the table between us and slowly rise from the chair. My nipples are tight buds against my thin top, and I know he sees them. I want him to. For once, I'm not self-conscious about my breasts. In fact, they feel fuller than ever.

His eyes follow me as I walk to him, and I feel as I'm floating. When I reach his chair, he looks up through his lashes at me. Bending down, I ever so lightly lay my lips on his cheek. I do not rush to move away. Instead, I linger in his scent—an earthy, musky, clean, cinnamon scent from his tea. I glide my cheek across his, and let the abrasion of his rough stubble graze my skin. The roughness is erotic, and masculine— a simple pleasure I take delight in.

"Goodnight, Jonas," I whisper in his ear. He moans deep in his throat. I straighten up to move away when I'm grabbed by the wrist.

"Julia," he says, and then stands, still gripping my wrist. "I've had *ten* bad years." Pulling me in, he wraps his arm around my waist. My breasts push into his chest. He moves inches from my lips. "Tell me not to kiss you."

"Don't kiss me," I breathe.

"Say it... like you mean it."

"Ah... I can't." His lips cover mine, hard, bruising them with a fierce passion I have never felt before, because this... this is my *first* kiss.

His arms squeeze me tightly, and I wrap mine around his neck. He feels so strong, and warm, and safe. He opens my mouth with his tongue, and I welcome his taste. Wildly, my tongue dances with his.

I'm floating above and watching us both. I see my hands move down his shoulders and caress his strong biceps. Then they move back up into his hair. He places one hand firmly around my neck and with the other, pushes me into his groin, his hand squeezing my bottom. I feel that he is hard. This is the first erection I have ever felt. This is lust —and I've been taught, this is wrong. How can it be wrong? I don't feel awful like they say I should. I feel privileged... because it's for me. His hard erection is for me. My swollen breasts are for him. The wet ache between my legs is for us.

"Julia," he breathes across my throat. His lips caress my neck. "Make me stop. Don't let me take advantage of you just because I'm alone with a beautiful, young girl in my house," he says, kissing my lips and then moving down my jaw. Goosebumps cover my body when his mouth moves into the curve of my neck. I'm beyond all words. I couldn't speak if my life depended upon it. I'm on a lust autopilot, touching and caressing before I even know what I'm doing. My body is on its own journey of discovery. I'm too weak to stop this—nor do I ever want to.

"Jonas... I don't want you to stop. Please," I beg with a voice I don't recognize.

He picks me up with one swing, cradling me in his arms. Our eyes melt into each other's with a wondering lust. In this moment, my whole life, *my future life,* rests in the arms of this man. I don't need Paris... or French cuisine. His touch, and his voice, are my dream. I see the children—*our children,* the way I did the day we first crashed into each other. That little boy and little girl, clones of us, seeds of our lust for each other. But is this also love? Do I love him? This must be love, because... I'm dizzy and drunk without any form of alcohol.

He carries me across the room, and just as we begin to leave through the door, the phone on his desk rings. The loud ringing startles me, sobering me back into the logic that I don't want. So I say the stupidest thing. "Maybe you should get that."

Pausing to look at me, he walks over to his desk, with me still in his arms, and glances down at the caller ID. Indiana State Prison. Slowly, he sets me down on my feet. "Even from the grave," he mutters under his breath. "I'm going to take this call, Julia. I... I need to take this call. Goodnight," he says, and waits for me to leave.

"Goodnight," I say in disappointment. I walk toward the door as he watches me. The phone rings again, and it's clear that I am to leave. I cross the threshold and shut the door behind me.

I exhale in frustration and lean against the wall. Starting towards the back staircase, my curiosity pulls me back, and I find myself propped against the door, straining to hear.

"Yes, I will accept the call."

A slight pause. "I'm only accepting this call to let you know... it is the last," I hear him say. I hold my breath to better hear. My breathing is muted.

"I don't want to hear you're sorry. Your apology means nothing to me." Another pause. "Because it doesn't. It will never change what you've done. What you've done to us."

I take a small step back and inhale a sharp breath, then return my ear to the door. "She will *never* know her mother," I hear him say.

Is this the drunk driver that killed his wife, and a call to make amends?

"Well, that's the situation *you* put me in," I hear him continue. "Trust me... it would have been a lot worse for you if *I* hadn't."

Situation? What could be worse than killing someone while drinking and driving?

"No, no you won't," he says to the person on the other end. "I will have every law-enforcement officer here if I *ever* catch you coming around." Another pause. "Yes, I do understand, because I've been living my own hell." Another pause. "Well, at least you have *medication* to help you. I have to *deal* with it."

He's moved away to the other end of the room, making it harder for me to hear. I turn my head, and press my other ear against the door. I just hope I don't cast a shadow to be seen under the door.

"Now why in the hell would I do that?" he asks. "You deserve nothing. You took a life, and knowing you—it was intentional." Another pause. "Yes, I know it's being recorded. That's why I said it. Don't give me shit about second chances. *Jail* is your second chance—and even *that* is too good for you."

He knows the person who killed his wife? Were they friends at one time?

"You want to see me someday? See you in hell. I'll be waiting."

A slam against the wall makes me jump from the door. I think that he just threw the phone. I rush quietly to the back-stair entrance and hide in the shadows. I only hope he walks into the great room and takes the stairs to his room. I would die if he knew I was listening.

Light floods the dining area when he opens the door. I melt into the wall of the stairs, hoping he doesn't see me. He has the tea tray, and sets it on the worktop. I crane my neck when he walks back to the study. I hear the top of the glass decanter open, and the sound of glass clinking. He's pouring another scotch. Then, I hear the sound of the top being place back on the decanter. The light goes off, and I watch his dark image pass by. His footsteps echo up the wooden stairs, and then I hear his bedroom door slam shut.

I think about rinsing the mugs out before heading to my room, but then decide not to. I turn and pad up the stairs, walk to my door, and close it softly behind me.

Once I'm inside, I lean my back against the cool wood of the door, and exhale. *What a tortured soul.* I think back to the letters that he burned in the fireplace. When he said he wasn't the one Sidney needed protection from, he too, had looked over at those burnt letters. Why would someone want to hurt an innocent little girl?

I shake the thought away and walk over to the closet. Turning on the light, I step in to change into my nightshirt when my toe is stubbed, hard, on a loosened floorboard. "Ouch! Shit, that hurt," I whisper. Great, now I'm swearing... swearing and lusting. *Get a grip, Julia.*

I bend down to grab my throbbing toe when I notice that the board has lifted. I remove the floorboard and see something below it. A stack of letters, tied with a ribbon, lies between the floor joists. I pull it out and find there are at least eight letters, or so. The ribbon is unraveling, and faded. It looks like it may have been a bright red at one time, from where it is twisted around the letters—but now it's a faded pink.

I untie the ribbon, and read the name that is handwritten on the front of the envelopes—Eve. *Who is Eve?*

I fight with my conscience not to pull the letters out of the opened envelopes and read them. However, my conscience loses the battle when my fingers slip in, and pull out the first letter. I begin to read.

Dear Eve,

I know it is not proper for a person in my position, or for a person who is a "nothing," to take such an astounding notice of you. But, I cannot let my feelings go undeclared any longer. You are truly the most beautiful being I have ever laid my eyes on. You make me feel a true bewilderment that cannot be explained. The moment I saw you, blood ran through my heart once again.

J x

8

THESE MUST BE LETTERS FROM JONAS, SIGNED WITH A *J*. AND THE "*x*"
must be a kiss. He signs his letters with a kiss. Who's Eve? His wife?
His *dead* wife? Why are they hidden in the floor? Who put them here?
"Oh, Jonas. You are more than a tortured soul," I whisper. *A mystery.*
"Why haven't you wanted to move on? Why can't you live for your
daughter? How was life with your wife, before she died? Why did
she leave?"

Maybe these aren't letters he wrote to his wife. Is it possible that Eve
is a woman he was having an affair with? The reason his wife left him.
Perhaps she caught them together, left that night, and was killed by a
drunk driver. He was never able to apologize. But, they have a baby
together. Possibly, he's one of those men who become scared when
faced with fatherhood, and find solace in the arms of another woman.
"*The other woman.*"

I remember Pastor Tom counseling a couple having marriage problems. It was my month to clean the church. I was getting supplies from
the closet, which was in Tom's office. Minutes later, the door to the
office was shut, and I heard Pastor Tom having a moment of prayer, like
he always does before starting his counseling sessions, with a couple
that sat down. I didn't want to interrupt his prayer, and by the time he

was finished, it was too late to announce myself. The couple started right in.

The wife's cries were so full of despair. I remember feeling so sorry for her. Her voice reminded me of a scared child's. The husband sat in silence. I imagined him sitting in shame, with his head bowed. She was repeating over and over through choking sobs, "How could you do this to me. How could you?" Then at one point, he must have tried to console her, because she cried out, "Don't touch me, you son of a bitch." And then she apologized for swearing in the Lord's house. I became so curious to know what he did.

She was in her last trimester of pregnancy, and caught him in the act of having sex with another woman. She was even being descriptive about what she saw. My ears perked up. I imagined Pastor Tom cringing. Just the thought of her husband having an affair killed her, but witnessing it had caused her such trauma, she began bleeding, and feared the baby would be premature.

The husband continued to apologize, over and over. At one point, he, too, began to cry. I thought things were going to calm down, but then he started to give excuses for his philandering behavior. "You were so tired every day. I didn't want to pressure you for sex," he said. Where at this point she said, "Pressure me? You never even asked. Maybe if you just would have at least acted... I don't know... attracted to me?" she cried. "I feel like a big, fat whale. Do you know how badly that makes me feel? Of course not—you're too busy fucking around." And then she apologized again for dropping the "F" bomb. Pastor Tom tried to console her with the excuse that sometimes, men act out when faced with fatherhood for the first time. I thought, *Well, that's bullshit.*

I thought—what an awful thing for him to do. I think that's what has kept me from getting involved with anyone. Just the thought of that happening to me, made me say, "No" to most dates. And also the fact that I wasn't attracted to any of the men who asked me out.

Yes, that's exactly what Jonas is, a philandering, pompous ass. He was having an affair, she caught him, she left, and then she died. And now, that all weighs heavily on him. And it should. Just look how he behaves around me. I'd seen the lustful way he watched as I cleaned the broken glass in the dining room. *Of course, I was in my panties.* The way he says my name—*which I love.* The way he touches me—*and my skin melts with pleasure.* I'm not convincing myself very well. He's such a master at seducing, leaving me, *women...* helpless. But that doesn't explain why letters he wrote to his mistress would be hidden in *his* house, and not in hers.

I tuck the letter back into the envelope and tie the worn ribbon around the stack of letters, placing them back in between the floor joists, and then I secure the loose board. I take off my yoga pants, leaving my tank on, and crawl into bed.

I lie in the dark, full of suspicion, and wonder what happened all those years ago. There are so many unanswered questions that have no logical answer. I am living in a mystery by Agatha Christie. The only problem... how does the book end?

I'M CRUMBLING THE TOPPING FOR BLUEBERRY MUFFINS. I PROMISED SIDNEY that she could sprinkle it on before we bake. Yesterday, while at the store picking up sugar cubes for Holly, a table of muffins, cookies, and cakes greeted us at the entrance of the supermarket—for pure temptation, I'm sure. Sidney wanted to buy Holly muffins, too. I told her, "How about we make some for your class, since it's the last day of school?" The dimples came out.

"You didn't start without me, did you?" Sidney yells, while running down the stairs. I turn and see a spunky, beautiful little girl with wide eyes, and an infectious smile.

"Only the batter. You get to sprinkle on the crumbs. Grab an apron and pull up a chair." She pulls open the linen drawer, and rifles through the dishtowels until she finds an apron. I help her tie it, and then she pulls a dining chair across the wooden floor. The chair screeches all the way. Once she is standing on it at the table, I pull her long hair back. I stroke her dark, shiny, chocolate locks while admiring her innocent exuberance, and then contemplate the strange mystery that surrounds her. "You want me to braid your hair again, like I did yesterday?"

"Yes, please," she says, then sticks her finger in the batter. I, too, stick my finger in, before popping it in my mouth. Our eyes meet, and we both say, "Mmm."

"So, Little Miss Sidney, what shall we plan for summer vacation?" Last night I tried to shift gears in an attempt to let go of the whole Jonas saga, and move in a positive direction for Sidney. Gardening can give you such a feeling of accomplishment—working the soil with your hands, planting the seeds, and nurturing the new life. It's early June, so there's still some time left. Plus... the bare landscape around the manor could use the touch of a green thumb.

"I want to ride Holly all summer," she says. Of course, I knew that was coming, and had prepared my answer ahead of time.

"You can't all the time—she needs her rest. But, there is something else you can do to involve her," I say.

"What's that?" she asks, while sprinkling topping on each muffin. I think more crumbs are on the counter than on the muffins.

"How about we grow carrots for Holly?"

"Grow? Isn't it easier just to buy them?" she protests.

"Yes, but this way we could give her fresh ones. And she will know they are special carrots, because you worked hard to grow them for her."

"Yes. I want to do that for her. I want her to love me."

"Oh, don't worry, she loves you very much," I say, and finish braiding her hair. "Sidney, what made you want a horse in the first place?"

"My teacher. She would read us stories she wrote about her horse when she was a little girl," she says, and continues with the muffins. "The horse lived at her grandma's house, and she would miss her when she was away. One of my favorite stories is when she went to the park where big, red poppies grew. The poppies would only be there for a short time. She would pick them as a treat for her horse. I wonder if Holly would like poppies?" She finishes topping her last muffin and licks her fingers.

"Maybe, that's what you can do, write a book about you and Holly," I say, handing her a washcloth. "Here, wipe your face."

I take the muffins and turn around to put them in the preheated oven. I'm startled when I find Jonas leaning against the frame of the kitchen doorway. He's been watching and listening the whole time. He's dressed in navy trousers, a white linen shirt—sans tie, with the collar unbuttoned, exposing a small part of his chest—along with a navy sport coat. *Why does he have to look so... amazing?*

"Good morning, Mr. Fairbanks," I say, and then assess my appearance in the oven glass. My hair is knotted up in a messy bun. Loose strands hang around my face, tickling the tops of my shoulders. And again, I'm in a tank and yoga pants. "Do you have a meeting, or something, this morning?" I ask, crossing my arms, like I can hide my hideous look.

"Yes, I do. May I have a word with you in my study?"

"Sure." I inwardly chide myself for looking so awful in his presence. He walks across the kitchen floor to grab a cup of coffee, and his black, polished, leather shoes tap out each precise step. How did I not hear him walk up to the doorway?

"I will also need a ride to the airport, if that's all right," he says, pouring his coffee.

"Yes, I guess." Why doesn't he just take his own car and leave it at the airport? But I don't ask. "I have to take Sidney to school first."

"That will work. I will ride with you, and then you can drop me off afterwards." He walks away, shoes tapping. I tell Sidney to eat her breakfast, and then go to his study.

He's at his computer when I walk in, and tells me to have a seat. I do, and then look to the clock. One hour remains for me to shower before leaving. *How long is this going to take?*

He shuts the laptop and then looks at me. "Julia, I want to apologize for everything yesterday, especially last night." He takes a deep breath and continues. "Something has come up... unexpectedly, and I need to act fast."

"Another acquisition?" I query.

He laughs under his breath, reaching for his coffee. "I wish it were.

That would be a lot easier." And even though I promised myself last night before falling asleep that I'd try to forget the letters from the prison, and the letters under my closet floor... I'm right back in that little book titled *The Mysterious Jonas.*

"Look, Mr. Fairbanks," I charge in. "I know yesterday was... well I don't even know *what* it was. But, I have decided my main focus is Sidney. Whatever you have going on at the prison, and your bad ten years, is between you and... whomever."

Lie.

"This is about Sidney... and I'm going to need your help." His words are palpable. The foreboding I felt when I first entered this house once again makes itself known.

"Yes, of course," I say, now feeling even more confused. "Is she in danger?"

"I like to think not. However, I need to make provisions to assure that she isn't. So, I will be leaving today and hopefully, will be back in a day or so. After that, I have some business in Maine. If things do not work the way I—" he hesitates, searching his words. "What I'm trying to say is that you and Sidney will be accompanying me in Maine."

Now, I'm being pulled into something when I haven't got a clue what it is. I am even more curious. "This has to do with the person in the prison?" I ask. He remains silent while looking at me, then turns his chair, swiveling to the side. He crosses his legs, with one foot atop his other knee, and rests his elbows on the arms of the chair. He's quiet, bumping his fist against his lips. *Will he tell me?*

"This is something I buried a long time ago, and I plan for it to stay buried. To open it up now, would only start another bad chapter in my life. Unfortunately, I made a mistake many years ago of thinking it was for the best. However, the person I did this for, couldn't speak for themselves. Now... I must continue to hold my silence." He spins his chair back. "But, I will need you to trust in me, Julia. Trust my silence, and my silence to you. The life I see you giving Sidney is what I want for her. So, when I refuse to tell you... respect my decision."

I need to decide if I can trust him. Do I? I am willing to stand by this innocent little girl no matter what. When I reply with a dry, "Of course," my stoic response gains me a respected nod, followed by, "Thank you... Julia."

~

MAYBE IT WAS THE WAY HE SAID, "THE LIFE I'M GIVING TO SIDNEY IS WHAT he wants for her," made me feel the respect he *does* have for me. So, an explanation was not needed. *Yet.*

Looking in the rearview mirror of my Mini, I see his handsome face, covered with sunglasses, as he stares back at me. He is sitting in the backseat, and, on his lap, he balances a box of thirty-six blueberry crumble muffins. I smile, because his six-foot, six-inch frame barely fits in the tiny car. Sidney is singing along with Adel in the front with me.

"Look at your father, Sidney. Doesn't he look silly back there?" She twists around and looks at him.

"Ha, ha. You look like a dork, Jonas," she says, laughing.

"Why thank you, Sidney. Glad I can make your day," he says dryly.

I pull into the parking lot of the school and find a parking spot. Jonas tries to hand me the box of muffins.

"Oh no you don't, Mr. Fairbanks. You are coming in to meet Sidney's class. We have plenty of time to make your flight," I say, glancing down at my watch. I open the door, and pull the front seat forward, and he reluctantly climbs out. Somehow, I have reached a level of leverage with him that if he's not willing to give me an explanation to the past, he at least has to succumb to my wishes of parenting for the future. After all, he needs my help—he said so himself. *And I only hope we run into Mrs. Anderson.*

We walk into the main lobby, and Jonas gets pleasurable stares from all the moms. *Yes, that's right, ladies. Hot dad coming through with muffins.*

Sidney leads us to her classroom, where she tells Jonas to place the box of muffins on a table in the back of the room.

"Good morning, Sidney. What do we have here?" Mrs. Gensinger asks.

"Since it's the last day of school, and you said we could celebrate, Julia and I made muffins."

"Oh, how wonderful," she says, but she's looking at Jonas.

"This is Sidney's father," I say, feeling a slight jealousy of how she is ogling him. He removes his sunglasses, and then shakes her hand.

"Hello, it's nice to meet you, I'm Jonas Fairbanks." His voice oozes sexiness. I feel that she is hanging onto his hand a little *too* long. I can see that she is completely besotted with him, and I suddenly feel the need to claim him.

"Well, Jonas," I say, using his first name, "you have a plane to catch." She finally releases his hand. "And I must get you there on time. Kiss your daughter goodbye," I coo, and feel a slight shame for laying claim to him. He looks at me and smiles, and I just *know*... he *knows*.

He bends down to Sidney, who is standing beside me. "Be a good girl for Julia," he says, and then looks up to me. "I'll be back in a few days." She shrugs as if to say, "Okay... whatever." Then, while still looking straight up at me, he kisses her on the cheek. I feel it's meant for me, or that he's looking for approval.

We leave the classroom and see Mrs. Anderson and London coming down the hall. London looks at me and waves. I give a happy, little wave back, then turn to Jonas. "This is the Mrs. Anderson I was telling you about yesterday," I say as she approaches. She looks at him with a suggestive smile. "Mrs. Anderson," I say when she's about to pass. "Mr. Fairbanks would like to have a word with you." She pulls her sunglasses down, looking over the top of them at me. Jonas looks at me, too, raising his eyebrows as if to say, "I do?" I raise one eyebrow. *Yes, you do.*

"It's been told to me that you have a problem with my daughter," he states.

That's right. Tell her off, Jonas.

"Your daughter," she says with a smirk, and rolls her eyes.

She's about to walk away, when Jonas asks, "How are you enjoying your new vacation home in the Keys?" She stops, and turns around.

"What?" she asks, pulling off her sunglasses. Her expression is unsure. "We don't have a vacation home in the Keys. You must be mistaken."

"Oh, I believe you do, Mrs. Anderson. I sold your husband one last year. He came to my investor when we were scouting potential building sites for condos," Jonas says with a smug smile. "Maybe it's a surprise. Well, I hope I didn't ruin it," he says, brushing fake lint from his jacket. "He said that you have been wanting one." He tugs on the cuffs of his shirt, and then glances at his watch. "I just figured that by now, he would have told you."

She shakes her head and blinks rapidly. Her mouth gapes open and shut like a fish breathing out of water. "He... he has to travel a lot... and maybe bought it to stay when he's there," she says, as if trying to convince herself.

"Yes, perhaps. What major hospital does he sell to? He said he was an orthopedic salesman and had the West Coast regions.

"Ah... maybe he's taken on another region," she stammers.

"And he didn't tell you? Hmm... imagine that," he says, putting his sunglasses back on. He turns back around and holds out his elbow, gesturing for me to take it. "We need to get to the airport, Julia." I straighten my shoulders and take his arm. "She won't be bothering you any longer... her *agenda* just became full." I'm dying to look back as we walk out, but I don't.

"Oh, my God. That was excellent," I say, as we get in the car. Jonas folds his long body up and pushes the front seat all the way back. He still looks cramped. "I thought you didn't know Mrs. Anderson?"

"I don't. I know Mr. Anderson—and his mistress."

My mouth makes an "O" shape. I start my Mini and drive out of the parking lot.

I pull up to the drop-off area in front of the terminal, but Jonas asks me to park in the parking lot and come inside with him.

"My plane doesn't leave for another hour, and I thought we could talk."

"Okay," I say, and make the turn to the parking garage. I'm dying with curiosity about our brief talk this morning in his study. I know I came off cool about not needing to know more. However, that feeling has faded fast. Plus, I'd like to know who Eve is.

I park my Mini and we exit the car. Jonas grabs his bag from the trunk, and we walk into the terminal. Once he prints his ticket from the kiosk and checks his bag, we find a small coffee bar and sit at a table in the corner.

I take a sip of my latte and wait for him to speak first, but all he has done for the last five minutes is to stare at me. *Why?* He wanted me to come in and... *talk.* So, I start.

"You said you like the way I take care of Sidney. What exactly do you like?" I ask, sipping my latte again.

He leans back in his chair and folds his arms. "You are protective of her, and you include her in things. Your desire to make her a priority is genuine. I think you would do it even if you weren't being paid. It seems to come naturally to you, as opposed to..."

"As opposed to what?"

"As opposed to something you might want for a while, and then—" he reaches for his cup, "and then move onto something else trending at the moment." He takes a sip of his coffee, looking over the rim of the cup at me.

"Trending?" I ask incredulously.

"Yes, trendy—fashionable, something everyone is doing."

"I know what the word 'trendy' means. I just don't know how it applies to the care of a child."

"It doesn't," he allows.

"Well, of course not," I say with a smirk, wrinkling my nose to show how ludicrous that is. Will I ever have a normal conversation with this man? He is so clandestine. I feel he is testing me. *For what?*

I tilt my head slightly to the side, squinting my eyes. I am hoping for an explanation, hoping he will elaborate on the *trending* comment.

"People do things their friends do. Boys go to war, and become men. Girls fall in love with them, and write to them. All the girls want boyfriends who can talk about serving their country, getting shot at in Iraq, Afghanistan, or any other ass-smelling, third-world country. It's so glamorous for the girls... but it's *hell* for the men. Because they are millions of miles away, missing their girls and living in fear, while the girls shop at the mall."

"Okay," I say slowly. "I guess I see your point. People talk about how

America is at war. But yes, America is at the mall, and our soldiers are at war."

"Exactly," he says, and takes a sip of his latte. Setting it back down, he continues. "People have affairs because their friends are having affairs. People have kids—"

"Because their friends are getting pregnant," I interrupt. "Yes, I know what you mean. Our youth group had a discussion about peer pressure. How girls get pressured into having sex and doing..."

"Not all girls get pressured." This time he interrupts. I start to feel uncomfortable. Where's he going with this?

"Oh, I know. I was just saying that maybe a few do. Not all," I concede. I smile, and try to clear the air between us. "Well, anyway... I'm glad you approve of how I care for your daughter. Thank you. So... what's in Maine?"

"Just some property I need to check out." He doesn't elaborate. I just nod and make a small noise in my throat.

"Huh."

I hold my paper coffee cup between both hands and run my thumbs up and down the sleeve. "What was your wife's name?" I ask, acting nonchalant.

He suddenly looks guarded. "Why? Is there some reason you need to know?" he asks.

"Attention, passengers of flight two thirty-one to Indianapolis. We will be boarding in twenty minutes."

"Well, that's my flight, and I still need to go through security," he says.

"I thought you were flying to Maine?"

"I will be, once I connect flights." He stands and tosses his paper cup in the trash.

"Oh, yes... and then onto Maine," I say. I stand, and toss my cup in the trash, also. "Well... have a safe flight, Mr. Fairbanks. Don't worry about Sidney. I'll make sure she's fine." I start to walk away when he takes me by the arm.

"You want to know the good thing about airports?" he says, looking into my eyes.

I swallow and say, "Sure."

"It's the one place you're allowed a PDA."

"A PDA?"

"Yes, a public display of affection," he says with a smile. "Everyone knows someone is saying goodbye to someone else here. So, two people kissing passionately is accepted either by a thumbs-up, or by turning away to allow privacy."

"Oh," I breathe.

"So... which do you think we'll get?" He whispers the warm words in my ear.

"Which what?" My heart beats faster as he draws me closer.

"Privacy," he says, running the back of his fingers along my cheek, "or a thumbs-up." He lifts my chin and brings his lips to mine. I think it's just going to be a small peck, but when he wraps me in his arms, the kiss goes deeper.

He kisses me, hard, and my mouth opens to taste him. Just as he did last night, he fully covers my mouth with his, and the passion builds in my belly. Despite everything I told myself last night, all bets are now off. I want him more than ever—and I don't even know why. His predatory kiss only puts me in a state of lust, and animal desire.

He releases me slowly and gazes into my eyes. "Turn around," he says.

Lightheaded, and in a lust-induced haze, I turn and see two men giving Jonas a thumbs-up. "They approve," he whispers in my ear, and his hot breath warms me all the way down to the wetness between my legs. I move into him, my back nestling into his chest, like he is mine, and smile inside.

"I have to go, Julia," he says, and kisses me on the cheek from behind. "I'll call you tonight," he whispers in my ear. The smell of his amaretto latte fills my senses, along with his warm, erotic breath. I feel the cold void the moment he moves from my body. He walks out into the hall toward the security gate, turns, and gives me a wink. I watch as he moves through security and then out of sight. He eluded my question with his seducing, philandering ways... and I let him. *Not fair.* Spinning on my heel, I walk out of the airport in a dizzy, lovesick stupor. I need to get control of myself.

Once I'm back in my car, I decide to stop at the mall before picking Sidney up from school. There really isn't enough time to go home first, and I have fallen in love with these skinny jeans I'm wearing today. I need a few more pairs. How did I go so long without them? They give my body a much younger, hotter look than the long dresses I've covered my body with for all my teen, and young adult, life. *Slut,* my conscience mutters.

Yes... well that's the spell he has on me! I inwardly retort.

~

I'M SINGING ALONG WITH LADY GAGA WHEN I PULL INTO THE SCHOOL parking lot. My back seat is full of shopping bags, and I feel somewhat guilty spending two hundred dollars on three more pairs of the jeans, along with some red high heels. I couldn't resist once I saw them paired on the mannequin. The idea of wearing the jeans with the heels when I pick Jonas back up in a few days is tempting me. I just hope I have the courage to wear them. *I better practice.*

Sidney is not on the sidewalk when I pull up to the curb. I know I'm not late—or early, for that matter. Parents are still walking out with their children. I silence the radio and look around. Maybe she is dawdling inside. But that's not like her. She is always anxious to get home to her horse. But then I remember the muffins we brought in this morning, and realize that she probably needs help carrying out any leftovers.

Pulling away from the curb, I park my car in the parking lot, get out, and walk to her classroom. Mrs. Anderson passes by, hiding behind large sunglasses, but I know the look on her face. I now kind of feel sorry for her. *Kind of.* But I smile and say, "Hello." She doesn't acknowledge me. I'm not surprised.

When I get to the classroom, all the children are gone, and Mrs. Gensinger looks at me, strangely. I look around for Sidney, but she is not there.

"Ms. Ellis, I'm surprised to see you," she says. This confuses me.

"Why? I'm here to pick up Sidney. Where is she?" I ask, with a bit of concern now in my voice.

"I don't understand," she says.

"What don't you understand, Mrs. Gensinger?" I'm now starting to panic.

"Why you are here. Her grandmother picked her up. She said that Sidney's father had to go out of town, and I remembered you saying this morning that he was catching a plane. I just figured…"

"No! I mean—yes, he did. But I was still picking her up today." I'm now in full panic mode.

"Well… her grandmother must have been confused. She said Mr. Fairbanks was leaving for Indianapolis, and she was to pick Sidney up. So, you didn't call anyone to pick Sidney up, Ms. Ellis?"

"No. As far as I know, Sidney doesn't have a grandmother. It's never been mentioned to me."

"Well, I did find it odd she didn't want to go at first, even after her grandmother—"

"Stop saying grandmother!" I yell. My body shakes, and my heart is about to burst out of my chest. "Okay," I say, trying to sound calm. "What did she say?"

"She said they were going to the park, and at first Sidney didn't want to go. But then she asked if they could get something for her horse. After that, she was all smiles, and willing to go. So I let Sidney go with her. I'm terribly sorry if I wasn't supposed to."

"Did she say which park?"

"No, she didn't. I'm so sorry."

"How long ago did she leave? Maybe I can still find her out in the parking lot."

"Oh," she hesitates. "She took Sidney out of school early."

My knees weaken, and I fall to the floor.

9

THIS IS NOT HAPPENING. I CAN'T BREATHE OR THINK.

What... how do I find her? I don't even know who took her. "Don't you have some sort of policy about who can take a child out of school?" I demand in a panic. "There has to be a list of the names of the people who can take her."

"Yes, there is. Let's go to the office and check. They also have to sign her out."

We run to the office, both in a panic. I push open the glass door, pound my fist on the counter in front of the receptionist, and scream, "I need to see who signed Sidney Fairbanks out today... NOW!" I try to breathe, and even though I'm hyperventilating, I take another deep breath. "Where is it? Where's the list?" I scream again. The receptionist looks at me, confused, and turns to Mrs. Gensinger.

"Sidney's grandmother picked her up during second period today. We need to see her name and the address she wrote down," Mrs. Gensinger explains.

The receptionist gets up from behind her desk and walks to the end of the counter, where three sheets of paper lay. "Second period, you say?" she asks.

"Yes," Mrs. Gensinger responds.

God, this is taking too long. "Hurry up! Is that it?" I yank the paper from her. My eyes scan every name... all *two* of them. "It's not here. Maybe they signed the wrong one."

"Perhaps. It's possible," she says calmly, and I go into a rage.

"Perhaps!" I scream, and take the other two sign-out sheets. Only five children were signed out today, and Sidney is not one of them.

"I'm sure I would have remembered if someone signed Sidney out," she says. "With it being the last day of school, most parents have already made arrangements for their child's absence. Today was a very low attendance."

"Then why isn't she on the list?" I scream again.

"Does Sidney have on file who is allowed to take her out of school?" Mrs. Gensinger asks.

"Let me check." She walks back to her desk. After pulling up Sidney's account, she looks up over her computer. "I have a Lisa O'Shea."

"She was her former nanny," I say.

She glances back down. "A Julia Ellis, and... that's it." Glancing back up, she looks at me like I should be satisfied with her information.

"I'm Julia Ellis, the only one left on that list. So, tell me why someone walked out with her besides me," I say. She only looks to Mrs. Gensinger and shrugs her shoulders.

"That's all you can do—shrug your shoulders? It's your job," I spit at her.

"Okay, Julia, calm down. Let's call the police."

"Oh God, oh God, I can't believe this." I'm pacing, with my hands covering my mouth. "I think I'm going to be sick." Mrs. Gensinger grabs me by the shoulders.

"Julia—look at me. We're going to call the police, and we will find her."

I nod robotically. It's all a bad dream. I listen as Mrs. Gensinger calls 911, and I know I need to think fast. I have to be strong so that I can find her. *Think, think, Julia.* Then it hits me. Sidney's revelation of why she wanted a horse.

"You had a horse," I state. She looks at me, bewildered.

"Yes," she says.

"You used to tell the classroom stories about your horse. Sidney was telling me this morning."

"Yes, that's true. But what does this have to do with this situation?"

"There was a park... a park you used to..."

"Get poppies for her. Yes, I did tell them that."

"And you said she didn't want to go to the park. Then she said she *would*, if she could get something for her horse," I say in a rush, trying to put it all together. My hands are trembling. I'm freezing and shaking, yet my armpits are damp from fear.

"Yes, that's what she said."

"Where is this park? Does Sidney know where this park is? Did you ever tell her where? Please think," I beg.

"Well, there's a park on Coldwater that everyone calls Poppy Park, because for a short time in the summer, red poppies grow wild at the park's edge, near the woods."

I grab her arm. "Take me there now. Have the police meet us there."

"But they're on the way to the school now."

"We don't have time." I look at the receptionist. "Tell them to meet us at Poppy Park," I say, and rush out the door. Mrs. Gensinger follows behind me.

We get in her car, and I scream for her to hurry. "God, let this be where she's at," I say, and pray for real that God forgives me. Deep down, I know this is my fault for the lust I have felt for Jonas. The shallow vanity I have shown by spending my extra time shopping for clothes to entice him even more. I should have come right back and spent the day at school with her. But no... I didn't. I was selfish and behaved like a lustful whore.

It only takes ten minutes to get there, yet feels like a century. Pulling in, I already see the flashing lights of police cars lined up at the park. She stops, and I get out of the car and run to the police.

"Oh God, please help me. She's a little girl with chestnut hair in braids. Her name is Sidney. She's only ten years old. She was wearing blue-jean shorts, with a pink tank top," I say in one big rush, before they even have a chance to question me.

"Are you her mother, Miss?" one of the officers asks.

"No. I'm her nanny. Someone took her from school today."

"Can I get your name, Miss?"

"Julia... Julia Ellis. Look, we don't have time for this. I have to find her. I believe she wanted to come here to get poppies for her horse," I say, and then leave them and run to the park's edge, where I see a line of trees. As I run, I look at every child and what they are wearing.

What if they changed her clothes?

As I get closer to the line of trees, I see red dots scattered among the weeds. *It's the poppies.* I see the flowers, and yell her name. "Sidney! Sidney, are you here? Please answer me. Sidney, its Julia, I'm not mad at you," I say, trying not to let the fear in my voice scare her away. I stop and listen. The police follow behind, along with Mrs. Gensinger. "Sidney... Baby, please answer me. We need to get home to Holly. Don't you want to see your horse? I'm sure she misses you," I say, and my voice breaks. I start to cry. I drop to my knees. "Dear God, please bring my baby back, please let her be here," I pray, and then... I hear a small voice.

"Julia?" I open my eyes, and there in the distance is a little face, framed by braids... *Sidney.* She stands, and walks out of the long grass holding a bouquet of poppies.

"Oh, thank God... Sidney!" I run and wrap her in my arms, crushing the poppies.

"I got these for Holly," she says innocently.

My voice strangles. "Yes... yes, you did." My throat tightens. "Oh, God, Sidney. I was so scared." A rush of air hits my lungs as I start to cry with joy. "Oh, Sidney... my sweet Sidney... you wanted to get Holly poppies." Tears run down my face, and I wipe them away with the back of my hand. She nods her head and smiles.

"Do you think she will like them?"

Down on my knees, and still holding onto her, I look up into her face. She's beaming with pride for collecting poppies as a gift for her horse. I cry into her chest. "Yes—she will love them."

Now encircled by the police, and an assemblage of people

witnessing this mother-and-child reunion, I hear heavy chatter. One of the officers talks into the radio clipped to his shoulder.

"Child has been located and is now reunited with her guardian."

I hear the dispatcher respond. *"Copy that."*

"Sidney?" A small, frail voice speaks from behind. "Sidney, it's time to go." I look up, and see an old lady walk into the circle. She looks confused, like a troglodyte who just walked out of the woods. Her hair is unkempt, and yellowing, perhaps from hard water or chain-smoking. She shuffles into the crowd, oblivious of everyone but Sidney. I grab Sidney tightly, and pull her away from the woman.

"Who are you? Why did you take her?"

She shakes her head, startled, and looks at me. Her eyes are filled with a deep loss. She *herself* appears lost.

"Come, Sidney. It's time to go home," she says again, and takes Sidney by the arm. The police grab her and pull her away.

"Ma'am, step away from the child," one of the officers says. "You are being arrested for the abduction of a minor."

She looks more confused when he puts the handcuffs on her. "I didn't hurt her," she says in a small voice. "Please—it's a miracle, another chance. I wasn't a good mother then, but now I will be the best mother."

"I'm sorry, but you are being arrested. Do you understand?" he tells her.

She looks at Sidney and then back to me. "She belongs with me... not you," she says. I pull Sidney to me tightly, wrapping my arms around her, and holding her head to my chest. I don't know what to say. Surely, this old woman is mentally unstable.

The police officer leads her away, like a child. As she's being led away, I hear her say, "But Eve told me to come get her."

Eve!

"Wait... stop," I call out, and walk over to the police car, holding Sidney by the hand. The officer is helping the woman into the backseat, and explaining her rights. "You said, 'Eve.'" The officer turns to me.

"Ma'am, step away from the car. She's had her rights read to her, and will be handed over to the prosecutor.

"Please, I need to ask who Eve is." I plead.

"I'm sorry Ma'am. I cannot allow you to speak to, or have contact with, her. If you have any questions, you can bring them down to the station once she has been booked into custody." His radio goes off on his shoulder, which he responds to while getting into the car. Though I cannot hear the old woman, she says something to Sidney as the car drives away.

With Sidney's hand still gripped tightly in mine, I bend down to be on her level. "Did you know that woman?" She shakes her head no.

I have forgotten about all the people standing among us, when Mrs. Gensinger touches me lightly on the arm. "Julia, let's get back to the school, okay? We'll make sure she wasn't hurt, and talk to her—maybe find out what happened. Then we can have her talk to the guidance counselor."

"What?" I say, perturbed. "She's ten years old, and was abducted from your school. She's not making out her junior schedule." I am angry.

"I know," she says, contrite. "Come on, let's just get her back."

I hold Sidney's hand tightly as we walk back to her car. Once inside, I buckle Sidney in. "Am I in trouble?" she asks. Her face is full of confusion.

"No, Sweetie. You're not in trouble. But we are going to talk about what happened, and why you went with her. From now on, you *never* go with anyone you don't know."

"I'm sorry," she says, and her bottom lip begins to tremble. Her big eyes fill with tears, and I hold her in my arms as the car drives away. The shock has hit us both, and I'm crying just as much.

I need to call Jonas right away and let him know what happened. Maybe he has an explanation of who this woman is, though given the sight of her... I highly doubt it. My purse is spilled all over the floor from when I threw it into the car, leaving in a panic. "I need my phone," I say when she stops at a light. Mrs. Gensinger reaches down, and hands it back to me. I scroll through the saved numbers I put in from the list Lisa left me. I only hope his phone is not on airplane mode. I need to talk to him. Now. I'm expecting it to go to voicemail, but he answers.

"Jonas Fairbanks," he says, not recognizing my number. In my head, I have rehearsed this conversation in a rational, calm voice. But the moment my mouth opens to speak, I'm a complete sobbing mess.

"Julia? Is that you? What's wrong? Calm down—I can't understand a thing you're saying."

"Jonas... Jonas, someone took Sidney today." My throat tightens. I try to hold back the sobs. "I was so scared."

"What?" he yells.

"I got her back... she's with me now. Oh, Jonas... what's going on?"

"Wait. Tell me what happened."

"After I left the airport... I... I went shopping first. Oh, god I'm so sorry, I should have—"

"Tell me who took her, and where," he interrupts.

"They took her from her classroom. It was an old lady who was claiming to be her grandmother."

"That's impossible. Her grandmother on her mother's side is deceased, and my mother has been out of the picture for years. She doesn't even know that Sidney exists."

"She knew that you were in Indianapolis. How did she know that, Jonas?" *Silence.* "Jonas? Are you there?"

"Yes. I don't know, Julia. Do you have Sidney now?"

"Yes, we are with her teacher, driving back to the school," I say, looking down at Sidney.

"Julia, listen to me. I'm still in Indy. I'm not going to fly on to Maine. I'm going to rent a car and drive home as soon as possible. You take Sidney home, and lock all the doors and windows. Do not open the door until you see me pull in. Okay?"

"Okay, I will. Jonas?" I ask quietly.

"Yes?"

"Does this have anything to do with the person in prison?"

I hear him take a deep breath.

"I'm not really sure. Just go home and lock all the doors. I'll be home in a few hours."

"Okay. Bye, Jonas."

"Bye."

Once we reach the school, we meet in the library with the counselor, and the superintendent. Sidney is frightened over all the fuss being made about her. So I tell her to pick out some books to take home, and say I will read to her tonight. She asks if she can bring home some books about horses. I tell her that would be a good choice, and maybe some gardening books, too. She shyly nods, and walks over to the bookshelves.

I wait until her full attention is on looking for the books, and then start with my concerns. "Mrs. Gensinger, from day one, I have witnessed some strange reactions that Sidney gets from the other students, and from some of their parents. Mrs. Anderson called her the devil's spawn. Just the other day, we came across a lady who also made some distasteful remarks. I don't understand what's going on. I'm hoping you have an explanation. I mean, I don't really see her being a bully, or even a mean girl, for that matter. She's only a ten-year-old little girl."

The superintendent looks sternly at the teacher, and I feel she is being intimidated. She's about to open her mouth, when he speaks for her. "This is Mrs. Gensinger's first year teaching here at Wayne Elementary. I'm sure she hasn't had enough background of Sidney's history as a student to give you a valid answer."

I look over at her. "He's right. I'm just beginning to know the students and faculty. Sidney is a wonderful student. I just think maybe she's a little shy, and with her mother not in the picture—"

"All I can say," the superintendent interrupts, "is that we are very sorry this happened today, and we need to focus on having a stronger policy that guarantees this never happens again." I'm about to speak up when Sidney walks over with her books.

"I found some," she says, holding the books up to me. "I want to go home now and see Holly. I'm afraid the poppies will die."

"Yes, let's go home," I tell her.

The superintendent stands. "Well, I think we are done here. I will file a report. Let's all go home, and have a nice summer vacation." He then turns and leaves the library.

I'm putting Sidney's stuff in the car when Mrs. Gensinger pulls up beside me and rolls down her window. She motions for me to come over.

"Buckle up, Sidney," I tell her, and walk over to the teacher's car.

"I really am sorry about today. I really do think Sidney is a sweet girl, but there was one thing I think maybe I should tell you. I didn't want to say anything in front of Mr. Grant, because I was afraid of getting her in trouble. But last Christmas we had a nativity display in our room." She looks over at Sidney in the car. I move closer to hear what she has to say. "Sidney was always playing with the Mother Mary, Joseph, and baby Jesus. She was, like, obsessed with them."

I frown at her, not understanding why this would get her in trouble. She's a little girl—a little girl who I'm sure likes to play with dolls. But then again, I have never seen her play with dolls. "Yes, what about it?"

"They went missing. Sidney was the last child seen with them," she says, almost apologetic.

"Did you ask her if she took them?" I ask.

"I did. She said no. I can't think of anything else that would have happened to them. So, I took it as a sign."

"A sign?"

"Yes—like if you saw someone steal a Bible, would you tell on them?"

"No, I wouldn't. I see what you mean." We both look at each other with understanding. God's word is always free... no matter how it's obtained. And with Sidney, it came as a nativity scene.

～

SIDNEY IS IN THE BATH, AND I ONCE AGAIN CHECK ALL THE DOORS AND windows, reassuring myself that they are locked. I poured bubble bath in the tub, hoping it will keep her in the bath for a while. I need to search for something—anything—to clarify what happened today. I'm about to pull off the floorboard in my closet and read some more of the letters, the letters to Eve, when Sidney comes walking in.

"Okay, I want to read the books now. *May* we read them in your bed?" she asks, remembering my correction.

"Of course," I say, quickly dropping the board back in. "In fact, I'm not letting you out of my sight tonight. You want to sleep in my bed?"

"Yes!" she says joyously. Now smiling and showing those dimples, she runs and jumps onto my bed. I snuggle with her and open the book *True Blue,* by Jane Smiley.

I'm three chapters in, when I decide to try my chance of asking her about the Nativity scene. "Sidney, may I ask you something? I promise you're not in any trouble, but I would like the truth. Okay?"

She looks up at me, concern in her eyes. "Mrs. Gensinger said you liked to play with the baby Jesus, Mother Mary, and Joseph from the Nativity last Christmas," I begin cautiously.

"Yes," she says, and sticks a finger in her mouth.

"Did you like them so much that you wanted to bring them home?"

She sucks her lips in, and looks back into the book. She's considering my question.

"It's okay," I say. "You can tell me the truth."

"Yes, I wanted to have a mommy and daddy in the house. Like baby Jesus did," she says. "I play with them in my closet. It's like our house."

"Oh, so that's what I heard in your closet that day. You were talking in a mommy voice."

"Yes, and then I take Joseph—because he's the daddy—and talk like him."

My heart is breaking. She's created her own little family. Her little family she keeps in the closet. Something she is teaching herself. This makes me even more furious with Jonas. Why does he not see this? He's wrapped up in self-loathing, drowning himself by taking over companies, and all while ignoring his daughter's needs.

I hug her tight. "Thanks for telling me the truth, Sidney. Can I come into your closet and play house with you sometime?"

She smiles, shaking her head. "You mean, *may* you?"

I love this little girl.

Glancing over at the clock, I see it's almost nine. I would think Jonas would have been here by now. Surely, it's not that long of a drive from Indy to Fort Wayne? A three-hour drive, tops.

Sidney has fallen asleep, and I kiss the top of her head, tucking the covers around her. I slip out gently, and pad over to my closet. Quietly, I lift the floorboard and reach in to grab the letters. I then tiptoe out of the room, leaving the door cracked, in case she wakes up.

When I reach the front entrance, I look out the side window to see if a car is parked in the horseshoe drive. There is no car, so I head to the great room, and sit down in the leather chair. I untie the frayed ribbon, and pull out the second letter.

Oh, my beautiful Eve,

Dream. That's all I do—dream of you. Your face is the center of my world. Your body is my temple I worship. Tonight, I will have you. You will be mine. It will be just as in my dreams. Before I discover you, you come to me, touching my bare skin. My chest jumps from the electricity of your hands finally on me. Your lips start at my mouth, and hungrily move down my chest to my abdomen. I feel you lick across my belly, and my cock jumps. You feel the hardness of my lust for you, and lay your cheek against my aching cock. You nuzzle into it, and I feel your hot breath through my pants. You're on your knees, looking up at me with those loving eyes of yours. Your eyes are begging for me to take you, and you reach for my fly, and unbutton my pants. You pull them down gently, and my cock springs out, wanting what it has longed for—YOU.

Ah, my God, you take your hands and gently stroke my hard, aching cock. I try and hold back, but then you run the head across your lips, and my body stiffens. You lick the glistening bead now dripping from my opening. That slick moisture that is meant only for you. You take me in your mouth, and I'm about to explode, so I pull back and throw you on the bed. You're breathing hard, and your eyes are full of want. Your legs open, and I smile with delight at the wet shiny arousal that is just for me. I run my finger along your hard, swollen clit, and you moan. I slide my fingers into you; you're soaking for me, and I run your wetness back up, circling your clit. I taste you, sucking my fingers and breathing in the scent of your sweetness. You beg me to take you now, so I remove my pants and guide my cock between your legs. You cry out the minute my head touches your wet opening, but I don't slide in yet. I circle it around, increasing your need. You're begging now, begging for my cock inside you, and I push in. Your scream is full of release, and desire for me. I push inside you so deeply, and I know I will not last. You call out my name, and your fingers scratch my back, demanding more. I lose control, and spill all my love inside you. We are one now, and I feel you come, your pussy pulsating around my cock. We lie there, and fall asleep, with me still inside you. You are mine, now —always mine.

Jx

I'M A HORMONAL, EROTICIZED MESS. I FEEL AS THOUGH I'VE ALREADY made love to Jonas, although I've never been with any man. My insides are screaming to be made love to... to make love. I'm shaking, and I don't know why. I don't know the truth about any of it. About Eve, about why these letters are hidden, or about why someone claiming to be Sidney's grandmother would take her. There has got to be an answer in this house—something.

I jump up from the chair and hurry into Jonas's study. Opening all the drawers of his desk, I search through every folder and document, but they all pertain to the banking and household finances, nothing else. My eyes move to the bookshelf, and I think that maybe something —a picture, perhaps—might be enclosed in a book.

I pull out several books, stacking them on his desk, and quickly flip through the first five. When I begin fanning through the sixth book, it pops open to a place where a few pictures are tucked into the pages. There are three. My fingers tremble as I pull them out. Turning them over, I see in the first photograph three men, wearing Marine Corps, dress-blue uniforms. They're on a large ship, and are toasting with cocktail glasses. However, none of them are Jonas.

I pull out the second picture. It's Jonas, also in uniform. I remember now his talk at the airport. How all the girls want to date a soldier. He is dressed as a Marine, and wrapped in his arms is a girl in a wedding dress... *his wife*. All I can see is the back of her. She is facing the other way, her cheek pressed to his, and he is smiling at the camera. A smile that radiates happiness, and pride. It's his wedding day. Her hair is long, and pulled to the side. All I can see is the slender profile of her neck, and just a slight bit of her brow, and cheekbone.

I quickly pull out the third photo, hoping to see the front of her. But the image is of them both, facing the opposite way, and watching the sun go down over the water. There in the background of the photo, is the Sydney Opera House.

This is where they married. This is Eve. Although I can't see her, I can tell by her slim, petite body and long, blonde hair flowing in the wind... she is beautiful. Like he says in his letters, and the possessive way his arm holds her... she is his. *Is this where they met? Was she Australian?*

Lights reflecting across the wall in the dining room catch my eye. A car is coming up the drive. I shove the pictures back into the book and quickly put all the books back on the shelf. Grabbing the letters, I run to the kitchen, pull open the linen drawer, and shove them under the tea towels. I will have to remember them in the morning, and put them back in the floor.

Moving into the foyer, I look out the side window and see Jonas coming up the walk. My emotions are out of control, and I unlock the door, running straight into his arms.

He squeezes me in his strong arms. I'm trembling and crying his name.

"Shh," he says. "It's okay, Julia. I'm here now. Don't be scared."

"Jonas," I cry out. "What's going on? Why won't you tell me anything?"

"Julia, I promise you—I don't know who this woman who took Sidney is, but I plan to find out. Let's go inside."

As I look up into his face and piece together what little information I have gathered, my emotions turn heated and angry and—without warning, even to myself—I slap him, hard, across the face. He looks baffled, and I haul off and slap him again. Then, from out of nowhere, torrents of words come spewing out of my mouth, like vomit. "You're such a selfish son of a bitch. Your fairytale of a life ended early, and you have given up on everything else. You've left your daughter behind," I scream, and beat on his chest. "You've forgotten about her—the only thing that should matter to you. The piece of your life given to you as a gift, and you have forsaken her." I take a deep breath, only to continue with my foul accusations. "So what if your life didn't end up happily-ever-after. Whose does? You think I liked being an orphan when I was twelve?" I step back and cover my face with my hands.

"Hey... come here," he says, trying to hug me to comfort me. But I'm angry for so many reasons, I don't want his comfort right now. I want to scream in anger, and I pull back, not wanting him to touch me.

"Do you know she took the Joseph, Mary, and Baby Jesus just so she could have a family in the house?" I say through clenched teeth. "Christ, it's no wonder she left with a stranger today. She's never been taught any differently. What the hell's wrong with you, Jonas? She doesn't even call you 'Daddy.' I would give anything right now to have my dad with me. Someone I could run to, making me feel safe. She doesn't even have that." I'm now bawling like a child, full of rage and anger. I have no idea where this pent-up emotion is coming from.

He grabs my wrists, which are swinging wildly in the air, and pins me up against the door. My wrists are locked above me, held tightly in his hands. "Yes, I know I've made so many mistakes, Julia," he says, and there's sorrow in his voice. "Please, help me. Help me, Julia." There's so much pain in his eyes. My heart shifts, and I cry for him.

"Jonas," I say, and his mouth comes crashing in onto mine.

"I need you, Julia," he says, his words moving on my lips. He picks me up and opens the door. My arms and legs wrap tightly around him as he carries me across the threshold and into the great room. When we reach the stairs, he releases me, only to pick me up again, and I'm cradled in his arms as he takes me upstairs and into his room.

My arms are wrapped around his neck, and my eyes lost in his when he sets me gently on his bed. I lie back and watch as he removes his shirt. He is so gorgeous and manly—and I want him. I'm about to move and reach out for him when he covers me with his body.

"Julia," he says breathlessly. His hands move up my tank top, reaching my breasts, and I cry out his name.

"Jonas."

His mouth moves to my neck, and my body burns with every touch. "Julia, tell me how you like it. Tell me what you want me to do. I want to please you," he says, his breath hot on my neck.

I'm so dizzy with desire for him. I feel as if I'm floating. "Jonas, I want you... please," I breathe out.

"I want to please you, Baby. What do you like?" he asks, meeting my lips with hungry kisses.

"I don't know, Jonas. Teach me. I've never been with a man before."
Everything stops.

He moves off me, slowly. My eyes beg him to stay. His eyes are full of disbelief.

"What? What's wrong, Jonas? What did I do?"

He moves off the bed and backs away. "Nothing, Julia. It's what *I* was about to do," he says, and there is regret in his voice. I sit up on my elbows, and my look must be full of confusion, still mixed with want. I watch him stand there—shirtless, and almost... vulnerable. Then... I remember the words in his letter.
I know what he wants.

Moving slowly towards him, I stare into his eyes as my hand reaches out and gently touches his chest. He breathes in, as if someone just knocked the air out of him. His hand covers mine as I move along his abdomen. I kneel, still looking up into his eyes. I break eye contact, moving in to press my lips low along his belly, and I can still smell his familiar scent.

"Ah fuck, Julia," he hisses. I feel his hands stroking my hair. "You should stop." I don't. I only nuzzle my face into his erection. I cover it with my mouth, releasing hot breath, and he moans deep in his throat. "Fuck," he breathes out. "Julia... why are you doing this?"

I reach up, unbutton his trousers, and slowly unzip his fly. His erection is spilling out of his pants and, just like in his letters, I pull it out, releasing it when it springs onto my face. I touch it, curiously. It's hard, yet the skin is the softest thing I've ever felt. He moves back against the wall. "God, Julia, Please stop." But I don't—I want to feel it on my lips. And even though I know from his letter that it's exactly what he wants, it's exactly what I want, too.

I part my lips and take in the head. I feel the bead of moisture at the tip and lick it gently with the end of my tongue. He gasps, and his abdomen tightens. "Ah shit... Julia. Oh, God." I begin to take him in my mouth, when he pulls it away. I look up.

"Please, Jonas... take me!" I plead.

He breathes heavily and licks his lips. "Go to the bed and remove your clothes... slowly," he orders. I go to the bed and pull down my yoga pants, revealing my bare backside to him. When my bottom half is bare, I crawl onto the bed, turn, and sit on my knees. Slowly, I pull the tank top over my head, and my breasts spill out, full and heavy. I drop the tank top to the floor and cup my swollen breasts. I'm aching inside with such need for him.

"Please, Jonas. Make me yours," I gasp.

"God, Julia... you're so beautiful," he says, as his eyes feast on my body. He walks over to the bed, stands over me, and gently slides one finger down my shoulder. Goosebumps prickle my heated flesh. He lifts my chin with his finger and moves slowly down, placing a kiss on my lips. "You're a virgin?" he asks, gliding his lips along my neck.

"Yes," I breathe.

"You want to give your virginity to me?" He looks into my eyes.

"Yes, Jonas. You were my first kiss. Be my first love," I beg. "Please."

He takes a step backward and removes his trousers. His cock is so erect, it touches his navel. Standing before me, he strokes it gently with his hand, and moans deep in his throat. "Lie down and open your legs for me. Show me how wet you are," he orders.

I do, and I can already feel my wetness on the inside of my thighs. My knees are bent, and I spread my legs. His chest heaves, and he licks his bottom lip before biting it. "Fuck," he breathes out. He slides one finger from my clit to my opening, and my back arches up to his touch.

"Oh, Jonas," I cry out.

"This is for me?" he asks, sucking my juices off his finger.

"Yes," I whisper. My chest heaves. "You do this to me, Jonas. Only you."

He slides two fingers inside me, then spreads my juices back up to my clit. "I'm going to make you come with my fingers first, because my cock will probably hurt you... and I want you to have some pleasure."

His fingers enter me again, and I feel him pressing on a spot I didn't know existed. I feel so sinful—full of want, and desire. Something is building inside my core, and I can't help but squeeze my thighs together to increase the pleasure. He cups my pussy, and I begin to ride his hand.

"Open your legs for me, Julia." I do, and this time he circles my wet clit with his thumb. His fingers stroke that spot just inside me. My body begins to buck uncontrollably, and I call out his name in strangled breaths.

"Oh, Jonas. Oh, God—Jonas. I... I." I can't manage to bring words together to even make a sentence. I'm full of carnal lust, and my body quivers.

He straddles me, his elbows on either side of my head. "God, Julia. You came so fast. You're so wet... I need you wet." With his knee, he opens my legs again, because I'm squeezing them together, enjoying the aftershocks of my orgasm. I feel the head of his cock at my entrance. "I'm going to push my cock in slow, and you let me know if it's too much."

"Okay," I say in a rush. He starts, and already my muscles tighten. He notices, and pulls out.

"Relax. I'm going to take my time with you," he reassures me. I swallow, and nod my head. I feel him enter me again, and this time I will myself to relax. I feel him slide in deeper, and I cry out.

"Oh, God, Jonas." He pulls out, and I think he's going to push back in slowly, but he doesn't. He pushes hard, and I cry out in pain, and with pleasure.

"Sorry, Julia. I don't mean to hurt you. This is new to me, too. Being with a virgin," he says, seeming to correct himself. "I will try to go slowly. Are you okay?"

"Yes. It hurts... but I like it," I say, not understanding why. He starts to pump slowly, not removing his cock all the way, letting me get used to his size. With each slow push, he thrusts in a little deeper. I feel myself being stretched by him.

"God, Julia. I need to stop. I don't keep condoms here. If I continue, I will explode inside you," he says regretfully.

"I'm on birth control. Have been since I was fifteen." His look is perplexed, and still mixed with desire. "It's to regulate my periods."

"Oh. God, Julia." He begins pumping in a little faster and deeper. "You feel so good." As a natural response, I push up into his thrust. "Take it all, Julia. Take it all," he repeats, and pushes in and out with a rhythm I follow, pushing up to him. It hurts, but the kind of hurt that is only satisfied with each painful thrust he gives me, because I know I am filling his need with pure pleasure. I hear our souls say, *Welcome home.*

He increases his thrust and with one last push, releases himself in me. "Oh, Julia," he says out of breath. Ironically, I feel so whole, with him splitting me inside. I'm his, I want to be his. But what truly makes my heart flood with bliss, is what he says next.

"I'm yours, Julia... I'm yours," he says, and kisses me on the lips.

10

MY HEART SINGS WITH THE CHORUS OF A THOUSAND ANGELS. I WANT TO
become his, but the second he says he is mine, it seals my fate forever—
our fate. This man will be my first, and last. I feel it, and I know it is
meant to be. However, there is still so much I don't know about him.

He lies heavily on my chest, his breathing still labored from our
lovemaking. I still feel an ache inside me—I am swollen and throbbing
from his taking of me.

"Julia," he whispers, looking me in the eyes. "Are you okay? Do you
regret what we have just done?" He kisses me on the forehead.

"No, Jonas. I feel satisfied, and whole." He kisses me on the lips.

"Me, too, Julia... me, too. Are you tender? Let me run you a hot bath
to soothe the swelling between your legs." He pulls out slowly, and I
feel the painful ache left by him. He stands beside the bed and looks
down at me. "You're bleeding." His smile exudes satisfaction. "It won't
last," he says, and walks into the bathroom. I hear the water start.

I sit up. I look at the blood between my legs, and on the sheets, and
feel a slight embarrassment. But I shouldn't—this is natural. It's the
proof of the gift I have given him, and the gift of becoming each other's.

He walks back in, and, strangely, I cover myself with the sheet.
"You're not going to become shy, are you? Here, give me your hand." He

extends his hand, and I take it as he pulls me up. As soon as my feet hit the floor, he picks me up. I wrap my arms around his neck, as he walks me to the bath. I gaze into his handsome face.

He sets me down, and steps into the tub, reaching for my hand. "Come here—let's relax and soak." I take his hand, and step into the bath. The water is warm, with a scent of lavender. He rests his back against the tub, as I stand naked before him. "Come here, let me hold you." I turn, and slowly ease down into the water. My back leans into his chest, and I rest my head in the crook of his neck.

"This feels nice," I say, when his arms wrap around me.

"Yes, it does." He kisses the back of my head.

The mirrors begin to steam over, and through the silence I hear the light trickle of the faucet dripping into our bath. I can't believe I'm here —naked, and lying in his arms. I close my eyes and let my body enjoy the feeling of being wrapped in him.

His fingers move in between my legs and gently rub my swollen labia. "Do you hurt?" he asks, lightly stroking his fingers up and down on the area. "Your tight pussy is swollen."

"It's tender," I whisper. And even as he strokes over the tender area, I become aroused.

"How does this feel?" he says in a seductive whisper. His thumb then brushes against my clit, and I discover it's still sensitive to the touch. "I want to make you come again. Like this... not with my cock." He rubs my swollen labia while circling my clit. I'm building up again, and for some reason the pain, mixed with his touch, enhances the feeling. With the pleasure building up in my core, I squeeze my legs together, increasing the pleasure as I rub against his hand. I'm so close, and air escapes from my lungs as my orgasm releases in his hand.

"Oh... Jonas," I cry out, and my body quivers. "God, how do you do that?" My breathing is labored.

"Because it's you." I'm not sure what he means. I turn my head, resting my cheek in his chest. He holds me in his arms.

"But you don't even know me."

"I know that you're twenty-one, you were homeschooled, play

piano, and teach swimming. Now, I know you want to be a chef in Paris."

"How'd you know about the other stuff?" I turn to face him. His smile is devious.

"Okay, I have a confession," he says.

"A confession?"

"I didn't exactly come home because someone bought a horse out of the household finances." He cups water in his hand, and lightly drips it down my back.

"But you said..."

"Ms. O'Shea sent me your info, and your picture was included with it, and I couldn't believe it was you." He runs his finger along my cheek.

"So, you knew it was me who became your nanny?" His roguish smile slowly appears. His eyes light up, with their blue, glistening irises. "But you didn't say anything."

"No, I didn't." He pauses and studies me. "I wanted to watch you."

"Oh," I whisper. He looks at me so sincerely.

"We spend our lives searching for our other half." He traces my cheek with his finger. "You're it," he says, and lifts my chin to meet his lips.

"Oh, Jonas," I say the words on his lips. I turn completely, straddling his lap. The water splashes over the edge and puddles on the floor.

"I was always thinking of another person," he confesses. "I was thinking of you... and I found you. You just needed to find me."

"And I did." I hug him into my breasts, kissing the top of his head.

"You asked me once if I ever prayed."

"Yes, I remember. You said once."

"That's right." My hair has loosened from the messy bun I tied it in. Long strands stick to my face and shoulders. With his hand, he gently strokes my face and places the loose strands behind my ear. "That day on the boardwalk, when I went crashing over the side."

How could I ever forget? "Our first encounter," I laugh.

"Yes... our first encounter. That was the first time I prayed." I turn my head slightly, waiting for him to go on. "Can I tell you a story? And promise you'll keep an open mind?"

"Yes. Of course, Jonas."

He pulls his knees up, and I lean back on his thighs. His thumbs caress small circles around my nipples. If they weren't hard before, they are steel buds now. "That day, something happened that I've been dreading for a long time." I wonder if it has anything to do with the person in prison. "I needed to escape and clear my head. Mostly, I was angry with myself for never moving on."

Moving on after the death of his wife?

"I jumped on my bike and rode for miles. Hours went by, and I ended up on that boardwalk." He tilts his head and looks sweetly at me. "Yes, *that* boardwalk," he says with smiling eyes, and runs the back of his finger along my cheek. My fingers pet the hairs curled across his chest. "There was a lady there that day, an older lady. She noticed me standing against the wooden rail. I was taking a break, leaning over the side. I must have looked distressed or something, because of what she said."

I sit up, wrap my arms around his neck, and hook my fingers. He leans back, resting his head on the side of the tub. "What did she say?"

"At first, I thought I was hearing things, because no one was around. Then I looked up and saw an old lady. I asked if she was talking to me. She smiled and said, 'We're the only ones here.' I asked what she said— if she could repeat it. She did, and what she said astounded me. She had read my mind, or heard my prayer. She said, "It's not too late. In fact, this is the day."

"Did you know what she was talking about?"

"I was about to ask, but then it hit me, what she meant. Somehow, she saw in me all the regrets and mistakes I've been carrying around, and now was the time to let go. Not only for myself, but Sidney, too." He tilts his head and looks at the ceiling. "I know. It sounds crazy, right?"

"Not at all. I believe we all have a guardian angel looking after us."

"Well, here's where it gets really strange. She was feeding birds out of her hand. Literally, they landed and ate out of her hand. Then, when she turned to me, I discovered that she was blind."

My breath catches in my throat. This is the same woman I met on the boardwalk. I've never told anyone about her. The lady who said he was thinking of me, too. *Was it Jonas?*

"Well, you are right about her maybe being a guardian angel, because she told me what I needed... that I would come crashing into it," he says, and cups my face in his hands. "You're it."

"Oh, Jonas," I gasp, and meet him with a kiss. *We are meant to be.* "I went back the next day to look for you, hoping you would be there looking for me."

"I had to be in Florida the next day, for business. The Florida Keys, showing a certain person a vacation home, if you know what I mean," he winks, and I frown at my inner-bitch for the little bit of pleasure of Mr. Anderson's betrayal. "But when Ms. O'Shea sent me your profile for her replacement, I couldn't believe my eyes. I stared at your picture for an hour, making sure I wasn't seeing things. There it was—your beautiful, innocent, I-hope-we-didn't-smash-a-groundhog face."

"I had no idea my profile picture would show up."

His roguish smile appears. "That's the real reason I came home... hoping to find you here."

"And then I greeted you with a fire poker over the head," I say with a grimace.

"Yes, another just-knock-me-over greeting. It's getting pretty late. We should get some sleep."

I stand and step out of the tub, grabbing a towel off the shelf. Instead of drying off, I wrap it around me and turn, watching Jonas wrap himself with a towel low on his hips. He walks to the bedroom and pulls down the duvet. His towel drops to the floor.

Hugging my towel, I walk over to retrieve my clothes from the floor and glance around, taking in the memory of what happened between us. I know it's real, because I still feel sore from him from being inside me. He watches as I start to walk out.

"Where are you going?"

I hesitate. "To bed."

He pulls the covers down beside him. "Right here, Julia. You sleep here—next to me."

I look down to the floor. *What is wrong with me?* I can make love to him, but feel too shy to crawl into bed with him? "Maybe I should check on Sidney," I say as an excuse for my hesitation. I should be happy he wants to share his bed with me. Not just for his sexual pleasure. Of course, I'm the one who... initiated it. *What does that say about me?*

"She's fine. Now, come here and lie next to me. Please," he whispers.

I have given up all self-control for this man. Slowly, I walk to him, and let the towel fall to the floor. He admires what is now his, and reaches for me. I take his hand, crawling up onto the bed, and lay into the arms of this man. My man—*Jonas.*

∾

I WAKE WITH THE SUN ON MY FACE. THE SILK CURTAIN IS RUFFLED BY A light breeze drifting in through the window. The pink sun in the horizon still lies low in the pasture, and I suddenly sit up, realizing where I am.

Jonas's bed.

Hugging the sheet around my chest, I touch the empty spot in bed where he laid, and feel an ache in my heart with his absence. When I look to the nightstand to check the time on the clock, I find a folded note with my name written on it. I reach for it and open it up.

Good morning, Beautiful. I'm wearing the smile you gave me.

I smile and bring the note to my lips, giving it a gentle kiss. I look again to see if he signed it with his signature, *Jx* like in the love letters, but he didn't. I can't tell if the writing looks the same. Then thinking of the letters I stuffed in the linen drawer, I quickly jump up out of bed, and scramble putting my clothes on. I need to get them back into their secret hiding place. Then I think of Sidney who is in *my* bed. *Crap.*

I rush down the stairs and into the kitchen. I hear Jonas on the phone in his study and want to use this time to sneak the letters back to their hiding spot. Opening the drawer, I reach under the towels, pull them out, and then wrap them inside a dishtowel. I'm about to run up the back stairs when I hear yelling coming from his study.

"You're going to sign it. You don't have a choice." It's silent, and I walk over to the study door. "Well, then it will have to be signed by the judge," he says to whomever he's talking to. "Yes... this is my final decision. Well, this is what I have decided. Look, I have made some very attractive provisions that you'd be crazy to ignore. It's the best I can offer."

Placing my hand on the door, I gently push it open, and see him pacing, talking on his phone. He is shirtless, and wearing only jeans. He sees me and smiles. "I have to go. Take the offer," he says, and ends the call.

I smile and hold the wrapped letters close to my chest. "Good morning," I say.

He leans against the front of his desk and sweetly smiles at me. "Come here, you." Looking down at the towel squeezed into my chest, I set it carefully on a side table before walking in. He holds out his arms, welcoming me, and I cuddle into his embrace. "Good morning," he says, and kisses the top of my head. "How do you feel this morning? Are you okay?"

I snuggle into his chest, and feel his light hairs tickle my face. He still smells of lavender from our bath. "Yes," I say, and look up into his eyes. He smiles a smile I've never seen before—not roguish nor sweet. It's... different. It's as if there is a whole life behind that smile. A dream, maybe? *The smile I gave him.*

"It's going to be a great summer," he says, before meeting my lips with a soft, gentle kiss. My arms wrap around his neck as I move in, deepening the kiss. He pulls, squeezes me into him. I love being here— here in his embrace.

His arms move up my back, pulling me in tighter. My fingers run through his hair, and I'm once again feeling dizzy and drunk from the lust I feel for him—*or is it love?*

His hands slide down my back and move under my tank top. They feel warm, and strong, as he caresses me. His lips move to my neck, and goosebumps prickle my skin.

"Are we going to grow the carrots today for my horse?" Quickly jumping out of Jonas's embrace, I turn and see Sidney, rubbing her eyes. *God, did she catch us kissing?* e

"Well, good morning Little One," I say, and look back to Jonas, who now has the roguish grin. I'm suddenly aware of the affect my nipples are having on him, and quickly cross my arms. *Who am I becoming?* "Yeah. We will need to make a list of all the things we want to plant before going to the farmers' market." I look back to Jonas. "I thought we could plant a garden this summer. I hope you don't mind."

He reaches out for me, and I hesitate a little, because of Sidney's presence. He pulls me in, anyway. "Like I said, it's going to be a great summer," he says, and kisses me on the forehead. "However, where do you plan to plant this garden? You'll need to till the ground first."

I look out the big window. "I was thinking maybe Gus could build some boxes that we can fill with dirt. Boxes are a lot easier to maintain than open land. That's if you don't mind."

"I think it's a great idea," he says with smiling eyes, and kisses me. He looks genuinely happy for once in the short time I've known him.

"Jonas having another bad day," Sidney says sarcastically as she walks back to the kitchen. I'm sure it's a reference to the kiss I made her give him the day before. I quietly giggle, and Jonas places his forehead on mine.

"I'd better get breakfast ready." I start to leave, then turn around. "Jonas, I think we need to talk to Sidney about yesterday. I want to know who this person is who took her."

He drops back against his desk, runs his hands through his hair, and then begins rubbing his face. He's agitated. "Yes, I'm going to go down to the police station to get some answers."

"Good. We can go after breakfast."

"No, Julia, you stay out of this. Let me handle it." He looks troubled.

"But I was there. I have questions. The old woman said things that were impossible for her to know unless she really knew Sidney."

"Like what?"

"She knew that you were in Indianapolis. How would she know that, Jonas?"

He turns and looks out the window. "It could have been through a business contact."

"By the looks of her, I highly doubt that. She was lost and confused, and even looked homeless—yet she had information connected to Sidney." I now have a reason to mention Eve's name without revealing that I've read the letters. "She said Eve told her to pick her up," I say cautiously, watching his response. "That proves this woman is someone from the past. Does she even know Eve is dead?"

He turns around, looking confused. "Who's Eve?"

In my head, I'm screaming—*Eve, Sidney's mother. Your dead wife. The wife you wrote beautiful letters to.*" But I stand with my mouth slightly open, and my eyes blinking rapidly. "She said Eve. I thought you would know." Am I now back to nowhere in this mystery I thought I was solving?

"Well, there you go. She must be some crazy woman wanting to steal a child." He walks around to the back of his desk.

"So... you don't know who Eve is?"

"No."

"Then will you please tell me what Sidney's mother's name was?"

"Jenna."

"Jenna?"

"Yes."

Jenna... who was Eve?

11

My heart sinks, and suddenly I'm back to zero as I walk out of the study. Jonas sits behind his desk and watches me leave. I grab the letters, which are still wrapped in the towel, and make my way to the kitchen. Sidney is rummaging through the pantry for breakfast.

"Sidney, let me get dressed, and we'll make breakfast," I say, climbing the back stairs to my room.

"I just want cereal. Cereal won't take long, and then we can get to the store to buy carrot seeds."

"Okay," I holler, running up the stairs.

Once in my room, I rush to the closet and place the letters back in the floor. I wish now that I had never discovered them. Why does knowing about them make me feel so... reserved towards Jonas? This is really none of my business, and I certainly shouldn't be reading them. But *who* put them here, and *why?*

My phone pings with a notification, and I go to the dresser to pick it up. A Facebook reminder alerting tomorrow is Natalie's birthday. Her *sixteenth* birthday. I can't miss this. I tap the notification and leave an early happy birthday message, along with a smiley face and birthday cake. Setting my phone back down, I turn to get dressed, and jump when I find Jonas leaning against the doorframe. *God, did he see me put the letters back?*

"Jonas, you startled me."

"I see that. Is everything okay?"

"Yes... I just didn't know you were there, that's all." I feel he sees right through my deception.

"I'm sorry. I didn't mean to startle you. You ran out so fast, so I feel maybe you are," he hesitates, "regretting last night?" His eyes have lost that shine they had earlier, and his sweet smile is gone.

"No, of course not. It's just... well, Sidney walked in on us, and I'm not sure she should see us like that." I cover myself, wrapping my arms across my chest. *Am I regretting it, after all?*

"I meant what I said last night, Julia. I know this is sudden, and I only hope that what I *can't* say, you will believe me when I say, *I'm yours.* This probably means more to me than it does you." He walks into the room and reaches for me. Slowly, I unfold my arms, and move into him. My eyes glance at the closet. *Eve.*

"Jonas, it meant everything to me—honestly. But, why *can't* you tell me everything?"

He squeezes me tight. "It's to protect Sidney." Is he saying this because he knows I will agree to defend a helpless child? Or is there another reason?

"All right, I'll agree not to ask questions about... well, I don't even know what I'm *not* supposed to ask about. However, I do want to talk about what happened yesterday with Sidney. Maybe, this lady said something that could be helpful. Also, Sidney needs to know *never* to go with strangers," I state, as a matter of fact.

He looks down and cups my face in his hands. "Okay, we'll talk to her right after breakfast. And then I'm going to the police station to see what I can find out." He smiles sweetly and kisses me on the lips.

When he releases me and turns to leave, I stop him. "Jonas?"

"Yes?" He turns around.

"Last night... before... before we went upstairs, you said to help you."

"Yes, I remember."

"What exactly did you mean? I mean... how can I help you—if I don't know what I'm supposed to help you with?"

He walks back in and sits on the bed. He reaches for me. "You were right about my not being a father. Being selfish, and leaving her behind. But..." he exhales and stands up, walking over to the window. "The decision I made years ago—well, I had other plans for Sidney, about her future." He turns around, and rubs his face. "It's complicated, and I really can't talk about it. All I can say now is—I was wrong and I need to fix it. For her... not for me." He looks at me, intently. "Please—trust me, and understand."

My heart is breaking for the pain on his face. I want to give him his smile back. The smile *I* gave him. I walk over, and touch his chest with my fingers. I make the symbol of a cross and kiss the center of it. "I will trust you, Jonas."

"Thank you." he says, and kisses the top of my head.

I look up into his eyes. "I better get breakfast ready," I say, and pull away. He grabs my wrist.

"She's fine. I made her a bowl of cereal. Now... I want to make love to you." He walks to the door, locks it, and moves to the bed. "Come here," he says, patting the bed. I gingerly approach him, and he pulls me down.

THE MORNING SUN WARMS THE PATIO AS I SET TWO CUPS OF COFFEE ON the table. Sidney is becoming impatient about our trip to the farmer's market, and we promise her that as soon as we have this talk, we can go.

"I told you guys—I have no idea who she was," Sidney says, frustrated. "You said I wasn't in trouble."

"You're not, Sidney. We just need to know what she said to you when you were together. But most of all, you never *ever* go with somebody you don't know." She winces, and slumps in her chair. Jonas sits across the table, observing her.

"Did she say anything about a person named Eve?" I ask, and look at Jonas. I hope to catch a hint of recognition when I say her name. But he doesn't waver.

"Eve?" she repeats, squinting her eyes. "No, she never said anything like that."

"Sidney," Jonas now pipes in. "Please, tell Daddy and Julia everything you remember." She looks incredulously at him. *Daddy* sounds so foreign coming out of his mouth.

She exhales with boredom, and then begins talking, seemingly just to get the interrogation over with. She reminds me of a little Natalie. *Natalie. Birthday.* "She said I was pretty, and how she was so happy to meet me," she says, waving her hands in the air. "I told her I have a horse, and she said how nice." She rolls her eyes.

"Did she tell you her name?" I ask.

"Yes," she says, nodding. "Grandma."

I look over to Jonas. "Is this possible? Could she be Sidney's grandmother?"

"Like I said... no. Now, I'm going down to the police station to see what I can find out." He finishes his coffee and leaves the patio.

"Good. Can we go now?" Sidney exclaims.

With Jonas's exit, I guess this is all the information I will get. "Yes. Thank you, Sidney. Now, promise me you will never do this again," I say, bending down and tapping her nose.

"I promise. I'm going to tell Holly about the carrots," she says, and disappears into the barn. My gut tells me that Jonas is not telling the truth about Eve. But I said I would trust him. Trust him is what I must do, if it's to keep Sidney safe.

When I walk back to the kitchen, Jonas is on his phone, talking to the police. He says he will be at the station in twenty minutes, and expects to get some answers. He ends the call and then looks at me. He's about to say something when my phone goes off. I see Natalie's picture displayed on the screen. "Excuse me," I say, and take the call.

"Hey, girl. What's up?"

"Tell me you're coming to take me out for my birthday!" she states, not asking.

"Yes, of course. I just need to make arrangements with... Jonas." He looks at me.

"Jonas?" she teases.

"Yes. He's the little girl's father."

"Wait... and her mother?"

"Um... there is none." And I know exactly where she's going with this.

"Okay, then at least tell me he's hot." *I was right.*

"Hey, we'll catch up this weekend. Let me call you back, and I will let you know what time. Be thinking of where you want to go."

"Hey...

"Bye, Natalie." I quickly end the call and set my phone on the counter.

"Is there a problem?"

"No. But I need to ask you something."

"Yes?"

"Since you cancelled your trip to Maine, will you be home all weekend?" He furrows his brows, considering my question.

"Yes. But I will need to reschedule. I have an investment project we need to get on, fast. I'm currently working on a condo project my boss wants in on," he says, while rinsing out his coffee cup.

"I was hoping to go home just this weekend. Natalie, the daughter of the people who took me in—well, it's her sixteenth birthday, and I would like to spend it with her." I hope he understands.

He walks over, and takes me in his arms. This is beginning to be my favorite place—here in his arms. I look into his eyes. "On one condition. You promise to come back to me. You may have given me your innocence, but I have given you my heart."

"Oh, Jonas." Guilt stabs at my heart. Why can't I just forget about those letters? Everyone has a past—skeletons in the closet. Except his is alive, in the floor of my closet!

I wrap my arms around his neck, and my fingers smooth the back of his hair. "I promise I'll be back. I could never leave you, or Sidney. Why would you think that?" Even as I say this, I know it's too soon for either of us to be talking like this. Yet, I feel I've always been with him. He is the only man I have ever fantasized about, even before I knew him. How strange that I ended up in his bed.

"Sometimes, you never really know someone," he says, taking my hands and kissing my knuckles. Is he talking about someone in his past? *Eve?*

I run my hands down the front of his chest, feeling the hardness of his muscles. "I have an excellent idea," I say. He tilts his head and narrows his eyes. "You asked for my help in becoming a better father."

"Yes," he whispers.

"Well, to become a better father—or a father at all—you need to spend some time with her. Be proactive. Some *alone* time. I mean... why does she call you Jonas?"

He backs up and exhales, placing his hands on his hips. "Well, that's my fault. Ever since the day I picked her up, she's constantly been with nannies. I guess I should be thankful she doesn't call me Mr. Fairbanks," he laughs half-heartedly. "Since that is what they all called me."

"How many nannies has she had?" I sound sarcastic.

"You're her fourth. You need to understand, my whole career, since she was born, has required traveling. There's no way I could be dragging a little girl around with me. I've done my best to see that she has great care. I just haven't done well as a father." He sounds genuinely regretful.

"Then this will give you the perfect opportunity to start. I will go home this weekend, and you will spend 'alone' time with Sidney," I say, using air quotes.

His lips tighten and his shoulders straighten as he inhales heavily before speaking. "Okay. Two things concern me about that statement."

I tilt my head, considering this. *What two things concern him?* "And those would be?"

"Home, and alone."

"Home, and alone?" I repeat.

"I would like for you to refer as *this* place as your *home*. As for being alone with Sidney... well, I don't know the first thing about taking care of a little girl."

"Oh, for crying out loud, Jonas. It's not like she's a scary, green-eyed monster with fangs," I laugh. "She's just a little girl who needs love. To know her daddy wants the best for her. You've said it yourself: 'I've done the best to see she is cared for.' So, just put those words into action. Get to know her, what she likes, what makes her sad, what makes her angry, and what she wants to be. Start to see the world through her eyes—the eyes of a child. Sometimes, the world is a much brighter place seen that way. A happy place. A child's view has not been distorted with all the disappointment life can bring. Sometimes, if we can look at the world through a child's eyes, we can see magic in everything."

He drops his head, then looks back up with a small smile. "It's just... I can stand up to the most ruthless person while doing business, and feel right at home. But... to go up against a little girl, well... I'm just not equipped for that."

"Who says it has to be an argument? Is that what you think raising a little girl is all about? Arguing?" *Like with Natalie. He has a few years before that.*

"Hmm, I guess I never saw it that way," he concedes.

Walking over, I take his hands in mine. "Look, let's break it down to what it really is. A relationship with a unique little person that God entrusted to you. To nurture, love, and raise her. After all, he's the one who gave her to you. So, he must have known that *you* are what she needs."

He takes in a deep breath. "To the alternative," he mumbles.

"What?"

He snaps back to the current moment, feigning an expression of understanding. "You're right."

"No, wait a minute. What'd you just say? What'd you mean by that? Alternative."

"Nothing. Now, let's talk about *home*." He walks to the counter, grabs his cell phone, and checks the screen before shoving it into the pocket of his jeans.

Letters. Eve. Grandmother. Sidney. Alternative. I let it go—for now. It's true, all I've wanted to do since the first meeting with Lisa was to put a little *home* in this house. "Like I said, life needs to grow here. The garden boxes will be perfect for you and Sidney to start with."

"Me and Sidney?" He has that scared look again.

"Yes... your *alone* time. This is something she is excited to do, and *you* will be the person doing it with her. It's a good start, don't you think?" I walk to the kitchen sink and rinse my coffee cup. Noticing the bare dirt in the window box underneath the kitchen window, I turn and say, "You should put some bright, colorful annuals in every box, at each window. This house needs some love and attention, too."

"What, all twenty-four of them?" he mocks.

Twenty-four? I was only thinking of the ones in the front. I never notice the ones in back. "Yes. All. Twenty. Four."

Sidney comes running up to the patio door. She opens it, not bothering to close it behind her, and starts with her demands. "Okay, I'm tired of waiting. Let's go already." *Little monster.*

"Sidney, close the door, please, and then ask politely if we may go," I say in a motherly tone. Her eyes widen for a moment, and then —*without* reluctance—she gently closes the door.

"Julia, may we go buy carrots seeds now?" she says in her politest voice.

There's potential. I smile.

❧

"BUT WHY DO YOU HAVE TO LEAVE THIS WEEKEND?" SIDNEY WHINES. SHE is riding on the side of the cart down the aisle of garden seeds as I push "Jonas doesn't know how to take care of me."

"Well, Sidney I'm not leaving him in charge of you." She looks baffled. And this is my plan, because I have apparently now piqued her interest. "I'm leaving *you* in charge of *him*. And starting today, you will refer to him as your father."

"You've got to be kidding me," she says, and I see Natalie all over again. And if Natalie could get away with it, she'd be calling her father, Tom. She tried it once—it did not go over well.

"No, I'm not kidding you. He needs you, Sidney. You need to show him how we do things, and how to take care of Holly. You don't want to leave your horse for the weekend, do you?"

She jumps down from the cart, and places her hands on her little hips. "I think he would rather have *you* take care of him." I sense sarcasm, and I cringe. She saw us kissing. God, do I have to have this talk with her now, *here?*

"Sidney... why do you say that?" I ask, knowing exactly why.

"Because, you like kissing him. And I think he likes kissing you, too," she says, as a matter of fact, and the lady next to us giggles.

"Let's get coffee, and a milkshake." We will have this talk in the car.

"I want chocolate," she says, and races down the aisle.

"Sidney, don't run. Wait for me." The lady next to me smiles, watching her.

"Your daughter is *so* adorable." I start to correct her, and then feel proud thinking of Sidney as my daughter.

"Thanks," I say, and run after... *my daughter.*

"This shake is too thick, Julia. I need a spoon to eat it," Sidney says, struggling to suck up her Wendy's Frosty.

"Take the lid off, and I will show you how to eat a Wendy's Frosty." Instead of handing her a spoon, I take a French fry from the box, and dip in the ice cream. "Mmm, this is how you eat a Frosty," I say. She smiles and then tries it herself.

Now that she is distracted with her Frosty and fries, I decide I need to make use of this time and find out how she really feels about seeing Jonas and me kissing. *I hope that is all she saw.* I take a sip of my cappuccino. "Sidney... so you saw us kissing?"

"Yep." She dips another French fry.

"Did... that bother you?"

"Nope. Somebody should kiss him. I *don't* want to." She wrinkles her nose. I giggle.

"Are you sure? Because... I really like Jo... your dad," I say quickly, using the right term. "And you might see us kissing again."

"Good." She grabs another fry.

"Good?"

"Yes. I want you to kiss him... like a thousand times." I start to laugh.

"Really? Well, I'm glad you're okay with this. But why a thousand times?"

"I want you to kiss him a thousand times, and him to kiss you a thousand times," she chimes. "That way you guys can make a baby, and I will have a little brother or sister."

I choke on my cappuccino.

12

WE PULL INTO THE HORSESHOE DRIVE OF THE MANOR. MY MINI IS STUFFED with bright, colorful, flowering plants. Sidney is holding a tray of marigolds on her lap, complaining about how they stink.

"That's the point," I tell her. "The smell will keep the rabbits away."

"But why do we want to keep them away? Couldn't we just keep them? Don't rabbits eat carrots, too?" she argues.

Huh! "Yes, they do. But rabbits can go anywhere and get food. We don't want them eating all of Holly's carrots, do we?"

"No, I guess not."

I eluded the discussion of baby-making by telling her I am not ready to have babies, and that I and Jonas would like to have some time just with her. She seemed to like that idea. I just hope she doesn't start with him about babies this weekend. After all, this is his time being alone with his daughter, and *that* talk needs to come years later.

We carry the plants to the back of the house, and set them on the patio. I can see Jonas through the glass doors, talking on his phone. I wonder what he found out at the police station. When I walk into the house, he ends the call and shoves the phone into his pocket.

"Looks like you bought the whole store," he says, coming to meet me at the door.

"No, only what I could fit in my little car. There is much more we need. So, what did you find out? Did you see her, or talk to her?"

He looks over at Sidney, then motions me to his study. I set the planter down and follow him, wiping my hands on my jeans. "So, what did you find out?" I ask, sounding anxious.

"She wasn't there, but I did find out her name." He leans back against the edge of his desk.

"And?"

"Kay Owens. She has quite a rap sheet. Prostitution, drugs, and multiple dealings with the CPS."

"So, she has children? She did say she wasn't a good mother, and this was another chance for her. What happened to her children? Did they say?" I'm rattling out my questions without taking a breath in between them.

"No, they wouldn't give out that information, I suppose for the protection of the children. They're probably grown by now"

"So... she's out now?"

"No. She's been transferred to a detox center, rehab. It appears she's a drug addict—heroin. She was high when they arrested her, and had paraphernalia on her. Needles, and two bags of dope."

"Oh, my God," I say, putting my hands over my mouth. "Jonas—to think she had Sidney!" I start to cry. "What if I had never found her?"

He takes me in his arms. "Shh. You did find her. She's fine."

"But, Jonas—"

"Don't worry, Julia. I will fix this." He squeezes me tighter.

I wipe my eyes, and look up at him. "Did you ask about who Eve is?" He looks at me for a bit, and I can tell that there is something he knows. But, he's not going to say so.

"No, I didn't ask about Eve."

"Why not? This Eve knew that you were in Indianapolis. Explain that to me," I order him.

"I can't."

"You can't, or you won't?"

He takes me by the shoulders. "Julia, trust me, please. I said I'm going to take care of it."

"How? What do you mean?" I know that's something I am *not* supposed to ask.

His eyes plead with me. "I promise to keep you and Sidney safe. It's all going to be okay. This woman cannot get to her again. She is locked up in a facility, going through withdrawals. Okay?" I nod my head, and he kisses my lips. His hands stroke my back, and his tongue parts my lips. His kiss turns passionate, and I once again lose control to his seduction.

"Kissing again?" I turn around and find Sidney in the doorway. "That's two times. Nine hundred and nighty-eight to go."

BEFORE THROWING MY PACKED BAG IN THE CAR, SIDNEY PROMISED THAT she'd take good care of her dad. Jonas told Gus about the garden boxes, and promised me they be completed and planted by the time I returned on Sunday night. It is hard leaving them, only if it's just for two days. But I am excited to see the girls again.

I thought for sure that when Jonas returned from the jail, there would be answers clearing everything up, and I could forget about the letters. I told myself to let it go, and have a great summer, just like he said. However, right before walking out of my room, I threw them in my bag. *Traitor.* There was just something in his eyes telling me he knows more than he is telling. And those letters are my only hope of finding out what that is.

Before reaching the DeLucas' house, I pull over and yank out the long dress tucked inside my bag, slipping it over my skinny jeans. A precaution, in case Tom and Cathy are home. Natalie is going to flip.

I can already hear the music blasting from Natalie's room as I pull into the driveway. *I can't wait to see her!* Running up the stairs two at a time, I reach her door and open it. "Get Free" by the Vines is blasting from the speakers. She turns and sees me.

Screams.

We both run, jumping into each other's arms, and then fall onto the bed. "Oh, my God, Julia. I miss you so damn much!" she yells over the Vines.

"I miss you too," I yell back. She gets up, and turns off the music. *Better.* She turns around... and here it comes.

"All right, I want to know all about this... Jonas." God, there is so much to tell her. But I need to be very careful, remembering she *is* only sixteen. Even though I'm an adult, she is like a sister to me, and it's so hard not to want to share everything. But first, I will start with the clothes.

I stand, unzip the back of the dress, and shimmy out of it. It falls to the floor, exposing the tight skinny jeans and a tank top. Her mouth drops open. "Wait until you see the red heels I bought." I stand on my tiptoes, imitating them in my white trainers.

"Oh, my God. Your tits look amazing in that shirt. And you do have an ass," she blurts out, as only Natalie would. "Okay... you have just told me he's hot."

"I never said that."

"You don't have to. Your body language is screaming it. And you also say there's no mother?"

"Let's go see Paige, and then I will tell you... some stuff." She's totally reading me right now.

I climb the ladder to the tree house, lift the trap door, and see Paige. As usual, she's wearing her Beats, and drawing in her sketchpad. She looks up, sees me, and her eyes widen. She drops her sketchpad, removes her Beats, and takes my hand. I stand up, and bump my head on the ceiling. God, it's been a few years since I've been inside. Natalie climbs in behind me.

"Are you home for the weekend?" Paige asks.

"Yep, I am. For Natalie's birthday. And to see you, too. I've missed you guys." I give her a hug. I know it's only been a few weeks, but she already looks older. Her hair is blonder than I remember. Must be all the sunshine.

We sit in a circle on the floor of the tree house, just like we did when we were little. All the signs we made—*No Boys Allowed, Paige Superstar Only, Princess Natalie Only* and *Queen Julia Only* still hang on the wall. The pink, lacy curtains with sparkles still flutter in the summer breeze. The scent of fresh-mowed grass wafts in, and I am once again a little girl. A little girl who is home for the summer. But... I'm not a little girl anymore. I'm now a woman. A woman belonging to Jonas. *To be a little girl again, simple. Eve. Letters.*

"How are things going here?" I ask.

"Shitty," Natalie retorts. I see her potty mouth hasn't changed. *Did I expect it to?* "Mom and Dad totally don't trust me. I'm barely allowed to see Sebastian—only when he comes to church with us, and he's going to be leaving to go home soon. I mean, how unfair!" she says, like it's the end of the world. "I'm also embarrassed when Mom invites him over after church for dinner. Oh, my God! Her cooking is the worst. I suggest she just order pizza, and tell her to relax on her day off. No working on the Lord's day!"

"It's true, Julia. Her cooking sucks," Paige chimes in. "I think Dad secretly eats at the club house at the golf range. She thinks his extra weight is coming from all her good cooking." We laugh.

"So, Paige is there any new romance in your life?" I ask, knowing she is not into boys yet. She smiles shyly. I'm wrong on this. "You are!" I gasp.

"Even I am," Natalie says. "He's totally good looking. Notice her hair? I'm having so much fun with the metamorphosis. Changing Paige into a glamour girl—and erasing the tomboy—has been my way of dealing with Mom and Dad ever since you left."

"Yes, I see the subtle changes." I run my fingers through Paige's hair. "But, don't go overboard, Natalie. Sometimes, staying young—and innocent—is not always a bad thing." *Jonas. Eve. Letters. Sex.*

"I totally have the perfect place for us to go tonight," Natalie says. "There's this new place that just opened... and it's French."

"French?"

"Yes, and it's so glamorous, and romantic. The three of us need to get dressed up and go. It will be so fun. Like we are in France, dining with all the Parisians."

"Sounds great, Natalie. What's the name of it?"

"L'il Paree."

～

THE THREE OF US WALK IN DRESSED LIKE WE JUST CAME FROM THE Oscars. Natalie is in a pink, hugging dress that barely covers her thighs. Paige is in a blue, sleeveless, form-fitting dress. And I'm in what every woman calls—*that little black dress*. Yes, it's *little,* and my boobs are spilling out of the top. We flat-ironed our hair, and it spills like shiny, spun silk over our shoulders. *We are gorgeous!*

Heads turn, and there's no doubt we've overdressed. But there is something to be said about fashion, and how it changes you from the inside out. In this little black dress, I could be anyone—and maybe right now, I want to be someone else, and someone else would like to be. Dress like you're already famous, I once read.

The maître d' escorts us to a table, and it's everything Natalie said. We *are* in Paris. "Is this table all right for you ladies?" the young man asks. We smile and nod, and he helps each of us be seated. I feel pampered.

Grabbing the menu, I see that all items are written in French. Both girls look to me, raising their eyebrows. "What? You think just because I want to study French cuisine in Paris, I know how to speak French?" Luckily, I do recognize the names of some of the entrées, along with the chef's recommendations.

"I suppose I can't get a cheeseburger," says Paige. Natalie rolls her eyes.

"Julia will recommend dishes for us, Paige," Natalie says, trying to sound all sophisticated.

When the waitress comes and fills our water glasses, I tell her we need a little more time. Looking over the menu, I suggest the Chicken Provençal and gougeres.

"What are gougères?" Paige asks.

"French cheese puffs. I made them once before, remember?"

"Oh yeah. I remember. They were good."

"And how about French lemonade as our beverage? Dessert... chocolate, French silk pie," I say with crazed eyes, peeking over my menu. Both girls return my enthusiasm with big smiles.

My cell phone rings, and when I pull it out of my clutch purse, I see Jonas's name on the screen. "Hello?" Both girls listen in.

"Hi, Julia." There's disappointment in his voice.

"Is something wrong? Is Sidney okay?" *Is she being a little monster?*

"She's fine. We're fine. But..."

"But what?" *Say you miss me!*

"But, something's come up that I need to take care of. I know you have plans and I don't want to ruin them, but is it possible for me to bring Sidney to you? I cannot take her with me on this trip. I wouldn't ask if it weren't important, Julia."

"Ah... sure." I cover the phone. "Girls, Jonas needs to bring Sidney by. Is it okay if we turn this girl's threesome night out into a foursome?" They both agree. "All right. We just sat down to order at L'il Paree. Can you bring her here? I will text you the address."

"Yes. And thanks, Julia. I appreciate it."

"Jonas, have her put on her yellow dress. It's hanging in her closet."

"Oh... Okay. I will pack her bag with her night stuff. I'm really sorry about this."

"No. Don't worry about it. She was wanting to meet the girls anyway. It will be fun."

"Okay, I will see you in about thirty minutes. Julia?"

"Yes?"

"I miss you."

My heart smiles.

I know the minute he arrives. All the ladies of the house turn toward the man walking down the corridor. He's wearing grey, twill slacks with a white button-up shirt. His cuffs are rolled just below the elbow, and in his hand, he holds the hand of his beautiful daughter. She's wearing her lacy, yellow dress, and hanging off her shoulders is a Hello Kitty backpack. She sees me and smiles big.

"Julia!" She lets go of his hand. I stand, stretching my arms out to her. She gives me a big hug. "We got the boxes planted. Daddy says you're going to like it." I'm shocked she called him *Daddy*. I look at Jonas with a look of *"Wow."* Not only for the fact she called him daddy, but also just the way he takes my breath away every time I see him. And to put this moment over the top—*this little black dress I'm wearing.*

The look on his face is more than I could ever ask for. His eyes scan every curve of my body, and if my boobs weren't spilling out before, they are *so* standing at attention now. "Julia." His voice is low. "You look... amazing." I smile, biting my bottom lip like a shy schoolgirl.

God! Those blue eyes of his. I hope our babies have those blue eyes.

Natalie clears her throat, jolting me out of my reverie.

"Girls, this is Jonas Fairbanks and his little girl, Sidney," I say. They sit, mouths agape and eyes wide. "Girls?"

"Hi, I'm Natalie." She stands and holds out her hand. "And this is my little sister, Paige." Paige remains seated, but holds out her hand, giving Natalie the *look* for calling her the *little* sister.

"It's nice to meet you both," Jonas says. "Can I speak with you for a minute, Julia?" I seat Sidney in the extra chair we had brought for her, and walk with Jonas down the corridor to the entrance. My body tingles when his arm wraps my waist. He turns and looks me in the eyes. "You really do look beautiful." He takes both my hands in his and kisses the tops of them.

"Thank you, Jonas. You look *killer* also. Are you traveling for work?"

"Not exactly. But I promise I will be back tomorrow. Will you and Sidney both be home tomorrow? She's excited to show you our work. You were right—it was great spending time getting to know my daughter."

"Really? I'm glad." His eyes shine. *Oh, those eyes!*

"She really is quite an amazing person. We have a surprise for you when you come home." I like the way he says "home."

"Oh? Well, I can't wait then." He kisses me on the lips.

"See you tomorrow. Okay?"

"Yes." He walks out the door, and as I turn walking back to the table, Natalie is looking at me with arms crossed, and a look that says, "We are *so* talking tonight."

13

UNKNOWN

THE NURSE SHUTS OFF THE LIGHTS. "GOOD NIGHT, KAY. YOU STAY IN YOUR bed, now. No messing about," she says, and shuts the door. Kay tries to fall asleep, but her withdrawals from the heroin keep her irritated. She sits up in her bed and scratches profusely—arms, face, and chest.

"Please, please somebody help me. I just need some. Just a little. Just enough to fall asleep. I haven't slept for two days," Kay cries. She tries again to fall asleep, and then sees the little girl's face. Sidney's face. "Oh, she was so beautiful. I must get clean for her. So I can have her," the old woman says. But then she can't remember if it was real, or not. "Yes, yes she was real. She told me about her horse. She told me about Julia, how Julia bought her a horse. I can buy her things now. I will get clean and have her, and make her happy... like Julia. I must get her away from Julia."

She hears the door open, and sees light spill in from the hall. "Hello? Are you the nurse?" she calls out. She hears footsteps approach her bed. Someone stands over her.

"Hello, stupid old woman."

"Who's there?"

"A friend. Someone who came to help you." The visitor walks back and turns the lights on.

"Help me?" Kay asks.

"Uh, huh. You need some help, don't you?" Kay looks up and sees the smiling face above her. She does not recognize the person.

"Who are you? What are you doing here?" She then sees the three vials of heroin being waved in front of her face.

"Why, Kay, I'm here to help you. I heard you calling from outside. Is this what you want?" Kay looks at the vials.

"I do. But I must get clean for Sidney. She needs me." She wants the heroin more than anything. Maybe just a little. Just a little to sleep, and then she can go back and get her. She will get clean after she has the little girl. Sidney will be her new drug. Her second chance to be a good mother.

"Do you want me to help you, stupid woman? You almost ruined everything for me. She was *not* supposed to know about Eve." The visitor puts on a pair of rubber gloves, then wraps the old woman's arm with a rubber band. Next, a needle comes out from the pocket of a lab coat. "You were always so stupid. Now, you, too, must be eliminated. No one gets in my way when I want something. Ever."

Kay pleads. "Just a little. Not too much." But it doesn't matter what the old woman says. All three vials are shot into her.

"Good night, Stupid. Old. Woman."

14

I HELP SIDNEY WITH HER PAJAMAS AND SHOW HER TO THE BATHROOM TO brush her teeth. The girls love her, and are doting on her at every moment. "Sidney, would you like more cake? Sidney, you want to play in our tree house? Sidney, you want to go shopping with us tomorrow?" It reminds me of when I first moved in with the girls. They were like my own living dolls, and little sisters at the same time. I couldn't get enough of them. Sidney's smile hasn't left since the minute she walked into our girls' party.

"I like Natalie and Paige," she says, spitting toothpaste into the sink.

"I'm pretty sure they are fond of you, too. Are your teeth clean?" She hops up on the vanity and smiles big into the mirror.

"Yep. Look." She inspects her pearly whites.

When we both move in close to the mirror, our breath fogs over, and I give her a peck on the cheek. "They look great. Good job, Sidney."

"Do I get to sleep with you?"

"Yep. But I'm sure the girls might fight over you to sleep with them." She smiles at my response. I feel it's probably the first time she's ever felt important.

We walk down the hall and into my old room. Sidney jumps onto my bed. "I still want to sleep with you, Julia." She bounces up and down. I turn down the covers, patting the bed for her to climb in. I start to cover her up, when she asks if I'm getting in.

"I will in a little bit, okay? Natalie wants to talk to me."

"What about?"

If I'm sleeping with your father.

"Oh... just girl talk, and stuff about you," I say, tweaking her nose. She smiles, and those beautiful green eyes shine. Her mother must have been a beauty. I wonder if Jonas thinks about her every day? Will there be room for me if she's kept him from moving on after all these years? How much does Sidney know about her mother? I must tread lightly. I don't think Jonas has kept her mother's spirit alive for Sidney.

"So, tell me what you and your dad did while I was gone. Sounds like you two had fun. I see you are calling him daddy now. That's good."

She rubs her nose, then responds. "Yes, he said I was to call him that from now on, because from now on and forever, he's going to be my daddy."

"Well... yes, that's true." *Strange reasoning.* "And how do you feel about that?"

"Okay, I guess. It's still the same number of syllables. We learned about syllables in school. Jon-as, dad-dy. So, it's kind of the same." She yawns. "Can I go in the tree house tomorrow?"

"Of course, and only girls are allowed. We will have a special initiation for you tomorrow."

"What's an initiation?"

"It's a special party just for you." I kiss her forehead. "Now, get some sleep." She tells me goodnight, and soon she's out cold. I study her beautiful, sleeping face—a face surrounded by so much mystery. Yet, she's so at peace, without a clue that she is the biggest piece of the puzzle. A puzzle I must piece together. I look over at my bag, and hear the letters whispering.

Natalie walks in and looks at the sleeping beauty in my bed. "Oh my, she is so adorable," she whispers. I smile, agreeing. "Let's go out on the roof," she says softly. I look over at my bag. *We will talk later.*

Natalie climbs out first, and I follow behind. Carefully, we crawl in between the dormers, lie back, and gaze up at the twinkling stars. Frogs sing in the distance, and I feel everything is the same... except me. I feel different. But I don't think I will tell Natalie. I feel years have passed, and yet it's only been a few weeks. Sometimes, I feel out of control, being directed into a war that had been going on for years, and I am supposed to settle it. I'm the definition of stupid. Knowing the truth, and seeing the truth—but still believing lies. And I don't even know what the truth is. *Letters.*

"So, how are things with you and Sebastian?"

"Oh, no you don't, Julia. That is not why we came out here."

Great. Here we go. I take a deep breath and let it out slowly. "Natalie," is all I say. My mouth remains partly open, and I fight with my head not to spill everything. She is young, and it's not fair for her to be the one to console me. But I have no one else. I know I can't talk to Cathy about this.

"So, tell me about Jonas, and what was that kiss all about?" Maybe I can keep this juvenile.

"Okay, yes we are attracted to one another. He is a widow, which is the reason Sidney has no mother. He travels the world for his job. He has asked for my help with his daddy-daughter issues. He's never moved on since the death of his wife, and he's a complete mystery," I say all in one breath.

"Ah... by the looks of that kiss and the way he looked at you... I say he's moving on... with *you*." She pokes me in the chest. *Good, it's staying in the juvenile zone.* "Oh, and those blue eyes of his." I haven't even told her that he's the man on the bike from the crash at the boardwalk.

"Okay, you are *so* not going to believe this," I say. Her eyes are the size of dinner plates. "Those are the eyes of the man that crashed into me that day at the boardwalk. The man riding the bike, who went over the railing."

"NO!"

"Yep. Can you believe that?"

"Oh. My. God."

I'm safe, and juvenile-friend-zone feels right. I will keep it here. "I know, right? I mean... is it fate, or what? And the next time I met him, I hit him over the head with a fire poker."

"A fire poker?"

"I'd only been at the house for a few days when a bad storm knocked the lights out. I thought someone had broken in." She laughs, and now I know I'm doing the right thing not telling her about the night I gave my virginity to him. *Because that was my choice.*

"Okay, now what's the great mystery? All men are full of mystery. That's what we like about them. Sometimes the deeper the mystery, the greater the chemistry." I have no idea what she means.

"How do you mean?" I ask, and sit up hugging my knees to my chest. She sits up, also.

"We all like to think there is some troubling past the man is dealing with, and you are the only one who can fix it. Like, you've got the magic key to their heart. No one else possesses that power. Only you."

I know this all sounds very juvenile, and I should be glad—however, she's totally correct. I do want to own the key to his happiness. There is a past—a bad past. *His bad ten years.*

"I mean... nobody wants a guy who is just so... cut and dried. What would be the fun in that? We want something more—that secret part of him no one else knows. Only *you,* when he's ready to share it, because you are his missing piece." If she only knew how it really feels. And maybe I will feel differently, when Jonas is ready to tell me. *Will he ever tell me?*

"I like to fantasize that Sebastian is really a secret spy for the government. He's working as a double agent between the United States and France, only posing as a foreign exchange student. He's torn between his country, and ours. He's here to gather information to take back to his government, but then he knows he could lose me in the process. He's so close to calling it quits, leaving his life as a double spy, and asking me to marry him. We will have to run off to a deserted island to live for our safety. He will have no regrets, because he will have me."

I burst out laughing. "Sebastian? A sixteen-year-old, double-agent spy?" We are so in the juvenile zone. *Stay in there, Natalie. Life's much easier.* She smacks me, and I suggest we get to bed. "I don't want Sidney to wake up, and not know where she is. And you better be packing for that deserted island you'll be moving to."

"Shut up, Jules," she laughs, and we crawl back in through the window. We both look at Sidney sleeping and then touch our hearts like they are melting. "So cute," she whispers. She turns to leave, and I stop her.

"Hey, Natalie?"

"Yes?"

"Thanks. I love you."

"I love you, too. Thanks for a wonderful birthday." She leaves, and I hear the secrets whispering from my bag. *The letters.*

I quietly pull the letters out, making sure not to disturb Sidney. Switching on the soft light over my desk, I open another letter, and let Pandora once again out of her box.

My beloved Eve,

The moon knows you are here, for only for you, he lets his light cascade down to watch you. Night is heavy, and I watch the ripples dance around your naked body as you swim like a song across the lake. For only you, the light from above shines. You are all that matters. You are all that is beautiful. You belong here with me. We belong together. The frogs are singing, and a deer approaches from the woods, admiring you. All of nature wants to be with you. I want to be in you. But I want to watch you for a while, and make love to you in my mind. I watch as you stand at the lake's edge. A summer night's breeze moves your long hair, giving me a chance to feast on your beautiful breasts. They are perfect. You are perfect. Perfect for me. It's times like this I'm glad we must hide our love, because I would miss seeing you out here in this beautiful moonlight if our love weren't hidden. It's also hard sometimes, especially when I'm with her. I could never tell her about you, she is too lost in herself to have ever cared for me. Only you make me feel loved. And for that, my beautiful Eve, I will love you long after my body returns to the earth. Even in death, I will go on loving you. Come to me now. We will make love in this beautiful place.

JX

My hands shake, and my heart feels broken. He was having an affair on his wife. Oh Jonas, I idealized you so much, and to think you would have an affair. It kills me. Who was she? What happened to her? Are you still in love with her? Dammit, why do I go on reading these letters? No good can come of it. Everything I learn is not what I want to know. Yet, I keep torturing myself. On one hand, the letters are so beautiful, so full of love. Then on the other, they are so wrong. Love for another woman—a woman who is not his wife.

Quietly as I can, I shove the letter back in my bag, and jump when my cell phone goes off. Sidney stirs just a little, then falls back to sleep. The clock reads 1:00 a.m., and I'm wondering who in the world is calling at this hour. Jonas.

Grabbing the phone, I climb back out the window, careful not to wake Sidney. I make my way between the dormers, and pray my voice does not to sound accusatory. I tap the accept button.

"Jonas? It's late. What's going on?"

"I know, I'm sorry. Did I wake you?"

"Well... actually, no. I... was doing some reading." *Letters. Eve.*

"There was something... something I needed to take care of. It's all going to be okay. I just wanted to call and hear your voice—just get some reassurance."

"Reassurance?" He's babbling. Has he been drinking?

"Jonas, are you drinking? Where are you? Are you home?"

"No, I'm not drinking. I'm on my way back home. I just had to take care of something from my past. Now, I'm ready to move forward. Forward with you, and Sidney. I meant what I said, Julia. I'm yours."

Oh, Jonas. Forget about Eve, Julia. Forget about his affair. Forget about the letters.

"Jonas... I'm yours, too. I'm yours."

"I miss you. I can't wait to be with you. Thank you for being on the boardwalk that day. Thank you for crashing my bike. Thank you for loving Sidney. And Julia," he says, and hesitates. "Thank you for giving me your innocence."

"I miss you, too. I can't wait to see you tomorrow."

"See you soon. Kiss Sidney for me, okay?"

"Yes, I will."

"Goodnight, my beautiful Julia," he says, and even though he says my name, I still hear, *Eve.*

"Goodnight, Jonas."

I climb back in through the window, and crawl into bed with Sidney. I kiss the top of her head. "That kiss is from your daddy," I say softly, and fall asleep next to her.

15

SIDNEY AND I ARE TRAVELING BACK HOME IN MY MINI. I CAME CLEAN about the skinny jeans, using the excuse that it's much easier teaching Sidney to ride her horse when I am wearing jeans. I think Tom and Cathy were just relieved to have some time alone, and took Natalie's advice about going away for the weekend. She said it was all she wanted for her birthday *Uh huh*. Tom did beg me to make one of my famous breakfasts before I left. I made zucchini quiche, along with a raspberry sauce. I found out a long time ago that it was the only way I could get the girls to eat quiche—smother it with something sweet.

I have butterflies in my tummy as I get closer to the manor. There was something different in Jonas's voice last night. While he talked, I could hear new beginnings. It was like a weight has been lifted—something is no longer in his way. And somehow, I feel it has something to do with the person in prison. Maybe, he has restricted the inmate from writing. Something about those letters disturbs him, like a ghost haunting him. And just like that, my ghost, Eve, comes and haunts me. The way he wrote about her, "Even in death I will go on loving you." If he felt so strongly he could love her from the grave, then he must truly still love her now. But he denies even knowing an Eve. They hid their love back then, are they still hiding it now? But his wife is dead. Why not be together?

And then there's the fact that he had an affair. *Dammit*, it still bothers me. I'm back in that cleaning closet, listening to the young, pregnant wife cry. Was Jenna pregnant with Sidney at the time? He did say she left him, taking all the pictures. When did he return to get his daughter—after she was killed by a drunk driver? Maybe he is punishing himself by *not* being with her. I can only tell him that the old lady said her name. I cannot tell him about the letters.

We pull up the horseshoe drive, and all those bad thoughts clear away like smoke the minute I see him leaning against a pillar of the porch, and my heart warms my soul—*Jonas*.

I park the car, and before I make my way out, he is at the door taking my hand, and pulling me into his embrace. "Julia," he says, smelling my hair. "I've missed you. Mmm, you smell so good." He's wearing the smile I gave him.

"I missed you too. I didn't think I would so much, but I did—and even the house." He kisses me sweetly at first, then becomes more eager for a deeper kiss. I know Sidney is watching, and what she's thinking is *babies*. "I'm very excited to see your and Sidney's work," I say, pulling back.

"I can't wait to show it to you."

Sidney comes around the car.

"You have to close your eyes. It's a surprise," she says, eagerly.

"Okay." I cover my eyes and begin to walk, when I'm scooped up into Jonas's arms. I squeal.

"This way, Daddy. I want her to see what we made for her first." Her voice trails off. She must be running to the back yard. I wrap my arms around Jonas's neck, lacing my fingers as he carries me to the back yard.

"Okay, Daddy. Now, Julia, open your eyes." Sidney's infectious excitement makes me giggle, and I can't even imagine what my surprise is. I knew of the garden boxes—they were my idea.

"No, don't open them yet," Jonas says. "I'm going to set you down—and then, on the count of three, open your eyes."

"Okay." I say with a laugh. I'm lowered down, and whatever he has sat me on, moves. It's a swing.

"One. Two. Three. Okay, open your eyes, Julia!" Sidney shouts.

I open my eyes, and before me is a small pond, complete with water lilies, pink and white. In window boxes bright, red geraniums bloom, with vinca vines hanging down. Three garden boxes filled with fresh dirt border the patio. One has a small sign that reads "Holly's carrots." Another has small signs for herbs, sage, thyme, rosemary, cilantro, and basil. The third box holds three tomato plants encased in cages. And what I'm sitting on is a beautiful, wooden swing hanging from a pergola. It's all so gorgeous. Like an outdoor-garden fairytale.

"Do you like it?" Jonas asks.

I'm in awe—speechless at the transformation. "Oh, Jonas, it's amazing. I can't believe you did all of this."

"Well, I only built the swing. Gus built the rest. And as you can see, Sidney has one whole box for carrots. She insisted. But I thought one should also be full of herbs... for your culinary work. I'm not sure if I picked the right ones." His eyes are full of hope, and promise, and sunshine.

"Daddy, show her the other thing!" Sidney is jumping up and down. I love how she calls him daddy now. Jonas walks behind the pond, and flips a switch on the outside wall. A waterspout sends bubbles up from the center of the pond. "He didn't want you to hear it when your eyes were closed."

"Oh, you guys—this is all so beautiful! I love it. Thank you so much." I get up from the swing and walk into Jonas's open arms. This is where I belong. Sidney is jumping up and down clapping, and I stand on my tiptoes to give Jonas a kiss on the lips. "Thank you."

"Sidney, let daddy have a moment with Julia, okay?" The pond is her only interest now. She places her hands over the spout, spilling water all over the patio. Jonas picks me up and carries me through the door.

"What are you doing?" I don't know why I ask. I know exactly what he's doing. Or going to do.

"I'm going to worship you." He runs me up the stairs and places me on his bed.

"Welcome home, my princess. I'm going to worship and adore you." He *is* my prince.

He walks toward the bed, pulling off his shirt. His chest is so perfect—I must sit up on my knees and touch him. I leave a small trail of kisses down his chest to his belly. I love feeling the soft hairs of his body lightly brushing my cheek. I look up into his eyes. "What if she comes in and hears us?"

He kisses me on the lips. "Got it covered." He pulls his phone from his pocket, taps in his code, swipes to his music app, and selects a song. The electric guitar of Ryan Adams's "Gimme Something Good" beats through the sound bar hanging off the wall. "Perfect," he says, dropping the phone on the nightstand, and then pulls my tank top off.

My breasts fall out, and he cups them in his hands. "God, you're so perfect!" He sucks one nipple in his mouth. It feels warm, and sensual. He squeezes my other breast gently as his tongue circles my nipple. He pulls it in and out of his mouth.

"Oh... Jonas!" I breathe out. My head falls back, and I watch the sound bar vibrate on the wall above me, like my body with every one of his touches. He's mine.

"I want to taste you, Julia." He lays me back, and my head sinks into the pillow. My jeans are unzipped, removed, and dropped to the floor. I feel my ankles being grabbed as he opens my legs. I look up and see him admiring my wet pussy, licking his lips. He crawls up the bed and gently kisses my wet entrance. His tongue slowly licks from bottom to top, and I cry out with pleasure.

"Ah, God!" With each velvety lap of his tongue, my body arches upward, out of control, and I'm lost in this subspace he is bringing me to. There are no letters. No Eve. No one in prison haunting him. It's only us. My prince. My... Jonas.

"God, I've missed you," he breathes the words on my opening. His hot breath increases my flowing juices. I'm already close. I've never felt like this before. "You're so wet. You respond so sweetly to my touch. Don't come yet. I want you to be in control. You're going to fuck me."

He moves off the bed, and I'm dying for release. How'd I go so long without experiencing this pleasure? Because he was not in my life yet, and I'm so grateful it is him who is giving me this amazing pleasure for the first time.

As I my body is missing his touch, I watch as he unbuttons his jeans and pulls them down. He is so hard. I have missed this. I am addicted now. To him. He removes his jeans, pushing them to the floor with his feet, and walks back to the bed. Standing over me, he reaches for my hands. I entwine my fingers with his as he lays over me, holding my arms above me. I feel his hard erection between my legs, and I'm dying for him to be inside me. I'm begging. "Please, Jonas," I pant out, greedily.

"I will let you have it soon." He makes a trail of kisses up my neck. What'd he mean, letting me be in control? I'm losing it. I want him.

"I want you now, please," I beg.

He rolls us over, and I'm now on top. "Sit on me, Julia. You will love this position. Let me help you find your sweet spot." *Sweet spot?* There's more for me to enjoy? "Sit up on your knees, and slowly sink your wet pussy down on my cock. You are so wet, and it will slide easily. I promise you, it will be better than before."

How can anything be better than what he has already done? I do as he says, and sit on my knees.

"That's it, Baby. Take my cock, and guide it in your tight pussy. Take your time."

Wrapping my hand around his thickness, I lift myself up, placing him at my entrance. He's right—I'm so wet. My arousal is soaking my inner thighs. He watches me with his beautiful blue eyes, so full of lust and desire. The head of his cock slides in, and his eyes roll back. "Yes," he moans, deep in his throat. I sink down a little more, and feel myself stretching to take him. The proof of him here before aches with pleasure, and I sink down. He places both hands on my hips, guiding me down a little more. I jump when it becomes too much.

"I'm sorry. I didn't mean to hurt you."

"It's okay. It just scared me a little, that's all." I gently move up and down, slowly taking all of him. He pushes up while holding my hips, sliding in deeper, letting me get used to him. Soon, the pressure is all pleasure, and I ride him while he pumps into me. Hard.

He pulls me forward, and I'm shocked when he spanks my bottom. "I'm going to make this sweet ass pink. Because it's mine." He spanks me again. "Ride my cock hard, or I will spank you harder." I let out a muffled cry and ride him hard. It feels so good. Better than before. His spanking me somehow increases my pleasure. "Yes. Fuck. Like that." My juices run between my legs. He spreads my cheeks and smears my wetness up my crack, pressing his finger into my anus. I jump. "Yes, I will have this, too." Then spanks me again.

I'm building inside with each spank, not sure why I feel this way, when he begins rubbing my clit with his thumb. "Oh!" I cry out, panting. "God, yes." He's right—I'm enjoying this so much more. Why?

My head falls back and my eyes roll upward with an insatiable hunger. "Ah... ah Jonas, I... I... it's coming. I can't make it stop." Each word comes out on a rush. Ryan Adams repeats, "Gimme something good, gimme something good," from the sound bar above my head. Jonas sits up, pushing deeper inside me, and sucks hard on my nipples. The double pleasure of him inside me, and of my nipples being sucked, hard, creates a strong feeling of madness—and I ride him with all the intensity of an experienced lover.

"Yes, Julia. I'm going to come. I'm going to come so fucking hard," he says through gritted teeth. And it shocks me, that his use of foul language triggers another explosion inside me. I try not to scream his name... but I do.

"Jonas!"

"Oh, yes. God, yes," he growls. I feel the strong pulsations of his cock inside me. "Oh, God. You feel so good." He pushes one last thrust. "Fuck."

The song ends, and we remain embraced in each other's arms. He buries his face in my breasts, and I kiss the top of his head. I taste and smell sweat—his sweat. The scent of my man... Jonas. Sweat. Sex. My scent on him... the scent of us.

He falls back on the bed, taking me with him. The smell of his skin fills my senses once again, and I can't get enough of him. He is my obsession. My drug. My alcohol. My Paris. Pushing myself up, I begin with light kisses on his chest. I lick small, slow, laps with my tongue and taste his sweat to satisfy my need for him. He responds with a light moan deep in his throat and traces small circles on my back.

"Mmm," he purrs. I look up and see my smile mirrored on his face.

My heart smiles, too.

Sidney is soaked by the time we return to the patio, and I'm so grateful the waterspout kept her preoccupied during our erotic welcoming home of each other. But when she looks up, giving me a fiendish grin, I hear her soul whisper, *Babies.*

I wince.

Jonas saunters past me, sans shirt—wearing only his jeans, and my smile. He sets himself down in the swing, sprawls one arm across the back of it, and holds a bottle of beer in the other hand. His legs are spread apart, and my eyes are fixated on his still somewhat-hard erection. He knows I'm looking when our eyes meet. My smile is gone from his face, only to be replaced with his roguish one. He reaches out and gestures for me. I joyfully accept and cuddle down next to him, and when he pulls me close, a warm ray of sunshine spills over the house. Sidney is splashing and singing a song she made up about Holly. The flowers in the window boxes kiss the house with love, and I drop my head onto Jonas's shoulder as I take in this tableau. *Us.*

MY FACE IS BEING SMOTHERED WITH OAKY-SCENTED KISSES, AS I WAKE TO moonlight shining in through the window. I'm naked in Jonas's bed. I feel my hair being gently smoothed away from my face. "Hey, Sleepy Head," he whispers in my ear.

"Hmm," I purr with a sleepy smile.

"I want to show you something," he says. I roll over and study the face of my obsession.

"What?" The moonlight is reflected in his blue eyes, giving them a glassy shine. His eyes seem to illuminate, like those of a night predator.

"There's something I want to share with you. It's something that—

only when shared at night—brings magic." When he says, "magic," he smiles, and his white teeth gleam in the dark.

"Magic?"

"Yes. That's why I need to take you there right now."

I glance at the clock. It's 1:00 a.m. "At this time of night?"

"Especially at this time." His eyes open wide, like he is crazed.

We quietly pad down the stairs after checking in on Sidney, and leave out the back-patio door. The moon is full, reflected in the water pond, and the nighttime, summer air smells of grass and rain. Jonas takes my hand and leads me out to the pasture.

"It's out here? I've already seen the pasture," I whisper like we are still inside.

"It's over there, past those trees." He points to the tree line. I've never considered walking through the trees while guiding Holly. We've always stayed in the pasture, keeping close to the fence line. What on earth could be past the trees? "Come on." He pulls my hand and we run blind through the pasture, like young lovers. I'm grateful for the full moon giving us light, as we make our way to the tree line's edge.

We reach the dark line of trees, and he grasps my hand a little tighter. "It's just a little farther, through these trees." He pushes back branches that might hamper our walking. The sound of an owl hooting nearby attracts my attention, and I stop for a moment to recall what it is.

"An owl. I haven't heard one in years."

"Yes. Sometimes, I stay awake at night, listening for them. They are nighttime hunters, too."

Too?

"Come on. It's just right around these trees." We walk through the woods, with the moon as our guide, and climb a small hill. Once we are to the top, I see it. The lake.

Letters. Eve. Lake. Deer. Moon. Affair.

16

THE MOON IS REFLECTED IN A PERFECT STREAM OF LIGHT THAT STREAKS across the lake. The water is so still, it could be glass. Frogs serenade all of the creatures of the night, us included. How I have never seen this lake before? Looking back, I see lights shining from the house. It's not that far away. This must have been where I heard the frogs at night.

When I walk a bit closer, something makes a splash in the water, startling me, and I jump back. "It's just a bullfrog. We frightened him more than he did you." Jonas reaches for my hand. "Come on. It's okay, there's nothing to fear here."

Old memories. Not my memories.

I take his hand as he leads me to the water's edge. The light from the moon shines at the exact spot where our feet stop. The moon is watching us, like it did Eve. Does he want to be here with me? Or is he reliving his love for her? *Stop it. Stop it. He's here with you.*

"Jonas, this is beautiful. I can't believe I've never seen it before."

"Well, the hill does hide it from the view of the house. That's not such a bad thing." He pulls my shirt up and over my head. Is this why he came here with Eve? A place to hide, where Jenna couldn't see them? He removes his shirt and jeans. "Your résumé did say you gave swim lessons, so you should have no problem swimming across this pond." The moon now illuminates his naked body, and I hear what he wrote in the letters. "How the moon is here to watch." Looking up, the great white orb in the sky whispers to me, "Now you know his secret, too." But I don't want to. I don't want these thoughts of my perfect Jonas sneaking around behind his pregnant wife's back.

He tugs at the button of my jeans, coaxing me to take them off. "Come on, I want to see you naked in this moonlight." I try to push the thought of Eve away—but she only goes to the back of my mind—and remove my jeans. I stand naked, and exposed to the creatures of the night, with the moon watching.

He picks me up, and carries me into the water, and—surprisingly— it's not all that cold. A light fog floats on top of it. My legs wrap around his waist, as he makes slow circles in the water. Small waves splash us from the ripples, and we are in the water up to our shoulders. My hair floats around us. He looks me in the eyes. "You truly are beautiful, Julia." He sounds sincere. However, his eyes look lost. I feel hypnotized by his gaze. The spell is finally broken when he hugs me close, and I lay my head on his shoulder.

"So, this is a special place for you?" Already, my motives are ulterior. He's quiet, and I'm not sure if he's going to respond. *Dammit.* Why couldn't I just keep this about *us*—what he wants to share with *me*?

"It was, at one time. I'm hoping it can be again." Now it's me who is silent. He's hoping. He's thinking of me... of us. "And at times... it was a place of bad memories." I look him in the eyes. Will he open up?

"Bad memories? After the death of your wife?" This could be a safe topic now. A wife deserves to be remembered—not an affair. And maybe, I'm on Jenna's side. "Can you tell me about her? I know she must have been beautiful by looking at Sidney."

"She was." I'm glad he thinks so. I know how he feels about Eve. I want to know about Jenna.

"Did you love her?"

"I did. But love can change into something else."

"What do you mean?"

He swirls us around, contemplating his answer.

"Love has many levels. There is blind love. You fall so deeply, that you see nothing but the good. There is growing love. The love you feel when you keep trying, through good times and bad, and you hope it will be good *again*. Then there is just love. The worst of all loves. This is when love turns into commitment only. You made a commitment, and it's the only thing left holding you to something..."

He doesn't finish, and I don't try to make him. I feel he is sharing more than he ever has with me. All I say is, "It must have been hard for you when she died."

He inhales deeply. "Yes. But then you discover scared love."

"Scared love?"

"Yes. Scared love. I'm falling in love with you Julia... and it's scaring the hell out of me." My breathing catches as I look him in the eyes. "I mean it. I haven't been in love for over ten years, and it is literally scaring the hell out of me.

"Jonas," I whisper.

"Everything about you is so perfect. Sometimes, I think you aren't real. You came to me when I needed you the most. A prayer that I prayed for the first time. A miracle that I crashed into one day on a boardwalk. You were dropped from the sky, and I can't fathom the fact that you were sent here for me. That... Julia... is scared love."

I WAKE STILL WRAPPED IN JONAS'S ARMS. I WATCH HIS CHEST RISE AND fall as he sleeps peacefully. It was nearly three in the morning when we returned from the pond, checked in on Sidney, who was still fast asleep, and tiptoed to his bed. He insisted once again that I stay when I turned to make my way downstairs. *Will this be where I sleep from now on?*

I still feel guilty for not saying that I love him back. I really can't say why I didn't. Does falling in love mean the same as *in* love? The more time I spend with him, the more I learn what is in his heart. How he hasn't been in love for ten years. Once again, the age of Sidney. And was he referring to Eve or... Jenna? And now, I'm growing a place in his heart. *Scared love.*

He stretches and opens one eye. "What time is it?"

Looking over at the clock, I see it's 7:00 a.m.

"It's seven. I need to get downstairs and start breakfast. I'm sure Sidney will be up soon." I start to get up when he pulls me back down.

"I meant what I said last night. And when I said I loved you, I didn't say it to hear it back. I said it because I wanted you to know."

"Oh, Jonas," I whisper.

"Shh." He covers my lips with his finger. "Don't say it until you're ready. That's what I want from you. When you're ready. I've waited a long time for you, Julia. I will wait longer, if I have your true love." I'm about to speak again when he stops me and gets up from the bed. I watch him walk, naked, to the shower.

Getting up, I start to put my clothes on, then stop when I see Jonas's T-shirt draped over a chair, and decide to throw it on. I look in the mirror, hugging the shirt, and smelling the scent of him. I then open the door and walk down the stairs, bouncing with a blissful sway in my step.

"Sidney, what are you doing?" I gasp, when I find her standing on a chair, making pancakes. God, I feel so guilty. *Who am I becoming?*

"I'm making you and Daddy breakfast in bed."

"Yes, I see that. But it's dangerous for you to be cooking by yourself." *And she knows I was in bed with her father?*

"I know what I'm doing. I watched you make them before. I watch *a lot* of things. Somebody has to make breakfast if you two are going to sleep all day."

"Sidney, it's only seven o'clock in the morning. That's not all day—and why am I arguing with a ten-year-old?"

"Are we arguing, Julia?" She is standing on a chair with one hand on her hip, while the other waves a spatula in the air. "And where are your pants?"

Placing both hands on my hips, I blow a strand of hair from my face. "No, we are not arguing, Sidney. And thank you for making breakfast."

"You're welcome, Julia," She turns and flips the pancake.

"Hey, it smells good in here," Jonas says, entering the kitchen. "Is the coffee ready, Sidney?" A ten-year-old making breakfast... and coffee? And I'm shocked when she points to a full pot.

"Hey, all right." He kisses my cheek and then pours himself a cup.

'Daddy, I need to talk to you about something." I fear the word *babies* will come out of her mouth. He turns and leans on the counter.

"Yes?"

"I want a tree house like the one at Julia's old house." *Whew.*

TODAY IS SIDNEY'S THIRD SWIM LESSON, WHICH I HAVE ARRANGED AT THE public pool. I discovered on the city's website that they gave free lessons, and thought this would also give her a chance to play with other children. We are three weeks into June—and so far, this summer couldn't be less than a fairytale. *My fairytale summer.* The dynamics of this little family—our little family—are happening like a true miracle. Jonas is happy every day. Sidney is blossoming into his daughter—and he, her father. The tree house has been built, and no letters or calls from the prison disrupt our home anymore. We are happy.

Jonas has spent the last week in Maine for business, and it really seems strange without him now. And I still haven't told him, "I love you."

I'm sitting on a bench, watching Sidney and the other children take turns jumping off the side of the pool. She is the prettiest girl here. A woman sits down beside me. She smiles, and I'm about to say hello and ask which child is hers, when her phone rings. She takes the call.

"Why hello. I suppose this is your daily check-in," she says to the person on the other end, and rolls her eyes at me. I look back to the children in the pool as she continues her conversation. "And where are you today? Me? Well, currently I'm sitting on a park bench, trying to enjoy my day. Yes, I am. And thank you for your concern, but you didn't answer my question. Where are you?" She pauses. "Well, that sounds lovely."

I feel I should leave to give her privacy, but then she lays a hand on my knee and mouths the word, "No, stay," and it also sounds like she said, "A patient" under her breath. I sit back, pretending to scroll through my phone.

"Tell me—how are things are going for you?" she continues her questions to the person on the other end. "I'm happy for you. You've worked hard for your happiness. Are you continuing your therapy? Oh... that good, huh? Well, it's not exactly what I had planned—however, plans change, and so do people. I guess I will have to get used to this place. I'm glad you're moving on with your life, and I will be dealing with my own. Okay, thanks for calling. Anytime. Bye." She ends the call, and puts her phone back in her purse.

"I'm so sorry about that," she says, apparently feeling the need to apologize.

"Oh, that's all right. I should have given you some privacy."

She laughs. "That's why I'm here—privacy. I'm a therapist and, well... some patients just feel the need to keep you on speed dial, you know."

"Oh, I thought maybe that's what you are. Not that I meant to listen in." I cringe.

"Oh, please don't apologize. I'm Erin." She extends her hand.

"I'm Julia. Hi. What child is yours?" I ask, tipping my head toward the children in the pool. She looks at the children, and then strangely, tears up. She pulls a tissue from her purse, and blots under her eyes. *Oh God, she's lost a child.* "Oh... I'm sorry, I didn't mean..."

"No, I'm sorry. I have a daughter. However, she's spending the summer with her father. We... are getting divorced. I just didn't think I would miss her so much. I recently moved here, and thought it would be best if she stayed with him. Just until I get settled."

"Well, I'm still sorry for your situation."

"Thank you. But here's to new beginnings and new friendships." She smiles. "Which is your child?"

"That one right there. Pink diving suit in braids," I say, pointing at Sidney. She plugs her nose, waves at me, and jumps in. "Her name is Sidney and... actually, I'm her nanny."

"Oh, she's just beautiful. How old?"

"Ten. However, I feel sixteen is right around the corner."

She looks over at Sidney with admiration. "They grow up so fast," she says softly.

"How old is your daughter?"

"She, too, is ten. So, yes... I know what you are talking about. Hormones are right around the corner. And hopefully, she is using them on her father this summer. Payback," she says under her breath. I blanch, but remember the divorce. "Oh, listen to me. Julia, is it?"

"Yes."

"Like I said, new beginnings." She reaches for her purse, and pulls out a card. "Here's my card." She hands it to me, and I read it. *Erin Kelly. Kelly & Flynn Associates Suite 4B Hannover Street, Indianapolis (371) 245-8856.* "Oh, here." She takes the card, pulls a pen from her purse, and crosses out the phone number. She then flips the card over and writes a different number. "That was my office in Indianapolis."

Indianapolis? Hmm.

"Right now, I'm without an office. I'm thinking of starting my own counseling services from home. So, here is my cell." She hands the card back to me.

I take the card, and Sidney comes running up, wrapped in a towel. "Did you see me, Julia? Was I good?" she asks with chattering teeth.

"Yes. I think you were the best. You're freezing. Let's get you out of that wet swimsuit." Erin looks at Sidney, again with admiration. She must be missing her little girl. "Sidney, this is Erin. She just moved here."

"Hello, Sidney. I'm so glad to meet you," she says, and touches her face. "She really is a doll. I just love those dimples."

"Yes, I do, too. Well, it was nice to meet you, Erin. I need to get Sidney home and make her some lunch."

"Hey, I have an idea," she says when I start to get up. "Why don't you two come have lunch with me? My house is so lonely without my daughter, and I would love the company. Please, I insist. I haven't met anyone since moving here, and I would so enjoy the friendship."

"Oh, I wouldn't want to impose, if you're still getting settled."

"Not at all. In fact, it will be a good excuse to get some things unpacked. Please? And it's not far. Just around the corner."

"Well, if you're sure..."

She looks at Sidney and taps her nose. "I'm sure."

I give Erin a lift in my Mini, and she is right, her place is just around the corner. It is a small house, packed tightly in a row of houses in the shady side of town. Most of the houses are in dire need of some repair —hers included. Maybe she plans to remodel, or something. But with the rest of the houses in such a dilapidated state, what would be the point?

"I don't like this place," Sidney says, when Erin gets out, and walks up to her house.

"Sidney, don't be rude. She's going through a divorce, and maybe this is all she can afford right now."

"What's a divorce?"

I shake my head. "We'll talk later about it. Now, let's be polite and accept her hospitality."

"What's hospitality?"

"Come on," I say with a sigh. "Let's go be her friend." We walk up to her porch, and wait as she fumbles with the key, which doesn't seem to work.

"Excuse me. I'm still trying to figure out *which* key goes to *what* door," she says, and tries another key. The door finally unlocks, and she welcomes us in. The inside is not much better than the outside, and I look to Sidney with a stern look that says, "Be nice."

Erin walks to the kitchen area and begins opening cupboards. It surprises me when I don't see any boxes sitting around. Didn't she say she needed to unpack?

"How about some tuna salad?" she yells from the kitchen.

"That will be fine," I call back. Sidney makes a yuck face. "Be nice," I mouth.

"I haven't done much shopping yet," she says.

"Can I help you with anything? Maybe we can do a girls' shopping day and get some of the things you need," I say, trying to be friendly, as I look around the room.

"Oh, I would love that," she calls from the kitchen. I hear bowls and utensils being rattled around, and then the sound of an electric can opener.

"Are you sure I can't help?"

"No. Just make yourself at home, and I will make the lunch." She appears in the doorway holding a rubber spatula. Sidney stays tightly by my side as we walk over to the couch. As I look around, I notice something strange about the pictures on the wall. They are pictures of random stuff, such as a beach picture that with the caption, "Life is better at the beach." There are several framed sobriety quotes, but no pictures of a little girl—her daughter.

"What's your little girl's name?" She doesn't answer right away, and I think she didn't hear me. I'm about to ask again, when she yells from the kitchen.

"Roman."

"Oh... that's different."

"Yeah. When I was pregnant, I wanted her to have a strong name. So, when she grows up and puts her name on a résumé, people will assume she's a man, and not know her gender by her name. It means strength and power. Lunch is ready."

We get up and move into the kitchen. I stop when I see a school picture of a young boy on a small end table, maybe twelve to fifteen. *Strange.* She never mentioned having a son. "You also have a son?"

She looks a little confused and then follows my gaze to the picture. "Oh. That. No, I don't. It's..." she hesitates, wringing her hands on a towel. "It's a reminder. That's Jason. He was a young boy I tried to counsel. He had a very troubled life." She drops her head and looks to Sidney.

"Tried?" I ask, fearing there's a sad ending.

"He committed suicide not long after that picture was taken. He was only fourteen. So... I keep it with me to punish myself... for not trying harder."

"Oh... how sad." I feel horrible for asking.

"Yes. Now, to new beginnings," she says, and waves us to the table. I take a look closer at the picture. Something about him looks *so* familiar. Like I should know him. Something in his green eyes... and those two big dimples that are embedded on his cheeks with his smile.

17

I SHAKE AWAY THE NOTION THAT I KNEW THIS YOUNG BOY. IT'S JUST THAT something is so familiar about the look of him—I can't put my finger on it. We sit at the table, where Erin has placed three plates with tuna salad sandwiches, and I tell Sidney to take a seat and eat. She wrinkles her nose, and I raise my brows. She reluctantly sits and picks at her sandwich.

"I could make her something else," Erin says, noticing Sidney's reluctance.

"No, she's fine. She needs to try new things. I just haven't ever made it for her. I'm sure she will like it once she tries it." I look to Sidney. Slowly, she takes a small bite.

"It's not bad," she says. "But why is the bread brown?"

"It's supposed to be brown. It's just a different brand than you're used to," I say. "It's probably healthier for you, too." I look to Erin, giving her a smile. "I myself prefer brown bread."

She points to the loaf of bread on the counter—Roman Meal. "It was the only bread my grandmother would buy. Even to this day, when I taste it, I'm back in her kitchen, spending the weekend eating peanut butter and jelly sandwiches." Her voice is a little melancholy.

"Oh... how sweet."

"In fact, I think it's the real reason I named my daughter Roman." Her eyes are a bit teary, and I suddenly feel a deep sorrow for her. I feel that us being here, is companionship she really needs. She's lonely, and starting life over can feel solitary.

We will be her friends—a new beginning. I touch her hand.

"That's a wonderful reason for a beautiful name," I say, and she smiles.

"Sidney is a pretty name, too," she says, smoothing her hand down one of Sidney's braids.

"Her father was stationed in Sydney, Australia, when she was born, and so... he named her Sidney." I brush her cheek. Sidney rolls her eyes at this display of affection. I can see she is becoming a bit embarrassed, so I leave her alone, and we continue with our lunch.

Once we finish, I help clear the dishes, and then tell Erin we need to go home. She looks sad. Looking around the house, and remembering how the outside looked, I come up with an idea. "Erin, how about we do a girls' shopping day tomorrow? As a house-warming gift, Sidney and I would like to buy you some plants, and dress up the yard a little."

"Oh, I would love that. Not that you need to buy me anything—just spending time and becoming friends is enough of a gift.

"Then it's a date. We can meet you here tomorrow... at the same time? Sidney has swim lessons for the next four weeks."

"Yes. I will meet you at the pool. I enjoy watching Sidney swim. Strangely, it helps now that my little girl is away." I smile and take delight in the thought of us becoming friends. Every woman needs three friends. One who is younger, to mentor. One who is the same age, to experience life together. And one who is older, to give you wisdom and guidance. Like Erin.

"Thank you for lunch today, Erin. It was very thoughtful of you, and we enjoyed being your guest. Didn't we Sidney?" Sidney gets in the car and buckles up.

"Yes. Bye, and thank you." She waves through the car window.

"Looks like we have a new friend," I say, as I buckle my seatbelt. I pull out from the curb, when a crow hits the window. Sidney and I both scream. Looking out the side window, I see that the crow is fine. He is flapping his wings at us, cawing like the first time I came to the manor.

~

SIDNEY AND I HAVE OUR DINNER IN THE TREE HOUSE—NOTHING FANCY, just hot dogs and chips. It's probably the first unhealthy thing I've fed her since becoming her nanny. She said I owed her for making her eat Erin's tuna salad, and I caved. This tree house is special to me, because I watched Jonas build it with his own two hands. It was something he wanted to do for his daughter. I truly am so proud of him, and the changes I have seen in him. I know I do love him. And right now, I miss him. It's been a week since we've been together, and I wonder how I ever lived without him.

Sitting on the ledge of the tree-house window, with my legs dangling down, I look out and admire the beautiful flowers growing in the window boxes. I can hear the fountain from the little garden pond. The vegetables are growing into a beautiful bounty. And Holly grazes nearby, in the pasture. Then, I look at the swing and remember how Jonas looked that day, having a beer and admiring his work... his new life... his new beginning. *Our* new beginning.

My cell rings and, just like he was thinking of me too, I see his picture light up on the screen. My heart warms, and I answer it.

"Hi," I say, smiling. I'm sure he can hear it.

"Hi, there." I can *so* hear his smile. "What's my beautiful girl up to?"

"She's eating hot dogs and chips in the tree house."

He laughs. "I was referring to you."

"Oh. Well, actually, I'm doing the same."

"Sounds fun. Wish I could be there." A slight pause. "I miss you." *Exactly what I need to hear.*

"I miss you too, Jonas. How much longer are you going to be in Maine?"

"Maybe another week." I hear his disappointment.

"A week?" I whine.

"I know. I hate it, too. It's beautiful here, Julia. I want to bring you here. You would love it."

"Describe it to me." I get up and climb down the ladder of the tree, using one hand for support, the other still with the cellphone to my ear. house. Once I'm on the ground, I make my way over to sit in the swing. My feet push me off, and I swing, listening to him describe the scenery around him.

"It's a bed and breakfast on the top of a cliff, overlooking the ocean."

"I thought you were looking at property for building condos?" I ask, wondering why he's at a B&B.

"I am. My partner wants to buy this place, tear it down, and build condos." He must be outside. I can hear seagulls in the distance. "It's the perfect place. It's not too far from the water. A rocky trail leads down to the ocean, and people walk on the beach every morning. Yesterday, I talked to a lady walking her dogs. I told her about the project, and she was excited about it. We could make some great money with this one. My partner is flying in tomorrow with an architect, and a building engineer, to discuss the layout."

"Oh. So, this B&B is for sale?"

"Well," he exhales. "Yes and no. Yes, it's for sale and no, not for what we want to do. They would like to keep it operating as a B&B. But we are prepared to offer them double for what they are asking. You would love it here, Julia. The house itself reminds me of a quaint little inn that you would find in Paris."

"And you're just going to tear it down?" I'm sure he hears the disappointment in my voice.

"Well, yeah. That's business." He's quiet for a few seconds, and I'm afraid maybe I ruined his mood. His good news.

"Well, I'm sure that condos would look beautiful there too," I counter. He changes the subject.

"So, eating hot dogs in the tree house, huh?"

"Well, at the moment, right before you called, I was admiring all of your and Sidney's hard work. This place has truly transformed into a home. I can't wait for you to see it. It's all grown so much." I inhale, fighting back the words, *I love you.* "I miss you, Jonas."

"I miss you, too—so much." I know he's waiting to hear the words, but I want to say them to him face-to-face. I want to look him in the eye, and tell him how I have fallen in love with him.

"There's more I want to tell you, Jonas... but I want to tell you in person." I hear his breathing change, a then a sigh of relief.

"Well, then, I can't wait to get back and hear it. How's Sidney?"

"She's doing great at swim lessons. She's the best one there. And oh, we met a new friend today at the pool: Erin."

"A little friend of Sidney's? Do they swim together?"

"No, she's more like in her thirties, I would think. She just moved here, and it seems she's going through a rough patch. Going through a divorce, and her daughter is gone for the summer, staying with her ex. She invited us for lunch today. She seemed so appreciative of our friendship. I feel sorry for her. We're going to help plant some flowers in her yard. The place could really use some help."

"Well, that sounds really sweet of you and Sidney."

"She's a therapist, and recently left her practice in Indianapolis. She wants to start counseling out of her home—and, well, it's sort of a wreck. If you don't mind, I would like to spend some time getting to know her, and help her out. Fix the place up, give it some fresh paint, new window treatments, and maybe some small furnishings. Decorating the porch with some flowers could help the curb appeal. She hasn't really said so—however, it looks like her ex has taken everything, leaving her with nothing."

"Well, how can I ignore your kindness for wanting to help another in need? It's so *you*, Julia. I couldn't imagine you *not* helping. One of the many reasons why I fell in love with you."

My heart warms, and I can't wait for him to come home, just so I can tell him how much I love him. "Thank you, Jonas. Come home soon."

"Soon as I can, Baby. Talk to you soon, I have another call coming in."

"Okay, goodbye." He ends the call.

Getting up, I set my phone on the patio table and sit on the edge of the garden box. Holly's carrots now have green, feathery tops and I brush my hand over them, and feel their softness. I move the green tops to the side and see the orange numbs popping up from the ground. Running my fingers through the soil, I stop when I come across a small pile of rabbit fur. *Oh, she's going to love this.* "Sidney!" I yell.

She pops her head out of the tree house window. "What?"

"Come here. There's something I think you'll want to see." I carefully move the little patch of fur to the side.

"Really?" She climbs down the boards nailed to the tree, running as fast as her little legs can carry her, then stops in front of the box. She jumps up on the side and squats down. "What is it? What is it?" She's out of breath.

"Come closer." She moves next to me, and I carefully reveal the six little baby bunnies wiggling around in the small hole left by their mother. Her eyes go wide, and she's about to squeal with joy, so I quickly lay my finger on her mouth. "Shh. We don't want to scare them."

"Oh, there's so cute! Where's their mommy?"

"She'll be back. She keeps them here to be safe. So, we must be careful. She's probably out eating grass, and clover, to make milk for them.

"How does she make milk with grass and clover?"

I'm faced with explaining this to her. "Well, mommy rabbits nurse their babies like human mommies do. You've heard of breastfeeding, right?"

She nods. "Yes. Mrs. Gensinger had a baby and she said she had to pump milk for the baby. When she left, one of the girls said the milk comes from her boobs. She said she knew because her mom was breast feeding."

"Well, that's right."

"So, did the mommy rabbit go off to pump her boobs? And how would a rabbit pump her boobs?"

Inside, I'm dying with laughter. But I don't want to embarrass her, and begin to tactfully to address the subject. Also, I think with all the blossoming changes of this summer, my own included, now might be the best time, to enlighten her on the many miracles a young women will experience. After all, a beautiful miracle of life is right before her eyes, in a box of carrots she planted. This moment was meant for her, and I feel so blessed to be the one who gets to explain it to her.

"Well, you see, Sidney. Rabbits don't need pumps to get the milk out. And neither do human moms. That's only when they can't be with their babies, and want to save the milk for them to drink later. Normally, the baby sucks it out. Just like baby rabbits. Rabbit mothers nurse their babies for only five minutes a day, early in the morning, and then again later, before bedtime. That's because their milk is so rich, it fills the babies up fast."

"Oh, that's so neat. I want to breastfeed my baby when I grow up." I wonder if she ever had a chance to nurse from her mother. How soon did she die after Sidney was born? Feeling the need to mother this little girl, I wrap her in my arms. We both watch the little bunnies as they squirm in the furry nest.

"You're going to be a wonderful mom, Sidney."

18

ERIN

ERIN SORTS THROUGH THE MOVING BOXES, LOOKING FOR HER DAUGHTER'S picture. It just couldn't have left her desk on its own. But then, she cannot remember if it was on her desk when she packed up her office. The move has begun to stress her out, and she wonders if she is losing her mind. She, and Sasha Flynn, her partner for the last ten years of Kelly & Flynn Associates, are ending their practice together. She is happy for Sasha and her husband, who are starting a family, and decided that Sasha will stay home with the baby. However, she now can't afford the office complex on her own.

"We were celebrating a little too much," Erin says, mocking herself. remembering their last day together at the office. They had just finished their counseling sessions with patients, and marked the books "out early." They were going to celebrate their next adventures of life, but promised to keep in touch, especially after Sasha's baby was born. Erin had poured a glass of champagne for herself, and orange juice for Sasha. After that, she had mixed the champagne and orange juice, finishing the rest of the day with a mimosa.

She remembers closing the front door and securing the lock. There was no need to set the alarm, because they both would be leaving for day, and would only have to disarm it. She also remembers setting the phones to voicemail only. This would be their last day together, and there were to be no interruptions.

Pulling files and pictures from the boxes, Erin looks for a place to store them until her new office is ready. She hopes to be back in practice soon. However, taking the summer off didn't sound like such a bad idea... if only she could afford it. She stacks her patients' files on the kitchen table, then decides it's time for a break. *I could use a glass of wine right now* she thinks, and grabs the bottle of cabernet from the counter. After pouring her wine, she finds her phone, which is lost in the mess, and then calls Sasha. Sasha is due in a week, and Erin doesn't want to miss the birth of the baby.

"Hi, Sasha. How is everything going?" She takes a sip of the wine.

"Ugh... it's not. I was hoping the baby would come this week. I am so tired of being pregnant, and this summer is already heating up. I can't even wear shoes, Erin."

Erin laughs. "You never wore shoes when in the office."

"Yes. But now I would do anything just to wear a pair of cute, little heels. I feel like a fat, beached, walrus surrounded by skinny girls in bikinis."

Erin laughs.

"Sasha, you'll be back to your size six in no time. Maybe back in a bikini before the end of summer," Erin says, trying to encourage her. "After my daughter was born, I was back in my jeans in months. You'll be the same."

"Oh Erin, I just don't see it. Have you got your new office all set up yet?"

"No. It's been a slow process; I'm just now unpacking boxes. Hey, you didn't happen to see what box my daughter's picture was in, did you?"

"No, I didn't."

"Well, that's strange."

"What's strange?"

"I can't seem to find her picture. I thought maybe you packed it."

"No, I didn't."

"Oh well, I have plenty more boxes to go through. I'm sure it will turn up. You make sure to call me the minute you go into labor. Or when your water breaks."

"I think I'm more frightened of my water breaking than I am of the pain of labor," Sasha says. Erin laughs with her, and holds back expressing how she will soon change her mind once the labor pains start. She doesn't want to frighten her friend. She remembers how her own labor was excruciating—and it lasted three days. She hopes this will not happen to Sasha. "You will be the first I call."

Erin ends the call, then takes another sip of her wine. She begins to go through her patients' files and reorganize them back into alphabetic order before updating them on her computer. She was smart enough to pack the boxes that needed to be updated first, which were those for the patients she had seen last. Grabbing the top file, she opens it and sees the note she wrote to herself at the top of the page.

> ** Call in the next few days. Suspect patient may stop medication with lack of supervision. **

Erin sets the file down and grabs her phone. She only hopes the patient will answer and that she hasn't waited too long to call. She rolls to the saved number, and relief runs through her when the patient answers.

"Hello?"

"Hello, Eve."

19

I'm getting Sidney ready for bed. The baby bunnies are all she can talk about. She's still filled with the excitement of finding them, and is jumping up and down on her bed. "I can't wait to tell Daddy about the baby bunnies. When's he coming home?" My heart fills with joy that she now anticipates his homecoming. *And, so do I.*

"He called when you were in the tree house. Maybe next week."

She frowns. "That long? Why so long? He was actually becoming fun to be around, for a change."

"I'm glad you think so."

"Yeah. I think it's because of you." I cover her up with the blankets. My heart melts thinking it's me who's inspired Jonas to change. "That's why you can never leave, Julia." The thought of leaving, and going to Paris, now gives me a heavy feeling in my chest.

"I think it's *you* who changed him, Sidney. I only told him what a wonderful daughter you are. The changes he's making in his life, are for *your* benefit." I think back to his comment—that what he did years ago, was to protect her. At the time, I thought it just was his bad mood talking, but then she was taken by the old woman. I just wish he would open up more.

"Get some sleep. You have bunnies to care for now," I say, and kiss the top of her head.

"Do you think their mom is back? What if they're afraid of the dark... like me?"

"She's probably sleeping on the nest with them. I will leave the bathroom light on. Goodnight, Sidney." I leave the door cracked.

"Goodnight, Julia."

I don't go to my room, but instead make my way down the hall into Jonas's room. This has been my room, too, since the first time we made love. And even though he is gone, I can still feel and smell him here.

I remove my clothes, but I don't go to bed. Instead, I sit at the window seat, hugging my knees into my chest. Leaning my head against the window, I listen to the frogs from the pond, and recall our last lovemaking under the stars—as the moon watched. It was *me* that he made love to... not her... not Eve. Yet, his love for me scares him, and I have to wonder why. Maybe, after I tell him I love him, too, he will no longer feel afraid. But is that why I haven't told him? Because *I'm* afraid?

I look up at the moon and think of the pond. My sweet memories are there... and bad memories are there for Jonas. *Memories of no longer having Eve?*

"Oh Eve, why do you haunt me? I don't even know you," I whisper up to the moon. And just like that, she possesses my body. I reach for Jonas's T-shirt, pull it on, and, like I'm hypnotized, walk down to my room, and into my closet. She's calling me.

My beautiful Eve,

Tonight, you have me so scared. You have been so distant, and all I do is pace. Pace until you call for me. You have no idea what it's like for me when I can't be with you. You are my everything. My life. You say there is something you need to tell me. Something has made a change in you, and I'm so afraid you are leaving me. I can't lose you,

Eve. Ever. I have nothing, if I don't have you. Maybe, your news is that you are getting divorced. I hope for this to be true, though I know it's only wishful thinking. She is worse than ever now, and I can no longer stay here. She tells me I'm awful. A mistake. An obstacle in her way. I'm nothing to her. I've never been anything to her. But it doesn't matter now, Eve. Because I have you, but if I lose you, she will be right. I will be a nothing. Please, Eve. Please tell me there is hope for us. I will hide our love forever, if I know it's the only way to have you. It still hurts when he's home, and I can't be with you. But for you, I will suffer. You are worth it, Eve. I would die for you. I'm dying slowly every day until I hear from you. You call me, and there is fear and excitement in your voice. Hope is in there, too. Maybe it's only me hearing that hope, because I need it.

Hope won. I won. You are carrying my baby. Our child. The child we made together with our love. Oh, Eve, how perfect. I'm going to be a father. Nothing will ever separate us now. EVER. I will be the best father. I love you, Eve.

JX

Could Jonas have another child? A child with Eve? Where is this child? My hands shake as I carefully place the letters back in the floor. I need to go to bed, but all I can do is sit, curled up on the floor of my closet, and rock back and forth. I had thought I would learn more about him through reading the letters, but it has only deepened the mystery. The things I learn about him... I don't like. Yet, I'm in love with him. It's too late. And maybe that's why it hurts. It hurts to think he was having an affair, and now may have another child. And what did he mean, he could no longer stay with his wife? Why did she think he was so awful? Was it because of the affair? Did she know? Or was it the fact that she was so awful to him that drove him into the arms of Eve? *Where is this Eve?*

With mixed emotions, I slowly make my way to Jonas's room and crawl into his bed. I brush my hand along the spot he lays on, and smell his pillow. I know for a fact, I have lost all control, and he now owns my heart. I now am part of his web of secrets... and he has no idea I even know. The deeper I delve into his past, the deeper I fall for him. Yet, my feelings are such a jumble of love, hate, envy, and jealousy. My head screams, OVER WHAT? LETTERS! *Let it be, Julia. He has professed his love to you.* He professes much, yet denies even more. I roll over, hug his pillow, and listen to the frogs from the pond, reminding me of our love.

$\sim$

"SHH," I HEAR SOFTLY IN MY DREAM. MOIST TOUCHES TO MY FACE BRING my hand to my cheek. I breathe in, lick my dry lips, and cuddle back down into my pillow. I squeeze the other pillow I'm still hugging, and drift back to sleep. Something tickles my cheek, and I feel it move across my lips. Without opening my eyes, I move my face a little and snuggle more into the pillow. I swallow, quietly clear my throat, and begin to drift away again. "You're so beautiful," a hushed voice says.

Opening my eyes, my beautiful Jonas is smiling down at me. "Jonas," I whisper. "You're here. What time is it?" I try looking for the clock, but he is blocking its view.

"It's two in the morning. I knew I wouldn't be able to sleep missing you so much. I booked an express, and flew in. I can't stay long. I will have to fly back in the afternoon. But I had to see you, Julia," he says, and places his lips on mine.

As his kiss takes hold, so do my emotions. I sit up and pull his body to mine. "It's me, isn't it Jonas? It's me you love." My words sound panicky. I need to hear it—that I'm his.

"Yes, Julia. It's only you. You are my compass. Wherever you are, I will be," he says with tender kisses on my mouth, down my neck, and on my breasts. "I will always be where you are."

I worship these words, which are meant for me. No one else. Not Eve. Me. "Jonas... look at me," I breathe out. "Look me in the eyes, and tell me."

He moves his head from my chest, and with those special, blue eyes, now full of hunger and desire, he looks so deeply into me, I can hear his words before he speaks. "Julia, I've waited my whole life for you. I just needed to find you. And now that I have found you." He stops—then, very carefully, stresses each word individually. "I. Will. Never. Let. You. Go."

"Oh, Jonas. I love you. I want you to know it. I love you." Tears run down my face. "I wanted to say it to you. To your beautiful face, as you look me in the eyes. Those beautiful, blue eyes I saw that day I fell onto your chest." His eyes fill with such joy and light, like I have changed the world for him. His world.

"Julia, I have been dead to the world for years. Now, with your declaration of love to me, the world is dead to me. *You* are all that matters to me. My heart has purpose. You're my purpose. I love you." He takes me in his arms.

It's me he wants. He's not making love to a ghost. It's me he's going to make love to.

He picks me up. Is he taking me to the pond? I want him here now, in this bed. "Where are we going?" I ask, cradled in his arms.

"I need a shower first, and I don't want to spend a second without you. You're going to shower with me. I need to feel you on me, Julia. I need to feel you're real."

He carries me to the bathroom and sets me down on my feet. Before starting the spray, he pulls his T-shirt off me as I lift my arms. Kneeling, he slowly pulls my panties down, and I step out of them. He places a small kiss ever so gently on my pubis, and I gasp when his tongue licks the tip of my clit. "Mmm," he purrs as his face makes a trail of kisses, hip to hip. "I've missed this." I hold his head, my fingers squeezing in his hair. He looks up and raises his arms, gesturing for me to pull off his shirt. I toss it to the floor when he stands. He removes his jeans.

My hands, without hesitation, start at his chest and find their way down to his hard stomach. He truly is a beautiful man, and my eyes and hands cannot get enough of him. We kiss, and his erection burns between us, hot on my belly. He lifts me up, steps into the shower, and stands me under the falling water. Taking my hands, he holds them over my head, pinning me to the shower wall, and kisses me with such intensity, I forget that water is pouring onto our faces. With each hungry kiss, water flows into our mouths, and we share the warm liquid between us.

He lifts me again, and I wrap my legs around his waist. "Hang tight, Julia. I'm going to take you here. Now," he says breathlessly, and I squeeze tight around his neck. I feel him put his cock at my entrance and think he's going to enter me slowly. I cry out when, instead, he pushes deep inside me in one thrust.

"Ah." He begins with his torturous, demanding thrust driving in and out of me, and maybe it's just this position making it hurt, but I hope my pussy will relax and take him. My tailbone bangs the shower wall with every thrust. He's hitting me deep, and my breathing is nothing short of hyperventilating.

"God, yes, Julia. This is what I need," he groans between gritted teeth. His behavior is like the releasing a deep anger—the exorcism of a demon. He shouts my name over and over, and what should scare me, suddenly opens me to his will, and I'm his to use.

I relax my body, allowing in the wonderful ache he's driving into me, and I accept him. We all want him—my head, my heart, my building climax coming closer with each thrust—and I begin to scream his name.

"Jonas." Water muffles my screams as my orgasm burns close, and I shudder at my every being. "It's happening, Jonas," I say. "Yes. Yes. Jonas... I love you." He drives into me harder and harder, praising me for my release. With each shocking wave giving me such pleasure, I hear every word he has said to me. I'm his compass. Wherever I am, he will be. I have given his heart purpose. I'm his world. The world he's been waiting for. These words are *my* letters from *Jx*. I will no longer let what is in the past and dead, destroy the future I have with this man. My Jonas.

"Ah, Julia," he cries out, and releases himself deep inside me. With each pulse of his release, he squeezes my bottom tightly as his body stiffens. "God, yes. I love you."

I remain wrapped around him as our breathing slows, bringing our hypersexual energy down to a wondrous calm. We are at peace now. Whatever was possessing him, has left in a fit of raging love, and only *I* now possess him. His past no longer exists for him, or for me. It's only us now.

With no sounds, other than the water pelting on our heated bodies, we wash each other like precious pieces of art. We step out, and he takes a towel, and carefully pats me dry. I towel his body in the same, loving way. He picks me up and takes me to his bed. Laying me down gently, he lays himself next to me, then pulls me onto his chest.

I love you, our hearts say to each other.

We fall asleep.

JONAS IS LEANING AGAINST THE COUNTER WHEN SIDNEY COMES WALKING into the kitchen. "Daddy, you're home!" she says, for once showing excitement at seeing her father. She runs to him, and Jonas quickly sets his cup down right before she jumps in his arms.

"I have something to show you," she tells him.

"You do? What?" he asks, with a kiss to her forehead.

"It's outside. You won't believe it." He looks over to me, and I get up, and suggest we take our coffees outside. I sit down on the swing and watch as Sidney takes her father's hand, and leads him to the baby bunnies. She screams when the mother rabbit jumps out, hopping away.

"She did come back, Julia! Come here, Daddy. Look at the baby bunnies."

Jonas carefully moves the patch of hair, exposing six little babies squiggling in the tiny hole. "Wow," he says, to humor his daughter. "What are you going to do with them, Sidney?"

"Keep them," she says. "But, I will have share them with their mom." His expression looks strained when he hears the word "mom." Maybe it was hearing it from her for the first time. He kisses the top of her head.

"Well... that's thoughtful of you, Sidney," he says, and joins me on the swing. He wraps his arm around me, and I lay my head on his shoulder. We both watch Sidney jump around in her pajamas, pretending to be a mother rabbit. She's telling the babies they can eat as many carrots as they want.

"Oh, do you have to go?" I sound whiney.

He takes a deep breath. "God, I sure don't want to, but all four of us are meeting tonight over dinner." Referring to his partner, building engineer, and architect. "I've already booked a flight back to Maine. In fact, it leaves at twelve thirty," he says, looking at his watch. I groan into his bare chest, still smelling of the body wash I washed him with last night.

I think back to our lovemaking in the shower—how it was different, so intense. "You... seemed different last night when we made love in the shower," I say, still with my head on his chest. "Like you were trying to break away from something."

"Did I hurt you?" He lifts my chin, meeting his eyes.

"No—I mean yes, it hurt at first, but then when I became lost in us... well, I guess I looked past it. Maybe it was just me... still learning sex, and all its emotions."

"I wasn't trying to break away from something, Julia. I was breaking *into* something. *You.* I'm sorry if I got a little rough. It's just... I'm finally where I want to be. With you."

"Oh, Jonas," I say, and kiss his lips.

"God, I wish I didn't have to leave so soon," he says, and hugs me tight.

"It's just as well. I promised Erin we would meet her today after Sidney's swim lesson, for our girls' shopping trip for flowers, and other stuff she needs. I would hate to renege on her now. She seems so insistent on our being friends. I can tell she's lonely.

"Use the bankcard in the desk to buy whatever you think she needs. Just add it to the expense spreadsheet in the computer. The password for my computer is BonhomeR—one word, with a capital B, and a capital R."

"What's a BonhomeR?" I ask, thinking it's a strange password. "Is that even a word?"

"It's a navy carrier. The ship I was on while serving in the marines. The Bonhome Richard."

He's finally revealing a piece of his past, and I'm glad. I don't want to keep secrets. The letters tell me about his past, and they aren't secrets anymore. One fact remains—he doesn't know that I know. So, now it's only me holding secrets. I can no longer hold this against him. "I found pictures of you in a book, in your uniform," I confess. The letters I still keep secret. Letters from the jail have stopped, and I no longer want a past hurting him.

"Really? Wow, I didn't think I had any left. Do you still have them?" he asks, and I'm shocked. Does he know there are pictures of his wedding day? Before I tell him, I get up from the swing and head to his office. I pull out the book that they were stuffed into, pull them out, take them back out to him, and sit on his lap.

"Here, they were in a book I was beginning to read." *Lie*. I watch his expression as he looks at the pictures. The one of him and his wife are underneath, not yet exposed. But by the look on his face, he knows this day. *His wedding day*. "It was your wedding day," I say, sounding enthused. Like it was a memory that should be shared—not forgotten, and stuffed away in a book.

He stiffens and breathes in deeply. It's not a good memory for him, I can tell. "Yeah... that it was," he says, and pulls the bottom picture from the stack. I watch his face as he looks at the lost wife who is curled into his side. A face never revealed. A name never spoken. And a wife and mother... who never was.

20

I'M SITTING ON THE BENCH BY THE POOL WHEN ERIN COMES JOGGING UP, panting. She twists the cap off her water bottle, takes a long drink, and then wipes her mouth with the back of her hand. Her long, blonde hair is pulled tight in a high ponytail, giving her a more youthful look, and her black running shorts compliment her slender body. She's a very attractive lady, and has kept her figure. I only hope I look this good in ten years.

"Hey," she says, still breathing heavily from her run.

"Hi, Erin. So, you're a jogger?"

"Jack of all trades, master of none," she says with a laugh. "I've tried to do whatever it takes to keep in shape for the last ten years—yoga, weights, and some running."

"Well, it looks like it's paid off. You look great," I compliment her.

"Thanks, but tell that to my ex who left me for a younger woman," she says twisting the cap back on the bottle and dropping it to the ground. She smooths her hands through her hair, tightening up her ponytail, then lays it over her shoulder.

"Oh. That's awful. I can't imagine she'd be prettier than you."

She shrugs her shoulders, then places her hands on her hips. Her flat belly, exposed by her cropped sports top, shows evidence of routine crunches that have paid off. "She's not bad. But I can take her on," she laughs. "She'll learn eventually what she has gotten herself into."

"Well, by the looks of you, I'd hate to be her."

"Trust me," she says. She sits down next to me on the bench. "I've been so looking forward all morning to your and Sidney's arrival. I've got something for her back at the house—a horse figurine she can play with."

"Oh, she'll love it." Although I don't recall Sidney telling her about Holly. "How did you know she likes horses? I don't remember her mentioning it yesterday."

"Oh, you didn't? Sure she did. Maybe it was when you were looking at Jason's picture. She came into the kitchen and told me she had a horse."

"Jason?"

"Yes. The young boy in the picture you asked me about."

"Oh, I'm sorry. Yes. That must have been what happened." She looks at me expectantly.

"Yes, and after you left yesterday, I finished unpacking my boxes and found some of my daughter's horse figurines. Sidney can play with them when she's here."

"Oh, well, that's very kind of you. She will love them. I will make sure she is careful not to break them."

My phone sings Ryan Adam's, "Gimme Something Good," the ring-tone I put for Jonas, and I see his face light the screen. Erin sees the photo of the handsome man and gives a look of approval with the raise of her eyebrows.

"Excuse me," I say.

"Go right ahead, if that's who is on the other end," she says teasingly.

I smile coyly and accept his call. "Hello, Jonas."

"Hi, Julia. I'm getting ready to board soon and wanted to hear your voice one more time. I miss you already."

"I miss you, too," I say, and smile at Erin. She mouths, "Oh that's so sweet," and places her hands over her heart. I gently smack her arm. She laughs and reaches for her water bottle.

"Hey, I wanted to make sure you weren't upset after the way I reacted to the pictures you showed me," he says. He sounds regretful.

The look on his face when he saw the picture of his wife, Jenna, was that of seeing a ghost. He stood up from the swing and walked back into the house, throwing the picture into the trash. I tried to apologize, and said maybe Sidney should have it. Something to remember her mother by. Someday, she will be asking. He looked at me with anger in his eyes and said, "She is dead, and that's the way it will stay. Even in memory." After that, he ran upstairs and took a shower. When I walked him to his car before he left for the airport, he never said anything more about it. He just held me tight, kissed me, and said goodbye. I took the picture from the trash. It, too, is now a secret in the floor.

"I'm sorry, Jonas. I guess I wasn't thinking, and I should have warned you first." Recalling his letter to Eve, how his wife had said he was "awful," a "mistake," I hadn't taken that into consideration. And maybe to him, she should stay dead. But someday Sidney should have that choice.

"No, Baby. It's my fault. I shouldn't have acted so coldly. I have you now—my compass, my new life. A beginning," he says, and I hear the life in his words. "Well, anyway, I just wanted to talk before I board."

"Do you want to talk to Sidney first?" I ask, feeling the need to continue coaching his parenting.

"Yes. Put her on."

"Sidney," I yell, getting up from the bench. "Daddy wants to talk to you really quickly." Meeting her halfway to the pool, I hand her the phone.

"Hi, Daddy," she says with chattering teeth. "Yes, I just got out of the water. When you going to be back?" she asks, and I look back at Erin, who now has a very disapproving look on her face. Her arms are crossed, and it's clear she is upset... *at me.* "Okay, I love you, too, Daddy." She hands me back the phone. "Daddy says he loves you, Julia," she says, and runs back to the pool.

I put the phone back up to my ear. "Hello, Jonas?" He must have ended the call, and boarded the plane. I walk back to Erin, and yes...

she is displaying a defensive posture. Her arms are still locked over her chest as her eyes narrow judgingly at me, and she shakes her head.

"You're the nanny and you're fucking her dad?" she states loudly, and a group of women look over at us.

Now, very embarrassed, I try to explain. "No, it's not like that," I say, looking both at her, and the other women. She holds out a hand, stopping my next response.

"Save it for the therapist. I will soon have him and his wife both on my couch, each blaming the other until they both agree it was always *your* fault. Trust me. I see it all the time. And the fact he has the *balls* to let his *daughter* tell you he *loves* you. I'm telling you, Julia this has danger, with a capital D, written all over it."

"He's a widow. Sidney's mother is deceased. She never knew her mother," I say in one rushed breath. She still looks appalled—as if just saying Sidney's mother is dead is somehow offensive.

"Oh. So, there's the lacuna," she says quietly, as if speaking to herself.

The group of women is still gaping at us, so I pull out my inner chutzpah. "Keep looking, and *your* husbands will be next."

Erin laughs, and then apologizes. "Oh, God, I'm sorry. I'm still feeling the pain of my divorce, and I guess I took it out on you. Can you forgive me, Julia?"

"I guess I never explained my, *our,* situation. And I can see now how it must have looked to you. I understand, and, given what you're going through—no apology necessary."

She holds out her hand, and I shake it.

"Truce," she says, pulling me down to the bench. "Besides, now that I've seen his picture, I don't blame you," she says, wrapping her arm around me. "And I'm dying to hear all about this *situation*. Trust me, not much is happening in my bed lately. I want all the details," she says, coaxing me like a high-school girlfriend, wanting all the gossip. I smile shyly and tell her maybe when we're alone.

Erin rides with us back to her house, since she ran here today, and she and Sidney change clothes before we set out on our girls' shopping trip. She apologized numerous times for the "shaggin' the dad," comment, as she calls it, and it's now in the past. Now, "getting all the goods" on Jonas has become her new quest for furthering our friendship. And although her talk seems a bit juvenile, 'her shaggin' talk," I'm eager to discuss my whirlwind, passionate, love life that has taken on a soul of its own.

Our shopping trip starts at the local Target, where we buy window treatments, cleaning supplies, some paint, and a bathmat with matching towels. Sidney insists on the shower curtain with the unicorn with a rainbow mane and tail, along with the matching soap, and toothbrush holder. Erin agrees wholeheartedly.

After a few throw pillows and candles, I decide this is all that will fit in my Mini. So, we drive back to Erin's, make a drop off, and head to the open-air market for some flowers. Again, my car is stuffed to the gills with flowers, and we enjoy the aroma of summer as we ride back home.

"I have some chicken we can grill outside for dinner," Erin suggests from the kitchen window, as I complete my surprise.

"Awesome. I can make us a fresh salad." While at the open-air market, I bought fresh strawberries, along with some romaine lettuce to welcome in the summer with our new friend. This day has been *wonderful.* And I can't wait to show her the sign I painted while she and Sidney decorated the bathroom, and living room. I am truly enjoying my new friendship with Erin. And with Jonas away, any advice she can give me—a younger woman—I look forward to.

"Come and see what Erin and I did," Sidney calls to me. I grab some paper towels and wipe paint from my hands before meeting her at the back door. As I step in, Sidney tells me to cover my eyes. "We want to surprise you." I cover my eyes as she leads me to the living room. "Okay," she says. I open my eyes to a fresh new look—new pillows on the couch, and curtains that accent the room with a floral pattern. A big candle sits in the middle of the square coffee table, and smells of the beach.

"Wow! You guys did this? It's beautiful."

Erin bends down and hugs Sidney. "We make a great team, Sidney," she says.

"Come see the bathroom," Sidney says, running down the hall and into the small bathroom. The unicorn shower curtain hangs bright with rainbow colors. Somehow, Sidney even found a rainbow-colored, Glade plug-in for the outlet, which smells of candy.

"Okay, now for my surprise," I say, and we walk out to the back yard. "Stay right here and close your eyes—both of you." They close their eyes as I pick up the sign and turn it around. "Okay. You can open them." Erin looks at the sign I painted and covers her mouth in disbelief. I have painted "New Beginnings" in bold, rainbow colors on a large, wooden sign with turnbuckles screwed on top for hanging.

"Do you like it? I thought it would be appropriate for *your* new beginning, as well. If you don't like the name—"

"It's perfect, Julia. I love it. Thank you so much." She steps off the little concrete step and gives me a hug. We then walk around the front of the house, to hang the sign. Standing back, we hold hands, all three of us, and turn to see the sign for the first time together.

New Beginnings.

We sit at the kitchen table, eating our grilled chicken and fresh salad, proud of the day's hard work, and talking of our new friendship. Erin says she feels blessed to have had us come into her life. A true Godsend. Especially when she has been missing her daughter so much. She constantly watches Sidney—stroking her cheeks and playing with her braids.

"Oh, hey!" she says, getting up and leaving the kitchen. I look at Sidney and shrug my shoulders.

"Maybe she has another surprise for you," I say to her. "Did you thank her for the horse figurines? Remember to be careful with them. They belong to her little girl."

"She said I could have them, and how did she know I like horses?"

"Didn't you tell her about Holly?" I ask. Sidney is about to answer when Erin returns.

"I finally found it." She holds up a picture of a little girl. "Wouldn't you know—it was in the very last box I unpacked." She takes a kitchen towel and cleans the glass, setting the picture next to Jason's picture. "This is my daughter, Roman." The little girl looks nothing like her mother, who is so blonde, with blue eyes. Roman has , almost black hair, and eyes the color of chocolate.

"She's a very pretty girl. Her black hair is so pretty, and those big brown eyes!"

"Yes," Erin replies. "My daughter looks just like her father." She straightens Jason's picture, and looks again at Sidney. But I don't hold that against her," she laughs. "Sidney, would you like to come see Roman's picture a little closer? We will have to get you two together soon, for a play-date."

Sidney looks up at me, and I nudge her to go look at Roman's picture. She gets up from her chair, and walks over to where Erin is still fussing with the pictures, setting them just so. "This is Roman, Sidney. I bet she will like you. She's your same age," Erin says, patting Sidney's head.

"She looks nice," Sidney says. She turns back around and looks at me. Her green eyes are shining, and those dimples are showing. And then I look at Sidney's face next to the picture of Jason and I see four green eyes, and four dimples. The likeness is so uncanny, they could be brother and sister.

21

AFTER HELPING ERIN WITH THE DISHES, I TELL HER WE REALLY NEED TO go home. Sidney needs a bath, and her bedtime is soon.

"Oh, Julia. I would love if you and Sidney stay with me tonight. Give Sidney a bath here. You can also shower, and Sidney can have my bed. *You* and *I*," she stresses, "are going to have some wine, and then you are going to fill me in on that 'hot' dad," she says, mouthing the hot dad part, so Sidney doesn't overhear. After thinking it over, I accept her invitation, get Sidney ready for her bath, and put her to bed.

I pull on a long nightshirt Erin left for me in the bathroom after my shower, and meet her on the couch. There are two glasses of wine, along with the open bottle set next to the burning candle on the coffee table.

She gestures for me to sit and offers me a glass. I reach for it slowly, and have a seat. Erin tucks her feet under her and takes her wine.

"I've never had wine before," I tell her.

"It's a dry wine, so if you have never had wine, you might not like it," she says. "I have some sweet wine in the fridge, if you'd prefer."

"Actually, I've never had *any* alcohol." I laugh.

"Ah, I have a virgin drinker with me tonight." Her eyes tease me. "But seriously, you might like the sweet better." I take a small sip and pucker my face. It reminds me of vinegar, and she laughs. "Okay, I think that's a yes. I'll go grab the Moscato from the fridge." She gets up and takes my glass. I think she's going to dump it out, but instead, she downs it in one gulp. *Damn!*

She returns with the fresh glass and tells me to sample it. Holding the glass up to my nose, I find that the smell is more refreshing, and I take a sip. She's right. It's sweet, and smooth "Now this, I like," I say, and hold my glass up for her to fill.

"It's smooth, but don't be fooled. It will kick your ass if you have too much of it." Her eyes widen with her warning.

"I need to call Jonas first and let him know where I am."

"I thought you said he was gone on business?"

"Yes. I still feel I should let him know where I have his daughter."

"Okay. Go ahead, and then... I want the juicy details," she says, and smacks my butt when I get up to find my phone. When I find it, I'm surprised he hasn't called me already. But then I remember his dinner with the others tonight for the condo project. "Hey, tell him thank you for all the stuff. I appreciate it all so much," she says. I told her earlier it was Jonas who offered to buy the stuff she needed.

"Hey, Julia," he answers on the second ring.

"Is now a bad time to call?" I ask, thinking I might be interrupting his business dinner.

"No, it's perfect timing. Yes, we are still here going over the plans, but I needed a break—and I'm so glad to hear your voice. How'd your shopping day go with your friend?"

"It went great. Sidney and I are still at her house, and that's why I called. Erin invited us to stay tonight. She also said thank you for funding the shopping."

"No problem. Glad I can help."

"She's really happy. Thank you, Jonas."

"I miss you so much, Julia."

"I miss you too, Jonas. Do you know how much longer you'll be in Maine?"

"Maybe a day, or two. Some... new ideas might come up on this project. Ideas I don't think my partner will like. However, I'm going to propose them anyway."

"Ideas?"

"Something I'm kicking around in my head. I don't want to say too much right now."

"Not even to me?" My voice is whiny again.

"Well, once I propose this to him, you will be the first to know about it."

"How will I be the first, if you tell him first?" *Whine.*

"Just... trust me. I'm working out all the details for the perfect proposal."

"Okay, I guess I will have to wait," I say, sighing.

"How's Sidney? Did she have a good time?" I'm glad he asked about her.

"Yes, she did. Erin found some horse figurines for her to play with. Her daughter is Sidney's age, and Erin hopes Sidney can come for a play-date this summer."

"Sidney will like that. Someone to share her horse with," he says, and I just love all his talk of Sidney, and how he remembers her horse. "Hey, I have another call coming in that I need to take. I love you, Julia," he says quickly.

"Oh? Okay. I love you too, Jonas." I barely get the words out before he ends the call. I see that the time displayed is 9:30. *Strange time for a business call.*

I hear Erin in the kitchen, ranting obscenities. I make my way to the doorway and see that she is on the phone. Obviously, by the sound of her words, she must be talking to her soon-to-be-ex.

"I don't give a *fuck* what time it is. I want to speak with my daughter."

Pause.

"Oh, don't give me that shit—*she's asleep.* It's only nine thirty, for shit's sake. It's summer break, and she doesn't need to be up early for school." She paces back and forth, holding her glass of wine in her free hand. "The truth is, she's out with your *fuckin' whore.*"

Pause.

"Oh, bullshit, you don't think I know better? I know *a lot* more than you think I do."

She downs the rest of her wine, then looks to me, holding out her glass. I look back at the bottle of wine on the coffee table, then back at her. She nods her head toward her glass, letting me know I am to refill it. Quickly, I retrieve the bottle and pour. She mouths, "Thank you," then continues her tirade.

"Maybe it's your little *whore* who needs to be in bed. How old is she? Like, *twenty*?" She takes a big gulp of her wine. "I know exactly what I'm talking about." She begins pacing again, listening to her ex's response. I feel I should leave her be, and let her get out her angry emotions. But when I start to walk away, she grabs my arm. "I'm having a glass of wine with my new friend. I hardly call that getting smashed, and then calling you on a drunken whim. I just thought it'd be nice to tell my daughter goodnight, you *fuckin' asshole*. Rot in hell," she says as her last words, and ends the call, slamming her phone down on the counter.

I am a little shocked, and unsure what I should do next. She covers her face with both hands and begins to cry. Without further hesitation, I walk over and wrap her in a hug. "Hey, it will be okay. Sidney and I are here. Your new beginning, remember?"

"Oh, Julia. I'm so sorry you saw that. It's just... it's just that he brings out the worst in me. All I wanted was to talk to my daughter—and even at that, he has to be a fucker about it."

I don't think I've ever heard so many foul words used at one time before. "Don't let him upset you. You are starting over, and soon you'll have your daughter back. Then we'll spend many great days together," I tell her. She is shaking, and I feel sorry for her.

She wipes her face with her hands, and sniffs a few times. "You're right, Julia. I *will* have my daughter back. She needs me—you know?" She sounds unsure. Maybe it's the absence of her child making her—someone who counsels others—feel insecure. She doesn't seem to have herself together right now, but I know she is going through a lot. "I should have seen right through his lies. I guess I was just too wrapped up in my career to see them. But still, that's no excuse to throw away twelve years of marriage for some young slut who shakes her ass." She straightens herself up, and wipes her face once more with the back of her hands. "Hey, I don't want to ruin this night for us. I want to hear about your love life. Trust me, I need to know romance has not yet died," she says, and grabs her wine.

She walks back to the couch, sits down, and pats the spot beside her. I walk over and curl up next to her. She pours me another glass of Moscato and tucks her legs under her, hugging the pillow. "Spill the goods," she says. A smile replaces her tears.

"Are you sure? I mean... I hate to boast about my happiness, given... your situation."

"No. Please, Julia. I need to hear it."

I take in a deep breath, have a drink of wine... and then another drink. Peering over the top of the glass, I look at Erin's expression, which is full of anticipation. I giggle nervously and finish the rest. She laughs when I gesture for her to fill my glass again.

"Watch it. Just because something's sweet now, doesn't mean it won't bite later," she says, refilling my glass. I take a small sip and start with my girl talk. Although, it's deeper than that. *Much.* Finally, I have someone with whom I can share my real concerns about Jonas... and the *letters.*

"It really did start out as a nanny position, and I am still Sidney's nanny. However, somehow it turned into... *lovers?*" I sound like I'm asking for permission to use the word.

"Well, that's no surprise. You're a beautiful young woman living with a man who's gorgeous, and apparently... single," she says, lifting her glass as if toasting the moment. "And... what kind of lover is he?" she asks suspiciously.

"He's amazing. But to tell you the truth, he's my first. First crush. First kiss. First fight—and, honestly, that's how we became lovers one night. Feelings have been building up inside me, and I couldn't rationalize them. So, I hope with you being a therapist, you could explain them to me," I say with true sincerity.

She gently touches my arm. "I will listen all you want. And remember, I'm not here to judge. If you are having trouble interpreting your feelings, or if you become stuck, please feel free to ask if it's okay to feel this way." I now hear the professional counselor in her.

I relax and begin. "Sometimes, I feel he's all I need. And then, other times, what I know about him, that he's doesn't know I know..." She tilts her head.

"What is it he doesn't know?" she asks. "And how does it change what you feel for him?"

"When I first was interviewed for the job, I was told his wife had passed, and Sidney never knew her mother. It was just Sidney and me at the house for some time, before Jonas returned. In fact, I thought he was an intruder and hit him over the head with a fire poker." She laughs. "Maybe I should go back before I knew him as Sidney's father. One day in my hometown, while I was praying on the boardwalk, he came along on his bike and, to avoid hitting me, he crashed over the rail. When I went to help him up, I fell as well... on top of his chest. Bare chest."

"Oh my. And that's when he offered you the nanny position?" she says, teasing me.

"No. That's just the thing. It was the next day I got an offer on Angie's List for the ad I listed. I had no idea it was Jonas who had hired me until the night I hit him. It was his former nanny who replied to my ad."

"Okay, this sounds all so romanticized, but shit happens," she says. "Go on."

"I first noticed that he and Sidney didn't have quite the father-daughter relationship I expected when she didn't even call him *dad*. And Jonas, well he seemed to be... too preoccupied with his business to be a father. Some of the neighbors, and parents of the other schoolkids, looked at Sidney as some sort of a bad omen. I didn't quite understand why, and I tried to bring it to his attention. But he would dismiss it, then turn the situation around, using my *hormones* for his defense. He would touch my face, stare into my eyes, and ask me questions about my dreams. I would become so flustered. That's the part I don't understand," I tell her, looking for answers.

"I see. And you want me to interpret for you what he's doing?

Because I can tell you this: he knows *exactly* what he's doing. He's deflecting your concerns by charming you as his defense. He's bypassing your logic thought and trespassing into your heart, which then leads to your bed. Trust me, Julia. I've seen it too many times to count with my female patients. They all think it's love, when it's just a place for him to stick his contingent dick," she says ruthlessly, and takes a gulp of her wine. I feel the conversation has shifted to girl-friend talk, rather than counsel between a therapist and her patient. But that's okay—I'm not paying her, and we are in pajamas, drinking wine.

"Now, to construe what's going on with *you*. I can tell you're inno-cent and... clueless." She sips her wine, then sets it back on the table. "And, trust me—I'm saying this in your best interest." *Is she?* "You have done nothing wrong. Just don't get caught up in the whole happy-ever-after bullshit. Take what he has to offer—in bed, and when it comes to money, that is—and when it's over, just go on to the next man."

Her words do nothing to comfort me. First, I don't want to take anything from Jonas. All I want is his love. I hate to think of him using me as a place to put his dick until he finds another. Second, I'm sure—with her marriage ending, and for the painful reason why—she's jaded. I will excuse what she is saying as her personal feelings making them-selves known.

"Now, what's this about *you* knowing something about *him* that he doesn't know?" she pries, and now I could kick myself for bringing it up.

Letters. Eve.

She knows I am hesitating, so I reassess my strategy of how to address the subject of the letters. Now that she has given her opinion of Jonas, she will be even more judgmental of what's in them. "It's really none of my business, and I had no right," I start. "And it was quite by accident how I obtained... some information. And what happened was so many years ago and is all in the past now."

"Julia, do you want to know the best way to predict future behav-ior?" Erin cuts in. "And I'm talking about Jonas. If you found something in his past that's... *unsavory*, then let me be the first to tell you—past behavior predicts future behavior. Now please, I want to help *you*. What did you find?"

Just what I feared, and she is the professional. "I found these letters, and it really was by accident. I was in my closet and stubbed my toe on a loose floorboard." She leans in toward me, her eyes wide, and I have her full attention.

"Letters? Written to whom?"

I take a heavy breath before I reveal, for the first time, my secret knowledge of Jonas's secret. "They were love letters. At first, I enjoyed reading them because I thought they were written to his late wife. But I didn't understand why he would hide them."

"If they weren't letters to his wife, then who were they to?"

"Eve." And just like that, just by my saying her name out loud to someone, it feels like a heavy weight has been lifted off my chest.

"And you've never told him you read the letters, correct?"

"No, I haven't. But, I did mention the name Eve to him. He said he never knew an Eve."

"How did you mention her name without revealing that you read the letters?"

"That's another mystery. A woman took Sidney from school, claiming to be her grandmother. She said that Eve told her to pick Sidney up. Jonas was in Indianapolis that day on business, and she even knew that. At that time, I still thought Eve was his late wife, but then he told me her name had been Jenna. I continued to read the letters, thinking they were to an old girlfriend he had known before his wife." I grab my wine, before dropping the ball. "But as I read on, it became apparent he and Eve were hiding their affair because they each were married. The last letter I read revealed she was pregnant. And I hate knowing this without his knowledge." Lifting my glass to my mouth, I finish the wine in one gulp.

"Hmm, interesting," she says. And I can see by the look in her eyes that the wheels are spinning in her mind. "So, what happened to the baby?"

"I don't know. I haven't read any more, and I don't plan to. I've decided it's his past, and he wants it left there. It's not up to me to bring it up. He says he loves me. He says I'm his compass. *His* new beginning. And he's happy now, Erin. I see no reason to bring it up."

"Okay, I understand how you feel. But tell me this," she says, and picks up her wine glass. "How did his wife die?"

"She was killed by a drunk driver. And that too, is a sore subject, because they were separated at the time. I'm thinking right after Sidney was born. He said she never knew her mother."

"Okay. But where is she buried? Hasn't he ever taken Sidney to put flowers on her grave? She should have that right—don't you think?"

"I guess you're right. I never thought about that."

"Well, guess what we are doing tomorrow," she says, as a matter of fact. "We're going to find this woman's grave, and start unlocking this mystery." She winks, then downs the rest of her wine.

22

RAIN PELTS AGAINST THE WINDOW, WAKING ME FROM A COMA-LIKE SLEEP. My head pounds, and the room is spinning. *My first hangover?* I roll over and find Sidney still sleeping. She is curled on her side, and her hands are in a praying position, tucked under her cheek. I barely remember coming to bed last night. Erin agreed to take the couch, letting me sleep with Sidney in her bed. Sidney opens her eyes and smiles at me.

"Do I have swim lessons today?" she asks. I know she's talking softly, but her voice pounds in my head.

"Oh no," I say in a strangled voice. I close my eyes, rolling over on my back, and cover my face.

"What's wrong, Julia?"

"The room is spinning,"

"No, it's not. That's impossible," she states, and her high voice cracks in my head.

"Oh, Sidney... can you please just give me a minute or so? I don't feel well this morning." She gets up, and her weight shifts the bed. My stomach turns, and I know I'm going to be sick. "Sidney, pleassssse," I moan. I feel her lie back down, with caution. She pats my head tenderly.

"I think you need some pancakes," she whispers.

"Ahhh... no, I don't think so," I say, with my eyes still closed, and my hands bracing my head.

"That's exactly what you need." Erin's voice is nearby, and I open one eye slowly. She's leaning against the doorframe, wearing a smug smile, with her arms crossed. "I told you, girlfriend. What goes down sweet, will bite in the morning."

"Oh my God, Erin. I think I'm dying."

"No, you're not. But Sidney is right. You need some greasy food, and pancakes. That will help soak up the alcohol in your blood. Come on, Sidney, let's make some pancakes while Julia sleeps it off."

I feel Sidney removing the blanket, and—ever so carefully—she pushes herself to the side of the bed, and slides out. She is being so considerate... and *I* feel like a complete ass. *Never again!*

I lie still for a few more minutes, then curse myself for being such an irresponsible nanny. I'm so ashamed of myself. I deserve this misery.

I sit up, *slowly*, and feel for the floor. The room only spins faster. If I throw up, will I feel... *better?* Or does hangover-sick differ from regular-sick? But it doesn't matter what I think—because the moment I stand up, my mouth fills with saliva, and I'm running to the bathroom.

Dry heaves, mixed with sour bile, splash the water in the toilet as I retch. I feel the scolding my stomach is giving me by the torture I'm putting us both through. It's not yielding. How long will this go on? *Retch.*

She (my stomach) seems to be forgiving, and I relax against the side of the tub, worshiping the cold porcelain. I take a few deep, calming breaths, then reach to flush the toilet.

After rinsing my face with cold water, and flushing my mouth with *more* cold water, I manage to find my way to the kitchen. Erin is helping Sidney flip pancakes. Yet, Sidney seems to be the one giving the lesson, repeating techniques I taught her. "That's how Julia does it," she says.

"Well, I can show you some things, too," Erin says with a hint of jealousy. Her tone rather shocks me. But then again, it's her profession —highly suggesting people take her advice. That's what they pay her for.

"Hi," I say dryly. They both glance in my direction. Sidney smiles and hops down from the chair she was standing on. She meets me at the doorway.

"I'm glad you're up. I almost have your pancakes ready, Julia," she says, taking my hand and cuddling me. Erin throws a sneering look our way. The look in her eyes is almost contemptuous. Maybe she is angry with me, for leaving her in charge of Sidney while I pay gratitude to the toilet.

"I'm so sorry," I say, in the most apologetic way I can. "You were right, Erin. I should have listened to you." I hope to be back in her good graces soon. She smiles and brings a plate of pancakes to the table.

"No. My fault. I should have made you stop. But we were having such a blast last night—once you opened up and began to talk." She winks, and I'm fearful of what I might have said. *Damn it.* "Who needs to read smut? Just pour Julia at least two glasses of wine, and you have the next bestseller. Complete with sound effects." *Oh. Shit. What did I tell her?*

She pulls out a chair, inviting me to sit.

"Your phone was ringing, so I answered it," she tells me. "Because of the rain, Sidney's swim lessons have been moved to the YMCA. I'm going to take her while you recuperate. When we get back, we are heading to the courthouse to look up death and burial records."

RAIN GUSHES ONTO THE WINDSHIELD OF ERIN'S CAR, AND THE WIPERS struggle to keep up. I try not to watch, for my stomach is still doing flip-flops. I feel she is driving too fast in this downpour and I want to tell her so. But with my poor judgment of drinking excessively last night, who am I to give out orders? Maybe she isn't driving fast. Perhaps it's just my incapacitated state.

She parks right outside the courthouse, and we wait for the heavy rain to ease up before making a run for it.

"Thanks for taking Sidney to swim lessons," I say, still feeling like an ass.

She touches my cheek, like a mother. "No problem, Julia. That's what friends are for. Are you feeling better?"

"Somewhat. Guess I learned my lesson."

We make our way up the steps, and into the courthouse. We shake our umbrellas before we collapse them, and set them in a corner, where other umbrellas wait for their owners. We then walk to the county records office, as Erin leads with purposeful strides. She is on a mission, with a mystery to solve, but I am now having doubts. I feel I am betraying Jonas.

Before entering the county records office, I sit Sidney in a chair, giving her strict orders to stay right there. She shouldn't overhear us talking about her mother, and I feel ashamed at what we are doing— though I shouldn't. She should have the right to visit her mother's grave. I look to the old security officer with the hopes he, too, will watch over her. He smiles with fatherly concern, and I whisper a "thank you" to him.

"I have to use the bathroom," Sidney says.

"Okay, but can you hold it for a minute? We won't be long." She nods.

"I want to go home, and see the bunnies, and Holly," she says. I know how she feels. I miss home, too. And Jonas. Especially now.

Once inside the office, Erin takes over. "Oh, the rain is awful out there," she says, running her hands through her long hair, as if it's wet. She is making friendly weather talk with the clerk.

"It's supposed to dry up by this evening. We could still see some sunshine," the clerk responds. "What can I do for you?"

"Hi, my name is Erin Kelly. I just moved here, and my friend and I are looking up—" she clutches her fingers to her necklace, "we are looking up an old friend who died ten years ago. We would like to know where she's buried. We're not even sure of the date of her death. If you could locate that as well?" she asks in a sorrowful tone. "We lost touch and now would like to give tribute by visiting her grave."

"Sure. If you could give me her name, I could look in our database, and we could go from there."

"Great. Jenna Fairbanks."

The clerk types the name in the computer, and I watch her eyes move across the screen. I look at Erin and give her a questioning look. "Can you repeat the spelling? Is it spelled with a J? And with one N, or two?"

Erin looks to me as if I should know. I shake my head. "Well, I'm pretty sure she spelled it with a J, but you can try a G. And try two N's, if nothing comes up with one," Erin says.

The clerk tries both ways, but still squints at the screen. "You say ten years ago?"

"Yes," Erin says.

"I'm sorry. There is no Jenna Fairbanks in our records. Are you sure you have the right name?"

Erin, again, looks to me. "Yes, Jenna Fairbanks," I say. The clerk shakes her head.

"In fact, there aren't any Fairbanks in the death records at all. Are you sure she died in this county?"

"Yes," Erin says. But maybe she didn't, I think. Jonas just said she died. He never said where.

"I'm sorry. I'm not finding it," the clerk says sincerely, then looks up from her computer.

"Okay. Thank you for your time," I say, and take a step back. Erin looks at me, and gives me a something-is-rotten-in-the-state-of-Denmark look, with one eyebrow raised. She thanks the clerk, turns, and walks out, seemingly satisfied with our failed attempt to find records for a Jenna Fairbanks.

Sidney is still waiting in the chair where I left her, and I look around for the ladies' room. I take her by the hand, and we walk down the long hall. Our steps echo off the tall, historical ceiling, and tile floor. I open the heavy, wooden door with opaque glass, and we make our way into a restroom that looks like it hasn't changed since the twenties. I help her into one of the stalls and turn to Erin, who is assessing her face in the mirror. "So, what do you think about that?" she asks, wiping smudged mascara from under her eyes.

"What do you mean?" I say to her reflection.

"There are no Fairbanks in the death records," she replies.

"Well... I'm not really sure where she died. I just know she's dead," I say. "And how did you know it was ten years ago? And I don't recall mentioning the Fairbanks name to you." We gaze at one another, and her expression freezes. She breaks contact by pulling out her lipstick.

"Oh my," she laughs. "You don't remember anything you said last night, do you?" She runs the lipstick over her lips. Sidney then flushes the toilet and comes out to wash her hands. *What did I say?*

"Fairbanks," she says while washing her hands. "That's my name. Why do you want to know?" I look at Erin and give a "deer in the headlights" look, hoping she will end this, for Sidney's sake. But my efforts fail when Erin bends down to her and starts asking questions.

"Sidney, do you remember anything about your mother?"

"Erin," I scold. She raises her palm at me.

"No. I was just a baby when she died. I know nothing about her," she says, only as information. No emotion. That doesn't surprise me.

"Has your dad ever mentioned her to you?"

"Just that she died long time ago. That's all I know." She turns to me. "Can we go now?" She takes my hand and gives me an exhausted look.

"Erin, I really need to be getting her home. I don't think we should be involving her in this matter. So, if you please, let's go."

"Okay, but one more question," she says, and I cringe. "Sidney, did your dad ever tell you where—or how—your mom died?"

"That's it, Erin. I said, no more!" Erin pulls back, and presses her lips together tightly. Even through the freshly-applied lipstick, they're turning white. I take Sidney by the hand and leave the restroom. I hear Erin exhale before following us out.

"Look, Julia, I'm sorry. I didn't mean any harm. Especially to Sidney. I thought I was helping. After last night's talk... well, it sounded like you want answers. And it's just in my nature, as a therapist, to look for them. Yes, sometimes I can overstep my boundaries, but I am only acting in your best interests."

We grab our umbrellas before walking out. "Erin, I don't remember what I said last night. And I'm sorry if... if I was looking to you for answers. That's not what I was trying to do. And I surely don't think we need to be prying." I make a meaningful gesture with my eyes toward

Sidney. I open the door and walk out to the car with Sidney's hand in mine.

When Erin gets in the car, she's quiet, and I know I've upset her. She was only trying to help, and it's all my fault. If only I could remember what I said. She gently takes my hand. "Look, I'm sorry to you and Sidney, both. But let me tell you something. Something I fear for you, since you are... romantically involved." I look out the window, and wait for what she is about to say. "You would not believe the broken women who come into my office. Their stories are *Dateline* material. One woman found out, after several years of marriage, that her husband had another wife. Not just a wife, but kids—and a black lab named Duke." I don't know why it's necessary to tell me the dog's name. I guess it adds to the drama. "She knew he was married before, only she thought the previous wife had died. It was only when she intercepted his mail that she saw the next semester's payment was due for their son at Notre Dame. She called the university to say there must be some mistake. Because they didn't have any children. She then asked for a statement of previous payments made. There was a record that went back four years. The son was a senior."

"Erin, how does this pertain to me and Jonas?"

"How does it not?"

Letters. Eve. Baby.

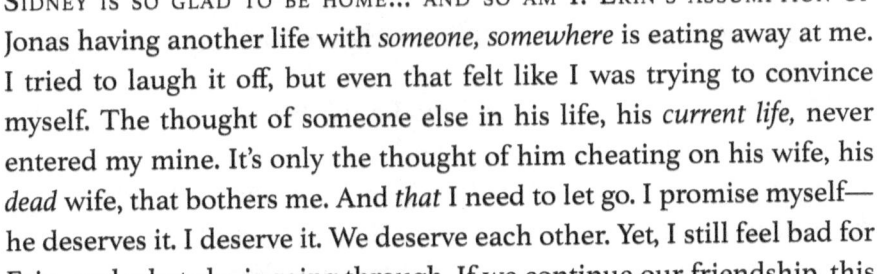

SIDNEY IS SO GLAD TO BE HOME... AND SO AM I. ERIN'S ASSUMPTION OF Jonas having another life with *someone, somewhere* is eating away at me. I tried to laugh it off, but even that felt like I was trying to convince myself. The thought of someone else in his life, his *current life,* never entered my mine. It's only the thought of him cheating on his wife, his *dead* wife, that bothers me. And *that* I need to let go. I promise myself— he deserves it. I deserve it. We deserve each other. Yet, I still feel bad for Erin, and what she is going through. If we continue our friendship, this kind of talk will have to stop. I really do want to be friends.

I'm watching Sidney with the bunnies, while I rock in the swing. In the last two days, the garden has grown, and the wildly-blooming window boxes have transformed this house into a home. This tableau speaks growth, and change, speaking to my heart. I, too, am growing and changing. When I first came here, it was full of gloom and sadness. Now, light shines down on this place, and love and happiness replace the darkness.

Ryan Adams sings from my phone, and I rejoice with excitement, knowing it's Jonas.

"Hello." My voice is joyful.

"Hi, Baby."

Just hearing his voice reassures me. "Hey. How did your proposal go?"

"I won't know yet. It's still on the table."

"Do you know when you'll be home? We miss you!"

"Yes, I do."

Silence.

"Hello? Jonas?"

"Yes, I'm here."

"Oh, I thought the call was dropped. So, when will you be home?" I ask again.

"I answered you, Baby. I'm already here."

"What?" I scream.

"Look up." Lifting my head and peering through the window, I see him looking down at me. "Come here," he says into the phone. I see his expression. It's full of suggestion. Without hesitation, I run into the house, and up the stairs. When I enter his door, he's standing there, waiting for me. I run and jump into his arms, wrapping my legs around his waist.

"I missed you, Jonas," I say, smothering his face with kisses. He swings us around, returning my kisses.

"God, I missed you, too. You don't know how much." He moves us to the bed, and pushes the suitcase to the floor. It pops open, spilling the contents. He sets me down, and unbuttons his shirt. I pull mine over my head, and toss it to the floor. It lands next to the spilled items—cologne, deodorant, body wash... and *condoms*. Erin's words echo in my head. *A wife, kids and a black lab named Duke.* He notices how I freeze and follows my eyes to the floor. Instantly, he sees the box of condoms, and immediately begins his explanation. "Julia, I had no idea those were in there. I promise you, they must be from a long time ago. If I'd remembered they were there, I would have used them our first time." He can tell by my look, I'm not convinced. "Please trust me. I'm not that kind of a guy."

"But you still have condoms in your suitcase. What kind of guy carries condoms on business trips?" I state. My voice is full of judgment.

"One who practices safe sex, Julia," he says as a matter of fact, with no apology for having them. "Yes. Okay, I lied when I said I didn't keep condoms here that night. I did remember I had some, but *this* is exactly what I didn't want you to think." He reaches for me, but I push back. His eyes show hurt, not for having the condoms, for me rejecting him. "You said you were on the pill. And if I remember correctly... Julia, you asked me to make love to you. I trusted you when you said you were on the pill. Now, I'm asking you to trust me. Those condoms are from a long time ago. Long before... you." He reaches for me again. I don't back away, but only hesitate. "Please, Baby. I love you."

"I want to believe you, Jonas... I do." My words catch, from the lump in my throat. "It's just... it's just there are so many questions you refuse to answer." He runs his hands through his hair. He's clearly frustrated.

"Julia, trust me. The things I don't tell you, are to protect you and Sidney. They aren't to hide things from you. You've got to believe me."

"Why? Why?" I raise my voice. "Why can't you tell me about Jenna, or the person in prison? Or Eve?" The minute her name is out of my mouth, his infuriated look makes my blood runs cold. It's taking me prisoner.

"Take off your clothes now," he orders. He speaks from behind gritted teeth. I swallow, and take off my shorts, along with my panties. He stands shirtless, and watches me. I'm waiting for him to do the same. He doesn't. "Come here." Another order.

I sit up from my knees and walk slowly over. "What are you going to do?" I ask, my voice trembling.

"I'm going to fuck some sense into you." His eyes are full of lust—and what should scare me, only turns me on more. I've never felt this wanton. In one movement, he picks me up and throws me over his shoulder. He smacks my bare ass, hard, and throws me on the bed. My body succumbs to his demands, and I'm now thrusting my hips up, wanting him... *more*. He removes his jeans and, in one leap, he's on me, pinning me down.

"Tell me who's in this room," he groans, pushing his hard erection between my legs.

"Me and you," I breathe out.

"That's right. Tell me your name," he says, sucking my neck.

"Julia," I pant out.

"Julia. Julia. Julia," he repeats over and over. My mouth and neck are tortured with his hard kisses. "What's my name... *Julia*?"

"Jonas," I cry out. "Jonas, please I want you. Now," I beg. "Please." His cock still teases my wet entrance. "You want it, too." My justification is breathy, and seductive.

"I only want you. I never want to hear the name *Eve*, or *Jenna*, or any other name again. Do you hear me... *Julia*?"

"Yes, Jonas. Please. I want you."

"Who? Who do you want... *Julia*?"

"You. You, Jonas." My words are begging, yet demanding.

"Who am I going to make love to right now?" he asks, looking deep in my eyes. "Look me in the eyes, and tell me. Who am I going to *fuck* on this bed?"

"Me. Julia," I say in a rush.

"Yes," he says, and pushes deep inside me. "Ah... fuck. Yes, *Julia*."

23

WE LIE MOTIONLESS, CLEAVED TIGHTLY TO ONE ANOTHER. HIS HEART beats in my ear, evidence of his passion for me. *Our passion.* He's peaceful now. Gone is his ravenous hunger that intensifies with each lovemaking. With each thrust he gave, he repeated my name, over and over. The look in his eyes was almost deranged when he demanded I say his name. "Say my name, Julia. Who's inside you?" he said. And each time I cried out, "Jonas," the more punishing were his thrusts. My body has fully accepted him, giving me waves of shocking orgasms I thought not possible.

His slow breathing tells me he's asleep. Sidney knocks on the door, and he jumps from his dream.

"Are you guys done kissing? I want us all in the tree house," she says from behind the closed door. I quietly laugh and look up from his chest. He smiles, with sleepy eyes.

"We'll be there in a minute," I say. Jonas squeezes me tightly and pulls me up to meet his lips.

"I love you," he says, perhaps fearing his lovemaking was too rough. I stroke his cheek as a silent answer to his concern. He smiles. "Well, I guess I have a date in the tree house with my two beautiful girls." I kiss his lips, and we help each other up from the bed.

I open the door, and Sidney runs down the stairs, yelling. "Come on Daddy, and Julia! I have dinner ready for us in the tree house." Jonas mimics her excitement, picking me up, and running behind her. She giggles as he chases her to the tree. I hold tightly around his neck and bury my face in his chest. *I'm so happy.*

She reaches the tree and climbs the ladder, scaling it like a monkey. "Come on, guys. Our hot dogs are getting cold," she says.

Oh, no. Hot dogs, again? "Sidney, I told you not to use the stove without me."

"I didn't. I used the microwave," she says, as a matter of fact. I pop my head into the tree house and see a picnic blanket, set for three. She even has our names written on a small piece of paper beside each paper plate—Julia, Daddy, and Princess Sidney. *Bless her little heart.* I crawl in and make my way to my reserved spot on the tree house floor.

"I haven't had a good hot dog in years," Jonas says, popping his head in.

"Come on, Daddy. I have yours right here," she says, playing the proud hostess. Jonas folds his long body, and sits, cramped, in an Indian position on the floor next to me.

"This looks really tasty, Sidney. I can't wait to eat it," he says. She sits in between us, and then tells us we may now start eating. All three of us pick up our hot dogs, and bite into them. "Mmm, very good, Sidney."

"Thank you, Daddy."

We sit, eating our hot dogs, and I couldn't be happier than I am right now. Not even Paris could bring me this much happiness. I haven't thought about going to Paris since the first night we made love. This is where I belong—right here with this man, and this little girl. This is my family. *Our little family.*

"How'd the girls' shopping trip go? Did you make your new friend happy?"

I cringe, thinking about what I might have told her. What she might try to dig up without my knowledge. "Yes, we did. She wanted me to thank you."

"Daddy, can you come to my swim lessons tomorrow?" Sidney asks, stuffing the last of her hot dog into her mouth.

"I have some calls and reports to get caught up on. But I will try, sweetie."

My heart bursts as I regard into the most beautiful, blue eyes I've ever seen. I lean over, and kiss him on the cheek.

"I'm so proud of you, Jonas," I say. "You have become such a good father." The expression in his eyes is thankful, as if all he wants is my appreciation. And I must wonder—is it because of what he wrote to Eve? *He's a mistake, an awful human being,* were the words his wife used. This is why I *will* let go, in my heart, of the fact that he had an affair. He's perfect. *I love him.*

We stand, lean over the side, and look out onto the pasture. Holly walks up under the tree, and Sidney climbs down to pet her horse.

"Daddy, you want to ride Holly?"

"Maybe later, Baby." He wraps his arms around me. "Mmm, I love the smell of your hair," he says, burying his face in it. I lean my head back into his chest and wrap my arms around his. "I'm so happy, Julia. For once... I'm happy. I want to take you somewhere. Not right away... but when the time is right. I want everything to be perfect."

"Things seem perfect right now."

"Yes, things are. But... I'm working on something... and I'm not quite sure how it's going to turn out. I just want to be sure, before I take you there." I turn in his embrace, face him, and lace my fingers around his neck. He lowers his forehead onto mine, as we look into each other's eyes.

"I can wait, then. Even though the suspense will kill me, I will wait." He kisses me. "You know what makes me happy, Jonas?"

"I want to know everything that makes you happy."

"That *you* are happy. That's what makes me happy." His eyes fill with tears, so I lift myself onto the tips of my toes and place a soft kiss on his lips. "I love you, Jonas."

"I love how you're so demure, and yet so strong. How one minute you're hiding behind your braid, but your lack of inhibitions reveals your true desires. How you turn anger into passion. Passion for me." With his thumb, he lightly brushes across my cheek. "You've made me so happy, Julia. This," he says, cupping my face in his hands, "is all I've ever wanted." His eyes are now full of tears, and what this could only mean is that it is... *the truth.* "I love you, Julia... always know this. Even if... even if something happens," a tear drips down his cheek, "just know I love you." He kisses me, pulling me tightly in his arms. He buries his head in my hair and holds the back of my head. I hear a slight choke, low in his throat. He anticipates that something will destroy my love for him. But nothing can destroy what I feel for him. I could never be like his wife, and belittle him, saying he's a nothing. I will never give him a reason to run into the arms of another woman. I can't believe how, at first, I was so supportive of Jenna. Now, I understand his love for Eve. *Eve.*

⁓

I DROP SIDNEY OFF AT SWIM LESSONS, AND IT'S NO SURPRISE—ERIN IS NOT there. I look around at the joggers in the park, thinking I might see her. I worry that when we last talked, that day in the courthouse, our friendship may have become strained. She was so insistent on finding Jenna's grave. And I'm still not certain how much I told her. If I don't see her at the park today, I will stop and check on her after Sidney's lessons, and plan for another lunch sometime.

Jonas was all ready to come with us today, but then, at the last minute, got an emergency call. Though I don't know what about, it seems he was needed in Indianapolis at the last minute. When he walked outside on his cell phone, to take the call in private, I watched his hands cut through the air in anger. The only words I could make out were, "I told you never to call me here," and "I don't know if I'll be able to control myself if I show up." He was full of rage and anger. Gone was the soft, gentle way he showed me in the tree house. The tears in his eyes—which, at the time, I took as tears of joy. Now, maybe they're tears of something else. Something he hides deep inside.

"Truce." A hand holding a large Starbucks coffee cup waves in my face. I look up and find Erin, dressed in her running clothes, holding two coffees. I smile and feel a bit of relief it isn't me waving the white flag.

"Sure," I say, and take the coffee. "I was going to stop by after Sidney's lesson. I promise. I did feel bad about how I left last time..."

She puts up her hand to stop me. "No, please don't apologize. It was none of my business. I guess you can say *wine* has its way with me, also," she jokes. "I was hoping to find you here, or else I was going to have to drink both coffees." We toast to our "starting over" with the coffees, and then take a drink. "Hey, I have some great news," she says. "My soon-to-be-ex is bringing my daughter up for the day, and I would love for Sidney to meet her."

"Oh, I have a lot of errands to run today. I'm sorry we won't be able to stay." I feel badly, then suggest some other time, perhaps.

"Besides," I say, "maybe you and your daughter would like to be alone."

"Oh... that's too bad. Roman was really looking forward to meeting Sidney. Hey, what if I take Sidney home with me after her lesson, and you can pick her up after your errands?" she asks. Her eyes are pleading.

I look over at Sidney, not sure how she will feel about it. "Well, just let me talk to her for a minute. Make sure she is up to it. She hasn't been feeling well lately," I lie, just in case she flat out won't go.

A cell phone rings, and Erin pulls it from her armband. Before looking at the incoming call, she says, "He better not be changing his mind." Then her face shows concern. "Oh, this can't be good. It's one of my patients." She answers the call. "Dr. Kelly here. What's wrong?" "Now wait... calm down." Erin speaks slowly, calming whomever is on the other end. "Did he hit you?" She listens. "How long ago was he there?" She listens. "Did you call the police? Good. Now, please listen to me. I'm no longer at my Indy office, and Sasha is gone, so..."

I begin to walk away. Erin grabs my arm to stop me.

"I'm going to come there, and we can talk," she says to the caller. "Give me your address, and I will make the trip, okay?" Erin waves her hands in the air. "I need a piece of paper and a pen," she says to me. I open my purse and rummage through until I find a small piece of paper. It's one of the receipts from our girls' shopping day, which I totally forgot to enter in Jonas's spreadsheet. I make a mental note of the amount, and where we shopped, and feel for a pen. I nod my head, letting her know I'm ready to write down the address.

"Okay, I'm ready," Erin says to her patient. "Tell me the address." Erin repeats it, and I write it down. 14615 Benfer Road, Indianapolis.

"Okay. I have it. Now listen to me," she says in a professional tone. "I'm going to be there first thing in the morning. Make sure you call the police if he threatens you again. Okay?" She listens, and then ends the call.

"I'm sorry, I didn't mean to listen in," I say.

"Don't worry about it. She's been a patient of mine for a long time. She is so fragile, and I hate to make her see another therapist. I shouldn't be telling you this, but since I won't reveal her name, let me tell you what she's been through. Her husband is a total control freak. He has her so beat down, she's afraid to do anything, right down to starting the dishwasher. He tells her she's incapable of starting it the correct way. Can you believe that?" she asks. "I mean, it's a damn dishwasher."

"Why doesn't she leave him?" I ask.

"Oh, believe me, she's tried. But he controls every aspect of her life. Even how she walks through a doorway."

"What? You've got to be kidding me."

"Nope. I noticed it the first time she came into my office. I thought maybe she had a problem with depth perception. She would always step wide over the threshold. When I asked her about it, she said her husband beat her up once for stepping on it."

"Oh, my God. That's awful."

"She believes now he has another woman."

"You'd think she be glad."

"Yes, except he will not give her up. It's like he gets off on controlling everything about her—what she eats, where she goes, and whom she's allowed to see. It has nearly ruined her. She once was finally brave enough to leave him, but then he took their daughter away and said she would never see her daughter again if she didn't come back to him."

"But he can't do that. She has rights, too."

"You don't understand. He's rich, and is looked upon highly in his community. No one will cross him. She would be out—with nothing. I guess I should be thankful that he pays for her counseling sessions. Of course, he thinks she's crazy. Like I'm doing *him* a favor."

"That's so sad," I say.

"Yes, it is. But that's tomorrow's worry. What about today?" she asks, getting back to the subject of Sidney going home with her.

"Yes, just let me go and get her." I begin to walk away, then remember the address on the back of the receipt. "Let me transfer this onto another piece of paper. I need to enter this transaction into the books." I pull another piece of paper out and transfer the address. "Here. I'll go get Sidney."

Sidney is shivering, and I wrap her in a towel. I describe the play date with Roman and tell her I will be back to pick her up. Not surprisingly, she isn't too eager to go. I then tell her maybe Roman could come to our house next time and ride Holly with her. And also, have hot dogs in the tree house. So, she agrees.

I kiss Sidney and tell her to be good.

"We're going to have so much fun, Sidney," Erin says. "Roman can't wait to meet you." She takes Erin's hand, and I watch as they walk out of the park, toward the sidewalk leading to Erin's house. I grab my purse, along with Sidney's swim bag and walk to my mini.

I check my shopping list, and mentally map my route. I flip my turn signal, showing I'm about to exit the curb, but then a crow lands on my windshield, and I jump. *What the hell is it with these crows?* It caws, flapping its wings at me. I honk the horn, scaring it away. "Damn crow."

Now on the road, I make my way through the city, and pick up speed once I merge onto the freeway. It's rush hour, and traffic is heavy. Pushing down on the gas pedal, I accelerate smoothly and keep up. I know my exit is coming up and make my way to the right lane, weaving in and out of traffic, not having to brake. Finally, when my exit arrives, I speed up, and signal to the car in front of me. It moves over and lets me pass. I hit the brakes to merge, but my car does not slow down. The brake pedal is completely to the floor, and my car still speeds up the ramp. I hit the brakes hard again, but nothing happens. They're gone. I have no brakes. The car starts to tip as I round the ramp. I hit the guardrail, which only bounces me back upright, and the car spins out of control. My hands have a death grip on the steering wheel, and I am preparing myself for a crash, when the car drives off the ramp, and down the hill into the median. The car flips upside down, and the last thing I remember is the airbags going off.

Black.

24

EVERYTHING IS WHITE. I'M IN A FOG. I HEAR THE SOUND OF A BABBLING brook that runs nearby. The air smells fresh. I feel so peaceful. The fog clears, and I'm standing in a field of beautiful sunflowers. I have the impression they are looking at me—and, if possible, they are singing. The sound of a child humming is close to me.

"Do you like it?" There, holding my hand, is a small child—a little girl. Her hair is golden, and she looks very familiar, but I can't place her. She waves her arm across the field, and it opens into a forest. The sunflowers turn their heads, and look to the trees. The child looks up at me and smiles. "Come on," she says. "It's okay."

"What is this place?"

"It's no place. Come on, someone wants to meet you." She leads me into the forest, holding my hand. Beams of shimmering sunlight cascade through the trees. Birds sing, harmonizing their songs with each other's. Her little hand feels so perfect in mine. All I feel is love.

She leads me to a small creek. This must have been where I heard the water rushing. It's so clear, and you can see the multicolored pebbles that line the bottom of the creek. Small, golden fish swim effortlessly up the stream. A raccoon walks up beside us and takes a drink from the creek, using his hands. She bends down to pet it.

"Oh, be careful," I tell her.

"It's okay. He loves us." *Is this normal?* "He says he wants you to pet him, too."

"He talks to you?" She nods. I kneel down next to her, and pet the small animal. He sits up on his hind legs, grasps my hand between his front paws, and licks it.

"He's kissing you," she says, so sweetly. I smile at her, and then at the raccoon. The creature scoops up another handful of water, and then scurries back into the forest.

"Who wants to meet me? Where are they?" I ask. She points across the stream. I look into the lighted forest—however, I see no one. She takes my hand and steps into the water.

"Wait, I have to take my shoes off," I tell her. She giggles.

"You don't have any shoes, because you don't need them." Although her voice is that of a child, it makes me trust her. I look at my feet. They *are* bare. I'm clothed in a white dress—the same as hers. "Come on," she says, taking my hand again.

We walk across in the stream, yet the water doesn't feel cold. It feels like I am walking on air. The pebbles don't even hurt the bottoms of my feet.

Once we've traveled to the other side, we climb a gentle hill that is filled with daisies, and other wild flowers. I can smell each one individually. The scent fills my nostrils, and lightens my soul with a feeling of bliss.

"This place is beautiful."

"We made it for you," she says.

"Who is we?"

"My brother and me."

"Your brother?" She nods, and points straight ahead. She walks in the direction she pointed, and I follow. We pass a few trees, and then she stops. She looks up at me.

"He's behind that tree," she says, pointing. "Go ahead. He's waiting for you." I look at her and then back at the tree. The forest floor is carpeted with light-green moss. As I walk on the moss, its softness feels heavenly under my feet.

Now at the tree, I reach out and lightly touch its bark. It feels smooth—varnished. Leaving my hands on the trunk, I crane my neck around the other side. My eyes scan the area, but I don't see a little boy.

"Do you see him?" she calls to me.

"No. No, I don't."

"Rah!" I'm startled, and jump, when a little boy grabs me from behind. He laughs, and so does the little girl. Their laughter is full of childhood memories—playful, innocent. Memories I feel, yet don't know why.

"Come on," the little boy says. He runs into the forest, and—as if I've done this a million times—I chase after him. And it's only when I've almost caught up with him, that I realize I have been laughing. We are playing a game of chase, and the little girl runs behind me, humming a childish tune. I feel like a child myself.

The little boy disappears, and we are left looking for him again.

"Where'd he go?" I ask the girl. She covers her mouth, giggling.

"Here I am." He walks from behind a tree—and for the first time, I really see him. His tan, little body is shirtless, and his skin is as smooth as a peach. He is so beautiful—and so familiar, it's eerie. Yet, I feel very close to him. His dark hair is sun-kissed, with gold high-lights. And his eyes... something about his eyes makes me reach out to touch him. He walks up, and I touch his face. I look deep into them—blue, with a hazel ring around the irises. I've seen these eyes before.

"Hello," I say. "It's nice to meet you." He smiles, and my heart melts. The little girl walks over to him, and he takes her hand. "What are your names?"

"We don't have any names," he says.

"What? Why don't you have names?" My legs start to hurt, and suddenly I fall on my knees. The green moss is no longer there. Instead, I'm kneeling on broken glass. There are cuts on my legs. I look at the children, but they are fading into the distance, down a tunnel. I hear the little boy yell out, "You haven't named us yet."

"She's breathing. I have a pulse." Voices, and a loud ringing, echo through the forest. The children, and the flowers, fade with each flash of bright light that stabs my eyes. I'm in so much pain. I reach for the little boy and girl, but they are gone.

"Please... help me," I cry out, but my voice doesn't make a sound. My head pounds, and something wet runs in my eyes. I open my mouth to speak again, but this time, only blood runs out.

"Somebody get me some suction over here. She's choking on her own blood." I feel something shoved in my mouth, and a suction starts. With the next cough, I take in a deep breath and open my eyes. I'm upside down, trapped in my car, and my feet are walking about in the air, with a sense of urgency. My head spins, and I pass out.

❧

Faint beeps sound in my ears, and something warm holds my arm. I open my eyes and find Erin's frightened face peering down at mine. Her eyes are red, and swollen. She sees my eyes open, and relief washes over her face.

"Oh, thank God, Julia," she says, and kisses my hand.

"Where am I?"

"You're at Lutheran Hospital. You were in a car accident," she says, smoothing my hair. "You had us so scared."

"Sidney? Where's Sidney?" I manage to say.

"She's fine—she's right outside. She's waiting for you to wake up. You want me to go get her?" She pats me on the arm, and leaves the room. When she returns, Sidney—along with a doctor—are with her. Sidney's eyes are red from crying, and the scared look on her face breaks my heart. She lays her head on my arm and begins to cry.

"Julia, I was so scared you left me," she sobs. She is so afraid of abandonment again—the loss of another mother.

"Oh. Thank God, Sidney, you weren't with me," I say, and stroke her hair. Erin holds her shoulders from behind.

"Hi, Julia. I'm Dr. Coulter. I was the ER surgeon when you were brought in. You're very lucky. No internal injuries," he says. I try to sit up, and wince. "You're going to be sore for a while. You have many lacerations to your arms, legs, and scalp. But other than that, you're going to be just fine." He smiles and pats my feet under the blanket.

"Oh, that's great," Erin says, and rubs my shoulder. I reach for my head, hoping I still have all my hair.

"The cuts to your scalp were minimal. Just a few stitches in the back. We didn't have to shave your head," he laughs, as if *that* would have been the main tragedy. "I've ordered an antibiotic drip for a day, and then I will give you a prescription when you are released tomorrow. Unless you feel you are unable to go home, I see no reason to keep you here. Any questions, Julia?"

"What exactly happened? Where's my car? And my purse, and belongings?"

"I have them right here, Julia," Erin says. "Your car is totaled. Oh, God, it was so awful."

"I'll be back to check on you when I end my rounds tonight. You will be in good hands with our nurses. Take care, now," he says, patting my legs under the blankets again. The moment he leaves, Erin starts talking again.

"We had just gotten back to the house when I turned on the TV and saw the accident live on channel 4 news. You don't know how scared we were when we saw your little car, smashed and upside down. God, Julia... just to see it. I mean..."

She starts to cry and holds my hand.

"Thank you for being here, Erin," I say.

"We came right to the hospital."

"Where's your daughter?" I ask, remembering Roman was having a playdate with Sidney.

"After I saw you on that highway... *wrecked*, I called my husband and told him there was an emergency. We'll reschedule."

"Oh, Erin. I'm so sorry. I feel awful."

"No, Julia. It's not your fault. Here, I was able to get your purse when the ambulance brought you in. I hope you don't mind—I kind of had to lie and say I was a close relative in order to get it back for you."

"Thank you, Erin," I say, feeling grateful for our friendship. I'm so glad she came to me today.

"Tomorrow, when you are released, I'm taking you to my house, until you are better. You're going to need help with Sidney," she says, and I thank her repeatedly.

"I need to call Jonas," I say, and try to reach for my purse. She pulls out my cell, and hands it to me.

"Tell him there's no need to come home. I'll take good care of you," she says.

"How do you know he's not home?"

She looks mortified. "Well, I don't. I just assumed he was away on business. You said he traveled a lot."

"Yes, I did. Well, I need to call him. At least let him know what happened, and that his daughter is okay."

"Of course. I'm going to take Sidney down to the cafeteria now, to get her something to eat. Can I get you anything?"

"No, thank you. Thanks again, Erin."

"No problem. We'll be back," she says, and takes Sidney out of the room.

I open my phone, and see several missed calls from Jonas.

"Hello? Julia, why haven't you returned any of my calls?" He sounds annoyed.

"I'm sorry, Jonas. I've been in a car accident."

"What! What happened? Where are you?" I now hear panic in his voice.

"Sidney's okay. She wasn't with me, thank God. I wrecked my car on the freeway. It's totaled, Jonas. But I'm okay. The doctor says I can go home tomorrow."

"What hospital are you in? I'll be there as soon as I can. I'm leaving right now."

"No, Jonas. Erin's here. She has Sidney, and will be taking me to her place tomorrow."

"Don't be absurd, Julia. I'm on my way. Now—what hospital?"

"Lutheran."

"I'll be there in less than three hours." I think he has ended the call. But then, I hear him say, "I love you, Julia."

"I love you too, Jonas. Thank you."

～

Erin stays with me most of the night. I tell her Jonas is on his way. Being such a good friend, she takes Sidney home with her, and tells me to get some rest. She says it would be a good idea if Sidney stays with her, in case Jonas has to leave town again, and that maybe we would like some alone time. I can tell she is feeling a bit remorseful over the whole situation. The heated conversation at the courthouse, her warning me about men—and, of course, the car accident. I feel she is overly trying to win back my affection. But she is truly a great friend, and I feel blessed to have met her.

I wake up a few hours later, and find Jonas asleep in the chair next to my bed. He's wearing the same clothes from the day before. He must have come straight here from Indy. His face is unshaven, but he looks just as handsome as if he were clean-shaven, and wearing a suit. I watch him for a bit, wanting to crawl onto his lap, and kiss his lips. He opens his eyes, and his smile warms my heart. *How does he do that?*

"Good morning, Beautiful," he whispers, like it's my name. My throat is dry, and I lick my lips before speaking.

"Hey," I say. "When did you get here?" My lips feel like sandpaper, and my voice cracks.

"It was late, maybe eleven o'clock. You were sleeping, and I didn't want to disturb you. You looked so peaceful. How are you feeling?"

"Like I'm ready to run a marathon," I joke, and roll my eyes. "God, I must look a mess."

"A beautiful mess," he says, and comes to sit beside me on the bed. He kisses my forehead, and I'm glad it's not on the lips. I'm sure I have dragon breath. "I listened to you dream last night. You were talking in your sleep." He takes my hand and presses a kiss to each fingertip.

"What was I talking about? I don't remember. Must have been the drugs they gave me."

"It sounded like you were playing with children. You sounded child-like yourself," he says. I then remember the little girl in the sunflower field, and her brother in the forest. It was so real. How my heart ached when I had to go away. I dreamed of them again.

"Something happened right after my car crashed on the freeway. I... went somewhere, because I have no memory of being in the car." He brushes my hair away from my face and kisses my cheek.

"You passed out. Of course, you don't remember. It's a way to protect you from the shock."

"Maybe. But it was so real. I was in a field, surrounded by sunflowers... and there was this little girl there. She knew me—and for some reason, I feel I know her, too. She wanted to take me into the forest to meet her brother."

"I was right," he says. "You were dreaming of children. Maybe you had Sidney on your mind when you fell sleep."

"Perhaps," I say. "But she wasn't in the sunflower field. This... brother and sister... they wanted me to be there—and somehow, they knew me. We played in the woods, chasing each other. It was so beautiful, and so peaceful. I didn't want to leave." He leans his head into mine, and I gaze out the window, thinking about the brother and sister. Who were they?

"Well, I'm glad you came back. I don't know what I would do if I lost you, Julia. I love you." I turn and look into his eyes. They are filled with genuine tears. "Can you tell me what you remember about the accident? Before you crashed?"

"I tried to slow down to exit the freeway, but the brakes wouldn't work. I pushed the pedal all the way to the floor. I remember hitting the guardrail, and spinning. After that... nothing."

He rubs his face. "Oh, God." He runs his hands roughly through his hair, and then stands, placing his hands on his hips. He looks angry, yet also concerned. "Julia, I'm going to have your car checked out. In the meantime, I'm not letting you out of my sight."

"Jonas, there's no reason to check the car. It's totaled. The brakes just quit working."

"Yes, but why? Where was your car before this happened?"

"At the park. I was with Sidney—we were at the pool, for her lessons. Why?" I watch his expression, which has become troubled. I'm about to ask what he is thinking, when Dr. Coulter walks in.

"Good morning, Julia. How are you feeling today?" He holds a clip-boards and searches through the papers attached.

"Better, but still a little sore." He sets the clipboard down on the bedside table and puts his stethoscope in his ears.

"Take a deep breath and let it out slowly," he says, listening to my lungs. "Your lungs are clear. I think you will make a full recovery." He removes the stethoscope and picks the clipboard back up. "I'm signing your release and writing a script for rifampin. Make sure you take these antibiotics as prescribed. Some of your lacerations were pretty deep. I don't want an infection setting in," he says, gives me the prescription slip, and puts the pen back into the pocket of his white lab coat. "You are free to go. I also want you to follow up with your GP in a week. Okay? Any questions?"

"Doctor, is it okay if she travels?" Jonas asks. "I'm Jonas Fairbanks, Julia's boyfriend."

Dr. Coulter shakes his head. "She should be fine. I wouldn't be doing any swimming or rock climbing, if your holiday consists of those things. But yes, she is free to travel in a comfortable environment."

"Thank you, Doctor," Jonas says.

He's taking me somewhere?

∽

JONAS DRIVES WITH THE CARE OF A SUNDAY DRIVER. NEVER HITTING THE brakes too hard or speeding up too fast. The drive home is taking much longer than it needs to. He's being overly cautious—to the point that other drivers are becoming irritated. One man even flipped us off when he passed us.

We pull up the horseshoe drive, and Jonas tells me to remain in the car as he walks around to help me out. When I get out of the car, he lifts me into his arms. "Jonas, I can still walk," I say, laughing at his overly caring self.

"Maybe I just like to hold you." We kiss, and he carries me to the door. Once the door is open, I'm expecting him to put me down. He doesn't, and carries me across the threshold... with one wide step. "That is how you walk through a door," he says. "Never step on the threshold.

I look at him sharply. "Why? Because it's bad luck?" I ask, remembering Erin's patient, whose husband told her never to step on the threshold.

"No. Because it's damaging to the frame of the door."

He still has me in his arms, and I stare at him. "You're kidding... right?"

"No. I'm not. It's one of my pet peeves." I wonder now how many times he's watched me walk on it. I blink several times, while staring at his face. *He's completely serious.* I shake my head, deciding this must be a more popular subject than I thought.

"Well, then, thanks for informing me."

"No problem." He sets me down, gently. "Why don't you go rest, while I take a shower? I don't want you doing anything today." He pulls off his shirt and begins walking up the stairs. "Don't worry about the dishes in the sink," he adds, when he's halfway up.

Sidney and I were running late yesterday, and I left the breakfast dishes in the sink. I was planning to wash them when we returned.

"I'll put them in the dishwasher. I know the proper way to start it." He's at the top of the stairs now, and it's a good thing he can't see my face, because I'm sure I look like I've seen a ghost.

"The proper way?" I call up the stairs. He leans over the banister.

"You have to set the dial to the proper setting before closing the door." I stare at him in disbelief, and he looks back at me, with concern. "Are you okay? You look... a bit lost."

"Uh... yeah. I just remembered something I need to do," I say, and turn toward the kitchen.

"Don't touch the dishwasher," he says, walking away from the banister.

This is all too uncanny. Setting my purse on the counter, I pull out the bottle of rifampin, grab a glass of water and take one. I pull out the paperwork from the hospital, and come across the receipts I have not yet entered into the spreadsheets. *I better get this done.* Who knows what obsessive-compulsive disorders he has on this matter?

I walk to the study and sit in front of the computer. When I type in his saved password, BonhomeR, it opens. I see two documents for household expenses, and wonder which one is the correct sheet. Clicking on one, I read the title at the top of the page: 5952 Oak Rd. Ft. Wayne. Assuming I have the correct document, I enter all the receipts for the things I bought for Erin's place. The numbers update themselves automatically, and I close the document. Curious as to what the second file of household expenses is for, I open and read the title at the top: 14615 Benfer Rd., Indianapolis. *Why does that address sound so familiar?* It shouldn't mean anything to me, but something about it does. I click my tongue a few times, pondering why this would be, then have an epiphany. I grab the receipts and turn them over. I find the one that I wrote the address on for Erin. 14615 Benfer Rd. Indianapolis.

This can't be. There has to be some explanation. I close the file, send a copy to my email, and then log out of the computer.

25

I OPEN THE DOOR TO LEAVE THE STUDY AND BUMP RIGHT INTO JONAS. "I thought you were taking a shower." My voice is a little shaky. He seems to notice my sudden change in behavior.

"I'm starting us a bath. I want to lie next to you, naked. I promise to be gentle, and wash you with tenderness." His eyes are full of love, and I try to match his look. If I don't, I'm afraid he will sense that something is wrong. *Is something wrong?* Why is it, *every* time I'm ready to let go of this mystery and relax in his love, a new mystery is unearthed, shadowing my feelings?

"Oh?" I ask. His eyes narrow in disapproval. I should have responded with, "Oh!" in a breathy tone, full of excitement. I sound... guilty.

"You're not feeling up to it? I wasn't hinting at sex, if that's what you thought. I just want to hold you, protect you, and know you are here." His hand strokes my hair, and puts strands behind my ear. He places a gentle kiss on my forehead.

"No... that's not what I thought. You just startled me, that's all." This time, my tone is contrite. "I'll be right there. I just need to get something from my room. Then I'll meet you in the bath." I stand on my tiptoes and kiss him on the lips.

"Okay. I see the accident has really upset you. I just want to wrap you in my arms and make it all go away. Ease your mind." He takes my hands and kisses the tips of my fingers. "Ease your pain. I love you, Julia."

"I love you too, Jonas," I say, placing both hands on his cheeks. "I'll be right back." I pass by him, and walk up the back stairs to my room.

I take out the receipt with the address written on it, and type it into Google maps on my phone, just in case I lose it. *But am I really going to go there?* How would I even manage that with Sidney? I need Erin to tell me the name of her patient who lives at this address. What are Jonas's ties to this address? I look to the closet and feel an impulse to read the next letter. *NO!* I said I was done. I have a beautiful, loving man waiting for me. A man who wants to worship me. What am I afraid of? The truth? I shake my head, and walk into the closet.

My Eve,

Where do I begin? What should be bringing us closer together, is tearing us apart. I painted our daughter's room, pink and lavender, yet you had no interest. Inside you, my precious daughter grows. Her little hands and feet move against your belly, and I want nothing more than to feel her. But you have changed, Eve. You need me one day, and the next... you loathe me. Why? Every scathing word from your mouth hurts me, and I know it hurts our daughter. You tell me I will never see my daughter. You lie to everyone about who her father is, and I know it's only to protect me, but I don't care anymore. I will have you and our daughter. If you continue with these threats, I will find a way to take my daughter away from you. Don't make me do this, Eve. My daughter.

Jx

This letter exposes a new aspect of their relationship. What happened? What did Eve do? This whole time, I've envied the love he had for her. Now, I feel almost... heartbroken there is trouble in paradise. I should be *gloating*. But why am I not? Is this baby Sidney, who Jonas has taken her from her mother? Is this when Jenna left him, after learning he has a child with another woman? Then she was... *killed*.

I'm ready to close this case—I have enough evidence. This last letter solves the mystery. But then I look at the address logged in my phone, and remember Jonas's plea. How's there's something he's protecting Sidney and I from. Something, he can't tell me. But what he thinks I don't know... I do.

He is lying on the bed when I walk into his room. I can smell the steam from the bath, with its lavender scent. He's still in his jeans, shirtless, and waiting for me. "Hey, Pretty Girl," he says, with light in his eyes. I'm about to turn that light out.

"Who is Sidney's mother?" My own voice shocks me.

"What do you mean? I told you, her name was Jenna." He gets up from the bed, placing his hands on his hips, defensively.

"Who lives in Indianapolis? You seem to go there... a lot."

"Julia, I don't want to have this discussion. You have been in a bad accident, and it's not good for you to get all upset."

"What makes you think I'm upset?" I ask. He smiles smugly, shakes his head, and then looks to the floor. "I can't believe this," he says. "All I want to do is be with you. We've had this discussion before. Do I need to fuck some sense into you?"

"Stop it! Stop saying that. Stop thinking all you have to do is shove your dick in me... and my mind goes senseless." *And it does.* "Because that's what you do, Jonas."

"I don't know what, or who, has told you shit, making you think I'm hiding something from you," he says through gritted teeth.

"You!" I scream. "You told me you were hiding something from me. Are you going to deny it?"

"That's not what I said," he hisses. "I said I was protecting you... and Sidney. There's a difference."

"How can I protect myself and Sidney, if I don't know what is trying to hurt us?"

"I am here to protect you and Sidney!" he yells.

"But you're not always here," I argue. "Where do you go?"

"You know I have to travel, Julia. That is why I need a nanny. Don't start accusing me of something other than making a living."

"Who. Lives. In. Indianapolis?" I stress each word.

"Lots of people live there, Julia." His mocking tone only infuriates me.

"Who do *you* know in Indianapolis?"

He lifts his hands in the air, bringing them down hard, with a slap to his thighs. "I have a lot of business contacts in Indy. Shall I pull up my contacts for you? Will that make you happy?"

I walk into his room a little farther. Standing tall, I fold my arms across my chest, and I say, "14615 Benfer Road. *That* should narrow it down."

His smile is insulting. "You're crazy. You know that? I think you hit your head a little too hard in that accident."

"Who?"

"Stop it, Julia. Just stop it, now."

"Are you denying you know this address? Because I saw it in your computer."

"What? Are you snooping around? Does having suspicions excite you?" His eyes have a glassy, crazed look in them. It's frightening.

"You gave me access, to enter expenses. Why do you have house-hold expenses at this address?"

"Julia, I have many properties. It's business." I want to scream, and tell him about Erin's patient, but that will only get her in trouble, and I don't want to ruin our friendship.

"What business is it, that you have to pay for the mortgage, cable, internet, and groceries? That doesn't sound like a business, Jonas. That sounds like a home. What are you hiding?"

In a fit of rage, he pounds his fist against the wall. A picture of Sidney that I hung falls to the floor, breaking the glass into a million pieces.

"I have nothing to hide!" he yells. I move back against the wall, now fearful of him. He slams his fist again, knocking over the porcelain lamp from the nightstand. "All I've done is protect that little girl. I'm guilty of protecting, and it has cost me the last ten years of my life." His voice is now sorrowful. He drops to his knees with painful, choking sobs. "You have no idea what I've been through," he says, dropping his face into his hands. I remain glued to the wall, speechless. "Oh, God, I just want to move on," he says, with more choking sobs. "I just want a simple life with someone."

I start to cry, and feel the need to hold him. He's so tortured, and I don't know why. Gone is the man I thought was *invincible*. Now, rocking back and forth on his knees and crying, he looks like a lost, broken child. I feel horrible. *What have I done?* This man has showed me nothing but love and compassion. He has changed himself for me and Sidney, and I have broken him. He has looked to me for guidance of how to be a loving father, and has showed he truly desires this. He has transformed for me... and I now have shattered him, just like the broken glass he's sitting in. *What have I done? What has he been through?*

"Oh. Jonas, I'm so sorry." Quickly, I go to his side, and take him in my arms, holding him tightly. He's trembling. "I'm so sorry I hurt you. You've have done so much for me and Sidney, and I have hurt you. Please forgive me, Jonas." I take his hands, pulling them away from his face. They are covered in blood. Glass is embedded in his hands, and a long gash on the side of his palm bleeds heavily. It must have come from the lamp. "Jonas, you're bleeding. I need to take care of this."

He continues rocking back and forth, and I'm not sure if he's even aware of me. "Jonas, look at me. Please, Jonas. I'm so sorry." My words catch in my throat. "Jonas, please look at me. I love you." He's not acknowledging me. I'm more scared than ever for us. "Jonas... I need you," I say, crying, and kiss him hard on the lips. I smell the metallic scent of blood, which is smeared on both our faces. The broken glass crunches under our knees. "Please. Jonas, I need you," I say.

He finally breaks from his fugue state, slowly coming out of the dark abyss. He looks me cautiously in the eyes—it's the look of a beaten dog that is begging not to be hit again. I kiss him tenderly on the lips. I taste his blood on my tongue. *His spilled blood.*

"Julia?" My name sounds foreign on his lips.

"Jonas. Are you with me?" I ask, fearing his mind is somewhere else.

"I need you, too, Julia." Relief overwhelms my entire being, and I kiss him, holding him tight. He responds, placing his hands on my face, and kissing me hard. The blood is in my hair, and our faces are covered with it.

"Come on, Jonas, let's get in the bath. I need to tend to your cuts." I stand, and help him like a child, leading him to the bathtub. I undo his jeans, pulling them down, and tap his ankle to lift his foot. Once his jeans are off, I move up his body slowly—touching his belly, and gliding my hands up his torso, to his chest. He takes my hands, and brings them to his mouth, kissing my palms.

"Come on, Jonas," I whisper, slipping off my clothes. I step into the bath first, and he follows. Before sitting down, we stand in the tub, and hold each other. The rage has exhausted us. The accident, my demand for answers, the details of his past—all have left like a bad storm, and cleaning up, and moving forward, are all that matter now. The past no longer exists, nor does the future. There is only now, right here in this moment, with each other.

I start to sit, pulling him down with me. He follows my lead, and his eyes show remorse and longing. He is in so much pain, and I have no idea if it's for what just occurred in the bedroom... or if it's what the past has done to him. But that dark past is over now, and all he wants to do is begin again. And all I do is keep bringing it up. I must stop. I *will* stop.

He leans his back against the tub, and I straddle his lap. "Close your eyes," I say. He closes his eyes, and I lift water to his face with my hands. Then, I splash my own face. The blood turns the bath water a light pink. I take his hand that has the gash and gently wipe it clean. The cut is not too deep, and I don't think it will need stitches, but I will need to use a butterfly bandage on it.

I arch my back, and dunk my head in the water, to clean away the blood. Holding my breath, I submerge completely under. The warm water rushes into my ears, and I hear the muffled sound of the faucet dripping. I remain there for a second longer, and when I rise out of the water, I open my eyes to his beautiful, blue irises, adoring me. "Hey." I take his face in my hands, and kiss him on the lips.

"Please don't be afraid to love me, Julia," he says, seeming fearful.

"I don't fear loving you, Jonas. I realize that all this time, I feared losing you. Losing you to... something I can't even name. But, I will no longer do that to us, Jonas. The phrase "Do not be afraid" is written in the bible 365 times. That's a daily reminder, from God, to live every day being fearless. I love you, Jonas."

"I want to take you somewhere," he says. "I was going to wait—but after your accident, I realized how precious you are to me, and how I could have lost you. I can't lose you, Julia. Sidney and I need you."

"Oh, Jonas."

"Tomorrow. Tomorrow we will jump on a plane and fly to Maine. There's something I want to show you."

"Maine? Where the condos are going to be built?" He pulls me close, wrapping me in his arms.

"Yes... where the condos are going to be built," he whispers. He kisses me gently at the center of my throat and then lays his head on my breasts. "I love you... Julia."

26

"First-class passengers flying nonstop to Bar Harbor, Maine, flight 437—we have started boarding. Please have your boarding passes ready." I feel butterflies in my stomach as I look at the man standing across from me, talking on his cell. He is cancelling all plans with his business partner for this week, and taking me on a romantic getaway. When I told Erin about the trip, she offered to watch Sidney. I half-expected her to be a bit hesitant about me flying off with Jonas. But I think having Sidney helps her with her loneliness. I hope her daughter, Roman, will come over, so Sidney will have a playmate. Leaving Sidney like this makes me feel guilty. *It's just a few days*, I tell myself.

Jonas ends his call, sliding his phone into the pocket of his sports coat. "You ready?" His smile is full of excitement.

"Yes," I say, and take his hand. He has booked us first class, and we slide our phones across the scanner at the gate, and walk hand-in-hand down the ramp. He offers me the window seat, and I slide in. He shoves our carry-ons into the overhead compartment before sitting and then takes my hand. He senses my nervousness.

"Are you still worried about going away and leaving Sidney?" he asks.

"I do feel badly for leaving her. She didn't sound very happy, either, when I told her we would be back soon. She also worries about her horse."

"Sidney will be fine, I promise. Besides, your friend Erin owes you for helping her out. Gus will take care of Holly. That's what I pay him for."

"I have another confession to make," I say, leaning into his arm. "I've never flown before." I look up, making a cheesy, overly-scared face, clenching my teeth tightly.

He wraps his arm around me, and holds me tightly. "Well, then, this will be even more exciting. Two surprises for you." He kisses my lips and gives me a quick squeeze.

"Well, good morning, Mr. Fairbanks." We look up at the person that is greeting only *Mr. Fairbanks*. A blonde, attractive woman, dressed as the flight attendant, smiles at us... at *him*. "Are you on business, or pleasure?" She asks, looking at me when the word "pleasure" comes out of the side of her mouth, as if she is giving some sort of inside signal. Clearly, she can see we are a couple. Why is she so familiar with him? *Why am I so possessive of him?*

"Good morning, Electra," Jonas greets her. *Electra*? Sounds like a stripper's name. "This is Julia. This trip is both. Business and pleasure," he says, giving me another quick squeeze. She smiles at me, and then her eyes slide back to Jonas. If it's possible to have sex with your eyes, she is doing it. She might as well take off her clothes, sit on his lap and say, "If there's anything I can do to make your flight more pleasurable, please let me assist you."

"Your friend looks a little nervous. May I offer her something calming?" she asks. Why are you asking him? Why don't you ask me, *Electra!*

"Thanks, Electra. How about two screwdrivers? Double."

"My pleasure, Mr. Fairbanks," she coos. Stop calling him *Mr. Fairbanks,* and stop calling her *Electra,* my insides scream. I think my period is on its way. Her green eyes are peering at me with envy.

She returns with two screwdrivers, and hands them to us with napkins. "On the house, as always, Mr. Fairbanks," she says again in her dripping-with-sex voice.

"Thank you," he tells her, and hands one to me.

"Just let me know if you need anything else. We'll be taking off shortly," she says, patting him on the shoulder, and then *finally* leaves.

"I didn't know you were a member of the mile-high club," I say, turning to look out the window while taking a sip of my cocktail. I cough. It's strong.

Jonas laughs. "Relax—she's harmless. She's just doing her job."

"Well, apparently, she only enjoys doing her *job* for men. I can talk, you know. She apparently thinks of me as a child, and treats me as such," I huff.

He smiles. "You're jealous."

"No, I'm not." *Lie.* "She was rude," I state, and take another sip of my *calming* drink.

"Jealousy equals—I care," he whispers in my ear. His hot breath rushes to my groin, and at the same time, the alcohol coats my empty stomach, causing a warming effect.

"Although, I hear she's fucking the pilot of this plane," he adds.

"Doesn't surprise me. And why would you know that?" I spit out.

"Good morning, passengers of flight 437. This is your captain speaking. I hope my wife, Electra, has you all comfortably seated, and ready for takeoff. We will be departing shortly. Our nonstop flight to Bar Harbor, Maine, will be approximately one hour and thirty minutes. I anticipate a smooth flight, with favorable weather conditions."

I smile and slap his arm.

～

A CAR IS WAITING AS WE STEP OUT OF THE AIRPORT. A MAN DRESSED IN A black suit and peaked cap welcomes us.

"Good afternoon, Mr. Fairbanks. I trust your flight was pleasurable?" he says, tipping his hat.

"Yes, Jack, as always." Jack takes the bags from Jonas and places them in the trunk. He then holds out his hand for me to shake.

"Hello, Ms. Ellis. It's a pleasure to meet you," he says.

I shake his hand and then look at Jonas.

"This is Jack," Jonas tells me. "One of my drivers, when I'm here on location. He was expecting us. I told him about you."

"Hi, Jack. It's nice to meet you, too. Thank you." Jack opens the door and gestures for me to climb in first. Jonas follows, and slides in next to me.

Maine is even more picturesque than I thought it would be. The little, seaside town we drive through looks old, with shanties near the water, and boats floating in the harbor. Seagulls herald our arrival from above. Colorful sailboats—blue, red, and yellow—float across the bay. Jonas rolls the window down, and I can smell the briny air as the breeze lifts my hair, flying it around. I sit up straight, with my hands on the back of the front seat, and gasp in amazement at its historical beauty.

"You like?" Jonas asks. His smile full of satisfaction, because he knows the joy he is giving me.

"Jonas, it's so beautiful. I've never seen the ocean, either." He pulls me down to his chest, and kisses the top of my head. "Thank you," I say, and meet his lips with a kiss. "It's no wonder you want to build condos here. It's like something you only see in the movies, or in paintings."

"I'm glad you like it." He takes my hand and kisses the back of it. I rest against his chest and continue to enjoy the sight of Maine.

The driver, Jack, pulls the car up to a Cape Cod cottage. It's huge, and sided in dark grey cedar. A sign hangs in front: The English Inn, Est. in 1939. He gets out and opens the door for us. Jonas climbs out and then reaches for my hand.

"I will bring your bags around, Mr. Fairbanks," Jack says.

"Thank you, Jack." Jonas hands him a stash of folded bills, and then lifts his arm, for me to take. "Shall we, my princess?" I smile and take his arm.

As we walk up the cobblestone path leading to the door, the scent of fresh roses wafts through the air. I see them climbing the trellis behind the small, wrought iron gate. Ivy covers the ground, and grows up the side of the house. Quaint, outside balconies adjoin each room. I hear the chatter of squirrels, and see a pile of acorns scattered under the tree.

We reach the door, where an older couple is waiting for us. "Welcome, Mr. Fairbanks," the older gentleman says. Jonas shakes his hand, and then takes the elderly lady's hand, and places a kiss on the back of it.

"Mr. and Mrs. Stanley," Jonas says with a nod. "This is Julia Ellis." They both smile and look to me expectantly. They both seem very pleased to meet me, though I don't know why.

"It's nice to meet you," I say, and accept their gracious hugs.

"Please come on in, Mr. Fairbanks, Ms. Ellis. Everything is ready," the older gentleman says. *Everything is ready?* Jonas has planned this whole trip, from the flight, and *Electra,* to the driver—and now to this inn. It's like I'm seeing him for the first time, in a whole new light. I used to think of him as a ruthless, lonely businessman, always on the move. Not so much anymore.

The inside is just as historical as the outside. It is elegantly detailed with nineteenth- and twentieth-century French and English antiques. Antique mantels surround warm, enchanting fireplaces, and classical piano music plays in the background. I walk over and look out an old, leaded window, and see a wooden patio with small, round tables that are covered in white linens. At least eight. Perhaps this inn has eight rooms?

When I look back, Jonas is pulling an envelope from the inside of his sport coat and handing it to the older gentleman. He then gives Jonas back something in another envelope, which Jonas then puts back into his pocket. They both look at me and smile. The older lady places her hands across her heart. The revelation that *this* is the bed-and-breakfast that he and his partner are buying to tear down sinks in. It will be such a shame to lose this historical beauty. And even as happy as I am to be here with Jonas, I feel sadness in my heart.

"I hope you'll be very happy here," the older lady says to me.

"I'm sure Julia will enjoy her stay here at the inn," Jonas says, coming to my side.

"Yes, then let me show you to your room," she says, and we follow her up a wooden staircase that creaks under our weight. Once upstairs, we are led to room down a far hall. "This is the Royalty King Balcony. It's one of our grandest rooms." She opens the door to a large room, with shiny wood floors, and a fireplace in the corner. French provincial furniture—a chair and a love seat—sit across from a four-poster bed that stands on an Asian rug. French doors lead out to a private balcony. It's breathtaking. Nostalgic. So set in the time of the early American settlers.

"It's gorgeous," I say, glancing in all directions.

"I'm so glad you think so. It's one of eighteen rooms," she says

"Eighteen?"

"Mr. Stanley will bring up your luggage. I do hope you join us for wine and cheese in the Fleur-de-Lis Lounge at five o'clock," she says with such a French air, it rolls off her tongue.

"Ms. Ellis and I will not miss it," Jonas says.

"Again, welcome, Mr. Fairbanks and Ms. Ellis. Thank you for being our guests." She leaves the room, and closes the door.

I open the French doors, and step out onto the balcony. I can hear the crashing of the sea from down below. I see a rocky cliff, and seagulls who fly in circular motions above me. As I lean over the balcony's edge, my hair blows free in the wind. I close my eyes, listen to the unfamiliar sounds, and breathe in the scents that are all new to me. It is a synesthesia of a life from long ago.

My eyes open when Jonas wraps me in his arms. His chin rests on my head, and I lean back into his chest. "Thank you for bringing me here, Jonas. Words cannot describe how I feel."

"Me, too, Julia... Me, too."

I turn and put my arms around his neck. "Make love to me. Right here, in this room. On that bed. In this place." He looks out over the sea. His lips press together, and I see something in his eyes. But it's not the response I am expecting.

"Maybe later," he says, and leads me back inside the room. "Let's go for a walk. I think you will enjoy this little town." His restraint concerns me. I know it's not because of our injuries—the cuts on my head, and his badly-gashed hand. We made love the day before, and he was ever so gentle. None of his demanding, or punishing, ways of "fucking some sense into me."

"Okay," I say, concerned. He must notice. However, he makes no effort to give an excuse. He seems a million miles away. Perhaps he's preparing to open up, after last night.

As we make our way through the small streets, I comment on the old, stately houses—on their history, and the many people who lived in them. In front of several houses, there are brass plaques attached to large trees telling of the house's history, starting with a timeline of 1492, with Christopher Columbus. "European explorers cruised the Maine coast in search of opportunities for their patrons, especially in the rich fisheries of the Gulf of Maine," Jonas says, enlightening me with this history lesson. "Soon after, missionaries and settlers followed, bringing diseases that devastated the Native American populations."

"You mean there were no diseases before that?"

"Not really. The Native Americans had never been exposed to anything. The Europeans had developed antibodies to fight such diseases."

"Wow, I guess I never thought of it that way. How this was just a vast land waiting to be discovered—although it was already somebody's land."

"That's business. One strives to be minted, while another only knows existence," he says, and walks on slowly, hands in his pockets.

"Minted?"

"Rich in wealth from your success."

"Oh." I ponder this. "Which are you?" I ask him, after a moment. "I mean, which do you consider yourself to be?" Although, I know he's *minted*, his manner sometimes shows he regrets his success.

"Neither," he says. "All I want is a new beginning, and I don't know if that's possible." He holds out his arm for me to take. I do, and we continue walking.

Our path leads us to the harbor of the bay, and we walk out onto a pier. Boats tied to poles are banged against the jetty by small waves. A pelican squats on top of a short pole. He watches us calmly. He looks old and weathered. I reach out, thinking maybe I can touch his head. In a flash, he raises himself up and backward, flapping his wings at me. His bill opens, and I scream and try to flee, running smack-dab into Jonas's chest.

"What were you thinking?" Jonas asks, laughing heartily. He holds me tight, still amused by my fear of being eaten by a bird.

"Well... he tried to swallow my arm."

"He thought you were going to give him a fish. That's why he opened his bill."

"Oh. Well, it's not a very attractive or inviting look, if he wants something from me."

We continue our walk, and pass by several fishermen coming in for the evening, securing their boats into slips. Some appear to have been out to sea for days. Their skin is sun-worn and leathery, and they reek of days without a shower. At best, the reward for a life out on the sea is some crabs, and shrimp.

We come to the end of the pier, and watch water crash up against the rocks that are stacked along the shoreline.

"I want to watch the sunset go down over the water," I say, squeezing Jonas's arm. I feel his chest quiver—he's holding in a laugh.

"What? What's so funny about wanting to watch a sunset? Is it *too* romantic for you?" I tease him, trying to bring out his pent-up laughter. Finally, he lets it out in one big laugh. "What is it?" I'm giggling, even though I have no idea what's so funny.

"Oh, Julia," he says when he can breathe. "How I so love you, and your total innocence."

"Yeah. Okay. But what's so funny?"

"We are on the East Coast, Baby. If you want to watch the sunset go down over the water, we will have to fly to the West Coast."

"Oh. That's true." Now I feel totally stupid. The sun rises in the east, and sets in the west. How that bit of knowledge, which *everybody* knows, slipped my mind is beyond me. *Duh!*

Jonas checks his watch. "I think it's time to make our way back. We don't want to miss the wine-and-cheese hour."

We walk up the cobblestone path and, surprisingly, there still aren't any other cars in the parking area. Surely, this is a prime location for a vacation? The lady of the inn, Mrs. Stanley, greets us again at the door. She looks full of anticipation when she sees us.

"Everything is ready, Mr. Fairbanks," she says by way of a greeting.

"Thank you." We walk in, and Mr. Stanley stands in front of a pair of double doors to a room that must be the Fleur-de-Lis where wine and cheese are served. He smiles, and nods to Jonas.

"Sir," he says, and then opens the doors. The room is furnished with dark, polished mahogany-wood tables, and red velvet lounge chairs. A table for two has been set with dinner plates, candles, and a bottle of champagne in an ice bucket.

"What's this?" I ask, looking up at Jonas.

"It's dinner," he says. "May I have the honor of being your guest?" I smile and take his arm. We walk into the room, and Mr. Stanley pulls the chair out for me.

"Thank you," I say. Jonas takes the seat across from me, and then Mr. Stanley bends down, and Jonas whispers something in his ear. Mr. Stanley agrees to something, and then nods to me, excusing himself. He shuts the double doors, and we are left alone in this room.

"Jonas, this is lovely—but why are there no other guests?"

"Because the inn has been bought. It's now privately owned by another proprietor. I guess you can say, it's under new management."

"So, this is the bed-and-breakfast you were staying at a few weeks ago? The place you described to me?"

"Yes, it is."

"Oh," I say, and there's sadness in my voice. "So, they have accepted your offer? And do they know of your plan to demolish this historic beauty to build condos?"

"The answer is yes, an offer has been accepted, and no, they know of no plans of condos."

"Oh. Well, I thank you for bringing me here to see it. I guess you wanted to show it to me before it's destroyed." I look around with a feeling of melancholy. How sad that years of history are once again erased by the cool hand of business. *To be minted.*

"You look sad. What are you thinking, Julia? You seem pensive. You don't think this will be a great place for condos?"

"Isn't there another place where you can build them? I mean... look at this place, Jonas. It would be such a shame to destroy it just to make deeper pockets for you and your partner. I'm sure there are many other places you could build condos."

"Tell me, what would you do with it?"

"Me?"

"Yes. If you had this place, what would you do with it? I'm curious."

"You seriously want to know?"

"I most definitely do," he says, leaning forward, and looking me straight in the eyes.

Shifting my gaze away from his hard stare, I take a long look around the room. I reflect on the outside, my first impression of the inn. The many rooms, and the people who could occupy it. And I'm sure he's referring to business.

"I would keep it as a B&B. I would keep most of what makes it historical, but focus on one region in particular. I've noticed some unique antique furniture from France, dating back to the early 1700s. So, maybe I would give it more of a French look all around, serve fine French cuisine, and call it 'Paris on the Bluff.'"

His stare doesn't waver from my eyes. It's a bit uncomfortable. "Really," he says.

"I know... it's a stupid idea, but you asked. Of course, I don't know a thing about business..."

He sits back, reaches into the pocket of his sports coat, and pulls out the envelope that was exchanged earlier with the Stanley's. "Here," he says, handing it to me.

"What's this?"

"It's for you."

"I... don't understand. What is in this envelope that's for me?"

"It's the deed to this inn, with the new owner's name. Open it up and read it to me."

I reach for the envelope with care, as if scared it could bite. Our eyes lock, with the envelope held above the center of the table by the tips of our fingers. He releases it, and I bring it to me. I look at it, and then back at him. A slight lift of his brow encourages me to open it. I pull out a folded document, and my eyes go wide when I read my name, Julia

Ellis, typed in bold, black letters as the sole proprietor of the English inn.

"Jonas... what... how... why—why would you do this?" I can barely speak.

"Because I love you."

"I love you, too. But you don't need to buy me an *inn* to prove it. I mean... you need this location to build your condos." He gets up, and walks around the table. I'm confused when he bends down on one knee, and pulls... *something* from his sports coat. A small, blue box. He opens it. There, shining like a beacon, is a diamond solitaire ring.

"I need you more. Marry me, Julia."

27

I'M DREAMING. I CAN'T SPEAK. AM I BREATHING? MY HANDS, WHICH HAVE been clutched to my throat for the last thirty... or sixty seconds—I've lost all sense of time—reach out and touch the blue, velvet box. I haven't even looked at Jonas, who is still holding it. The diamond is huge. I don't know much about jewelry—but just to look at this ring, one wouldn't have to.

Jonas removes it from the box, and now I see the entire band. It's wrapped in diamonds. "It's a double halo. I hope you like it," he says, holding it between his fingers. He's still on one knee. "Marry me, Julia. Make me the happiest man in the world, and I promise to spend the rest of my life making all your dreams come true. You don't have to—"

"Yes! Yes, Jonas, I will marry you," I say in a rush. "My hesitation was only because... it was so unexpected." He smiles from ear to ear as he slips the ring on. I, too, cannot smile any bigger. I extend my hand and look at the sparkling mass that twinkles with the twist of my hand. "Jonas, it's so beautiful."

He takes the end of my fingers, bringing them to his lips. "Thank you, Julia. I love you," he says, and kisses my knuckles.

"I love you, too—so much, Jonas." We stand, embracing each other and let the passion of our kiss seal this commitment. I feel the weight of the ring around my finger—a promise, a love, a dream that all started with a kiss. His kiss.

He pulls back. "I have one more surprise," he says. Disentangling himself from our embrace, he once again reaches inside his sports coat. *How many pockets does that coat have?* He removes another envelope. "Here, open it."

Seeing the excitement in his eyes, I take the envelope. "Jonas, I can't imagine—after all this—what it could possibly be." I open the envelope, and unfold the contents. Tuition in my name has been paid in full to Le Cordon Bleu. "Jonas, I can't believe this."

"I don't want you to give up your dream of becoming a chef, and studying in Paris. We can be engaged while you study. I can work from there. Sidney and I will move to Paris while you're completing your studies."

"Oh, Jonas. I'm speechless," I am shaking my head back and forth in disbelief.

"We can get married in Paris, if you want. We'll live here when your schooling is done. At this inn. Your inn."

I look at the ring, the deed, and the paid tuition to Le Cordon Bleu. "Yes! Yes!" I jump into his arms. "All of it, yes," I say, and smother his face with a thousand kisses.

"Now, do you still want to make love? It wasn't easy denying you, earlier. I had a lot on my mind," he says with a wink.

Still cradled in his arms, I press my forehead to his. "Yes. All of it... yes." He carries me to the door, and struggles momentarily to open it. The moment it opens, he rushes up the stairs with me still in his arms.

"Shall I keep your dinner warm?" Mrs. Stanley calls from below.

"Yes," Jonas says, kicking the door shut behind us. With me still held in his arms, we kiss tenderly, repeating "I love you's" between each one. He sets me on the bed, removes his sports coat, and crawls up to me. I'm pressed into the bed, when his body covers mine. My hands massage his strong back through his shirt. They move up and down, feeling every muscle. He's growing hard. My dress is pulled up to my hips. My panties are damp between my legs, and I rub that spot on his hard erection, pressing against the fabric of his trousers. He presses hard against my pubic bone, and I arch my hips to reach my sweet spot. My wetness now soaks my panties.

He pulls my panties to the side, and slides his fingers into my wet center, before circling the wetness around my clit. "Oh," I breathe. "It feels so good when you do that."

"You taste so sweet." I open my eyes, hazy with lust, and watch him suck my juices from his fingers. "All mine," he whispers, and puts his fingers back inside of me. They touch me with such a lightness and tenderness—it shocks me. With each velvety touch, my nerve endings cry out in ecstasy. He scarcely needs to touch me, and already an orgasm is building.

"Jonas," I breathe. "I'm close. Already."

"Mmm, Baby." He pulls his fingers from my moist center, and smears it along my lips. His tongue licks slowly across my lips, before crashing hard with a punishing kiss. "I want you, Julia," he moans from deep in his throat.

"I want you, too, Jonas," I manage. I spread my legs, my dress now hiked up around my belly. "Please."

He removes himself from the bed, and I'm lost without his weight on me. My hands go to my aching need, between my legs, and I rub my wet panties—now drenched with desire. I'm so wanton.

"Take your clothes off for me," he commands. "I want to watch you strip. For my eyes only."

I obey, sitting up on my knees, pulling the dress over my head, and tossing it to the floor. Reaching back, I unclasp my bra, and let my heavy breasts spill out. I hold out the bra, teasingly, and drop it to the floor. I tuck my thumbs into the waist of my panties, and roll them down slowly. I watch his eyes following them. Lying back, I maneuver and wiggle the panties off, and then return to my upright position, sitting on my knees.

"Like. This. Sir?" I ask, panting, and let the panties drop to the floor. I am completely naked.

"Just. Like. That." I watch as he unbuttons his shirt, removes it, and throws to the side. Next, he removes his trousers, along with his briefs, and stands naked before me. His erection stands to attention, and I'm dying for it. He strokes himself while bringing it toward me, and I swallow in anticipation. "Lie back," he orders, and I do. Once again, he crawls on top of me, and his erection grinds my belly. My neck is smothered with kisses, and then both breasts are tortured, when he sucks hard on my nipples. His teeth lightly graze my skin, and I cry out with pleasure.

"Oh, Jonas."

His lips once again meet mine, and then he looks me deep in the eyes. "Do you know how much I adore you?"

"Yes," I breathe out.

"Do you know how much I love you?"

"Yes."

"Remember that. Because I'm about to fuck you like I don't."

Without warning, he's up, and I'm grabbed by the ankles and flipped over onto my belly. He grabs my waist, pulling me up on all fours. *Hard.* My pulse quickens. Behind me on his knees, he holds my waist, and guides himself between the cheeks of my ass. "Do you feel how hard I am for you, Julia?"

"Yes." I'm still panting.

"Tell me how my cock feels on your ass," he says from behind clenched teeth.

"It feels hot and swollen," I say, as he glides it along my crack. He takes my hair, wraps it around his wrist—and, with a yank, pulls my head backward. His hot breath makes shivers run through my veins as he speaks in my ear.

"I love this hair, Julia. Never cut it," he says in a brutal tone. It's an order.

He reaches between my legs and spreads my wetness in slow circles, teasing my clit. I beg in my throat: "Ah."

"You have a greedy, little pussy, Julia. Who does this pussy belong to?" He yanks on my hair again.

"You, Jonas," I cry out.

"Who does this ass belong to?" He slaps my ass, hard, and I'm shocked. Shocked that it's turning me on.

"You, Jonas. I'm all yours." I've never seen this side of his lovemaking before. Yes, he was rough in the shower that one time. But this... this is different. This is primal.

"It's all mine. You have given me your virginity, and I'm going to fuck the hell out of it." He pulls my hair back again, and slaps my center. "I'm going to spank this wet pussy, and then I'm going to fuck it." What I think should offend me, only makes me more of a wanton mess. I'm aching inside for him to take me.

"Oh. God, Jonas. Yes, spank... my pussy," I plead. I don't recognize my own voice. He moans with the use of my language. He slaps my pussy again, and a rush of electricity runs deep in my core. I want more.

"Yes... more, please." He slaps twice more then circles his fingers, saturating them, and teasing my clit. I slide myself up and down his hand, dying to reach my orgasm. I'm rewarded with another slap, and a tug on my hair.

"Jonas," I say, out of breath. "How do you make this possible? How is it that your crude way of treating me, and your vulgar talk, turns me on?"

"Because it takes the type of woman who only shows her bad girl, when she believes in her good man. You are that girl, Julia. Every man wants a girl who is naughty only for him. You... are mine," he says, and shoves himself deep inside me. "This... is mine," he says, with another punishing thrust.

"Yes... I am yours, Jonas." He drives into me deep and hard, still holding my hair wrapped around his wrist. He moves in and out, harder and faster. My head is held tightly by the grip he has on my hair. His breathing is out of control, along with the thrusts he drives into me.

"Oh, Julia. I can't get enough of you." He pauses and grinds slow, deep circles in me. His fingers again tease my clit, and I come instantly. "Yes," he hisses, and returns to the deep, pounding thrusts. Just before he's about to come, he lets go of my hair, and spanks my ass, hard. "Yes. I'm coming. Take every bit of my cock, Julia," he growls through his teeth. He stiffens, and I feel the pulsations of his release as he comes inside me. "Ah, shit," he says, and collapses over me.

We breathe hard, as he holds me tight. He jerks a few more times from after-tremors of his orgasm, moaning my name—and it has never sounded so sweet. We lie for several minutes before speaking. I feel the rhythm of his heart as the pace of its beating slows down from our frantic state, bringing us back to the now.

"Are you okay, Julia? I know I got carried away. I didn't hurt you, did I?" he asks, now stroking my hair with great gentleness.

"No, Jonas. I'm fine. I... didn't know it could be like that. I mean, it was harsh... yet, I am on such a high from it."

"A girl can have respect for herself, and still want to fuck the hell out of you," he says, and places a kiss on my cheek.

"You're worth every sin," I whisper.

He gets up, gathering me in the blanket, and carries me out onto the balcony. He's still naked, and he sits down on the patio chair. "I want to hold you for a while before we go down to eat. Are you still hungry?"

"I'm famished."

"Me, too. We've worked up an appetite. But I'm going to hold you, until I know you are okay with what we just did. I love you, Julia," he says. "I fuck you, because I want you to know the desire and lust I have for you. I make love to you, because I want you to know that my connection to you, and to your heart, mean everything to me." He kisses the top of my head.

"I love you, too, Jonas."

∿

"WAKE UP. HE NEEDS YOU." MY EYES OPEN. THE ROOM IS DARK. I look to Jonas, who is sleeping beside me, peacefully. I swear I heard someone talking to me. A small voice. I know we are the only ones staying at the inn—*my inn*. I look at the red digital numbers of the clock next to the bed. *2:00 a. m.* Perhaps, I was only dreaming. I crawl onto Jonas's chest. He stirs a little and then wraps his arm around me, holding me close. I feel him drift back to sleep. I kiss his chest and close my eyes.

"He needs you. Please." *What?* My eyes open again. *Who is talking to me?* I blink, trying to focus on the darkness. I feel someone touch me.

Through the bright moonlight cascading into the room, I see a small hand on my arm. A child's hand.

"Please, he needs your help." The moonlight now shines bright on a little girl standing beside my bed. The little girl from the sunflower field. "Now," she says. I sit up. Jonas rolls over, but stays asleep.

"Who needs me?" I whisper back.

"My brother. He's out there." She points out the window. "You have to save him." She pulls on my hand, and I do what she wants. She walks me through the open door, which I know was shut, and locked, when we went to bed. She scurries down the stairs, but they don't make a sound like they did earlier.

She turns and looks up at me. "Please hurry. He needs you." I rush down the stairs, and this time they squeak. The front door is open, and she takes my hand, taking me down the cobblestone path at a run. I hear the sea, crashing against the rocky cliff below. I smell the briny air, drifting up from the shore. The wind blows my hair, blinding me as I hurry along with her.

She leads me to a rocky path, and I feel the painful stabs of the sharp rocks and stones on my feet, but, somehow, I manage the pain. We stand over a cliff, and I look out to the sea. Ribbons of moonbeams shine through the dark water as the waves crash against the rocky edge. She's still holding my hand. "Why are we here?" I look down and ask her.

She points down to the rocks. "He's down there. He's stuck."

"Your brother? Why is he down there?"

"Come on. He doesn't have much time." She pulls me to a path leading down the shore. A path made from nature's fury of a timeless, grueling crashing of water that has cut into the earth's crust. Sharp rocks, made smooth over the centuries, create a walkable pathway.

"Be careful," I tell her. But she seems to know exactly which stone or rock to place her foot on. Like she's been here many times before. Stepping over sharp stones, and jumping down, she guides me in the moonlight. I feel so trusting of her, and I don't know why. She stands now high on a rock, her hair whirling all around, just like mine. She points again.

"He's not far away. Can you hear him?"

I stand, motionless, and listen to whatever is howling out in the darkness. I hear the water rushing. The faint sound of seagulls looming above. The humming of a tugboat in the distance. And then I hear it. Ever so faint, and getting fainter. A heartbeat.

"Yes," I whisper. "I hear him."

"He's stuck. You have to do something."

"What can I do? How can I find him in the dark?" She points to me. "Yes. Me. What can I do?" I say again. She walks closer, and points again at my throat. I look down to where she is pointing. I grab the cross on my necklace. She smiles, and nods.

"Pray? That's what I must do?" She nods again, and places her hands together in prayer, dropping to her knees. I clench the cross tightly, fall to my knees, and cry out to God to save this little boy. I pray hard for him to be safe. I hear the heartbeat fading away.

I scream. "Oh, God. Please save this child of yours!" I feel the trickle of warm tears run down my face. I taste the salt, and cry for this little boy. I cry out again. "God, please forgive me. It's not his fault. Please, save him."

Please!

The heartbeat grows stronger. It's close. I feel it against my cheek. The vibrant rushing of life is running through his strong heart.

"Julia. Julia, please wake up!"

I open my eyes to a bright light. So bright, I must cover my face. The darkness is gone. I still hear the water crashing against the rocks. I peer through my fingers. Seagulls fly above. The sun shines through my fingers, and I can feel its warmth on my face.

"Julia, what are you doing down here?" I remove my hands, and look into Jonas's face—so concerned, looking down at me. There's such a look of fright on his face, it scares me. He holds me tightly to his chest. It's his heartbeat I heard thumping in my ear.

"Jonas, what's wrong?"

"Why are you here? Why did you leave me? I woke up this morning, and you were gone. The door was open, and I ran down the stairs, calling for you. You didn't answer me. Oh, God, Julia. I was so scared. I ran out and saw you down here, lying on the rocks. Oh, God," he cries, and squeezes me tightly. So tightly, I feel we have morphed into one being. "God, I thought you were dead." Choking sobs rush from his throat, and he begins to cry like a scared, lost child. Then I remember the little boy.

"There was a child down here who needed my help. His sister woke me in the night."

He moves his face from my chest, and looks at me in bewilderment. "Child? What child?"

"There was..." I sit up, and look across the rocks. Turning my head toward the sea, I squint, and look at the red-orange sun, floating ever so peacefully on top of the water. The sun is rising... and it's beautiful. I'm here in Jonas's arms, it's a new day—and, even if I don't understand what happened, I am at peace.

I smile.

"It's beautiful, isn't it?" I continue to gaze across the water and he slowly turns to look to the sun.

"Yes. You wanted to see the sunrise," he says. Still crying, he begins to laugh. "You couldn't see the sunset, so you came to see the sunrise."

"It's a miracle, isn't it?"

He relaxes his hold, and settles himself next to me. "Yes. It is. Just never leave me, Julia. Please." I lean my head on his shoulder, and we watch the sun come up. It's a new day.

"I promise."

WE CHECK OUR BAGS, AND WALK THROUGH SECURITY. THE MORNING SPENT watching the sunrise together hasn't lost its magic effect as we walk hand in hand, stronger than ever before. How things change so quickly —if either of us were to question every little mystery about the other, our own future could be jeopardized. I am now the wife-to-be of Jonas Fairbanks, and the owner of my own inn. We talked over breakfast about how soon to get married, and Jonas insisted that I complete my schooling in Paris first. I then told him I wanted to adopt Sidney. I want her to be my daughter, to be her mother. Although he seemed pleased, he never actually responded.

My cell phone rings, and I see Erin's name on the caller ID. A shiver runs through me, and my first instinct is that something has happened to Sidney. I answer with a shaky voice.

"Erin. Is everything okay? Is Sidney all right?" My sentences run together, without giving her a chance to answer.

"Julia, she's fine," she says, and I feel there's a "but" coming.

"Oh. Good. I'm sorry I didn't call and check in. I should have. Is she mad at me?"

"She might be, but that's not why I called. It's about one of my patients."

"Oh. We should be back in a few hours," I say, thinking she needs me to get Sidney soon, so she can go counsel one of her patients.

"It's not that," she says. "I think there's something you should know." Her tone is full of dread, and the sound of it fills me with fear. I know, with all my heart, that what she is about to say is a black cloud that looms above, waiting to destroy my happiness. *I must stop this.*

"Erin... there's something I need to tell you first. Please." I am trying to think of the best way to tell her my news, when it just comes flying out of my mouth. "Jonas has asked me to marry him. He proposed this weekend." *Silence.* I'm expecting her to either chastise me, or shrill with excitement. But I hear neither.

"I see. And what did you say?"

"I said yes, Erin. I love him. We love each other." I continue talking, like I need her to approve. "But it's going to be a long engagement. We are waiting until after I return from Paris. He bought me my own inn. Can you believe that? I'm going to run my own bed-and-breakfast in Maine. There's even enough land to bring Sidney's horse. I'm going to adopt Sidney. I love her, too, you know."

"Wow," she says. Yet, it is still not the kind of "wow" I'm expecting.

"Yes. I'm so happy, Erin. Please be happy for me." A few moments pass before she responds.

"I'm happy for you, Julia. I am, really. I tell you what—I'll bring

Sidney by, so you don't have to come get her. I'll have her waiting for you at the house. She's been missing her horse."

"Oh, thank you, Erin. And, Erin?"

"Yes?"

"Don't tell Sidney the news. We want to tell her together."

"I won't."

"I want it to be a surprise for her."

"Yes. A surprise. Perfect. Then I will see you two at the house."

"Thanks, Erin, for everything."

"Don't mention it. Goodbye."

"Bye." I end the call and take Jonas's hand as we head to the gate together.

We land two hours later in Ft. Wayne, and rush to the car to drive home, so we can tell Sidney the news. My phone was already in airplane mode when I remembered that I never gave Erin the address to the house. There were no missed calls or text, so I figured Sidney must have showed her how to get there. She is a smart little girl, and she's going to be mine.

Erin's car is parked in the horseshoe driveway as we come up the lane. We are beaming with the good news. I take Jonas's offered hand as he helps me out of the car. We're not even to the door, when Sidney comes running down the walk.

"Julia! Daddy! I missed you guys," she screams with excitement. Jonas bends down, holding out his arms to his daughter, and she jumps into them. I kiss her cheek.

"We've missed you, too," I say. "We have a surprise for you."

"You do?" Her dimples are showing.

"Yes. Tell her the surprise." Erin stands in the doorway. Her arms are crossed. "Tell her the surprise, Jonas," she says again, her tone condescending. But she's not looking at him, or at Sidney. She is looking straight at me. Her smile is confusing me. Surely, if she had something to tell me about Jonas, wouldn't she be rushing to me, as a friend? A friend who knows that what she must say... will hurt. However, it appears she wants to hurt *me*. Not Jonas.

I look to Jonas. His face is stone-cold. His eyes are full of hate. "What the fuck are you doing here?" he spits.

She saunters over. "Tell her, Jonas. I've been waiting for this surprise, too."

Jonas puts Sidney down, and tells me to take her into the house. "Now, Julia," he orders.

"Jonas, what's going on? What's she talking about?"

"Yes. Jonas. What am I talking about?" Erin mocks.

"Julia, go to the damn house now!"

"Sidney, I want you to go to your tree house. Stay there until I come and get you," I tell her.

"But I want my surprise now. Erin said you and Daddy have a surprise for me."

"Sidney—listen to me, Baby," my voice breaks as my throat tightens. I am choking back tears. "We will be there in a little bit. Okay?" My smile is strained. "Please?" She shrugs her little shoulders, and reluctantly leaves.

As soon as I see her disappear up the tree, I turn back to Jonas and Erin. "What's going on, Erin? You said you were happy for me. If this is because of your failed marriage, then I'm sorry about that."

"Oh, trust me, Julia. I am at my *happiest* right at this very moment. But it really should be Jonas telling you. He knows exactly what's going on." I look at him. There is fear in his eyes. They are pleading with me. But I don't know what they are pleading about. *Oh, God.*

"Jonas." My voice quivers. My lips vibrate against my teeth.

"Tell her who I am, Jonas. We're all waiting."

"Her name isn't Erin," Jonas says.

"That's a start," Erin says. "Then who am I, Jonas?"

My heart pounds. I hear blood rushing through my ears. Erin, or whoever she is, smiles like a predator, trapping me in her web. Jonas looks so lost, like I'm supposed to reach out and save him. But from what? And how?

"Who. Am. I. Jonas," she says, poking him in the arm with each word.

His mouth opens several times, trying to form the word. "Julia," he says with such sadness.

"Jonas?" My voice is reaching out to him, like a drowning person reaching for a lifeline.

"She's... my wife."

End of Book 1

ABOUT THE AUTHOR

Gina A. Jones was born in Northern Indiana, where she still lives today with her husband, Robert. Her profession for the last thirty years has been in orthopedics. She believes, that while working under the strict guidelines of a government regulated industry, her writing was a way to unleash and discover her creative side. Her first novel, 'FACES', was the work of a bet between her and her husband. It was self-published, but never released. In the beginning, he discouraged her writing of which made her press on to receive an outstanding review from the Kirkus. Since then, he's been her biggest supporter, and has allowed her to leave her career in orthopedics to pursue her dream. She loves to write about intense characters, with deep conflicts and an over the edge mystery. Putting several genres in her stories, such as romance, erotica, and suspense, create her own unique style. A romantic at heart, she strives to bring her world into the lives of those who enjoy her books.

To learn more about Gina, and updates of her upcoming novels,
you can find and follow her here:
www.ginaajones.com
gajonesauthor@outlook.com
Facebook @ginaaauthorjones
Twitter @GinaAnnJones2

www.ingramcontent.com/pod-product-compliance
Lightning Source LLC
Chambersburg PA
CBHW031223120726
47905CB00002B/451